THE SEASON OF THE PLOUGH

THE PLOUGH

being the first book of the *Travalaith Saga*

by **LUKE R. J. MAYNARD**

• **CYNEHELM PRESS** •

TORONTO

A Cynehelm Original
Published by Cynehelm Press
www.cynehelm.com

Our books may be purchased in bulk for promotional, educational, or business use. Please contact us directly.

To receive advance information, news, and exclusive offers online, please sign up for the Cynehelm newsletter on our website: www.cynehelm.com

Manufactured in the United States of America

Cover art & design by Luke R. J. Maynard

First Edition: July 2019
ISBN: 978-1-989542-00-2 (paperback)
978-1-989542-02-6 (hardcover)
978-1-989542-01-9 (e-book)

10 9 8 7 6 5 4 3 2 1

THE SEASON OF

THE PLOUGH

The Village of Widowvale

in the Year of Strangers a.m. 3413

N

To the
Serpent Craig

Grimstead

Cotter's
Oak

Village Green

Alic's
House

Maddric
Watch

Miller's
Riffle

Herric's Mill

Oltman's Farm

Bram &
Robyn's
house

Moot-hall

Darrad's Farm

Minter's Rock

To the
Iron Road

Scale (in feet)

0   250   500   750   1000

from the *Uliri Imidactuai,*
the *Mysteries of the Unwatchers*:

Ulira Kedwana othuriamillas
Şar burund mi bethal kitad,
Fusun iralila ap kirilamaillas
Ic finiamaira golad.

Ali li umilda êtrila havila
Ai fulcon iarthona fenast
Şar gurinda Ionai umaliamaillas
Othuril Tûrtha caivectast.

The Riddle of Kedwyn was spoken
On wind that was choked into dust.
The Chain of the Night shall be broken,
And so will have earned its mistrust.

But born of the womb of a maid of the wood,
O, sword of the people, you stand;
In you shall the will of all folk rise anew
And Tûr's will be brought fully to hand.

—*Uliri Imidactuai* Book IV:2

ONE

TRAIL OF HOT BLOOD dappled and cratered the virgin snow, etching a grisly path deep into the heart of the ancient wood. Still red and gleaming, it had been warm enough to dimple the smooth surface of the year's first squall when it fell. Robyn was the first of them to crest the hill, and she knelt so close to the poacher's tracks that she could smell the fresh blood beneath the chill of the air.

She put a gloved hand to her nose as she studied the marks. The smell of it called back a distant memory, threatening to lure her mind away to a place she did not want to go. *It's only sheep's blood*, she reminded herself. She grounded her restless thoughts in the sting of the wind, feeling it in her ears and the tops of her cheeks. The crisp snow crunched and squeaked beneath her boots as she rose to her feet.

"I have his trail," she called, but not too loudly. There was no use in alerting the quarry too soon. When it was clear the wind had drowned her out, she gripped her bladed spear low on its haft and brandished the weapon high overhead to signal the men below.

The wickedly barbed heads of three identical polearms shot up in answer, and the men advanced. The wind howled fiercely on the crest of the ridge, whipping at their faces as they came up out of the hill's shadow. Their cloaks of green and brown were patched against the cold with motley scraps of a dozen fabrics from a dozen lands, but few of those lands had ever faced the naked chill of a Haveïl winter: their colourful garments took the bite out of the gusting wind, but not much more.

Only twenty Havenari remained in Haveïl now, keeping watch over the border towns. Of those twenty, only four had scaled the nameless escarpment—and not the strongest four, either. Those square-jawed, brawny warriors who were still in the bloom of their youth had taken their horses up the Serpent Trail. Eager for action, glad as falcons to be uncaged at last, the strongest men had sped along the poacher's most likely route, fully mailed and spoiling for a fight, if a fight could be had.

For now, Robyn was pleased to be rid of them. Most of the Havenari were noisy men, Imperial veterans weighed down by the trappings and tools of war. Life in the Havenari was nobler than desertion and paid better than retirement, and so their ranks had often swelled with the old and cowardly—neither of whom ever seemed to last the winter. The three men at her back were too young, too old, too sick to stand shoulder-to-shoulder with the big men of the vanguard—but here on the hunt, they moved with an easy grace and an altogether different cunning.

Her captain, Toren, was first up the hill behind her: he was no coward, and he was determined to prove he was a few winters yet from being old. His steps, while far from spry, were cautious and swift. His pitted coat of battle-worn Travalaithi chainmail was as much a part of him as his own skin, and he mounted the hill in silence where the younger men might have rustled and clanked fiercely on the ascent.

"Here," said Robyn, pointing to the blood. There were footprints, too, though a few minutes of gentle snow had started to fill them.

Toren frowned. "I thought for sure he'd have taken the trail with an animal that size."

"We'll lose the tracks if the snow picks up," Robyn urged.

Toren narrowed his steely eyes at the sky. "It's about to," he said—then, under his breath, "get your brother moving or we're leaving him for the others."

Robyn met his hard gaze for a moment, but bit her tongue and moved to the edge of the plateau. Bram was predictably struggling on the slope, crawling upward with both hands in the snowy earth. Young Tsúla, barely twenty summers old with the slight build of an Easterner, was shouldering Bram's pack and helping him over the top.

"Get up here," she barked. "We're losing him." She took Bram's arm in hers and tried to haul him up, but in those early days she was still lean and spindly, and he did not offer much help. Bram's hollow face was pale and frustrated as he found his footing. Tsúla, focusing quickly on the blood, was beaming with excitement.

"We've got him!" he whispered sharply. "Venser's going to be jealous."

"We haven't caught him yet," Robyn said. She clapped a hand on Bram's shoulder and met his wavering gaze.

"Bram," she pleaded. "Focus. We have a job to do."

"I...I don't want to fight," he pleaded.

She could not embrace him, not in front of the captain. But there was a firmness in her eyes.

"You won't have to," she said. "But we have to keep moving. How's your head?"

Bram shrugged. "No worse than most mornings. I just…this isn't how I start most mornings."

"Afternoons," Tsúla corrected him, patting him on the back without a hint of judgment. He bounded toward Toren, who knelt in the fading tracks trying to make sense of them.

"Thought he'd be dragging the sheep," said Toren. "He's *carrying* it. Big man."

Tsúla whistled low. "How big was the ewe?"

"Darmod says two hundred."

Tsúla looked up at the treeline, his dark eyes wide. "Big man," he agreed.

Toren stood up as the brother and sister approached. "You two ready to move?"

"We are," Robyn told him—but Toren didn't look convinced.

"I'll take point," he said. "If you lot have any dignity left, you'll keep up with me. At this rate, we'll be lucky to catch him before he's dyed and spun the wool for market." The pace Toren set, grunting and breathing hard in his armour, was meant to punish them—and maybe, she thought, to punish himself, for doing something as foolish as aging.

Bram took a moment to steady himself and took a deep breath. His tremors were quiet this morning, but there was an unsteadiness in him that only a sister could see.

"You ready?" she asked him.

"Come on," said Bram, and started off after Toren.

As they pushed deeper into the woods, the chimney-smoke coming up from Widowvale and the sound of the laughing river echoing up from Miller's Riffle were both lost to the wind. They passed away from all the places that had ever been named, into the oldest part of the forest.

"Stay close," Toren urged. His hand brushed the side of his neck absently, as it often did when he was nervous. "And keep that one quiet."

Robyn looked to Bram, who was doing all right for himself. He was moving swiftly and silently now, and seemed to pay Toren no mind, but still she fought the urge to say something in her brother's defense. Tsúla must have seen her set her jaw tightly with resentment, for he fell back from the captain and moved quietly to the young woman's side.

"He means well," Tsúla whispered.

"He's cruel," Robyn spat. "To both of us. To you, too. He's been like this for months."

Tsúla sighed. "It's getting colder. Could be his old wounds ache in the winter. I know mine do."

He pulled back his sleeve to expose the old scars that circled his wrist and forearm. In the cold, the marks stood out ghostly pale against his skin of burnished gold.

"You see these scars?"

Robyn nodded. "They're looking better this year."

"My scars will get a little better every year," said Tsúla. "His will get worse. They say he was ravaged by a Horror."

Robyn froze in her tracks for a moment. "Impossible," she whispered. "He's not old enough. The Siege of Shadow was eighty years ago."

"Sure," said Tsúla. "But no doubt some of the Horrors escaped. It was the Havenari who hunted down the last remnants and wiped them out."

Robyn shook her head. "I've never known the Havenari as anything but mercenaries. A militia for the border towns."

"Then you can imagine how unhappy this life makes him," said Tsúla.

"I can *feel* it," said Robyn. "You can feel it in the way he treats us.

It's not fair, and there's no reason for it."

Tsúla put a comforting hand on her shoulder. "I know what you're thinking," he said. "Don't do anything rash. Wait him out. Venser's likely to challenge him for First Spear next summer, soon as he's ready."

"When he's ready?"

"He reckons a captain of any sort, First Spear included, ought to be able to read and write. He's working on it."

"That's a long time to wait," Robyn said, frowning. "But he's a commander worth waiting for."

"He'll call us 'sorry rats,' quite often," Tsúla warned. "If you have no taste for criticism, he'll be no better." Ahead of them, Toren had stopped at the clearing's edge before disappearing into the thorns.

"Quit your chattering," he spat. "You're getting short-changed, Bram, to put up with a lovers' quarrel." He smirked at himself, then turned his back and kept up the climb, trying not to look fatigued.

"It's not the criticism," she said. "It's the disrespect. It's the way he makes us feel small."

"He's endured a lot," said Tsúla. "It's made him a difficult man."

She almost scoffed aloud. "I thought we came out here to get *away* from difficult men."

Tsúla rubbed his wrists in the cold. "We all came for different reasons, I think. Even Toren."

"He came," said Robyn, "because the Grand Army would've flogged him for bullying his own regiment." But Tsúla only smiled his thin smile and nodded in thought.

"Another season," he said. "Two seasons at most, and Venser will vie for command. He's got the support to win it, and he'll be a good sight more fair to everyone."

"I want to believe you," said Robyn. "I really do." She looked to Bram, who was breathing hard but keeping up.

"Let him fade out in his own time," Tsúla offered. "He was a great man, once. Let that go with him."

Robyn sighed. "Well, he's too much 'great man' for my tastes."

"Most men are," said Tsúla with a laugh. "Come on. Let's catch him that poacher."

Even where the wood was thickest, it was veined throughout with old and secret trails for those who knew how to seek them out. Beaten down by the vanished ancestors of the Vosi people, they lay dormant beneath the snow, the last hidden scars of an ancient age. Buildings could be hewn down, barrows looted, and monuments smashed into dust. But a road, once walked, could never be fully unmade.

Toren cared little enough for their history, but he had taken care to learn the old paths just the same. In recent years, the Havenari had seen deserters from the Grand Army and fugitives from the Iron City who thought the forests of Haveïl would bring them sanctuary. Toren delighted in outpacing them through the woods, surrounding them with his men, springing upon them when they thought they were safe. He took great pride in the rumours that his company had some hidden power to side-step, like wood fairies, through the very trees and emerge where they pleased, as he hoped to do with the poacher who fled from him now.

As the day wore on the snow was falling more steadily, and would bury the tracks in time, but the path cut by his quarry was clumsy and straight, establishing a clear direction of travel. With practiced eyes he sought out the hidden ways, clove through the bushes, and led his three whispering subordinates onto one of the ancient trails. A half-mile on that hidden way would put them well in front of the thief, where they could make an end of his crimes in a manner worth boasting about.

It was on this stealthy errand that the Havenari first discovered the mysterious child. Following the poacher's tracks, they might have missed her altogether. She was naked in the snow, nearly invisible where she crouched a hundred feet up the hidden pathway. She had gathered beside her some leaves and stems from a carpet of chickweed that shivered in the breeze where she had brushed the snow off it. She was perhaps nine or ten years old, and pale as snow herself—as pale as death, with the white hair of a grandmother—and she paid Toren no mind as he stood in mute astonishment, watching her forage until the others came in sight.

"You see something?" asked Tsúla. Jaw hanging open, Toren gripped the young man's shoulder and turned him toward the child.

"What is that?" Toren asked.

Tsúla blinked his dark eyes and looked again. "That is a naked girl," he pronounced. "I thought your years in the Grand Army would—"

"Shut up," Toren snapped. One hand rubbed thoughtfully at his neck, but the other tightened around the haft of his spear.

"What's she doing out here alone?" Tsúla asked. "She must be frozen to death. I wouldn't last the morning out here in naught but my armed-for-birth—"

He fell silent, voice trailing off, as he caught sight of Toren's white-knuckled grip on his weapon.

"That's not a human child," the old captain whispered. "It's a monster." He smoothly lowered the blade of his weapon toward the girl.

"What are you doing?" asked Tsúla.

"You heard me; that's no right child," said Toren. "Don't let your eyes fool you. There's some evil about her."

Tsúla narrowed his eyes, squinting down the trail toward her. "Is she an aeril?" he asked. "I've never met one, but I've heard a few of the Elder-kin still live and work in these parts."

"Something worse," said Toren. "A witch. A fairy. Maybe a Horror herself."

"She's not a Horror," said Tsúla. "She's a little girl. Look at her."

They looked. She had turned toward them, watching silently. Her eyes were a brilliant green, the only drops of colour on her whole pale body.

"Put up your blade," snapped Robyn. "Stop this madness."

Toren shot her a cold glare. "I don't like your tone."

"She's just a child." There was a sudden steely resolve in her. Tsúla caught sight of it and stepped away. Bram saw it and shuffled closer. His hands were shaking again.

"*You're* a child," Toren shot back. "You've not heard half the stories I've heard. You think every Horror comes at you ugly and slimy? Only those too weak to deceive you. You think the fairy-folk are weak because they're wee? This is a bad fairy-tale waiting to happen. I'll not go to green in these woods, never to be heard from again. We're knee-deep in winter. No human babe could long survive out here without a stitch of clothing on her. She's not human."

"She could have fallen away from a caravan," said Tsúla softly.

"Aye," said Toren. "Or we could all wake up on a hillside a thousand years from now, white-haired and robbed of our souls."

Tsúla stood his ground, breathing slowly, forcing down the loudness of the conversation with measured calm. "I'm not prepared to discuss the life or death of a child," he said. "None of us ought to be. Let's take her back to Widowvale. The Reeve can decide what sort of creature she is."

"If we take a vengeful fairy out of her wood," said Toren, "she might kill us all. Dryads used to live in these woods, they say. The fairies of old don't like to leave their home. Taking her to the village is the last thing I'd do."

"That's ridiculous," snapped Robyn. "Kill us all? I've seen pumpkins twice her size. Even Bram could handle her."

"I have an intuition about such things," said Toren. "I'll not take any chances with the people we're sworn to protect: our *own* people."

"Aye, that's how it starts, isn't it?" said Tsúla. "I've heard words like yours before." He turned his dark eyes aside before Toren could see the old memories welling in them.

"Bram, give me your cloak," said Robyn. Her brother doffed his patchwork mantle without a second thought, shaking the snow from it.

"She's not coming back with us," said Toren.

"She is," said Robyn. "Tsúla, go put this 'round her."

"Me? Why me?"

"Because you won't have the stomach for my part in this," she said. She turned her gaze back on Toren, who was positively fuming.

"I've made my decision," said Toren. "I hunted the Horrors. I'm the only one left in this sad little band who has. I've smelt their blood, and I tell you, I'm smelling it now. There's something vile in this little creature. Putting it to the sword is our duty as protectors of this land. I'll do it myself, if you're too soft for it. Stand aside."

"Mad," Robyn said. "You've gone mad."

"Maybe," said Toren. "But you'll do as you're told."

Robyn looked to the child, who watched them with a guileless, doe-eyed face, and to Toren's steely gaze. Tsúla approached the girl, cloak outstretched, but paused in his stride, turning back to the stand-off.

"Wait for the summer," he urged. "Wait for Venser." But Robyn laid down her bladed spear and reached for her sword. She was still growing in those days, and did not have the muscle to move the heavy polearm with speed. But the trail was narrow and the branches close on all sides; perhaps the sword would serve her better here.

Toren's jaw shook and he took a step back. He set down his own spear as his longsword sprang to life in his hands. "So it's mutiny, is it?"

"That's up to you," said Robyn. "Change your mind now. We're only following your orders if you come to your senses. The men don't even need to know you lost your wits with fear at the sight of a child."

"I'll not stand here and take—"

"Put away your sword," ordered Robyn. "The child comes with us."

"Do as she says," Bram said softly, stepping between them. His trembling hand was on the rusted hilt of his old sword, but Toren had never seen the boy draw steel, not even in practice. The battered hilt was so ruined that the old man wondered if the whole sword would shake apart in a shower of rust flakes on its way out of the scabbard.

"Do you need her?" Bram asked cryptically.

"I don't," whispered Robyn, and Bram's shoulders relaxed.

Toren spat in the dirt. "You think I'm so old I can't fight a woman, and the useless drunk she hides behind?"

"You're afraid of a tiny, naked, unarmed little girl," said Robyn. "I can only imagine you're scared to death of a grown woman in warm britches, with a sword of her own. I don't need to hide behind a useless drunkard to deal with the likes of you."

"You're too kind to me, dear sister," said Bram.

"Thank you for saying so," said Robyn, without taking her eyes from Toren's sword-point.

Ahead of them, Tsúla had reached the girl, who had come the last few steps to him with wide-eyed curiosity. He wrapped Bram's old woollen cloak around her tightly, and she delighted in its softness.

"This is absurd," said Toren. "We've got a poacher to find, and you're letting him get away. We'll leave her behind and press on, but be it on your head."

"She'll be dead of cold when the sun's gone."

"That's not our concern."

"We're taking her back to Widowvale," said Robyn. "Now. We're giving her food and shelter there, until we can find out whose child she is and where she came from."

"You're willing to die over this, girl?" said Toren.

Robyn rolled out the tension in her shoulders. "I'll take a slim chance of it, aye."

"Robyn," called Tsúla. "You'd better come listen to this."

"In a moment," called Robyn. "I'm fighting to the death just now." She raised her eyebrows at Toren, who had been holding his sword at the ready for a long moment—long enough to remind him how heavy it was. The last eight years had made it no lighter.

"I am, aren't I?" she asked. "Are we really crossing swords over whether or not the sworn protectors of Haveïl mean to butcher a lost child?"

They stood for a long moment, measuring each other's resolve. In the great war-poems of the Hanes, in sagas full of heroes, the challenge would have ended with a chorus of ringing steel. But Toren's boasting of his glory days had not been empty. He had spent enough years on true battlefields to know that killing was not much better than dying, and that it brought no pleasure to men of reason and honour when it could be avoided. With a derisive snort, he lowered his sword-point warily. Men who boasted of killing were fiercely proud of it, Robyn knew. But men like Toren, men who had truly done more than their share of it, knew just how little that pride was worth in the end.

In the long silence, Tsúla had tried to hoist the little girl and carry her over, but she slipped his grasp and insisted on running over herself. Fumbling and twisting free of Tsúla's grasp, she came directly over to the standoff, dragging Bram's long cloak like a bridal train, hood raised over her tangled white hair.

"My sword's meant for better blood than yours," warned Toren. "I've no weapon cheap enough to stain with the blood of a mutineer."

Robyn's arms and legs ached with fear. She fought to keep her breath steady, even as it jerked and pulled in her chest like a frightened horse pulling at the reins.

"I'm no mutineer," she breathed.

Toren jerked his head toward the point of her sword. "Really."

"I challenge you for First Spear. Fairly and formally, under the Code of Veritenh."

Toren, fuming, slipped his sword back into its sheath. If she had wanted to strike, that would have been the moment.

"First Spear!" he scoffed. "You're a stupid girl!"

"Call muster," she said. "We'll see."

"When the Havenari muster at—"

"I could challenge you for First Spear *now*," she said. "We've split up. Who knows where the others are? They're dead, for all we know. Eaten by Horrors."

"They're not dead," Toren muttered. "They're a mile away, dragging their tails up the Serpent Trail. And don't *ever* name the Horrors of Tamnor in jest."

"They've no voting rights until they return, Captain. Until they return, the four of us decide who leads, here and now. We'll tally the votes of the men later. So says the Code."

Toren clenched his jaw. "The gods have cursed me with a literate woman," he sighed. "Fine. The four of us will decide—"

"I stand with my sister," Bram offered.

"Of course you do," Toren spat. "Tsúla, put an end to this madness."

Tsúla shut his eyes and took a steadying breath. "I back Robyn for First Spear," he said softly. Toren's eyes widened with fury.

"You're not serious. After what I've done? I took you in. All of you!"

Tsúla was at a loss to say more, but did not recant.

"You don't want to be First Spear," Toren sneered. "No one wants that! Least of all you."

"You're right," said Robyn. "I don't. When we call muster, I'm sure the other men will side with you, and give you back your command. I'll be First Spear for all of an afternoon, I'm sure. But while the sun lasts, the girl lives, and she comes back to the village with us. The Reeve will decide what to do with her. Only when she's in his hands, not yours, will the men decide my fate."

Toren threw up his hands in defeat. "So be it," he said. "Until tonight. Even you can't destroy the Havenari that fast. But when I resume my command, you and your tosspot coward brother are out. Out of the Havenari and out of the villages I protect. You can go back to where I found you, begging and whoring for scraps on some deserted border road."

"Careful," she warned him.

"Tonight," he shot back. "Till then—I await your command, *sir*. Savour it while you can."

"We return to Widowvale," she said. "We bring the little girl with us. Alive, as if that needed to be said."

Tsúla bent down to the girl. "Hello, little one," he said.

The girl smiled. "*Ru valam*," she answered.

Tsúla looked back to Robyn with concern. "I—we don't understand," he said.

"*Ru valam*," the girl insisted. "*Ei, ru mith, sumorim, valam.*" She gestured at something—the trees, the snow, maybe the land itself.

"What language is that?" asked Tsúla. "Does anyone know? It's no eastern tongue."

"Viluri, I think," said Robyn.

Toren raised his eyebrows—but, cowed for the moment, said nothing.

"The old aeril tongue?" asked Tsúla. "Are you sure?"

"No."

"Can you speak it?"

"No."

"*Eloru, eloru anur lurit loamali*," said the girl. There was a spark of excitement in her eye that seemed, in all respects, utterly human.

"Oh, this is absurd," said Toren, frowning.

"Just the same," said Tsúla. He bent down to the girl. "We're taking you back to our village. To Widowvale. You'll be safe there. Do you understand?"

She touched her chest. "Aewyn," she said.

"Aewyn," said Tsúla. He pointed at her. "Is that your name? Aewyn?"

"Aewyn," she repeated, nodding.

"Good. She has a name."

"Look at her," said Toren. "Skinny as a wet rat. That's probably her word for *hungry*."

"All the more reason to get her back to the village," said Robyn. She looked up at the sky. It was not as cold as it had been in years past. Perhaps an ordinary child could have survived out here like this, at least for an hour or two. But the snow was coming down thick and heavy now, with great fat flakes clustering on their mail-coats and filling in the tracks they'd left coming onto the hidden trail.

"We've lost our quarry, no doubt," said Toren. "That poacher's halfway to the white moon by now, so you have my thanks for that, as well."

Tsúla nodded. "There's nothing to be done. This is the third sheep from Widowvale in three years. If we ride back early next year, before the first snow, we'll see him again."

"You sound awfully sure of that," said Toren.

"I am," said Tsúla, "unless we've got our little poacher right here. How about it, Aewyn? Did you carry a two-hundred-pound sheep up that hill with those twiggy little arms?"

She shook her head. "*Thirumalnu,*" she said. "*Lai lurit thirumal-nu.*"

Tsúla held his arms wide, as if to indicate a sheep. "*Baa,*" he said.

She laughed at that and bleated back. "*Baa,*" she replied.

"By all the gods," Toren spat, as he turned to begin the trek home.

Tsúla's hunting-horn was an heirloom of his vanished house, cut from some strange foreign beast, and sounded like no other horn west of Syrkyst. It was the finest of its kind in the West, and when he set it to his lips, its tremendous call shook the whole valley from the high plateau of the deep wood to the Iron Road far to the south. The Havenari heard it along the riverbank, where they combed the mud downstream of Miller's Riffle for signs of the poacher's crossing. They heard it on the Serpent Trail, the winding road that marked the only route to the other border towns without doubling back to the highway. They heard it across the sprawling floor of the little vale; and wherever they stood, they turned their horses or their feet to the great moot-hall of Widowvale. The townsfolk were hastening there, too, eager to look on the stranger who had been poaching Darmod's sheep and to see justice done.

From the steep slope of the escarpment, Tsúla took a quiet pride in watching them scurry across the snow-dusted fields. He led the girl by the hand for a time, until she at last suffered herself to be carried. Bundled in his cloak as they met the wind on the edge of the deep wood, she began to shiver a little—like an ordinary child, he thought, not like some fairy of another world. It brought him comfort, as did her silent, wide-eyed company. Behind them, with raw nerves and with their blood still up, the other three followed him down the hill at their own pace.

"Don't worry about them," he whispered to the girl, though she did not understand. He was mostly trying to quell his own nerves. Robyn's quarrels with the captain had never before come to naked steel—and he did not know how challenging Toren for First Spear now would affect Venser's challenge in the summer. Both of their swords were back in their scabbards now, and their spears hoisted like walking sticks rather than brandished like weapons—but no less sharp had been their words atop the hill: sharp words were not so easily put away once they had been unsheathed.

The village of Widowvale was larger and busier now than Tsúla remembered it. In just eight years since the first clearing of scrub, the industrious women and a few men had built a mill and a vineyard, cleared as much field and pasture for farming as they could ever hope to work, and raised an impressive grand moot-hall that could hold everyone in the village when the occasion called for it. He could spot the other Havenari at a distance, even before he could make out their faces in the snow. They were the seasonal visitors, men who took in the sights as they walked with awe. The locals hunched their heads in the cold and hurried past the rugged outriders to the warmth of the hall-fire.

"Taking your time, Venser?" he called.

Venser was a head above the others, a tall broad-shouldered man whose silhouette was hard to mistake. His long strides had put him well ahead of his own four-man search party as they trudged across a fallow field.

"Tsúla? Is that you?" He put his hand to his eyes and squinted through the snowfall. "What've you got there?"

"It's a naked girl," said Tsúla.

"Don't you wish," Venser began to laugh, but trailed off as the bundle shifted in the young man's arms.

"A foundling child, I mean. She was out in the thick, far from any trail now in use."

"That's our poacher?" asked Venser.

Tsúla shook his head. "He's still out there. We picked up his trail, but we couldn't leave her to freeze to death. We'll get her inside. There will be other chances to catch our poacher."

Venser seemed unconvinced. "Toren said that?"

"Toren wants nothing to do with her," said Tsúla, leaning in close as they came together. "Says she's dangerous."

"You can't be serious. Let me see her."

Tsúla pulled back the cloak from the little girl's hooded face. One green eye peeped out.

"*Otabia?*" she said.

Venser let out a deep laugh. "Hello, little one. Truly, a worthy adversary. No wonder it took all four of you to subdue her."

"Enough of that," said Tsúla. "There's been some real trouble about it."

"No trouble," barked Toren, who had caught up with them. "Just call muster outside," he said. "I've got something to say when the men are assembled." He said that word, *men*, with a sharp accent and a sidelong glance at Robyn, who glared defiantly back at him but seemed shaken by the whole business.

"Something happened," said Venser. "Something serious?"

Tsúla pushed him away from the old captain and lowered his voice. "Toren wanted to kill the girl," he whispered. "He would have, if not for Robyn."

"Three Maidens, he didn't," cursed Venser. "Why? He's a hard man, but even he's no butcher."

"I saw it with my own eyes," said Tsúla. "Out of the blue. No warning. No reason. The moment he laid eyes on her, he was ready to cut her down."

"That makes no sense," said Venser, shaking his head. "Even for him. There's something more to it; there must be."

"I only know what I saw. He looked ready to cut clear through us to get to her. I don't think he would have, but all the same—"

"Do the others know?"

"They will soon," said Tsúla. "Help me call muster." The two men set about wrangling the others; Venser's voice was as big as his broad barrel chest, and it did not take long.

They were met at the gates to the moot-hall by the newest Reeve of Widowvale, a portly clerk named Marin who had followed his sister out from the Iron City.

"You've got him!" he said with premature excitement.

"We've got something, at least," said Toren. "But not your poacher. Someone will be in to speak with you once we sort out our business."

Tsúla set down his squirming bundle to the Reeve's alarm. "This little lady could use some proper clothes, if there's anyone can spare them."

Marin looked down with some surprise. "I—oh, of course."

"Run along then, little lamb," said Tsúla. "In you go." She took the Reeve's hand and followed without complaint.

"Aewyn's her name," said Robyn. "At least, we think it—"

"So!" Toren barked, even before Aewyn and the Reeve had left them. Tsúla hastily shut the door after them and took a supportive stand beside Robyn, who looked ready to be sick.

"There has been a challenge for First Spear," he said. The men went silent.

"Some of you have served with me a long time," Toren went on. "Some of you will recall I took up the Leaf more than eight years ago. I served and trained to lead under Sumac of the Fairfold, himself called by Janus Veritenh on his deathbed. I fought and cleared Horrors in the Fairfold and the Wastes—real ones, left behind after the Siege of Shadow. Ere that, I served in the Grand Army for thirty-six years. I fought for our Imperator in the Annexation. I was blooded in Estelonne, and again in the Forty-Nine Day Siege. I fought the karach in the Verdant Wastes, and unlike most of those poor souls I lived to tell of it. I achieved the rank of Marshal of the Fifth Legion of the Blade. I am a proven captain, and I have lost no man to strife or accident in my eight years of command."

The others nodded with mixed appreciation. A few were already looking uneasily toward Venser, who was if anything more shocked than the rest of them.

"None here doubt your word," said Tsúla.

"I have been challenged," said Toren, "by this girl. By Robyn, of no right name. Twenty-four summers old, by our best guess. Most of you will recall when we took her on, some two years ago. And all of you, I think, will recall the circumstances."

The men were murmuring, and Toren paused to give them space to do it. Some had known Venser planned to challenge the old man when the easy summer came, but none had expected Robyn to vie for command. A few of them snickered under their breath. Venser cleared his throat.

"She has the right to boast her own credentials," he said, "as you've boasted yours."

Toren raised his eyebrows but stepped deferentially away from her.

"I am Robyn," she said. "You all know me. I'm—twenty-four summers old, as he says."

There was silence until one of the men coughed. Bram cocked his head at her, and she searched her wits for more words.

"I've no right experience," she admitted. "I've never served, nor been blooded anywhere. I've no proper name and no right to command. I challenged Toren for First Spear for one reason only: to save the life of that child. The foundling girl, whoever she is. The girl Toren had every mind to kill in cold blood."

"She's not human," Toren spat back, cutting off the unease of the assembled men. "She's a fell creature of some kind—a fae, or worse, a Horror of Tamnor. I felt it the moment I laid eyes on her. My old wounds ache when one of their kind is about."

"She's safe now," said Robyn. "The Reeve and the town widows will decide her fate, as you will decide mine. Toren is the more capable leader; that you know. I am content to follow him again. But I could not follow him this afternoon, not into what I am sure was the briefest lapse in judgment."

"That is not how the Code of Veritenh operates," warned Toren. "You can't simply invoke it as a civil substitute for mutiny. It's not a tool for disobedience. It's a declaration that I'm unfit for command. That I've failed to uphold the Vigil itself. That you would do a better job of it."

"I would uphold the Vigil with mercy," said Robyn.

"We'll see," said Toren. "All of you, remember your duties to the Havenari, and to the Vigil. You are more than a glorified town militia—at least, I've always said so. You are the spiritual descendants of the first vigilants, chosen to secure the outlands themselves from Horrors unnumbered. Do not be fooled by the peace we've kept in these villages—by these petty poachers, dowry disputes, pickpockets and deserters. You watch and wait with a higher purpose, and you have a duty to stand the commander who will best fulfill that purpose."

Venser met Robyn's eyes, then glanced at the men. But she shook her head.

"I've done all I meant to," she said, and backed down from speaking further. There were tears in her eyes when she turned away from them, to Bram.

"I'll get our things together from the cottage," he whispered. But big Venser laid a hand on his shoulder.

"Hold on," he said—and Bram held on.

The men were dividing—evenly, at first—into two lines, one before Toren, and one on the side of the moot-hall door where Robyn stood. The lines they formed were more or less the lines they expected, but there were a few surprises as they shuffled into place.

Tsúla made his stand at the head of Robyn's line and cast a scornful glance at the man across from him.

"Really, Hendec? For Toren?"

The other young soldier sighed. "He's the stronger leader. You know it. He's proven. But I'll follow whoever commands the Havenari."

"Well, I won't," snorted the older man behind him. "I've two daughters in the Iron City older than her. I'll not call a rover like her First Spear, not now, nor ever."

Tsúla looked to the back of the lines. "You may not have much of a choice."

Every man was accounted for now. The two lines stood in uneasy parallel as the men cast troubled glances at one another. Most were hardened veterans who had served under men like Toren their whole lives. Many had *been* men like Toren. But there, at the great door of Widowvale's moot-hall, ten men of the eighteen who stood muster before Toren and Robyn had chosen another path.

Toren looked down the two columns in disbelief. His mouth played at forming words. Venser shook his head, but not unhappily.

"I'm a little surprised," whispered Tsúla. "But not, you know, a lot." Robyn, stunned into silence, acknowledged him but could not speak.

"Betrayal!" Toren spluttered at last. "Mutiny! I've built this—"

"We have a new First Spear," said Venser, who could speak over nearly anyone when he chose to. The chaotic clatter of spear-hafts striking the ground served well enough for applause, but they did not drown out the mutters of discontent from Toren's line.

As the clamour died down, Venser leaned close to Tsúla.

"Go inside," he said softly. "Tell the Reeve what's happened."

Tsúla slipped away past Robyn, whose face was a mask of trouble and confusion. Toren's face, as he approached her, was tight with anger.

"They're all yours," he conceded. "As a veteran of this order, it is my duty to tell you, *Captain*, that you're making a grave mistake with that so-called child. Lead them any way you will. You've doomed this company already—though I won't be around to see it."

Robyn, nearly lost in panic, found her focus in his disrespect. "Am I to accept your resignation, Toren?"

Seething, he threw his spear to the snowy ground. "You are."

They stared each other down for the briefest of moments. Standing this close, her eyes were above his. She was still thin in those days, underfed and not well-muscled, but she had never been a small woman.

"Count out the price of your horse," she told him. "You leave tonight, and it's a long way up the Serpent Trail, to Aslea or Seton or wherever you're going."

Toren stuffed a heavy purse of unrefined silver into her hands. "Why wait?" He backed away from her, then paused.

"That's a fair price for a good riding-horse," he said. "A parting word of wisdom: be sure to collect what's due every time another man deserts you. I have a feeling I won't be the last."

Some of the Havenari were muttering to themselves and each other. Some, watching the two captains settle formalities, kept their distance. But Venser, eyeing them with the eyes of experience, came to put his big body almost between the two.

"You're paid out," said Venser. "It's time you were gone."

Toren looked up sharply. "Venser, did you just—"

"You're not my captain anymore either," he said. "I don't know what happened up there, but I know bad blood when I smell it. Through it all, I've been loyal to the First Spear. Loyalty and honour compel me to follow the order of command. But now, you see—now you're not my captain. You're just the little shit who's giving my new captain some trouble."

Toren spluttered for a moment, suddenly realized where he stood without his mantle of command, and backed away.

"You won't last a month," he called. "These men will turn on you, just as you turned on me. We'll see if mutiny serves you any better than it served me." With that, like an ill wind, he was gone to collect his things. Robyn's eyes were cloudy with tears, but the storm in her had not yet broken. At her side, Bram was in his own world, staring away to the horizon with haunted eyes. He had done too much today, Venser knew. He'd be lost in a jug of Grim's wine as soon as the business with the child was done. The veterans were looking at her now with anger and confusion, some muttering quietly to each other. Before they could approach her, he leaned down to her ear.

"Don't you dare cry," he whispered. "Don't let them smell it on you. Tonight, when all's settled, you go off into the woods and wail yourself hoarse. But if you keep face now, if you own your First Spear for even an hour, that'll be the end of it."

She looked up at him. "This is only the beginning," she said. "I'm twenty-four. I'm no commander."

"Not yet, maybe," said Venser. "But you're no beggar either, Lady Fane."

For a moment, that shocked the tears out of her eyes. "How did you—"

"I'm smart," said Venser. "That's how. I'm more clever than Toren ever gave me credit for. I've been doing this since I was a lad, and I see things the proper way. A woman who knows her way around a sword, fleeing west out of Creslyn Wood? I was born in Creslyn. Figured the two of you for Elgar's children from the beginning."

She was turning white. "Please don't tell the others."

"Hush, now," he said. "I only raise it to tell you one thing. You've got good blood for this. You'll be better suited to it than you know."

"The men won't stay," she whispered.

"Not all of them," Venser conceded. "But those that do—they'll help you. Whatever you said to him up on the trail, you're an impulsive fool for saying it. You both are. You've got a lot of growing up to do. But you have long years to get better at it, now. I'm afraid a fool's the best he'll ever be."

Robyn shook her head. "This is the worst thing he could do to me," she said. "To all of you. I'm so sorry."

"Here's what you fail to understand," said Venser. "What neither one of you understands, you because you're too green, and he—well, because he's too damned full of himself. Every man here knows how to fight, how to ride. There's paying work for men like us back east."

"The Mages' Uprising?" she asked.

"To begin with, aye," he answered. "The border vasilies are getting restless now that word's out the Mage is still alive. I could go home to Travalaith, and be an officer in a fortnight. Most of these men could—yet here they are, glorified militiamen to a handful of villages for little more than the food in their bellies. Men brought up in the hierarchy of war don't take a step down the ladder without good reason. Maybe a few of us are criminals. I haven't asked. Maybe they've seen so much war and bloodshed already that wrestling a poacher over a fat sheep is all they have the stomach for. What we all have in common is this: we've spent our lives taking orders from hard men like Toren. Every one of us is here because we're sick of it, whether we know it or not. That world—it's not for us. We needed a change."

Robyn looked back at the men, who had settled their chattering and begun, slowly, to look at her expectantly.

"It might be that you're the change we need," Venser finished. But meeting their eyes, the Havenari started to surround their new captain, and there was no time to say more.

Hendec had a sour look on his face as he approached—but true to his word, approached with deference. "Is there a reason now, Captain, he asked, "that we're still freezing our tails off out here?"

With a look to Venser for encouragement, Robyn nodded toward the moot-hall doors.

"Get your tails inside, then," she said. "I want us to have a voice in what's done with this child." To her surprise, with a steady string of grumbling, the men began to move.

"We'll help you," said Venser. "Most of us."

Robyn smiled at last. "You've a good heart as well," she said. "Now I know for certain you should have been made Captain."

Venser beamed as the others shuffled past him toward the door of the hall.

"It's kind of you to say so, sir," he said. "But you're my First Spear now. And I think no man is fit to lead who's too proud to serve."

He held open the heavy door of the moot-hall as the outriders began to stream into the council. At a silent nudge from her brother, Robyn took her place at their head as they entered the main hall. She heard the hushed murmurs as Tsúla recounted, more or less, the story of how they had come by the girl.

Tsúla, to his credit, was a fine storyteller. He was never fully at ease speaking the Merchants' Tongue, and the traces of an accent made even his mundane tales and jokes sound a touch exotic to her. Coming into the firelight, she thought back to the travelling skalds who came and went in her childhood, filling the tall keep of Draden Castle with song and story in trade for food and safe passage. She thought of the Blind

Riders, the stewards of the Hanes, who still roamed the outlands keeping their mysterious chronicles of town records. She wondered what they would make of this day in the end: whether her story was an epic or tragedy, or nothing more than a note in the margins of some greater adventure. The way Tsúla was telling it, though, he could not have been blamed for the latter.

"Here Toren lunged for the girl," he half-whispered, eyes blazing in the firelight. "But Robyn met him at his strength—turned his wicked blade with a flash of her own! Steel rang in the glade, and her voice rang out over the steel. 'By my life,' she swore, 'you shall not harm this child!'"

The townsfolk gasped and muttered among themselves. Startled by the story, the little girl hugged the Reeve close and hid her face in his great beard. Robyn smiled a little, in spite of herself, though her stomach was hot and sick with fear for the difficult season that lay ahead.

The Serpent Trail, if it could be called a trail, was interminably long. There were other and older ways through the heart of the old forest, and Toren knew them still. But there was darkness in those woods, now. He felt it in his bones; it chilled him worse than the wind, and the old scars ached in ways that had saved his life more than once. In his hot youth he had discovered an uncanny sense for the unspeakable dangers that still throve in the Travalaithi outlands—and those instincts had never been wrong before. It was almost painful, going through brush and broom, leading his horse through the thickest paths, searching for the ancient trails. For this reason alone, and certainly for no reason to do with his fear of the deep woods at night, Toren had come to the Serpent Trail, determined to ride it all the way to Aslea alone in the bitter cold of a moonless night.

Toren's story ends here. As the plain-speaking sagas of Silvalis dryly observe, "he appears in none of the later tales." It was a single fateful day in the deep wood above Widowvale that brought the end of Toren's story, the uneasy middle of Robyn's, and the beginning of Aewyn's. Unlike the heroic songs of the Hanes, the sagas have no heroes. They have no right beginning, and no proper end. And the saga in whose tapestry these three were woven does not rightly belong to any one of them. The people of this saga are many, their threads are small, and their tales are made large only in the weaving.

It was not until the light was lost and the cold had set in that Toren allowed himself the weakness of tears. Mostly they were the tears of a fallen man, once mighty, who had come in the end to meekness, and had never been taught how to shoulder its burden. But there was fear in him, too. On a high coil of the Serpent Trail, doubling nearly back on itself to look over the valley, he stopped long enough to watch the plume of smoke rising from the moot-hall and wondered what decision, if any, they would reach about the little girl.

There in the dark where none could see, he unlaced his collar and filled his gloved hand with frigid water from a waterskin nearly frozen through. Gritting his teeth against the cold, he slapped the pure water over the deep purple scar that skirted the edge of his neck. The chill did much to shock him from drowsiness, and to numb the queer ache that had come back to the scar. It had pained him most of the day, like the burning of a hot coal. Toren did not fancy himself a religious man; but there on the trail, his joints aching with age and cold, his neck and shoulder throbbing with an old and evil pain, he touched his fingers to his forehead and made the sign of the white crescent. As if in answer, the forest grew still. His horse nickered at the bit, tossing its head.

"Steady," he whispered. He prodded the animal's flank with his spur. "Don't you turn on me too."

The trees were silent, at first.

Then, the crack of a branch. Crisp leaves rustled.

Toren's neck burned fiercely. His hands were clammy. His horse was frozen in place, trembling helplessly beneath him.

"Mother of Sorcery, protect me," he whispered. He drew his old sword with the reluctant sigh of a man too full of despair for fear to keep a home in him for long.

With haunted eyes, Toren looked into the darkness. It returned his gaze.

"Lay on, then," he said. "Have done with it."

As the sagas say, no more was heard of him after that.

TWO

GRIM HAD COME DOWN from the far North for reasons some called mysterious. Unlike most of the villers and hillers, drawn out to the frontier by Widowvale's sudden and recent prosperity, Grim had been there from the very beginning—since the first huts were built, since a few miners with an overwhelming lack of imagination simply called the place "Silver." Those men had moved far into the hills now; the town that remained was almost wholly made up of women. Nearly all of them came from lands where men were afforded greater authority in political matters—but even so, it was Grim's seniority among the villagers that earned him respect when he spoke at moot.

It did not hurt his authority that his wife Karis, who was from Travalaith, was the Reeve's sister. As the village's only purveyors of ale and wine, the two of them held a tight grip on Widowvale's good cheer whether they meant to or not. The effect of it all was that when Grim talked, people listened—even though the name Grim, in the old language of his people, meant "mask," and he was known in Widowvale and many other places as a spinner of tall tales, unmatched in his talent for telling lies. He was a weighty man, too, and when the true-widow Oltman sat down and he replaced her at the fire, his presence filled even the vast moot-hall. He cleared his throat and waited for silence.

"The far North has ten thousand fairy-stories," he told the hushed assembly. "In the Age of Sun, the elders say, the world was hot with magic, like a pie fresh from the oven. A hundred fairies lived in every house, they say, and I've no reason to disbelieve them."

At the side of the hall, far from the fire and swathed in shadow, Tsúla watched him with what looked like approval. Bundled in the young outrider's cloak, draped in a set of farmer's clothes too big for her, the little white-haired girl listened to the stories with awe even though she seemed not to understand the words. Such was the power of Grim's voice when he was deep in his tales.

"Some of your grandsires, no doubt, were children of the Occupation," he went on. "They remember the Horrors that came to Travalaith. Men like Toren know of no magic but black magic—and who's to blame them? Not I, for one. But I tell you, north of the river Ban, there's magic a hundred colours thick. Wise women and fairies, seal-spirits and ghost bears and the restless dead, too. It's said the wastes of Cuinen get so cold at night that even Tûr and the Ten are afraid to walk there. But there are older gods than the Ten, and the dryads of old come even before them. They lived in the First Forest, and played among the vanished trees before the ice came. And mark my words, in your lucky summer lands, they live here still."

"A fairy-child, then," said one of the skeptical farmwives. "An estrel of the wood. This is your explanation?"

"Let him speak," said the Reeve.

"I'm sure your Southern tales warn you about the dangers of inviting a spirit into your home. But in the Banlands, to this very day, travelers live or die by the custom of hospitality. Many's the story of a family cursed when they let in a fairy. But those tales are outnumbered a hundredfold by the curses laid on families who turn away a traveler in need. You say she's fairy-touched? I'm no skeptic. I'll have you at your word. But if you say we take her in at our peril, I tell you all, you turn her away at yours."

The assembly murmured at that, and were still restless when the heavy door edged open just wide enough for Venser and Robyn to slip in. Robyn crept round to Tsúla's side like a cat, but Venser was too big for such tricks, and Grim waited for him to nudge his way through the crowd before he began again.

"She might grant us wishes," a woman called, "if we find the right kind of rope to bind her." A few chuckled uneasily; some gave it serious thought. Tsúla scoffed at the notion as Robyn, who seemed not to hear it, slid onto the bench beside him with a loud creak.

"Hush up, if you're joining us," snapped Karis, Grim's wife. "You all talk about this little girl as if she's some fairy you caught like a firebug in a glass lantern. Even you," she added to Grim, nudging her husband in good humour. Great talespinner though he was, Grim stumbled over a reply, the villagers laughed, and the tension in the room eased just a bit. He edged aside, gave her a little room at the fire.

"She's a living, breathing child," Karis went on. "Whatever else she may be, she's that above all else. I've six children myself; I know one when I see one. Forget what ought to be done with a fairy-blooded foundling. That's talk for other seasons. Ask yourselves, tonight, what ought to be done with an abandoned child. Start there." She moved to sit down, before turning back to the muttering assembly.

"And if it turns out you do get some wishes granted out of it," she finished, "ask the Lord of Forests for a little compassion, maybe."

"An ordinary child, then," shouted another voice. It was Darmod, the farmer whose ewe had been stolen, and whose poacher the Havenari had failed to catch on account of the girl. "And who will feed her, then? I'm in for a third lean winter, now. You've six little mouths of your own to feed, Karis. Can you afford a seventh?"

"If need be," she said proudly.

"Perhaps we'll raise the price of wine," said Grim, which took the wind out of Darmod's sails straight away.

"Now hold on," said Bram, who had crept in with the Havenari almost to no one's notice. "Let's not be hasty. I'll help you raise her before that happens."

"I'll not see a foundling raised by the town drunk," Karis snapped— but Grim, surprisingly, contradicted her.

"We'd be grateful for the help, lad," he said. There was always a natural friendship, to be sure, between the town vintner and the town drunk, but there was something more behind Grim's sad grey eyes that made even Karis reconsider the harshness of her words.

"The Havenari cannot offer much," said Robyn, "but when we winter in Widowvale, we'll do what we can." She hesitated. "I mean— those who'll stay with me."

The Reeve raised an eyebrow at the woman. "And you speak for the Havenari?"

Robyn swallowed hard. "I do," she said. Grim thought she looked terrified.

"We've no money," said one farmer.

"Neither have we," said another. "But we have a dry roof, and she's welcome to that—till it caves in, at least."

"We can spare a silver rider a year," came another voice. "Two, if my husband hits that vein he's going on about."

The clamour of the hall quickly grew as some villagers offered to pool what goods and coin they could for her welfare. Others, offering nothing, felt the need to be heard offering nothing as loudly as possible. The Reeve took the opportunity to whisper something to his sister Karis before thumping his staff on the moot-hall floor and demanding silence.

"I've heard enough," he said—then, stroking his chin, "nearly enough. Who's the clerk for the miners this year?"

"The foreigner," shouted Darmod.

"We're all foreigners," Tsúla snapped, his nerves struck. "His name is Fen'din."

"Fen'din," Marin repeated. "Where is he?"

"He hasn't come in for the season," said Grim. "None of them have."

"We should wait for the men," said one old woman. "It should be the villers and the hillers making these decisions together."

"We've had first snow," said Marin. "The census-tellers came and went weeks ago. There's not many who'd care to winter in the south hills, beyond the comfort of the village. They were late last year, and came home, every one of them, rich as border vasils. I'd like to think it's happened again."

A low murmur of approval went through the townsfolk.

"We've been uncommonly prosperous," said Marin. "And the miners have been uncommonly lucky when it comes to dodging the Imperial tax census. Widowvale indeed! We've made a good life here, and I've heard it said that we'd all be more noble if only our conditions were better. Well, conditions are fair to good. I think we can spare the cost of a child between us—and if your house will take her in, Grim, we'll see to it no one family shoulders the burden."

"Six children, seven children," muttered Karis. "It's not as if I've got any leisure to lose."

"Then I've made my judgment," Marin said. "The girl will live at

Grimstead, for as long as the house of Grim can feed her. The town will furnish any expense beyond what they can bear; the hillers shave more than enough off the Imperial Tax to absorb the cost."

A murmur of approval sifted through the crowd. The women seemed pleased enough with the idea of spending their husbands' coin before it was mined.

"You can all help save a poor orphan's life," Grim told the assembly, "by drinking all the wine you can."

At that, the townsfolk cheered. Marin cast a sideways glance at his brother-in-law, but a thin smile cracked his round face.

"It's settled," he said. "She goes to Grimstead. We'll revisit the matter in a year. When she's old enough, any of you willing to foster her to a trade will be compensated for your time."

"What if someone comes looking for her?" called Darmod.

"The Havenari will see to them," Robyn answered.

"Aye, and if they come in the summer while you're on the move?"

"It's been decided," Marin insisted. "We've other matters to discuss—unless the sheep-lord himself would prefer we forget the matter of the poacher who, it seems, has eluded old Toren again."

"Toren is gone," said Robyn. "He won't be back."

The crowd hushed itself at that. They had anticipated his parting of ways for some time, but its abruptness still shocked them into silence.

"Now, that's news to us all," said Marin. "I'd hear more of this sudden change."

Toren had been something of a necessary evil among the townsfolk, but he was not well-loved, being the sort of man many in Widowvale had come west to avoid. When the business of the girl was decided, the rest of the Havenari came in from the cold, though two men had already deserted straight away. As the moot wore on, the town sought reassurance that the remaining Havenari would not abandon them as Toren and the others had. Robyn did much of the speaking for them, and by the end of the night she had convinced a few of the skeptical young outriders that she might not collapse under the mantle of leadership. Only those who had aspired to First Spear themselves still bore her ill will: they would not follow, and even their own brethren did not expect them to last the season.

The discussion soon cycled back to the matter of the poacher, and at this many of the village women returned to their homes. In Toren's absence, and with the unity of the Havenari suffering in light of the little band's crisis of leadership, it was Venser who advised them not to chase the poacher too far into the heart of Haveïl. The Reeve agreed that the town, flush with the hillers' wealth and underreporting their Imperial taxes, could afford to compensate Darmod for his loss—a conceit contrived mostly to quiet the old man's complaints that the militia was not sent off into the deep woods at their peril for his own personal benefit.

Since the whole town had gone to the trouble of assembling on a cold night, the Reeve followed up the matter of the Havenari's change of leadership with some dull business about the partitioning of fields and meadows; a plea from the true-widow Oltman, who had taken sick and whose sons were not yet grown, for help in repairing the roof of her barn; and a few scattered rumours about a renewed uprising on the far east side of the Travalaithi Empire, which amounted to nothing more than gossip. It was past midnight when Grim and Karis trudged home to Grimstead with a new child in tow. She rode high on Karis's hip, shivering against the night's chill as if she had never known cold before.

"What do you make of the business with the Havenari?" Grim asked his wife.

"It'll do them some good," said Karis, "having a woman in charge."

"I'm inclined to think so," Grim agreed. "Half the men won't be able to stand it. Probably the half I like least. They'll likely stay the winter, ride out in the spring, and never come back. The rest will be the stronger for it."

"I worry about Toren," Karis said. "He was not a kind man."

"That's precisely why I don't worry about him," Grim said. "Rascal take him, for all I care."

"In the Iron City," said Karis, "there's plenty of pomp and politics to keep distasteful men in power. Out here in the thick, there's no such thing. I'm surprised he's lasted as long as he has, without the others jeering him out of command."

Grim nodded. "You think there's something to his worry?" he asked. "You think we've taken a dangerous monster into our home?"

At Karis's side, the little girl yawned.

"You remember when Arran and Glam were this age," she said. "All children are monsters, deep down. Her more than most, maybe."

Grim snorted with laughter. "Then why'd we take her in?"

"I'd sooner her be the monster," said Karis, "than me myself."

"I love my wife," said Grim, helping her through the snow.

"You're wise to," she said. As they trudged up away from the torches, her smile was hidden in the dark of night.

By Imperial reckoning, the year of Aewyn's arrival was 3407 in the Age of the Moon. At the last harvestmoot before her discovery, the Reeve had declared it the Year of High Trees, but by the time another harvest season had come and gone, it was known locally as the Year of the Child in spite of what was written in the town chronicle. In the season to come, many remarkable discoveries about Aewyn set the villagers' tongues wagging, and renewed their speculation that in spite of

Karis's urging, she was no ordinary girl, but a strange fey creature from beyond the mortal world.

She was a talkative little thing, though none could understand her; and though she taught the children a few words of her curious tongue, she was slow to learn the Tradespeak that united the exiles and foreigners of Widowvale under a common language. When she had learned it well enough to answer questions about her origins, her cryptic stories were fairy-tales in themselves, so full of nonsense that the villagers wondered whether Grim had put her up to spinning tall tales.

Grim was known in Widowvale for two uncanny talents: first, he was a master vintner and grower of grapes, able to call up rich vines from the ground as if by their own tongue. He sang to them, it was said, in a language old as the rocks, and where many had tried to coax hardy cold-weather grapes out of the unforgiving soil, only Grim had succeeded. But it was the second of his talents, as an unmatched liar and spinner of falsehoods, that the townsfolk heard echoed in Aewyn's mysterious tales. When she had learned the words to speak of her past, Aewyn told them that her mother had been a dryad, a fairy-spirit of unearthly beauty who dwelt still at the heart of the deep wood. She spoke of growing up under a massive, wounded tree—a towering oak with a missing limb—and of riding through the forests on the back of an immense beast called Poe, though what manner of creature it was she could not explain.

She spoke, too, of an old man named Celithrand who visited her in the woods as the seasons changed, teaching her the ways of the wood and bringing her little gifts from distant lands. These stories drew the most attention, for Celithrand's name was known to almost all who had grown up under the banner of the Travalaithi Empire. The Imperator himself, in the dark days of the Occupation, had fought alongside a druid of that name—an ancient advisor from across the sea who served at his right hand after the Siege of Shadow, then disappeared altogether. Aewyn's stories of the old man held just enough fact to be true, maybe. But then they remembered Grim's stories about the dragon he had slain in his youth—or the time he ate an entire sabercat, raw, in a single sitting—or the time he would have perished in the Hinterlands of Cuinen if the God of Forests had not personally brought him firewood.

Over time, the townsfolk came to discount most of her stories as they did Grim's, imagining that he put her up to them as an elaborate prank. This they did not begrudge him, for he was kind to her and they were glad to see her flourish in his care. But Grim was tormented that first year by the mysteries of her stories: he knew with certainty which tall tales he had put in her head, and which had come to her by unknown roads of the mind. Were they inventions of a child's imagination, tinted by unreliable memories? Or was there a true magic in her words as well? There was a veil of sorts, it was said, between the mundane world and the world of fairy-folk; and though she tried to articulate her memories of her mother, the longer she lived at Grimstead, the harder it became to put them into words.

It unsettled Grim that she claimed to know so much about Celithrand, as the druid was most known to him as a political figure, and he distrusted Imperial politics immensely. He was more alarmed yet when she described the skills in hunting, foraging, and woodcraft he had taught her—and when the Havenari, in the spring, took her out and tested these skills, and found them to be true. The Havenari spent much of the year on the move, making their way from town to town along the old forest trails, and even the youngest of them was something of an expert in woodland survival. Even so, Aewyn taught them the names of many new plants, and many new uses for old ones, and how to raise storm shelters of wattled wood with such haste and efficiency that it was how they built their temporary shelters ever after. In her surprising skills they took much delight, but every new discovery put Grim a little more out of sorts.

It was discovered one spring morning, not long after the Havenari had ridden out, that Aewyn's white hair had taken on a tinge of pale gold that deepened as the year went on. Like a ripening berry, she waxed from snowy white to the colour of corn, and after the last frost, as the carrots started to come up, it darkened further, first to a sandy brown, then to a deep chestnut in the height of summer. It was wondrous to behold, and the first true evidence beyond her fairy-stories that she was more than an ordinary girl. The absurdities Grim might have spun about her then would have been great indeed, but he was too unsettled by her mysteries to take much sport in her strangeness.

In the autumn, her hair turned the bright ginger colour of a Nalsian milkmaid's, before greying and going shock-white with the arrival of the frost, as it had been when they first found her. By the anniversary of her discovery she was speaking Tradespeak almost like a native, playing and sporting with Grim's natural children, who with the eyes of innocence had accepted her strangeness without judgment, and saw nothing magical in her queer appearance or the changing of her hair. But the census-tellers who rode out every year from the vasily of Haukmere would not be so quick to accept her, and the shadow of their visit hung unsteadily over Grim for weeks before their arrival. The roving merchants who found their way to Widowvale for the Harvest Fair had brought word of a full-blown rebellion in the East; rebellions were expensive, and the town's independence and continued prosperity depended in large part on Marin's ability to cheat the Imperial taxman by decrying the existence of the "hillers," the fifty-odd miners who lived and worked the hills south of Minter's Rock. It was imperative that the special attention of Haukmere's Censor not be drawn to the village. And so Grim wrestled with the many stories he might tell in the weeks leading up to the census about his new, strange child, who must have sprung fully-formed from his wife on the brink of adolescence, with hair as white as his grandmother's.

In the weeks leading up to the Harvest Fair and first frost, the miners watched and waited from their hidden claims and highland settlements for the Imperial census to be taken and for head taxes to be tallied. When the census-tellers arrived at last from Haukmere, fearsome and resplendent in their long purple tabards and blackened armour, they went about their business with the usual efficiency. A head count of the village found an uncommonly prosperous town of widows and orphans, with far fewer men of labouring age than might have been expected. By the second day, they found their way to Grimstead, where they discovered an undocumented child of some nine or ten years with the traces of an alien accent—a strange little thing who put them ill at ease.

They asked many questions about her origins, which Grim mostly deflected. With a face honest as granite, he swore by the Imperator, by Tûr and the Ten, and by whatever other gods they might muster, that Aewyn was his rightful child, begotten of the same good woman, and by the same delightful method, as the other six.

"There is no record of her," said one of the census-tellers. "Not in all the years we have come to your door. And any man with eyes can see she's not your right child. I see six children in the register. Here at your table, I see six fat little heads, as gold as harvest grain. And here, one bony wisp of a girl, as white-capped as the ocean waves. We would have the truth from you, winemonger."

"The records sometimes lie," said Grim. "Sometimes they are mistaken."

"Censor Stannon is a very precise man," said the census-teller.

"Even so," Grim said, "children come and go so fast in these lands, it's hard to keep tally. Life on the frontier is harsh for the wee'uns." Karis, who had just finished putting the other children to bed, laid a comforting hand on her husband's shoulder.

"You'd understand, soldier," she said with a boldness equal to Grim's, "the day you pass thirteen healthy babes of your own, and raise but six to their grown teeth. When you beget a fourteenth, it's hard enough work to squeeze out a sickly runt like her, I swear, leave alone a healthy one."

"Tûr's blessing on us," said Grim, cradling Aewyn's confused head, "that this wicked plague has not taken her from us as it took the others."

"Few in these parts survive the ravages," his wife agreed, brushing Aewyn's white hair away from the soft curve of her face. "Fewer still come through so unspoilt. We must be blessed by the gods. Two years now the sickness has come and gone through our house, every winter, without any more going shock white like her."

"And no more catching the rot like little Jorvin Half-Face either," said Grim approvingly. "I suppose once you've lived through the plague a few times, it leaves you be. If you survive it, that is."

His wife nodded solemnly. "Gods be praised. Poor Jorvin. You should have seen his face, m'lords. Looked like a horse kicked it in, at the end."

"Don't speak ill of the boy, woman," said Grim. "The sickness just came one too many years on our house. Explains why we can't foster off the little rats. If they stay at home much longer, we may lose them, too."

"Aye, best to wed the girls off before the rot sets in," said his wife. She exchanged a few silent, urging glances with Grim, who cleared his throat obligingly before addressing the census-tellers, his hands clasped before him entreatingly.

"My lords," he began with an earnest smile, "are you both married?"

The house of Grim had little trouble from the census-tellers after that. Each year after the harvest, a mounted soldier would halt at foot of the path up to Grimstead, record a nondescript *nine* for the farm's population, and return his findings to the Censor without comment. But the deception sat uneasily with Grim, and he knew even then it would not stand up forever.

The spring that followed, in what came to be known as the Year of Gardens, was one of the most pleasant and prosperous on record. Gladdened by the unusual warmth, and eager for a share of the coin set aside for it, the townsfolk one by one began to extend their help to Grim and Karis in the raising of Aewyn. She began to pass more of her time under the thatched roof of a half-dozen farmers and tradesmen, whose rudimentary apprenticeships began to transform her. Living alongside the millwife's daughters, Anna and Melia, she learned to bake bread in the big stone ovens, and over the course of several days with Jerrold the Mercer, she learned to measure, cut, and even sew—a skill for which Karis, with six other children to tend, was very grateful. Grim taught her the arts of vintning, about which he knew much, and conventional farming, about which he knew surprisingly little.

In the winters, when the Havenari returned from their rides, she learned to feed and groom and sit on Robyn's horse, a nut-brown mare named Acorn. The animals took to her with such calm that she exacted—then redeemed the following year—a promise to go out on little rides with them when her legs were long enough. More and more often, Bram was too deep into the wine by midday to ride, and Aewyn took to his spirited, late-gelded horse Jumper with such comfort that she had immediately earned the affection of the Havenari who remained. Two years after Aewyn's arrival, Toren's twenty men had dwindled to twelve: the others, jilted and bristling under Toren's successor, had deserted within the first few months. But those who remained were all the happier for it: Robyn had filled out to greater physical strength, and had proven herself a capable leader with time and counsel. When the smaller band rode out with their horses after the spring thaw, Aewyn was far from the only villager who lamented their parting.

Year after year, Aewyn's age, too, became something of a mystery. She was not quite a child, for the blush of Idis soon ripened her body like the first fruit of an early summer, but she remained small in stature as Grim's eldest boys shot up to the height (if not the width) of their father in the course of a summer. As the seasons passed she played with the daughters of the townsfolk, but they grew taller and fuller of shape, and each year another turned her attention to silks and suitors. Aewyn, though she slowly came to resemble a woman in the height of her springtime, had the look of a child about her face for long years after. She took no interest in the boys of the village (nor, as the millwife's eldest daughter noted sourly, in the girls). Those who were still wary of her origins, half-waiting for some terrible fairy king to reclaim her or some prophecy to call her to greatness, marked her disinterest the same way they marked everything about her—with cold suspicion under a false veil of prudence and concern.

Their words, over time, planted seeds of doubt in the mind of Karis, whose concern was genuine, and who had come to regard the strange foundling as something halfway between a benevolent house-spirit and one of her natural children. Her suspicions grew as Aewyn began to venture into the wooded hills alone whenever eyes were off her. She flitted from house to house, wherever there were a few coins to be made by teaching the affable young girl the rudiments of a new trade. For every stern guardian that absolutely forbade such reckless trips, another kind hand would give her leave—or, more likely, simply turn their back and let her disappear.

In time her excursions grew longer and more frequent, though the promise of a hot meal was usually enough to bring her back. But soon the trips extended into stays that would last nearly the whole night. In the colder seasons, it was more than Karis could bear, and she unburdened her thoughts to Grim. Still perplexed by the girl's stories, the vintner was a sympathetic ear to his wife, and though he made a manly show of resisting her she knew there was complete agreement buried in him, if only she could mine it out.

"It's not natural," she said one winter night, when Aewyn had gone to sup with Jerrold the Mercer's family. "A girl her age, in and out of the deep wood, such a winter as this."

"She's no child anymore," said Grim. "She's the most part of a grown woman, these days. And children are children, Karis. They will play in the wood as pleases them, with or without our leave."

"Aye," she returned, "and grown women will too. You call her a woman. What do you suppose she's up to, then?"

"Running about with druids and fairies," said Grim with his usual straight face. "Hunting her magical beasts, or whatever she says. She'll never catch any, and it does her no harm."

"Running about indeed," said Karis—then, whispering low so the children would not hear, "have you forgotten how I got big with Arran?"

Grim laughed. "Perhaps you'd better remind me tonight."

"It wouldn't be the first time you've forgot," she teased.

Grim clutched her and kissed her, but his fatherly concern was never far from his eyes. "Look, she's pure as the snow," he said. "I've no doubt of that. She's shown no interest in the village lads—enough that there's been some talk of it, if you want to know. Widowvale's a small enough town to fit on a barber's sovereign, and Aewyn's on the tongue of every gossip. If she's already had her strings loosened, I'm sure we'd have heard of it."

Karis took away the wooden bowls with a snort and put the stew back over the fire. "I wager she's the plaything of some bandit, then," she said. "Or someone who doesn't keep with the village. Maybe not a bandit, but a deserter from the Iron City. I've heard things from back east. Even high-ranking Imperials lose all heart for it, sometimes, and go to green in the Outlands. My sister says—"

"Your sister's a merchant and tells merchants' tales," said Grim, though he knew that wasn't to be the end of it.

"The Havenari haven't caught that poacher yet, have they?" she asked. That chilled him, as she knew it would.

"No they haven't," said Grim. "Every year we lose another stock-head or two. Widow Oltman's pig, this year."

"Now think. If Ali had become the plaything of some poacher, some brutish Travalaithi soldier turned hovel-dwelling ruffian—"

"Ali's *twelve*," Grim snapped, his fatherly protectiveness twinged.

"—I'm sure you'd never suffer it," Karis finished.

Grim frowned, then paced, then fumed, in exactly the order she suspected. She laid a hand on his shoulder, just the way he liked when the moots put him in an ill mood.

"It's not natural," she said again. "I worry for her, Grim."

He rose and led her away from the children. The house was dark in the gathering twilight—dark enough that Karis might still have passed for a young girl, laughing in the woods, tasting his winter wine.

"You don't suppose—they can't be true, all her stories," said Grim. "Dryads don't come into the world anymore, and they especially don't breed with menfolk. Never *could* breed with humans, as far as my legends go. That's why fairy types were always stealing children. But you don't suppose all that nonsense is real."

"I don't," Karis said, nodding. "But you do, my love."

Grim shook his head. "Fairy children? Miraculous foundlings? Things like that don't happen anymore. Not in the Age of the Moon, leastwise. They just don't come to be, these days."

"Not without reason," said Karis.

"Not without reason," Grim repeated. "Aye. That's what worries me."

The breathing of the children was quieter than the wind outside.

Karis leaned against the wall, still as a stone.

"There's ways you could find what she's up to," said Karis. "See if we've got bandits to fear, or monsters, or worse. My father fought in the Battle of Syrkyst, and his in the Siege of Shadow before him. I may not believe in your fairy-stories, but I know there's no end of things in this world to keep your babies safe from. And after six children, lover, I can see it in you when you've taken a babe to heart."

"It's not my business to follow her," Grim said weakly.

Her eyes were bright, powerful, concerned.

"The town looks out for her," he reasoned. "Anyone hurt her or brought an unkindness on her, we'd know of it straight away."

Karis said nothing.

"I've no care what she gets up to out there," he said finally. "And I've no care to be eaten by her magical monsters. She's not our born child, woman; her business is hers alone, and I want no part of it! That's all I've got to say on the matter."

But if there was a place to hide from his wife's eyes, Grim knew not where it lay, nor how to get there.

In the first six inches of an early Audnemaunt snowfall, with the winds spitting curses at one another overhead, Grim crouched against the shadowy trunk of a fir tree and shivered in his vigil. He couldn't have followed her from his own home, not across the vineyard, without his long shadow betraying him. He was too tall and too old to creep through the low empty trellises in silence, and the crunch of the snow would betray him in the open. But Robyn and Bram's cabin was built down close to the stream, by the narrow bend called Miller's Riffle, where the current was loud and the trees came down nearly to the water. It was here he waited, for Robyn was especially soft on the young girl, and Bram fell too easily and hard asleep to be much of a sentry. When Aewyn's care and feeding passed for a time to the young Havenari captain and her brother, her trips into the forest were frequent and long.

Aewyn was not late in coming. The edge of the sun was still brushing the tall pines to the west when she quitted the house and made for the tree line. Her long white hair caught the light of the sun and moons, and her youthful step on the snowy hill was sure, but far from silent.

Grim kept a safe distance as he trudged through the grove, trying to stay on the riverside where the laughing current covered the regular thud of his heavy strides. Aewyn's gait was long and her pace brisk; more than once Grim found himself breathing like an ox as he struggled to keep up. The biting cold meant little to an old Banlander; his armpits and the small of his back were damp and hot with sweat by the time he mounted the hill. It was all he could do to keep up with his prey, silent or otherwise, but she skipped with abandon up the hill and his presence seemed utterly unknown to her.

The hill was nameless, at least in Grim's tongue, but it stood on the north side of the highway and looked down on Miller's Riffle—and farther to the south and east, on Minter's Rock, where the first silver mines had been opened after the stream bed was panned clean. Minter's Rock was itself a tall enough hill, and looking down on it from the far side of Widowvale, Grim realized for the first time the real height of the north escarpment, and the roughness of the climb in the fresh snow.

If Aewyn was worried by the steepness of the slope, she did not show it. Her movements between the trees were eager and deliberate—she had come this way before, Grim knew, and no doubt knew the strange secrets of the hill, if her stories were to be believed. Grim resigned himself to greater distance, even though the wind at this height covered his footfalls and his laboured breath, and turned his attention to his own progress up the long hill.

The relief of level ground came some time later, and only then at the cost of torchlight. The fires of Widowvale, burning below, were obscured now by the lip of the escarpment; and although the deepening dusk was still bright enough to find his way, there was something uncomfortable about leaving the lights of the village behind. The rising smoke of the larger house-fires could still be faintly seen, steel-grey against an iron-grey sky, and brought Grim comfort. He gave silent thanks for them, and for the tree cover that thickened overhead as he moved deeper into the wood. In the Banlands, the open sky was a cruel goddess, with a cold unchanging face and a gaze that swept from one horizon to the other. He felt warmed and sheltered beneath the trees, and that feeling was no small part of his decision to set down pack in Haveïl. The forest was thick and growing dark, but to a Banlander of low birth it was preferable by far to a high, flat land under a naked sky.

Aewyn had stopped, somewhere up ahead, and Grim had to circle for some time before he again caught sight of her. The girl was stooped before a mound of wood and packed earth, shielded from the distant sea-wind by a single standing stone. Whatever its purpose, the mound and its stone reminded Grim of the old barrows of his homeland, small hills and monuments raised to the dead who were buried there—or sometimes, in tribute to those lost far away. A countryside rich with barrows was, to Grim, the sign of an old and prosperous family. He did not know what such sites meant here—but as he waited, his eyes fell upon the massive pile of bones that surrounded the hut. Some were fashioned into tools, others carved into wicked and threatening shapes. He waited in perfect stillness, less from strategy than from fear.

The girl's small voice, after so much silence, nearly shocked the vintner from the low bushes where he hid.

"*Otabia?*" Aewyn asked suddenly. Her voice raised at the end, like a question, though he could not guess at its meaning. He was about to give answer when something immense stirred in the darkness, and he knew the word was not meant for him. As he held his breath and advanced a step toward the clearing, the discovery did not relieve him.

A low, rattling voice, nearly too deep and far too guttural to be human, echoed from the mound. It spoke the same language, in stranger tones than Grim could distinguish, and sounded to Grim the way he always imagined a draugur, a restless corpse of Northern legend, to sound. The vintner trembled, wishing he had thought to bring his knife on this fool's errand, though he wondered what use it might be against a shambling corpse or restless spirit. In fairness, he thought, it would be little enough use against a bandit or Travalaithi deserter either. He was past his prime, and still winded from the hill. A highway robber, discovered with his booty, would be the end of him as surely as a draugur; and so he resolved himself to be no more afraid of one than the other. He held his breath and slowly advanced, crouched so low in the snow than his back pained him with every step.

Aewyn moved in fearlessly, speaking the strange tongue in familiar tones. The shape that rose from the mound, out of some opening on the far side, towered over her like a cat over a mouse. There was no mistaking it for a spirit then: its deep brown coat and steaming breath were too real against the night sky, and its sheer physical presence was too overwhelming to be some figment of the night. Karach they were called, tribal dog-men who still lived in remote parts of the Banlands. Grim had seen them at great distance, around the fires of their camps, in his youth; his father had traded with them when the winters were desperate enough. To men of the western Empire, at least those old enough to remember them, the karach were savage tribes that preyed on civilized folk—they were fierce creatures, bloodthirsty warriors, eaters of men. Grim knew at that moment that he loved the strange girl, for what it was worth: regardless of whether his knife sat idly rusting on the kitchen-block at home, he would die fighting the beast if it made a move on her.

But Aewyn spoke to it, and it seemed calmed by her presence. It returned her words in a delicate language unsuited to its deep growl and thin clumsy lips, crouching low to speak with her. It—he, Grim decided, for it was too big to be a female—was surprisingly gentle with her. There had always been something unseelie about her, he thought, something altogether otherworldly, and her discovery in the woods was like something out of legend. He should not have been surprised, he thought, that his fosterling had the power to quell such creatures. They seemed to be having some sort of conversation, her airy voice floating above the deep registers of his gravelly whisper. It occurred to him that the karach was speaking more quietly now, ears flicking warily, even as Aewyn chattered away in the strange tongue with her usual dinner-table exuberance.

If he had been a master hunter, like his blood father, Grim might have realized then that he stood upwind of the pair. He might even have had the instinct to take his first steps into the thicket, into brush too dense for the karach's larger frame to follow. But Grim was no hunter; his food came over the market-bench in exchange for bottles of wine. He could hardly read the alien features of the karach's doglike face, and he did not see the thing move until it was nearly upon him.

The attack was sudden, but not ferocious. Whether it recognized his man-smell or not, the karach pounced with the metered confidence that suggested that it knew it held the predatory advantage. It did not lead with its claws or its gaping jaws, but took him up with hands that looked, felt, uncomfortably human. Grim's back struck hard against a thick trunk; he folded at the waist like a sack of flour and pitched down into the snow. The karach was in close before he found his wits, its smoking breath and dagger teeth hot and real around his throat.

Aewyn's scream, a barely-articulated order, brought the woods to silence. Even the birds in the trees were stilled by the command, though Grim knew it was meant for the karach when the great beast relaxed its grip and moved warily away. Only then did a scream of his own leave his mouth: it had nearly died quivering in the snow, along with the rest of him.

"Run, girl," he said quietly, his courage rallying once the shock had passed. He was maybe half the creature's weight, and wore much of that around his middle, but he would make a fierce stand now that he was prepared.

"He's a friend!" Aewyn pleaded. "*Malal ei iara!*"

"Don't contradict me, child," he said through set teeth. A desperate fire burned hot in his veins.

"I wasn't speaking to you," she said, which caught him off guard enough to stay his hand for a moment.

Grim's laugh was as hostile as his balled fists. "That thing?" he snorted. "Your friend?"

Although he could not understand the karach's severe reply, he sensed it was similar in spirit. The beast was not quite naked, clad in coarse trousers and some tattered leathern mantle that resembled a travelling cloak. It watched him warily with an intelligence altogether unsettling. While Grim himself had never come so close to a karach in his youth, seeing one in the flesh took him back to a place he thought he had left behind him.

The creature sat back awkwardly on its haunches, a seemingly lazy pose that Grim took as an unthreatening one. It extended a hand—too human a hand, Grim thought again, hairy and clawed but with undeniable and disturbing fingers—and eyed the girl, not the vintner, as he did so.

"That thing, your friend," it mimicked. Did it misunderstand his words as greeting? Or was it looking to Aewyn for confirmation? Grim reached out a hand and clasped its wrist in his, felt its claws brush around his forearm. A handshake past the wrist, in the North, was a sign of greater trust than a limp Imperial handshake, held only at the fingers. He hoped it was so here.

Aewyn nodded, wide-eyed, and meekly approached the two as they stood predator-still in the clearing. Grim, out of his element with the towering karach but a dauntless father of six, tried a different tack, fixing his eyes sternly on the girl.

"You have one chance to explain this, young lady," he said. Aewyn's eyes fixed quietly on the ground, and the karach relaxed visibly. A parental threat had an altogether different tone to it, and Grim imagined the creature could read the nature of their relationship, even if it could not understand his words.

"This is Poe," she said. The karach barked out a similar sound, as if correcting her. "He is a friend. We lived together here, in the forest, before I was fostered in town. I've missed him. He protects me from the beasts and bad men."

"Your friend," Grim said again. The girl nodded. "And where did you get this…friend?"

"I've told you many a time," she said, though it wasn't meant to be precocious. "Celithrand brought him to me one spring."

"Celithrand," Grim said. Poe, if that was his name, pricked up his ears. "The lord of druids. The Imperator's ancient advisor. The hero of the Siege of Shadow. That Celithrand?"

"I suppose," she said, "unless there is another."

Grim threw up his hands. "You're my girl," he said, "if not by blood. I suppose you could have said 'what karach?' and still I'd have believed you."

"But it's true," she said, more earnestly. "He brings us gifts, every spring when the flat leaves come back, and he comes to Haveïl."

"And you drink tea with Naeïl the Fairy Queen, I suppose," he said.

"My tales of the beast-man were true," she said, looking to her companion. "Why not the rest?"

"Beast-man indeed. It's a karach, Aewyn—their kind exist here and there all through Silvalis, especially in the Northlands. They use them for mercenaries in the Iron City, I hear, those that can fight. Maybe your friend fell away from a Travalaithi legion. Maybe he deserted."

The karach tensed unhappily at that.

"He doesn't understand me, now, does he, girl?" Grim took a cautious step back.

"He speaks none of the Merchants' Tongue," she confirmed. "But we have both learned Viluri from Celithrand, and from my mother."

"Viluri," said Grim. "From your mother."

"Yes," said Aewyn.

"Not Karis or Robyn, you mean. Your real mother. The tree spirit who lives in the woods."

"Yes."

"Right," he said under his breath. "Come home, girl. I've heard enough. I was sent to solve this riddle, and now I have."

"This is home," she said, but saw his meaning and began to walk with him. "What about Poe?" she asked.

Grim was about to answer when he looked again at the bones surrounding the mound. A sheep's skull, beak-nosed and grinning, stared back at him.

"That's a sheep," he said. He looked to the karach, who seemed unconcerned with the bones—then to Aewyn. "Did Poe get this sheep from the village?"

She asked him in a string of strange words. Grim did not understand his reply, but he understood the nodding head.

"I think the town has been looking for him for a long time."

Aewyn's eyes brightened. "Can he come back and meet everyone?"

Grim sighed long and deep, but forced a smile. "Yes," he said. "Yes, he can." He looked to the karach, who snorted warily as Aewyn related the good news. There was no way he could compel the beast by force—but if he, a slow-moving old vintner, could bring a poacher to justice where even the Havenari had failed, it would win him the universal respect of the town. And perhaps some good apprenticeships for his six children, too, if they did not take well to winemaking.

"He will come," said Aewyn with delight.

"That's good," said Grim.

"You don't sound happy."

Grim cleared his throat. "I don't know what storybook you sprang from," he said, "or what business you have with druids and fairies and karach. But you're a child of Widowvale now, true and proper. I stuck my neck out for you, girl. I lied to the iron soldiers from Haukmere for you. Haukmere! The vasily of Ashimar. I reckon you're too young to know that name, and I'm thankful for it. But I could lose my head over you—if I've got a head to lose, when the Reeve is done with me."

"Why are you in trouble?" asked Aewyn, concerned. "Am *I* in trouble?"

Grim looked back to the karach, who had fallen obligingly in step behind them, much to his relief. He tried to make his motions as friendly-looking as possible, and smiled obligingly as only a master liar might.

"The village is your home now," he continued, "and a village has laws. When people come together, they live by the same rules. And now it seems old Darmod's sheep weren't poached by bandits or Adâni barbarians after all. Though in the circumstances, I don't expect that news to please him. We're taking this friend of yours to meet the Reeve. Maybe the village will take him in and adopt him, as it has with you."

Aewyn studied his face carefully. "You don't think they will," she said with the wisdom of a child.

"I have my doubts," said Grim. "But this is what's happening. It's what's right."

"Will Darmod Pick cut off my head?" she asked.

Grim laughed. "No, lass. No one's cutting off your head."

"Will they hurt Poe?"

Grim's heart sank in him, but he made sure to smile at the eyes as well as the mouth. "Tell him there will be food."

"Poe," she said softly, reaching back for the creature's massive hand, "*Fena femoiom, otabiam.*" The karach responded in kind, the words harsh in his throat.

"*Guri ionai wiwalia golandeom,*" the creature spat with a disdainful glare at the vintner. But he followed them willingly.

"What did he say?" asked Grim. "I don't understand a lick of aeril-speak."

"He cannot read the emotions of your face," she said, "but he says that parts of your body are weeping with fear, even if your eyes are not."

"He's not wrong," said Grim. "But you can tell him he's the least of my fears, now, if that puts him at ease."

"It puts me at ease," said Aewyn cheerfully.

"Wish I could say the same," Grim replied.

The journey down the hill, even in the bluest twilight, was faster than the climb. Aewyn was leading the way before too long, and although Grim puffed heavily behind her he had no trouble picking his way through the snowy rocks. By the time they had come down below the crown of Minter's Rock, the town fires were being extinguished, and in the dying glow of Widowvale's hearth-hour, they were met time and again by hastily armed townsfolk who were sure the beast was in pursuit of the vintner and the strange girl. Grim was forced to explain each time, sometimes at the point of a hayfork, just what had really happened on top of the hill; and with Aewyn busy calming the skittish karach, who spoke no Tradespeak at all, Grim's tongue was free to wander. By the time they had passed Grim's house-gates, and then the Reeve's, the vintner could hardly fault Aewyn for the tale of druids and forest folk she was sure to spin. Grim's second talent, after all, was that of a liar, and the stories of Grim's desperate battle with the savage creature remained the stuff of local legend for years to come—even after the Year of Strangers, when the town finally came to know Poe as one of their own.

There were not many Havenari in town that winter. The snows had come early and caught them on the coast, near Seton. Only Bram, too weak to ride, had remained behind; and so the men who took Poe prisoner for his crimes were no proper warriors. They plied him with food and drink, as promised, and he was gladdened for a long while by their treatment, as was Aewyn. When they bound him at last, he was more confused than enraged: looking down at the stout rope, he did not feel especially imprisoned by something so flimsy. And yet, like the bride at a handfasting, this tying seemed of ceremonial importance to them, so he suffered them to bind him with their strings of hemp: he understood by the symbolism of the rope, if not by its strength, they expected him to stay where he was.

When Bram was dragged reluctantly from his bed to stand for the absent Havenari, and the town had assembled to see the mighty poacher bound before the Reeve's justice, only then did Grim recount the story of how he succeeded where twenty armed men had failed for years—tracking his prey, subduing him after a mighty battle in the woods. The story passed for truth among all who heard it, right to the moment that the trial began. And in that moment, when the nature of the gathering became clear, there were bigger things to worry about than a boasting Northerner's tall tales.

THREE

THIS IS NOT THE STORY of Darmod Pick, son of Adel, or of his sheep; but he was a poor, proud man who pitied his father, and so a page of it must belong to him as well. His father's home, which had been named Pickstand after their ancestors, was a narrow, scrubby strip of meadow east of the capital, good for little more than grazing their own sheep and the oxen of the nearing families.

As a young man, Darmod had little enough love for anyone, and it seldom stood him to favour with his neighbours. But he had no love for the Imperial Grand Army, either, and that earned him some admiration among the poor farmers. During the Siege of Selik, when Adel had surrendered his grazing rights to the two Travalaithi Legions,

Darmod shouted himself out the door of his childhood home. He left his spineless father to the company of Travalaithi post-wardens and headed west to Haveïl, taking his birthright in the form of livestock. It was a difficult season for travel, and the journey was long for an angry boy with an unmanageable flock: he came to the valley as a hard young man with a dozen sickly sheep, and his hunger for prosperity never left him no matter how large and healthy the flock grew, no matter what fortune it bore him.

It was Darmod who first jeeringly dubbed the town "Widowvale" when the men moved into the hills and the women remained—and none of the men minded leaving him behind to tend his flock. He was too bitter to charm their wives, and the young women especially took an easy comfort in a man too spiteful to have designs on them. They preferred his company, at times, to that of more pleasant men—and later, in their efforts to find something kind to say of him, the women simply agreed that old Darmod was "honest."

As a sheep farmer and a sheep farmer's son, Darmod was an unlettered man, and not particularly well-spoken. But when Grim brought a ferocious karach before the Reeve, who determined it had been poaching his sheep for years, he became so uncommonly articulate in his outrage that another moot was called at once to determine the facts—and hopefully, to exact justice from the creature's hide.

When the tally was complete, and Aewyn had coaxed the truth from the creature, Darmod counted four sheep he had lost to it in the past three years, and only two to the lower predators—wolves and cougars—that came down from the high hills. In more difficult lands, a man could be hanged for less; and Darmod saw no reason to let the hammer of justice fall lightly just because the soil here was generous and the weather forgiving. The kindness of the land, he said, was a blessing meant for those who earned it by toil and diligence, and granting clemency to a beast who fed on the labours of others made light of those who had built the town by sweat and struggle.

Darmod left the moot-hall when he knew the argument had been lost. Marin the Reeve made several inquiries about the karach's origins, and the weird forest-girl who had come to live with Grim made such a shameless defense of the beast's ignorance that it was clear Marin's heart would be swayed by those wide green eyes. Darmod stopped short of accusing the Reeve of a conflict of interest—though as Karis's brother he was virtually uncle to the sickeningly naïve girl—but he was sorely hurt by the opinion of the townsfolk, which had been so easily swayed against him by the sincerity of the girl speaking in the monster's defense. Many still clamoured for blood, but Darmod knew before any of them that they were not likely to get it. He stormed out in disgust once it was clear that Poe would not be put down for the offense; it mattered little to him what final blow befell the beast after that. As the heavy moot-hall door slammed shut behind him, he cursed the softness of the townsfolk, though perhaps it was his father's softness he saw in them. Whatever notions of law and justice they had brought with them coming west had been abandoned somewhere on the road from Travalaith, or on trails more distant, like so many sheep too weak to make the trek.

If he had stayed, Darmod might have heard the wisdom of Alec Steel, who ran horses and kept bees in the meadow adjacent to Darmod's lands, and who had spent more years in the company of karach than any in the village, even Aewyn herself. He had served once, long ago, in the feared Legions of the Blade out of Travalaith; and in those times the karach of many tribes provided frequent and powerful mercenaries for the Travalaithi host. He, more than any, knew that the karach was yet young and had not reached his full size—and more importantly, that his kind were capable of honour and could be taught what things were of value to men. That familiarity, and his unimpeachable regard in the community, were the chief reasons he was called on to speak in defense of a creature that could not speak for itself.

"You have heard the crimes from Darmod Pick," he began, "a man who has a right to be angry. And this is no crime of slander, no simple trespass, no offense against a single man or woman. This is poaching, and poaching by an outsider. Every one of us has a right to be angry. This year has been a year of plenty, but other years may be lean."

"Poacher!" someone cried. The Reeve waved his hands dismissively at the assembled villagers.

"Who among us," Alec asked, "has tasted neither milk nor meat of Darmod's flock? Who has worn no cloth spun from his wool? Blacken Darmod's eye or steal his shoes, and you victimize one man. But a theft from his flock is a theft from all of us—from our chandler, who goes without tallow, and from our children, who go without blankets in the night."

"Your words are wise," the Reeve said, "but you do a poor job of speaking in its defense."

"Let me finish," answered Alec. "This is no city court and I am no tribune. I am a simple man with simple facts. The karach has lived like a beast, and must be punished like one. But our judgment cannot be so clouded by thirst for revenge that we forget our own wounds. If we kill him, as might well be done, even in less barbaric times and lands than these, Darmod will be avenged. But vengeance puts right no wrongs. It makes none of us whole, and will not restore what was lost. I know not how much tallow comes from four fat sheep, but we'll not get it from the karach's body."

"Burn him!" someone cried. Aewyn, who sat near the karach and translated Alec's words in a trembling whisper, neglected to repeat it.

"Aye, burn him?" Alec said. "And then starve, three winters from now, when we've had no more lambs of those four ewes? No. Put him to work, I say, in the fields. We will need the food, with those sheep gone. Let the karach live, and let him put his strong back to such hard work that no one will mistake our prudence for mercy."

"Let him live," some murmured in half-agreement, including Grim, though he did not know why.

"Burn him!" another woman shouted from the back. Grim's wife, Karis, clearly recognized her.

"Burn him yourself then, you old busybody," she snapped. The din of the crowd rose until the Reeve stood, hands outstretched as if he were preparing to wrestle the whole moot-hall.

"Enough!" he shouted, his deep voice rumbling below the rising noise of the townsfolk. "That's enough!" He sat again as the noise receded. "I did not call this assembly to hear the shrill grot of shrewish women. I need not have left my house for that honour." Those who knew well the Reeve's wife and daughter stifled their laughter, and order was again restored.

"Alec Steel has made a reasonable point," he said. "What can a karach do? Can it pull a plough?"

"I cannot say," said Alec, "but during the Annexation, I saw them lift and throw down animals that could."

"This winter may be unkind to Darmod," said the Reeve, "and unkind to us all. We'll want a large spring crop, and that means expanding the south fields. Perhaps we'll plant east of the Rock too, if we can draw water that far. That's hard work—brush that needs clearing, furrows that need ploughing. Those who hold land, or make oath to work it, will pay tribute to Darmod for use of the karach."

The crowd murmured in mixed assent.

"That is my judgment," he said with firmness. "I'll suffer my heart to ache a single day for vengeance, before I'll suffer my belly to ache for hunger the whole next year. The silver price of four ewes, last told by the markets in the Iron City, will be Darmod's remedy," he went on. "If more homesteads contribute, each man pays less—but the karach's time will be divided accordingly, among more households. Who makes use of him will pay down his debt to Darmod."

"We can pay," shouted Marta, wife to one of the miners. "If the karach does my husband's work, he may as well winter in the hills too."

A few of the tradeswomen laughed.

"Most of your husband's work, leastwise," one added. The comment seemed lost on Marta.

"We already have oxen," someone cried. "What can it do that an ox cannot?"

"How many oxen?" answered the Reeve. "At an acre a day per ox, with new fields to water all the way from Miller's Riffle, it will be a hard season." His stern gaze lingered long on the karach, who hunched low over the young girl and seemed to sense more than understand the thrust of the conversation. "A season of labour may pay us what we've lost. Two seasons certainly will."

"Two seasons at the plough, then," Grim shouted, "and call it settled!" Aewyn looked to him with a look of betrayal as the hall shouted their agreement.

"You told me he would be a welcome friend here," she said.

"I said nothing of the sort," he protested. "I said there would be food, and there was. I said he could meet everyone. Well, he's met them."

"You tricked him," she said, glaring. "You tricked me."

"This is how it has to be," he whispered to her. "He stole. Do you understand? He stole those sheep from Darmod. Stole and killed what didn't belong to him. That's a crime."

"I don't see how you can own another creature."

"Well, you can," said Grim. "Sheep, at least."

She shook her head. "That's like saying you own a wife."

Grim shrugged. "There's places like that, too," he said. "Be glad we don't live in one. Look, two seasons is the wink of an eye. Nothing but a cuff on the ear, as punishments go. They'd have killed him, if we'd let them. Do you understand? If they'd caught him in the wild instead of me—if Robyn had caught him on patrol, she would have killed him. Stuck her big spear right through him. Or maybe he'd have killed her. Would you prefer either one of those?"

"He'd be free in the wild but for you," said the girl, teary eyes blazing. "This is all your fault." Grim snorted and moved away, back to Karis's side, trying to look smug about the whole thing. Better that she blamed him than herself.

"Two seasons at the plough," said the Reeve finally. "But no man or woman takes the karach until fair coin has been given. The township of Widowvale will advance the sum, and pay Darmod the price of two ewes at once, and two ewes after the next census from Travalaith."

Aewyn cast pleading eyes on Grim. "It's not fair!" she called, though her small voice was lost beneath the crowd, which grew increasingly noisy in the wake of what sounded like a final decision.

"Two seasons at the plough!" many shouted.

"Burn him!" some still called out. The karach shifted uneasily, eyes and ears darting. Aewyn had stopped translating for him in her distress. The shouts of rage could mean anything, now.

"We are adjourned," the Reeve roared over the crowd, "if Alec's mercy has been satisfied."

"Mercy," someone shouted mockingly at Alec, as he rose with patient satisfaction.

"Mercy!" they all cried. The Reeve, his own bellow drowned out now in the noise, pounded his staff and pushed the rowdy hall-goers toward the door. Two burly farmers brought a yoke and chain for the karach, since the town had no manacles to fit him, and there were none who seriously thought the rope would serve.

Grim was adept at reading people, and it may have saved Aewyn's hide that night. He left his wife's side, pushed back toward the girl, clapped a firm hand on her shoulder as the karach crouched low and sucked in his breath.

"Don't touch me," she said. But he tightened his grip—his fat fingers were suddenly as serious as a wound by the heart—and hauled her backwards at the last moment.

With two huge hands Poe met the yoke straight on and pushed hard, shoving it back against the men who carried it. Their shouts of surprise were lost in the noise; and by the time they had drawn their knives, he was past them. He touched the crowd gently, as if handling glass, but they were easily scattered and could not hold him, and he reached the doors of the moot-hall in a few long strides. Aewyn strained against Grim's hand, but in spite of his age the vintner's grip was hard as stone when it had to be.

"Poe!" she called after him.

The farmers who had been elected to yoke him were somewhat prepared for this, and they started after him, but the townsfolk were unready, and the confusion had driven many to their feet, and some into the center aisle.

"Call the riders!" shouted Marta. "Where are the Havenari?"

"Wintered at Seton," the true-widow Oltman cried. "Bram *is* the Havenari. Think he'll stop it?"

"Gods and fishes," said Marta, "somebody do *something*!"

"After it!" the Reeve shouted, caught in spite of himself in the growing frenzy. Aewyn was only too eager to go, but Grim would not be evaded; he would not be bargained with, and even the kick she launched into his leg as he dragged her away brought only a grunt of stoic resignation. His pace was slow but sure, as if he were standing still amidst the chaos—but Aewyn knew he was taking her to his home, to the house at Grimstead where she knew not what punishment awaited her. She wanted nothing more than to start after Poe with the others, whose shouts grew distant now as they chased the karach up the escarpment and into the wood.

The golden heads of Grim's youngest children peeped quietly from the loft as he trudged into the cottage. Karis was still at the moot-hall, or somewhere along the way; he had no doubt she'd take care of herself.

"I hate you," Aewyn spat. "You're a liar and it's all your fault."

"You're upset," Grim grunted as he set her down. "We all speak nonsense when we're angry."

"You've always hated me," Aewyn cried. "I'm not like Ali and Gray and your other right children. I'm not your real child and you've always wanted to make me different. All you want is to get me in trouble."

Grim sighed sadly. "You're not in trouble," he said. Then, in a tone of warning, "not yet, leastwise."

The girl looked ready to bolt, but knew she dared not try it.

"They're going to kill him," she pleaded.

"He's a criminal," Grim said. "He's broken our laws."

"They're not his laws," said Aewyn.

"Then he's worse than a criminal. He's an outlaw."

"What's the difference?"

Grim thought about it. "A viller who lives in town—a man who acts lawfully every day but one—that's a criminal. A raider, a bandit who comes and goes without regard for any of it—that's an outlaw. It's a fair sight worse."

"They're going to kill him," she said again. She slumped against the cottage wall numbly, and Grim's stony face softened when he saw that she really believed it.

"One or two might try, if they had the chance," he acknowledged. "But I don't think they'll catch him. How long have you known him, lass?"

"Six summers," she said. "Since he was small. Celithrand brought—"

"There's to be none of that," Grim snapped, "not today. This is serious business. No more fairy folk, no tall tales."

She was silent.

"Six summers," he breathed. "And five of those summers, you've lived among us and told us that story. And you see what happens? Tell enough stories, and no one believes you when you speak the truth. Tûr's breath, I wish now I'd listened to you. Might have been a time I could counsel these damn fool ideas out of your head, or lash them out, if you were too damned stubborn for counsel."

"W-will I be lashed?" she asked.

"Would you really learn anything?" he answered sharply. "My father always told me, 'Grim,' he said,

> It pays no help to raise a welt
> Unless you weal a foe;
> You whip a whelp, the welt you dealt
> Will only heal to woe.

Aewyn looked at him in confusion and some fear.

"No, you'll not be lashed," he clarified. "Well, you may be yet, but not by my hand. There's folk enough in this town who treat you like their own child, and have a strong enough arm to prove it. You're damned lucky Darmod Pick's never taken a hand in your raising, or he'd take a hard hand to you now. Man's fit to be tied, and I can't say I blame him."

"What's going to happen to me?" she asked. "Am I an outlaw too?"

"You're a child," said Grim. "Too young to have had a part in this. If anyone's to blame, it's me, for not teaching you better."

"They won't kill me?"

"What's all this killing nonsense about?" Grim asked. "We're none of us killers out here in the thick. That's *why* we came out here, some of us. Even the Havenari—Travalaithi soldiers, most of them, or else men of soldiering age. Killers who got tired of killing, or boys who didn't want to grow up into it. Out here, we need every man we've got, every woman. We need you."

"Me? For what?"

Grim furrowed his brow. "I'll think of something," he said. "Somehow, you're going to make this right—and not by dying, lass. There's no killing or beating for you. That's not who we are."

"Poe says that's all you are," she whispered.

"Is that right?" Grim snapped. "Even me?"

"Even you. All city-men."

"City-men—" Grim stopped and composed himself at that. "Who digs holes for the spring trellises? Who digs a thousand holes every Idismaunt thaw?"

"You do. You and Arran, and Glam, and me."

"And what do your little—what do Gray and Ali do?"

"They bring us the mouse-sticks."

"What for?"

"To put down the holes," Aewyn said. "So if a mouse gets caught in a post-hole in the spring floods, he can climb out."

Grim nodded, let her weigh the experience in her mind, let her feel the memory of loamy earth on her fingers.

"D'you really think we kill each other here?"

She shook her head, but no words came.

"You've known all along he was taking Darmod's sheep. You should have told someone. If he's hungry in the hills, we might have found fair work for him. They're not beasts, are they, the karach? If he can think and speak like a man, he can learn to do fair work, and earn an honest day's pay. At least, he could have done, before all this foolishness."

For all her hateful words against him, she clung to him now and would not let go. "What must I do?" she sobbed. "How do I make things right for him, with the town?"

Grim put a big arm around her. "Now you're asking wise questions. But it's more questions than I've got answers."

They sat in silence for a time. Grim put water on the fire for tea, and the children who woke when he stormed in grew weary and crept back to their beds. It was not long before Karis returned home; she took immediately to sweeping the floor and clearing the wooden bowls from the table. There was no hiding what that meant. She was making the place presentable.

"It's a late hour for civilized visitors," Grim said.

"The karach got over the top," said Karis. "They lost him in the deep woods, of course, as you knew they would. If they're still civilized after all that, you're a lucky man."

Grim stood wearily, laid a gentle hand on her shoulder, reached for a bowl. "I am a lucky man," he said. The smile they nearly shared would have been fleeting, if it had come at all.

"You see that?" he said to Aewyn. "I told you they wouldn't catch him."

"But they'll catch me," she said.

"Aye," said Grim. "That they will. Run along up to bed now. Take care not to wake the others."

"I...you're not going to punish me?"

Grim sighed. "This is bigger than punishment," he said. "Off to bed with you."

They had time enough to clear the table, steep some root tea, and check on each of the children before the knock came. It was a slow, ponderous knock, not as forceful as Grim expected; it was the growing murmur outside more than the knock that told the vintner his door would soon be thrown open, whether or not he unlatched it himself.

Grim came to the door with a long candle, as if he had just come from bed, and was surprised to find Alec Steel at the threshold, his face bright next to a blazing torch.

"I'd expected the Reeve," said Grim, "or worse."

"I am worse," said Alec. "I'm the closest friend you've got, Grim, and I'm here to tell you that Widowvale's making an unhappy stand on it."

Grim looked past him to the dim faces in the darkness, none daring to step forward to accuse him, all waiting for the first punch or torch to be thrown.

"The karach is gone," Grim said. "You've seen them run, haven't you? You remember the Annexation. You waved your sword about a few times in the Clearances, I recall. You know the karach fear death, like any living thing, and you know what ground they can cover when they flee from it. He could be thirty miles gone by tomorrow afternoon. And judging by the size of your very impressive mob," he added, looking out over the whispering line of townsfolk, "he'd be a fool not to cover twenty of them."

"They're not my mob," Alec said. "The Reeve has made his judgment and wants no more of it. But these people want justice. They want the girl to answer for this."

"Not Aewyn," Grim protested, his voice lowering. "Not that poor drowned cat of a girl. That's not justice; where I come from, folks call that revenge."

"She brought him on us," Alec insisted. "Forget for a moment what manner of creature he is. Forget that he could tear your head off with those jaws. The girl befriended an outlaw, and led him straight to our village. He poaches our stock. He flees from what little we have to pass for a court. He could have killed one of Oltman's sons, if they'd been faster fetching the yoke and chain. She's consorted with that trouble, and had a heavy hand in bringing it."

"She's a child," said Grim.

"A fairy-child," Alec countered. "That's what they're whispering now. They're saying that Toren was *right*, and that's no good for any-one. It's no good for Robyn, Grim. She's lost half her men already. Did you think of her?"

"I didn't—"

"Do you suppose Aewyn's seen twelve summers, Grim? Or fifteen? Or how about a thousand, like Celithrand himself?"

"She doesn't say," Grim sighed.

"Listen, friend," said Alec, frowning. "These men and women—every one of them comes from across the Empire, no few of them from lands far beyond. Halgeir's a Banlander like you. Robyn and Bram—she won't talk of where they're from, but I'll wager it's somewhere un-friendly."

"It's nobody's business where those two are from," said Grim sharp-ly. "They're from nowhere, far as I'm concerned. Bastards of Kyric, the both of them, born in some alehouse, or popped out of the ocean like the aerils themselves. Where all these folk are from, it's got nothing to do with the trouble my girl is in."

"But it does," said Alec. "They come from all across Silvalis, and they've brought their stories with them—stories about creatures of magic, creatures like your girl, that live on after magic's gone. Those are the stories they're telling tonight, Grim. And they don't end so well. An ordinary girl with hair that happens to change with the seasons like the fyltree leaves—they can turn a blind eye to a pretty thing like that. But if the Poe exists, if it's really just a karach that survived the Clearances, those stories she tells are starting to come true. We can't ignore them forever. Maybe she's cursed. Maybe she's got some terrible destiny, as magical children of miraculous birth always seem to have. You know how the sagas always go. And people come out in the thick to flee their destinies, not to face them. You of all people should know that."

At Alec's back, Grim could hear the crowd growing restless as Alec went on for longer than they would have liked.

"There's no escaping this particular destiny, is there?" Grim said. "What do they want?"

"Justice," said Alec. "But more than that, they want to go on believing there's nothing special about this girl."

"She is special," said Grim. "She needs no fairy magic for that."

Alec would not be moved. "Let her take the karach's punishment. Let her get her hands dirty, like a real farmer. There's plenty of women working the land here—plenty who will train her up, if you won't. If she's a communal child, let her do communal chores. Let her work off the debt to Darmod in the karach's place, and I swear to you they'll let the matter go."

"Put the yoke on her?" Grim asked. "Are you mad? She can't pull a plough. I've owned dogs that outweigh her."

"Ah, but old Orin has birthed horses that weighed less," countered Alec. "No one's expecting her to pull a plough. They just want to see her stop being an ill omen, and start being a farmer's daughter. No more fairy-folk and monsters, Grim. Just a girl in a field."

"A girl in a field," repeated Grim.

"That's all they want. A normal village of normal people."

Grim scowled at him. "Alec Steel, you are a mercenary, and a mercenary's son."

"Call me Alec Mercy," Alec countered. "That's what the moot decided, after you fled. They think the name suits me, after all I've said to quench their fires. A poor name for one who fought in the war, I think." He leaned in close—his beard was close enough to Grim's ear to scratch it. "Mercy or no," he said then, "these people must see something real, something unpleasant, happen to the poor wretches tangled up in the fabric of this misfortune. They need to know, above all, that they do not live in a lawless society. Do not be fooled by the warm summers: we are frontier folk, here in Widowvale. We have no tribunals, no magistrates, no proper courts but what Marin gives us. And those things make justice more important, Grim...not less."

For a rare and brief moment, Grim's face softened. "Alec Mercy," he breathed. "The name suits you, I think. A worthy name."

"Let me come in and speak with you about your punishment," said Alec. "Yours and the girl's, in exacting detail. We'll talk all night if we must, until the cold and the wind take the fire out of these people, and they stagger off home to their beds. And we'd better be damned sure we arrive at a suitable answer before they come back in the warmth of day."

Aewyn's hands were small and thin, with clever fingers, and her eyesight was strangely keen even in the dark. They were made, Grim said, for the planting of carrot seeds. Romaunt was a bleak month in the mildest of climes; in Haveïl, it was meant for carrot seeds and not much else. The bold favoured cabbage, but the largest fields were unprotected, and the weather of late winter and early spring was unpredictable at best, unforgiving at worst. Carrots were dependable, Grim said, like a good mace. Unlike a sword, he said, a good mace never needed sharpening or oiling. The little seeds were flanged like tiny mace-heads, which he explained was the source of their hardiness in the early season.

Aewyn's childhood had ended suddenly over that winter, and she knew Grim's lies now when she heard them. What did a vintner know of carrots, after all? He would tell her any and all stories he could to keep her tired legs moving, her chilled hands placing seed after seed in his grunting, sweating wake. Three seeds to a hole and a full step. Three seeds to a hole. Even for the hardy carrot, life in this land was uncertain.

A few paces ahead of her, Grim leaned hard against the push-plough, moiling against the strain of the barely-thawed soil. "Keep up," he scolded.

For two weeks, now, they had risen in the night to till and sow their way across the fields of Widowvale, leaving as much pregnant soil behind them as they could manage before the sun rose to announce the start of Grim's own workday. The old push-plough, a narrow-wheeled wooden frame with a scrap of bellmetal for a share, cut hardly more than a harrow's depth in the cold soil. But it was as much as Grim could manage by hand—and so here they were at sowing time, crossing fields already turned and furrowed to lay seeds of carrots, collards, and peas in shallow tracks. A night of planting, from the small hours to sunrise, was counted half a day; and a day of planting was counted half a day again of ploughing. So it was that Grim and Aewyn together began to serve the karach's sentence with conviction and patience, for his two seasons at the plough would cost them eight.

The tense silence of winter and the unquenched anger of the town itself had faded now; but gone, too, were Aewyn's days under the trees, taking shelter with the great karach for warmth, taking what delightful food and drink the forest was pleased to give her. There were no karach left in the land west of the Capital, now, and none really knew how much work could be done by one karach in two seasons. It was certainly more, however, than one portly vintner and a whelp of a girl could account for. Grim never told her (it was part of her punishment) how long the work was to last. Perhaps forever, she thought. Perhaps they would forget, in time, the life of freedom they had lived before the Reeve had accepted Grim's settlement. Grim himself seemed to have forgotten his former life already, just as he had forgotten the one before that, before he left the inhospitable Banlands for a life no less friendly.

"You're not counting stars, Princess," Grim barked again. "Three seeds to a hole, take a step. Come on."

Aewyn sourly doubled her speed, but pushing her resentment out of mind only seemed to bring it to her mouth. "Why the hurry?" she said. "We'll be here for a whole season, even if we could plant the whole Empire in a night."

"I'm not about to waste my breath explaining justice," he said. "This field will teach you justice soon enough. I'd expect that kind of yowling if you were big enough to push the plough. But your work, sprinkling seeds and patting the earth, that's nothing-work. That's child-work. If we're at this a whole season, maybe you'll get big enough to push for a while, maybe find out what real work is."

"It's real enough work, this many hours for a small bag of seeds," said Aewyn. "That's hardly more than a stick in the ground. They mean to insult you, else they'd have given you a real plough."

"It's every bit as much as I can handle," he said. "And a fair sight more than you can. You need beasts to pull the heavy plough, Aewyn. Oxen, big horses. Or maybe a karach, like that pet of yours."

"Poe," she said softly. "My friend has a name."

"Poe," Grim repeated with stoic acceptance. "Well, your 'friend' certainly left you—left us, I venture—to handle his debt for him."

"I'll be leaving too, someday," she said suddenly. "I'm a child of destiny. Celithrand told me so, once. Someday the druids will take me away and I'll become a great warrior, like—like in the songs."

Grim shrugged with his eyebrows, since his shoulders were hard at use.

"Warriors need muscles," he said, "and you've clearly got no interest in growing yourself any. There's a thousand songs of heroes in the Hanes of the North, and not one about a sickly runt who whines at the touch of steel. If the druids are coming to take you away to their magic kingdom, well, then get your arms and legs moving, and give 'em something worth taking. Otherwise, you can ask Robyn when she comes back to the village what it really means to be a warrior-woman. Feel the muscles in her bow-arm some time, and ask her if it's a nice break from farm work to go do something easy like soldiering."

Aewyn had a retort, but dared not utter it.

"Go ask your friend the karach, while you're at it," he added, "what kind of work a warrior gets up to. He's no doubt seen plenty of their work with his own eyes."

"He won't come back," she said. "I won't see him again, after what's been done to him."

Grim snorted at that. "What's been done? It's been done to you in his stead," he reminded her. "And I'd call no one 'friend' who left me holding the honey when the bees came home. If that's what passes for a friend in these lands, ye princess of the druids… I suppose I should be glad he's seen to it I've no friends left in Widowvale, either." The remark stung her almost as much as the long silence that followed.

All that season and into the next, they talked little and laughed less. It was not all planting, of course. Some of it was harder work still—but as time passed and forgiveness began to take root, some of it was hardly work at all. A few of the year's more fortunate townsfolk, their purses overflowing with silver or their carts too heavily laden with foodstuffs, bought days of their field-labour from Darmod Pick, then bade them sit in the shade with a cup of Grim's wine and a few of his tall tales, as long as he was generous with both. Despite her growing renown as the town's youngest criminal mad-woman (to be touched by the wood folk was not, after all, universally smiled upon), Aewyn was a likeable girl. She had been fostered in many homes, and made many friends, and while they would not give public voice to their hearts, it pained them to see her toil without end.

That year was later remembered as the Year of Twins, for Alec Mercy's mares foaled very late in the spring, but no less than three of them foaled healthy twins. Even Orin, the old groom who was called upon to attend the births, could remember no such occurrence. He had seen only four sets of twins in all his travels between Travalaith and Widowvale; always with horses one twin was too weak, he said, and had to be slain. But this season the birthing was easy, if long, and they were of good stock and grew mightily. The foals were a fair sight in Alec's fields, and he knew that in time he would prosper well beyond his expectations, for the Mages' Uprising left the Iron City in great need of horses, and pure hot-blood breeds were high in demand. It was an implausible, even miraculous windfall, with some saying that the gods had seen fit to reward Alec for his kindness.

One of the six twins he gave to Darmod Pick, when it was hale enough—a black-maned filly with a coat of burnished gold, the larger of the twins from her mother. This was considered far too generous a trade for the several days of Aewyn's labour he took in barter. Many of the townsfolk were still wroth with Alec for his easy judgment of the karach at Darmod's expense, but in the hearts of many, the foal settled those accounts. Darmod was a hard man, but his anger grieved him, and when he named the young filly Shimble, or "gold-thorn," after a plant used in the healing of old wounds, it gladdened the hearts of many. For many seasons thereafter, it was said—though never too loudly—that Darmod in secret was a kind man. Even more quietly, it was said that Alec Mercy was wise.

By this shrewd gift of his good fortune, Alec bought many days of relief for Aewyn and Grim over the hottest crest of the summer. He was well off and growing wealthier with no need of their labour, and so they would sit in back of his house, which was large and had a loft, and drink Grim's wine, and tell stories until there was no light to work by. Alec, too, was a fine storyteller, with tales from the city that seemed inexhaustible. But the stories that interested him most were not his own, nor even Grim's, but Aewyn's; and for the relief it afforded his toil-weary back and hands, Grim learned to suffer her fairy-stories gladly.

"The matter of the karach is still unsettled," Alec warned them, "and I am unsettled as well. I would like to hear everything I can about how this has all come to pass. And this time I promise to believe you, Aewyn, no less than a little—and more, if I can."

FOUR

Sing, Spirit, of companies, seasoned   campaigners of yore
Who brandished bright weapons and banners   in service of war,
Who warred not for glory, though glory   by weapons they won,
Sing out of the sign of the Owl, of   the worm-liquor spun,
Of the Four of the North, unchained from   the fetters of fear,
Who strove with their strength, who struggled   with knife against spear
In the long siege at Travost; sing true of   the travails and trials
Of the four allied forces, who fighting   won fame for their styles
And peace for their families, proud of   the price that they paid:
By craft they were mighty; by might the   false Craftsman unmade.

Sing, Spirit, of Celithrand's sacrifice!   Sing of the Gift
That he rendered, rejecting his fate, and   by rending a rift
Between a life lasting for ever   beloved by the Fei
Who were family to him, for forsaking   their undying way
On the waves, he who would not on water   be merged with his folk
At their yearly return—how unyielding   he took up the yoke
Of the young, of the Ox, who by effort   and suffering strove
To contend with the terror of Men. Thus   he tarried for love
With great strength and a steely resolve on   the steps of the dawn,
And was tied to the Earth, and was hailed, but would never sail on.

LEC MERCY HAD GROWN UP the son of a soldier,
and the soldiers of Travalaith knew a very particular family of songs.
The Ballad of the Bannered Owl, as it was known, was a pompous and
ponderous song, winding on some forty or fifty verses from beginning
to end. Most soldiers knew five or ten verses—the ones most directly
concerned with battle and valour—but Alec was wiser than most, and
could sing the first half or so from memory. This he did only reluctantly, after Aewyn had asked him every day for a week; but when he
unlocked the singing-voice long chained up in his throat, it was melo-
dious and deep, like the voice of a grandfather or distant uncle in his
fiery prime. In song his voice belied his origins east of the Iron City,
and it rang with the proud wonder of a child raised on heroic stories
of war, tempered only slightly by the uneasy sadness of a man who had
grown to see such grisly times firsthand.

From Alec, Aewyn heard of Celithrand's efforts in the war—how he had fought with the Company of the Owl to end the Siege of Shadow, how he had come to the Northlands from the long-lived aerils, and forsaken the natural fate of his people to continue to serve as the Imperator's chief counsel and spiritual advisor. Such grandiose stories, told in sweeping lines of bloated court poetry, seemed passing strange to her: the Celithrand she knew was a kindly old man who came to Haveïl in the springtime, regular as the moons, and brought her trinkets and treasures from distant lands, and taught her the words and ways of his people as she grew.

In the height of summer, Grim walked her as far as the old shelter—Poe was nowhere to be found—where she gathered these few possessions and brought them to show Alec Mercy with a sense of pride utterly detached from their worth. A black-bladed knife, cut from a single block of obsidian, was to Grim's eyes the jewel of the collection: the stone was mined in far-off Shadowsand and in Seythe across the sea, and trace amounts of it had been found in the deadlands north of North. The rest of her little treasures—a crude game-piece carved of petrified wood from Estellone, bright seashells from the Rahastan coast, tumbled stones of streaked amber—were curiosities of far less worth, but she spoke of them with no less wonder.

The karach himself had been one of these seasonal gifts—a companion and playmate brought to the child one spring for reasons then unknown to her. He was a cub then, young even by the measure of his short-lived kind: in those days he was smaller than Aewyn, and he never forgot this even in the years he towered over her. His strange speech, when he tried it upon her, was halting and came with a yelp and a high-pitched whine he was slow to shed. His name was something close to Poe—a sound in his own tongue that even Celithrand could pronounce only with difficulty. It was not a natural human sound, and "Poe" was the closest she could come to it.

Eventually, he resigned himself to it and answered to her best efforts, though the sound of his name never pleased him. In time he learned to speak Viluri, the ancient language of the aerils, though it was harsh and deep in his throat, and with a shared language their friendship deepened into family. In the long days of winter, when Aewyn's hair turned white and the forest was quiet, the two would go walking in the deep woods together, weaving from their thoughts a spring of sounds that never ran dry.

It was Poe who first told her of the land beyond the trees, a warm lowland rich in birds and flowers, where he had been born among others of his kind, and grown among the karach. He told her also of those called the Iun in Viluri—people shaped like her, who lived male and female together in vast camps of stone and wood. He spoke most frequently of them, though not without pain. When he spoke of his own people, the hurt deepened, and he was quick to move on.

Of her mother, though, Aewyn could remember little. It was, Grim insisted, the way of fairies and wood-spirits that the farther out a man ventured from their magic world, the less distinct his memories became, like a dream remembered too long after waking. In Celithrand's native tongue she was called Aelissraia, though between them the two spoke some other tongue of the wood, some ancient whisper that seemed to Aewyn as the sound of wind through the leaves.

To Aewyn she spoke little if at all, and her green eyes, though full of love, were wild and alien in their way. Her skin had the colour and smoothness of naked birch, and her hair, like Aewyn's, changed with the seasons. Aewyn's memory was that she smelled always of wildflowers, and her milk was woody and sweet. But she was not like a human mother, and the silly rhymes and stern warnings Karis heaped on her children were foreign to Aewyn at first. The motherhood of the Iun was altogether different. Half-imagined through a wistful veil, Aewyn had, in the end, only fleeting impressions of her mother—that she was gentle and sad; that she was inattentive, by the standards of mundane folk; that she had unseen ways of going within the deep wood, and was ever more often away.

Celithrand was frequently on the move as well, and as her connection to Poe deepened she came to fully inhabit his mundane world. The food of the forest that had once been so plentiful was replaced by pangs of hunger and the need to forage and hunt—skills Poe taught her from his own childhood. The closer she stayed to the heart of the wood, the better she endured the cold of winter: the chilling climate did not trouble her in the deep wood, but pained her like a normal child when she ventured too far. The chill of the winter and the sparseness of food outside the heart of the forest served to keep her from coming too near the village until she was discovered. Poe's hunger could not be sated by the magic of the wood, and he was forced to roam wider in search of food. The notion that he was a poacher—wrapped as it was in strange ideas about livestock, possession, and crime—was foreign to him. And like a soft-hearted shepherd who preferred cheese to mutton, Poe soon shed his natural inclination to hunt those domesticated herd-creatures that walked on two legs and looked too much like Aewyn. She was of human form, if not quite human spirit, and the prospect of manhunting made him uncomfortable.

In the lazy evenings behind Alec Mercy's house, tasting Grim's wine and sharing stories, Grim asked her most often about her mother. Was she really a fairy? Did she have extraordinary powers? Did she really go about the woods as naked as a toad? Had she ever lured a mortal man like in the ballads? She must have, he reasoned, to birth a child; but Aewyn had answers to none of these questions. Her mother was a distant figure, a weak memory growing weaker with each day she spent in Widowvale.

"It's not natural," Grim said, "for a girl to grow and not know her mother, nor father."

"Fawns leave their mother after two winters," said Aewyn. "Besides which, Karis has been my mother, and you are as sure a father to me as any."

"I'm surprised you recall as much as you do," said Alec. "Men who get bewitched these days mostly don't know it. You know Robyn's brother, Bram? He was gone all through the last muster of the Havenari. I've heard he was taken by a woodkin, lived a year and a day with her, and returned home that same week. He's got that great sadness in him, like a man who loved a fairy once, and can never find his way home to her."

"Bram's a good man," said Grim. "Or the better part of one, at least. But just the same, I think it was a brown jug, not a green lady, that kept him from muster."

"It's just as well he doesn't ride out with them," said Alec. "I'll not trust the borderlands to a man in that condition. It's shameful the way he embarrasses his sister."

"She doesn't seem embarrassed," Grim noted.

"She's had enough trouble bringing that bunch to heel without his reputation weighing on her. Eight men deserted in five years, that's more than she deserves. She's not weak, Grim. It's her fool brother makes her look so."

Grim scoffed. "It's all polished plate and pageantry, anywise," he said. "Not one of the Havenari is a true soldier. Not anymore, whatever they were supposed to be, long ago."

"Robyn's the finest archer in Haveïl just the same," Alec said. "Better than I am, and I've loosed arrows on men in battle. I've seen her thread a ring at thirty yards. She's won the tourney in the fall fair six years running."

"Then we'll be safe," Grim replied, smiling, "when the prophecies come true and the Tourney Rings rise and walk again."

Alec shrugged and left it at that, turning back to Aewyn. "Did your mother have—a taste for ordinary men?" he asked. "Like they say in the fairy ballads?"

Aewyn shook her head. "I don't know," she said. "There were never men who came to see us, except Celithrand, but I remember so little about her."

"That baffles me," said Grim. "I find it hard to believe you remember so little of your old life."

"I don't," Alec countered. "We've all come here, give or take, to forget our old lives. I was seventeen when I joined the Grand Army."

"I thought you played the horn," said Aewyn. "That's what Arran and Glam say."

"I did," said Alec. "I was what's called a bannerhorn—a signal-carrier for the legions during the Stonewind Clearances."

Grim nodded. "You were in one of the Blades, weren't you?"

"Tenth Legion of the Blade," said Alec. "They called us the Blood Dogs, and not because we made good manor pets. I fought in the Wastes under Harrod, long before he ever became Master General of the Blade. And you know what? I remember very little of that life—and I'd like to keep it that way."

"Can't say I blame you," said Grim.

"And you, Grim? What were you in your former life?"

Grim chuckled. "I see your point," he admitted. But a shadow passed over his features and he said no more.

"You're safe at home here, Aewyn," said Alec. "Do the children tease you, being different?"

"Only Glam," she said, naming Grim's second-oldest. "And I wallop him for it."

Alec smiled. "We're all outsiders in the end, girl. You. Me. Grim. Maybe I was a soldier once. Maybe you were a magical dryad, or a dryad's kin. Maybe you were born under a star of fate, as you say. But Widowvale's a young town—probably no older than you—and it's a new home for us all. You can make a new fate here, if it suits you."

"I don't know what suits me," she said.

"I know what doesn't suit you," said Grim. "That'd be farm-work. But it's where you're at for now. We've taken enough of Alec's time. Hettie Oltman's greens aren't going to grow themselves. Plenty of time to figure out the rest later."

Aewyn turned back to Alec as she stood up. "Do you miss your home, though? Or your family, if you have any?"

Alec thought about it for a long moment. "I miss my family," he said. "They're spread all over, now. But I never miss the Iron City. My home is my horses, and my pasture, and the bees I keep in the high or-chard. It's blue skies and clean snows, roads that smell of autumn cedar rather than rubbish and window-shit. Pardon me, girl. Grim."

"She's not my daughter," Grim said off-handedly. "Speak as you like."

"Come fall, my home will be the Harvest Fair," said Alec. "Music on the hill. Children under the oak. Bram sleepy with wine on the steps of the moot-hall, Grim here all the richer for it. Robyn in a skirt, the one night of the year, barefoot on the green, dancing the halling as well as any man."

Aewyn's eyes brightened at the mention of the young woman. "I can't wait to see Robyn again," she said. "It's been so long, now, since she's come through town. The patrols or the seasons, or both, grow too long when she's gone away."

"That," said Grim knowingly, "is not a lesson you need teach Alec Mercy."

If there was a Harvest Fair that year, Aewyn had little memory of it. She worked through the fair, too exhausted from her labours to make much of an appearance. She heard only later from Arran, Grim's oldest son, that it was a particularly good one: the Year of the Twins, after all, was treated by all as a year of plenty. After the census had made their head count, the miners all came in from Minter's Rock and lands farther afield, their clothes black with dust and their sacks heavy with smelted silver. They bathed at the Riffle, and Grim's daughter Ali was old enough that year to climb to Maiden's Watch with the older girls. On Baker's Day, the ceremonial loaf of autumn bread was brought to the moot-hall, signaling the beginning of the fall harvest season. When the fair finally came, the Reeve led the young children on the mushroom hunt; the balefire burned as the few who worshipped the Banlanders' gods (and a fair number of opportunistic young couples) took to the fields and gave thanks in the old way. Grim again sold twice his weight in wine during the festival alone, an achievement that grew more impressive with each passing year—though it was Arran, mostly, who managed the sales. Grim, for his part, was no better off than Aewyn, and spent most of the festival on his back in bed, saving his strength for the work that would not end.

Not all was as it should have been, however. For reasons unknown, the Havenari did not return. Robyn did not come to the village green; she wore no green dress, danced no dances, and for the first time in years the annual archery contest was won by someone new. Halgeir the Tall, a yellow-bearded Banlander who had come down to seek his fortune in the mines, bested Alec Mercy by a hair in the final shootout. His luck with a bow on the archery butts was evidently better than his luck in the mines, but most said it was only natural, since he'd hunted ghost hawks in some far-off northern vasily in his former life.

That whole season was lost to Aewyn, in any case, and before long it was time again to prepare for seeding the last winter forage, a sign that the season had come to an end. Her hair, a stunning red through the autumn, had gone the pale white of old bone. Grim's hair, too, was more grey than it once was, though its colour was not so likely to return with the spring.

The third ploughing of the year meant real work, especially in a field the size of Hettie Oltman's. Her farm was a large one, plotted long and lean in the shadow of the escarpment, upriver from the mill. She was called the "true-widow" for she was one of the few women whose husbands had well and truly died, and the field was as large a piece as she and her three sons could work. It had grown further since Darmod Pick had gained the good fortune of indentured help: Hettie Oltman was a shrewd woman and went hungry one season to hire Aewyn and Grim for the next. The swell of her harvest was testament to her wisdom and patience, and she was ever after sought out by the other farmers for advice and counsel.

The seeding of her winter oats did not have to be deep, and so it was determined that the ploughing of the fallow field in preparation could be done without ox or horse. Alec Mercy had done the kindness of hauling over the larger of the two push ploughs from Grimstead with his stud horse the night before. But even under two near-full moons, the night was a dark one as Grim struggled to push his wife's arm off him. It seemed heavier on him every night.

"You're going," she managed to moan. "You only just came back."

"It won't be much longer," he said. "Shut your eyes and dream, sweetling."

"I'm dreaming of toys," she said cryptically. "Leather horses, like Rinnie's."

Grim kissed his wife on the forehead. "You're mad," he said.

"I'll get over it," she groaned into the straw pillow.

Aewyn was ready for him, as she had been all week, by the time he puffed his way down from the little loft. "Quiet as a mouse, now," he whispered, and led her to the door. "But quick. We're late."

"I was ready," said Aewyn.

"Well, I wasn't," mumbled Grim. "But the morning comes just the same. Hurry on."

The two shut the door of the house gently, then took to a steady jog down the main road, Aewyn light as a doe, Grim huffing to keep up. "Solstice near," he said between ragged breaths. "Sun comes up later—every day."

They set to work again, Grim leaning hard on the plough as Aewyn followed him with spade and seeds. It was slow going at first; Grim struggled with the plough more than usual, and the cobwebs of dream hung over Aewyn's eyes, though she tried to sweep them away. She had been dreaming of her mother, and of a terrible chase through the deep wood. At first, it was something like a bear chasing her mother; then, the bear's eyes and skin were changed, slick to the touch as if turned inside-out for curing, and fire roiled in its hanging mouth. She saw the flames lick at her mother's heels, closer this time. Though she dared not tell Grim, the dreams were getting worse. Rising before dawn, even hours before, was a pleasure to her after dreams like that.

Aewyn wondered, sometimes, if she had the gift for prophecy. There were certainly stories about it. Karis's sister, a merchant who still lived in the Capital, swore that the true Travosti kings, in ancient times, had been a bloodline of seers and prophets. Why not, then, the child of a dryad? She dared not think of herself as a dryad—she felt too much like the children of Widowvale now. She took too much after Glam and Gray, Grim's second and third sons, to be anything near as strange as her mother. But she had been thinking, lately, of what it meant to have an extraordinary birth. She had considered that the facts of her life might to some be called legends—that Celithrand and her wood-spirit mother, both of whom she knew in her heart were real, were things others disbelieved in as freely as monsters or dragons. Perhaps a dryad was, in fact, a monster, in some men's ways of thinking. And if a dryad could exist, why not a seer? Why not a dragon, or a sea monster, or...

She was jolted from her reverie as she ran hard against Grim's broad back where he leaned against the plough.

"I caught up!" she said, rather proud of herself. Grim nodded slowly.

"I must be getting faster," she beamed, unsure of how much ground she had covered as her thoughts ran away with her. She looked back to make sure she had not been too careless in her planting. The long row stretched out as straight as an arrow shaft.

"Aewyn."

Grim rolled himself around to face her. His jaw was slack, and his arms were draped limply over the cross-bar, twisted inward like a dead spider's legs. She felt suddenly cold—and he looked it.

"I'm tired," he said. "I think I'm tired."

She didn't think she'd be strong enough to catch him as he fell. She wasn't. But she slowed his descent with her straining arms, staggered with her load, and he fell to the earth not like a stone, but like a dancing leaf. She called his name and he nodded.

"Karis," he said, his voice very small on his tongue. "Tell her I just had to come back, and meet the woman who made this soup..."

When his lips stopped moving, the night was still, as if the whole Empire had stopped with them, and Aewyn's heaving chest was the only thing in all the world that still moved. She screamed his name, or something like it, more than once; each time the scream was a little less like his name, as Grim, too, was a little less like himself.

A light—first a candle, then a torch—was kindled in the window of the Oltman house. Somewhere the trees rustled as a night-bird started. Hettie Oltman's sons were big men, and Corran was the biggest of them. His body almost filled the whole door frame. He was a fast runner. The bag of seeds had fallen all in one place. Someone, probably

Corran's brother Ard, had brought a blanket for her. Grim's face was the colour of mottled stone. There was no wind. The night was cloudless and the stars were beyond count. Aewyn's feet were heavy and the voices of Oltman's sons were deep rumblings around her, muddled as if heard through water. She had never seen Corran Oltman cry before. He had seemed, for many years, so much older than she was. He had come out of doors in his bare feet, and they were soon muddy from the field.

Aewyn's eyesight was keen as a knife's edge, even in the dark—made, as Grim had said, for the planting of carrot seeds. There was no mistaking the gleam staring back at her from the trees, watching her. Poe's eyes were the yellow of mashed yams by day; but in firelight the back of his eyes shone emerald green; Corran's torch gave him away easily. She wondered what he would make of the death of a man. She wondered if a man smelled different dead than alive—wondered if a karach could smell your soul going on its way, even before the rot set in. In the days to come, she remembered nothing that transpired after they took her into the house; but she heard later that once Grim's death was beyond doubt, they left him face-down in the field for a time, and carried her indoors instead, and gave her food and drink, warmed her, held her hands, staunched the flow of her tears with soft rags. Their first duty was to care for the living; and like many who lived in such border towns, the sons of the widow Oltman were practical young men.

The weekday of Grim's death was not recorded in the Chronicles of Widowvale—at least, not at first, and not by the Reeve. There was no need, in such a small and new place, for such luxuries as weeks: worship in the town, for those who cared for it, happened daily and followed the hours of the sun. Days of work and payment followed the white moon and her changing faces. But when Karis emerged from her days of mourning, she went straight away to the moot-hall to meet with the Reeve, seeking permission to alter the book in accordance with what would have been Grim's wishes. He ought to have refused her; but he was her brother, after all—and in truth, that stood him as a potential heir to Grimstead if the laws of inheritance in the Empire, the laws of men and men alone, overruled the old laws of men and women alike. So out of courtesy, deference, greed, even brotherly love, Marin the Reeve acceded and took her to his home, where she recorded in the margins that Grim died on Jornsday—the last Jornsday before the start of winter. At the time of the last crop, before the soil could freeze, he was laid in the ground by his oldest boys. It was a custom foreign to his ancestors, but one he would have wanted, and a fitting end for a man who lived and died on rich tilled earth.

We know, then, that Poe returned on Jornsday also. For six days, Grim's family mourned, and Aewyn worked the field alone. Darmod Pick refused to release her from service to mourn, for she was not Grim's natural child, nor even a child of Karis, and she had no legal claim to a day of mourning. Twice a bastard, he called her, a child with no right father, nor mother either; and though it was thought unkind, the debt was hers to shoulder—sixteen seasons it would be, now, twice the indenture of the two of them together, for half the work would come of it. Corran Oltman brought food and drink to her in the field, which he need not have done, and for that most called him a kind man like his father before him. But for six days Aewyn laboured feebly, alone with her tears in the desolate field. When she was too weak to walk the heavy hand-plough, Alec Mercy towed it away and brought her the light one; when she was too weak for that, he brought her a hand-held loy spade; and with little else but that loy and determination, she made the Oltmans' south field ready for winter seed in the days after Grim's death. Her hair had gone shock-white now with the change of seasons, and her eyes hard; often she wept, and in the odd hours between her efforts she would fall to her knees and pine loudly for Grim, for she had never known death and was slow to comprehend it.

On the morning of the seventh day, when Corran Oltman walked out to the south field with apples and cheese, he saw the karach crouched in the field with her, stroking her head as a mother soothes a child, speaking some strange tongue as she wept against its broad chest. Although it had grown a head taller than it had been the previous year, it was definitely the same one as before, judging from the way it turned and stiffened at his approach. It remembered the smell of him, perhaps, or remembered the ox-yoke he had carried for it, and suddenly big Corran felt very small and ventured no closer.

Whatever words it might have shared with Aewyn, he saw it the next day also; and on the third day, it took up the loy and began to work for her, though the silly tool looked like a toy in its clawed hands. When it proved too strong for the loy, it turned to the little push-plough; when it was too strong for that, Alec Mercy brought the heavier one; when that proved little challenge, Alec came for the first time with a proper cart-plough of the sort drawn by an ox or bull, and Corran brought up the yoke. Finally, the karach bent his head low and suffered the big man to tighten it over his shoulders.

"I unarrstan," the karach growled to Corran, pointing at the yoke, which put the big man not even slightly at ease. But it was clear he had been made to practice the words.

Through much of the autumn, the karach laboured with Aewyn. They planted Oltman's south field and ploughed in the north and west before the frosts of Teurmaunt came. Then was the time for gathering acorns in Alec Mercy's fields; when that was done, and the snows had come, they returned to Darmod Pick's farm. The sheep would come nowhere near their old foe, knowing the karach's looming shadow all too well, but the two worked in the gardens around Darmod's home and replaced the shoddy fences between meadows with walls of waste stone quarried from the mines. Aewyn's hands were skillful at stacking, her walls stood the old way, without mortar or pitch, and the karach tirelessly brought enormous loads of rubble in a great bronze-banded wheelbarrow. In the cold of the winter, Aewyn would sometimes sleep at the Oltman farm, though her work was done there, and bring the karach there for a few hours after nightfall. Corran and Ard would serve them winter cider and the meat of the fall slaughter. The karach, whose name they learned was something like Poe, learned to say "hello" and "welcome" and "thank you" in the Merchants' Tongue, though it never sounded smooth, and it found their well-furnished home a place of much curiosity as it stooped through the hall, asking the names of things.

Word of the karach's return was, of course, quick to circulate. Stout men came at first with spears and board-shields, but these men had been hand-picked by the Reeve, who chose cool-blooded men with level heads. One of them, Aewyn was sure, was Alec Mercy, though he kept his distance and only watched a little from the field's edge. He looked sad, though at what she could not tell; perhaps he had felt Grim's death as a heavy weight on his breast, as she did. In any event he came for a few minutes every day, with two or three other men elected to watch the beast. But after the first day he came no more with weapons—only with grey eyes that seemed jewels of sadness.

The townsfolk of Widowvale took the whole winter to decide what was to be done with Aewyn after that, and especially with Poe, though he did not shelter with them, retreating to the trees after dark to work some unknown mischief in the woods. Aewyn Half-Dryad (or, as she was less charitably known, Aewyn Twice-Bastard) was something of a communal child, but it was known that she had taken strongest to the family of Grim. Word was sent from the house of the widow Karis that she remained welcome in their home as one of their own. But that news came by way of fair-haired Arran, and not by way of Karis herself, who stayed at Grimstead. Except for the one meeting with her brother to record Grim's day of death, she would not come down from her house.

Aewyn, for her part, was quite insistent she could survive in the wild. She had grown up there, after all, and had grown taller and stronger from her work in the field. But this was not given real consideration by the Reeve or anyone else. When Darmod Pick offered to make her up a bed in his home, even the Reeve was surprised. His argument landed on sound points: she did most of her work for him, and his own house was closest to his lands. When her debt was paid, she could simply stay on, earning her keep (and perhaps even meat for her friend). And yet there was something in him that had changed; or else he saw something changed in her, now that some of the adversity that had hardened him against the world had come to wound her as well.

She must have spoken to Darmod in private, for as the cold winter wore on it seemed she was living with him. Rumors swirled, for a time, that the sour old man had taken the girl to his bed, but they did not last: so keen was his dislike for her that few imagined a love, or even a lust, could be kindled there. Like the girl, Darmod had never shown any real interest in women before, or even in men. They had a queer sort of kinship in that, and the townsfolk who speculated that Aewyn's soul was too pure for the love of ordinary folk were equally quick to judge Darmod's as too stained for it.

This arrangement also meant that Aewyn had her share of freedom, and spent the long evening hours in the woods with Poe. The karach still came down to the fields, still tirelessly did the work of five or six men—and in his cleverness under Darmod's cautious tutelage, he learned the arts of the fields and furrows; thinking like a man and pulling like an ox, he worked better than either one alone. The spring lambing, when it came, was bountiful for Darmod Pick, but now that he had added through his unlikely servants a considerable vegetable crop, he would share now in the riches of the late summer harvest too. With two seasons of plenty to look forward to, Darmod's temperament seemed to ease, and few were troubled by Aewyn's presence in his home for long. Corran still brought her lunch in the fields, and Alec Mercy still came to look with sad wonder at the towering beast, hauling earth in the fields as he practiced his halting speech.

One day in the spring, Darmod came out to meet Alec by the meadow-fence as Aewyn and Poe were transplanting the onion bulbs. A smile, and not an insincere one, split his craggy face nearly in half.

"Alec Mercy indeed," he said. "You've made me a wealthy man with your mercy."

"I haven't," Alec said dismissively.

"Well enough," said Darmod. "Less poor, then. The whole town talks of that brute; his shadow falls halfway to Minter's Rock, when the sun's low. But that wee nothing of a girl—she's determined, I'll give her that. Good arms on her, like yew, spindly enough, but they'll be strong one day if she keeps at the work."

"She has the span of a little archer," Alec said, smiling. "I'll have Robyn teach her when she rides back." He looked away wistfully, then. "When she rides *home*."

"Has that to do with the whole prophecy business?" asked Dar-mod.

"What prophecy?"

Darmod waved a hand dismissively in her direction, as if to punc-tuate his speech with cynicism before he spoke.

"She tells of it, sometimes," said Darmod. "Twice-bastard that she is, she swears some king of the druids found her in the woods, and like every foundling in every story, he's supposed to come fetch her one day and take her away to some great destiny."

"Do you believe it?" said Alec.

"The world doesn't work that way anymore," said Darmod, "if it ever did. This mysterious-birth business is no great wonder in my family. I grew up in the First Revolt, and believe me, children who don't know their fathers are nothing special in these times. Sons of Kyric, they're called, after the old trickster." He paused thoughtfully. "Always wished I was one. If you'd known my father, you'd understand. But past that, a mysterious birth means no great destiny. All it means is she'll have a hard time getting wedded and bedded when the time comes, with no name and no dowry to speak of."

"Perhaps that's why she belongs with Robyn," said Alec wistfully. "The Havenari certainly do behave themselves better when they ride out with an old maid on point. And Robyn won't stay unwed forever."

"Where I come from," Darmod said, "archery and militia duty are a man's work."

"We are a long way from Pickstand, sheep-lord," Alec warned him. "And I'd suffer no one in these woods—man, woman, or child—without a proper longbow. I wouldn't send a dog into those woods unless he could shoot with his wagging tail."

"The woods are safe enough," said Darmod, "now that the karach's come down out of them and knows his place and his punishment. I wouldn't go far as to call him civilized, but we have no more to fear from him. Much to gain from his work, too, and I'm more surprised by it than any. I may even keep him fed on mutton, if he'll stay on and work when his time is up."

But Alec Mercy was far away in his mind, grey eyes fixed on, but not really watching, the movements of Aewyn and Poe in the next field.

"There are worse things in those trees than karach," he said, and left it at that.

FIVE

HE TWILIGHT OF THAT SUMMER was a time of leisure and bounty for everyone but Arran, the eldest son of Grim. At eighteen years of age, he was as broad as a bull across the shoulders, and so well-muscled from his farm work that he had overtaken Ard Oltman as the largest young man among the generation coming up. Arran the Strong, some called him already—the eldest and healthiest of the first generation of children to be raised in Widowvale. He was well-liked enough, though he was quiet and withdrawn.

In solitude he walked the rolling fields of Grimstead, though he dared not go too near his reflection in the pond there. He could not bear the sight of himself, come into his full strength. His father, he had come to remember, was not particularly tall, large only around the middle, run to fat at the end of his life, and yet in the sparse hours outside his indenture, Grim whispered and sang up one of the richest crops the vineyards at Grimstead ever produced. Arran had toiled long and hard, and earned his calloused hands and his corded shoulders by sweat in the field—but as the summer wore on, the grapes on the vine struggled against the cool nights and came in uneven clusters of large and small berries, spoiling much of the season's yield.

When the fattest berries became sweet to the taste, he left the picking in the hands of the younger children and came more often to the village, trading as he did in place of Karis, who no more came down from the farm. He crossed paths often among the storehouses with Alys, the miller, whose husband Aeric was miller before her. When news of the silver came in the first days, he had schooled her in the trade and gone off to the mines. In time, Arran crossed paths not with Alys, but with her eldest daughter Anna, who had grown tired of Aewyn's aloofness and taken some notice of him. But though she admired his strength and made a moontouched fool of herself in his broad shadow, he did not at first return her affections: he had grown strong exhausting himself to half-perform the work Grim had seemed to accomplish in near-laziness. The chiseled shape of his young body, in his own grey eyes, was a monument to that failure.

Anna, now twice-rebuked from the family at Grimstead, leaned heavily on her mother's ear in those days, and they lamented together the arrogance and aloofness of insensitive farm boys. It was in this way, through the smallest of ripples rather than the great splash of his death, that Grim's end came to stir the peace and happiness of the town. As the misshapen and underripe grapes were left to the crows, the town's attention turned to the harvest of the staple crops. An uneasy discontent tempered the bounty of the season, though few really understood why.

Anna, who only understood that she was the plainest, most unlovable girl in all of Silvalis, stayed close to Alys's side through the grinding of the first wheat and the baking of the ceremonial loaf for Baker's Day. While her sister Melia lay idly in the summer grass, awaiting the return of the Havenari, Anna threshed the wheat with frustration and brought it to Miller's Riffle, where the river bent over the rocks and ran fast enough to grind it for bread.

The millhouse lay close by Robyn and Bram's cottage, and in the last hours of summer it smelt morning and night of fresh-baked bread. The Millers had a dog, a talbot hound that had been born lame and could not go with Aeric into the hills. So great was his love for the poor limping creature, and so great Alys's love for her absent husband, that she made two loaves for Baker's Day. The first she gave to the dog in its entirety; the second, only she and Anna knew, was carried to town to be given up to the gods.

So it was to be this year, she knew; for the dog was old and mostly blind, but Aeric's love for it only grew as its health faded. When Anna came at last to the moot-hall with the first Baker's Day loaf, she knew that somewhere old Banning was enjoying a holy feast.

It was tradition in Widowvale that the bread on Baker's Day came to the Reeve's wife, who watched over it in the moot-hall, selling slices for a silver rider and morsels for a copper skatt. There were few in town who made worship to gods of any kind—Tûr has no use for bread, said Alys, and the Ten only fight over it—but for many, it was customary to give up the first bread of the season in sacrifice. A few from the Banlands—Grim among them, when he had been alive—bought bread from the Baker's Loaf and burned it or buried it in a place sacred to their gods, and so gave thanks for the harvest already begun, the wheat and the hay, and for the crops still to come.

The year that followed the Year of the Twins, known locally as the Year of Strangers, saw the first time that Poe came to the moot-hall unbidden. He furnished the Reeve's wife, properly called the Lady, with two silver riders for two slices of bread. It was nearly his whole season's wages, once his considerable appetite had been sated—and he sat for some evenings on the village green feeding it all to the birds. For this he was thought quite mad—but even the songbirds came to him freely, and the sight of the imposing creature sitting so peacefully and gently with them seemed to put many at ease. Few of the townsfolk gave him such a wide berth after that, and fewer still clutched their children when he passed. Anna stood near the green for some time, feeling kinship in the beast's solitude. She was careful to keep her distance from old Darmod Pick and Alec Mercy, who had scrutinized the karach since his return and perhaps knew him better for it.

"He is much changed," said Darmod Pick approvingly, "from the monster Grim captured all those seasons ago."

"Perhaps it is we who have changed," said Alec Mercy. It was all Anna could hear of their conversation before Aewyn came to be with them, and she returned to Miller's Riffle in sullen silence.

In the previous year, the Year of the Twins, the Harvest Fair had passed quickly and without incident, and left hardly a mark on Aewyn's memory. Her thoughts had been on Grim and his family, and on the lessons of the tilled earth. There had been freshly emptied fields to work, and winter grains to put down, and that year the Havenari did not return. But in the Year of Strangers, they came at last with the season, as suddenly and surely as thunder with lightning. It was well known that the Harvest Fair came three weeks after Baker's Day, once the seasonal census had been taken, and it was three days in advance of the Fair that Tsúla's roaring horn sounded its unmistakable signal of greeting from the highway.

As far out as Darmod's farm Aewyn heard their call, and she ran all the way to the highway to meet them. Time had grown her legs some, and her toil in the field had made her hardy for such a spindly girl. Even over distance, she was one of the first to arrive as the company crossed the south grass and passed the signpost of Widowvale at a trot.

Robyn rode at their head, resplendent in her steely coat of plate and chain, oiled and polished where the sun struck it, dull and pitted only in a few of the joints—a reminder, perhaps, that it was no parade armour in spite of the pageantry of the day's ride. She had grown into it some, broader and stronger, and it seemed lighter on her powerful shoulders than it had been two years past. Her brother Bram, when he staggered up the hill to meet the riders, had roughly thrown on his own arms—for he had ridden out with the Havenari too, once, in the years before the drink took him. He had clearly taken the care to clean and polish his plate, and in a moment of brotherly pride, decked in matching arms, he looked as dignified and noble as he was ever going to look.

Ten more riders came on her heels, following in something like a formation. But years on the trail had changed them from the tight muster kept by Toren in earlier days. They were none of them quite alike in appearance; they rode not in the tight formation of the Grand Army, but in the easy manner of merchants or pilgrims. An unfamiliar lad, maybe fourteen or fifteen with skin dark as burnished chestnut, brought up the rear somewhat awkwardly, as if he had never sat a horse before, and Venser rode at his side guiding his skittish mount with a firm hand.

The children came out to watch the procession as they trotted through town, falling steadily behind as they rode past the moot-hall and onward toward the mill. Only Aewyn kept pace with them, long legs pumping feverishly with excitement, her heart lightened by something she did not quite understand.

Alec Mercy was shaking hands with Alys the millwife as they rode toward the mill, as if taking his leave of her. When he came up the hill, it was with some speed, though he was not nearly as winded as Aewyn when the horses pulled up short.

"Hail, fellows, and welcome," he called, mounting the hill.

"Providence to you," said Robyn, softly.

"Providence," the riders echoed.

Alec's smile was short-lived. "Providence," he said flatly. "Am I so soon a stranger?"

"It has been two years," said Robyn. "The memory of most men is short-lived." She dismounted and offered her arm at the elbow; he shook it as one man who meets another.

"You are not like most men, Captain," he said. She smiled at that, and it was all the invitation Aewyn needed to run and embrace her. She had run nearly twice the length of town, from Darmod Pick's to the highway and back to Miller's Riffle, but she was not too winded for words.

"Welcome back!" said Aewyn. Robyn put a mailed arm around her as if seeing her for the first time.

"You've grown," was all she said. Then, to Alec: "Will the miller see us?"

"She welcomes and thanks you," said Alec. "As do we all."

Bram, some paces behind Aewyn, caught up in time to embrace his sister coarsely. She received him with warmth, as she always did.

"You must be hungry," said Alec. "Your horses need water. Come down with us to the river."

The men dismounted and led their horses down to Miller's Riffle, with Bram awkwardly leading Robyn's horse so that she might be free to speak with Alec. Aewyn followed them, moving from one rider to the next, and her tongue was a tangle of questions.

"How far was your ride?" she asked. "Where were you at last year's harvest? Did you go to the deep wood? Did you go to the Iron City? Was there fighting? Have you seen any karach? What word of the Grand Army? Did you see any monsters? Were there bandits? Did you draw steel? What news from Adân?" Their responses, for the most part, were noncommittal, though they treated her gently and with patience.

From atop the tallest horse, Venser reached down to ruffle her hair. He had shaved his beard for the occasion and looked a few years younger, though his hair had greyed at the temples all of a sudden, like an overnight snowfall.

"There will be time for all your questions," he said. "But we've had a long ride, and few stories fit for a young lady's ears. Not much to show for all the months and miles, I'm afraid—save a few sores in unlikely places and a wicked thirst for Grim's best."

Aewyn looked away from him. "This will be a special year for Grim's wine," she said, but she had not the heart to tell him that Grim was gone, especially with Bram so near. Even though he had remained in town the whole season, she was not sure he had heard.

The company walked down to the mill itself, and back to the yard of Alys's modest millhouse, where her daughters had fired cakes for them in their massive outdoor oven. Although the harvest cakes were symbolic, the first gesture of thanks to the riders for another year of their protection, the men ate them with hunger and delight that was clearly more than ceremonial. After that, they passed upstream of the Riffle to water their horses, clean their gear, and bathe in the warm spring that came through the rock just above the bend. It was here that Alec took Aewyn away, back toward her home, and freed the Havenari from the endless assault of her questions. While she had only one question for him, it was one more than he was prepared for.

"Are you going up to Maiden's Watch?" she asked him flatly. He lost his step on the hill, then, and nearly turned his ankle.

"What do you mean?" he asked.

"When the miners come in," she said, as if explaining something he did not know, "after a long season in the south hills, they bathe at Miller's Riffle. And the maids old enough to fancy them go up the escarpment and climb out on Maiden's Watch to see them bathing."

"That is so," he said, quickening his pace.

"Only you fancy Robyn," she said. "And in the Havenari, she is just as one of the men. Does that make you like one of the maidens?"

"I'll not pay that the honour of a response," he said. But the innocence of Aewyn's eyes wore on him some, and at last he said, "I'm no maiden, child. Nor is your Robyn, for what it's worth. A man gets…or a woman, or anyone…gets to know such things, after a time."

"I think this year when the miners come, I'll make the climb."

"Perhaps it's time you do," said Alec. "Only don't *talk* of it so much."

When Aewyn returned to Darmod Pick's house, he was sitting by the hearth counting his money, as he often did. Only this time he was counting *out* of it, setting aside the proper price of something. He didn't look up when she came in. No one but Aewyn entered a room in that leaping gait, and only then at a special time of year.

"You're awfully glad at heart," he said dryly. "The Havenari?"

"They've come back!" she said, and he nodded. Her eyes fixed on Darmod's counting-table in spite of herself. The sight of silver was a common enough sight in a silver-mining town. Only Darmod kept his coin in gold.

"I heard Tsúla's horn a mile away," he said. "Ugly thing. No better than the lowing of the milk-cow that grew it."

"It'll be a fair to remember, this year," she said. "You'll have a fat winter, with all you can sell."

Darmod allowed himself a cracked smile; only its warmth, and its rarity, made it an attractive sight. "I know it," he said. "You've done me a good service, girl."

Aewyn nodded and thought no more of it, until she asked: "What is that you're counting?"

"A fitting payment," he said, if only because the word *gift* stuck uncomfortably in his sinewy throat. "The Havenari still have that new boy with them? The southling, the brown boy?"

"Aye, he was there. You know of him?"

"I hear things," said Darmod. "Last I changed my silver for gold in Haukmere, they'd picked him up. Fletch, they call him, since none of them can pronounce his right name. Hendec says he's a fine bowyer."

"I wouldn't know," said Aewyn, "but Hendec tells no lies. Honest to a fault, they call him."

"We'll find out soon enough," said Darmod, "when he makes a bow for you."

Aewyn was delighted and confused at once. "What have I done to please him?"

"Nothing," said Darmod, "unless he has a queer attraction to the homely and underfed. But you've pleased *me* well enough. Took your hardship like a man. Brought me good fortune. I'll keep more lambs in the spring than I ever have before. I owe you a true debt, girl. And for all the nonsense you've told me about Celithrand and the druids of Nalsin, they're archers of great renown. Wouldn't do to turn you over to them in the state you're in. If I feed this silly prophecy of yours, if I can give you a bow and the first thing about using it, I'll consider us square."

"I didn't think you believed in prophecies," said Aewyn.

"I don't," said Darmod, stuffing the rest of his gold back into a velvet-lined box. "But if you're not stolen away for such fancies, what'll become of you? You fancy any of the men in town will wed you?"

"I hadn't thought—"

"I don't suppose you ever did," said Darmod. "But I tell you this, a grown woman who takes no husband has a hard time of it in these lands. Imperial law will not be kind to you. So if you won't wed, or if there's none will have you, your old legends had better come through after all. I've no time for prophecies—no old rhymes can tell the future—but destiny's another thing entirely. You're bound for one end, or another. You're either a shieldmaiden of the Hanes, or some ploughman's wife. There's no middle ground. And since I can think of no ploughman mad enough to breed a twice-bastard with bad luck for hair, I'd best get over myself and buy you something you can use."

"I'll use it," said Aewyn, thinking already of Robyn's majestic stance in the fall archery tournaments. "I'll practice every day!"

"And Robyn will teach you," he said. "One girl shooter ought to teach another. Maybe a lot like hers is the only happy end you've got coming. And you do deserve one."

"I—thank you," she said, a little uneasily.

"Nothing to thank me for," said Darmod. "Makes good sense. When you're practiced up, you'll keep an eye on my flocks. Shoot anything that comes near them."

It was then that Poe filled the doorway behind them, having come down from the woods in the late morning. The yoke of the plough was on his neck already, for the wheat had already come up at Hettie Oltman's, and there was work to be done before the field was left fallow.

Darmod leveled his narrow gaze at the karach. "Anything," he repeated dryly.

True to his word, Darmod counted out a generous price for a stout bow of elm, and the next morning Aewyn went down to Robyn's house, where the Havenari had barracked. The young Southling was not hard to pick out: he was a head shorter than any of them, darker-skinned even than Tsúla, and looked to be a year or two at most older than she was.

"Are you the boy they call Fletch?" she asked him.

"I am," he said. "Are you Aewyn? I heard you were coming."

She handed him the little bag of coins from Darmod, which he threw to Venser. The older man weighed it in his hands sourly, until he glanced inside and caught the glint of gold.

"You got this from Darmod?" he asked. "For one bow?" Aewyn nodded and he whistled with appreciation.

"This way, please," said Fletch.

He led her before the fireplace, where he took a piece of white string and some wood ash and marked the length of her arms. He felt the strength of her back with his hands, which were calloused from the road already, though it was his first season with them.

"Your draw is two foot, one inch to the ear," he said proudly and with precision. "It's two foot nothing, to your lips. You are a small thing."

"Am I too small to shoot a bow?" she asked.

"For any bow we carry, too small," he replied. "But your shoulders are strong, more than I would expect. And you will still grow some. But better I make one you can use now."

"Shouldn't I grow into it?"

Fletch smiled. "The first bow never lasts forever. We don't care for it right, or comes bad weather and here, the wet summer, the dry winter, it is no good. But if you learn well, and practice every day, I will make you another."

"How long does it take to make a bow?"

"It changes. Several hours, some times. Several days, depending on what you want. Making from wood, it is faster. In Khihana, where I am from, we make bows from horn and animal bindings. Seasoning, it can take months."

"Will mine take months?"

"No."

"Can I help?"

"No."

"Can I see your tools?"

"Yes. Come."

Fletch kept his tools in a leather satchel on one of the saddlebags, and Venser knew where. He slipped them out, handed them over, and did all he could to retreat to the shadowy end of the long cottage without breaking the spell Fletch's craft seemed to have over the girl. Bram was there, nursing a cup of mutton stew with shaking hands as he watched them with a smile.

"He stays," Venser insisted. "Every year, that girl has more questions. If he'll field them, if Fletch will keep her curiosity from waking the rest of us at all hours when we winter here, I don't care if he's ever tall enough for a spear or quick on a horse."

"She's that age," said Bram, a little dismissively. "At least, we think she is."

"How's the stew?"

Bram took another swig. "Good as Robyn's. Better, maybe. But then, she never learned how to cook."

"I suppose not," said Venser, and poured a bowl for himself. "But it's not stew that keeps a company together."

"It can be," said Bram. "You cook well, Venser. You speak well. You read well, now."

"Well enough."

"You're a fine rider," said Bram, "and in your old age you'll make a decent swordsman, yet."

Venser smiled broadly, but tried not to look proud. "The sword's just a journey, a wise man once said."

Bram let the hint of a smile peer over the rim of his cup. But it was gone so fast it might have been some trick of the steam.

"You should be First Spear," he said, suddenly serious. "You're the best man for it, on all fronts."

"That's a popular opinion," said Venser, deflecting. He sighed, and might have left it at that; but Bram leaned in close, though Fletch was too busy fencing with Aewyn's questions to hear.

"Challenge her," he whispered. "The men love you both. *I* love you both. But they know in their hearts you were meant to lead."

"You don't mean for me to lead," said Venser. "You mean for Robyn not to."

"She never asked for this," said Bram. "She did what was necessary. She took care of me. She took care of Aewyn, there. That girl was why this happened, and the town loves her. She'll never be in danger again, fairy-child or not. Robyn's done right by the Havenari, but she's done enough. She'd settle here, in Widowvale, if we let her. Make a life for herself. A real one. A happy one."

Venser shook his head. "Are you a leader?" Bram hesitated, but said nothing.

"Do you know the first thing about what you're asking me to do?"

Bram took a long draught of his stew. It was less sweet than before.

"Have you ever been the master of a thing you couldn't hold in your own hand?"

"No," said Bram. He seemed very small, then. Venser's size and weight, and the weight of his words, seemed to dominate their corner of the long cottage.

"Then keep your mutiny to yourself," he said. "I'll not turn on your sister, not to give her some merry little farm life you think she deserves. A challenge under the Code is not the claim of a better leader over a lesser one. It's the claim of a man who can do the job over one who can't."

"It's wearing on her," said Bram.

"Can she do the job? That's the meat of it. Can she?"

Bram set his bowl down hard. His eyes were dark angry gems in the firelight.

"Of course she can," he said.

Venser shrugged. "Then I don't see how I can help you," he said at last. "Though you're free to go on telling me how good I am at things."

"Forget I asked you," said Bram.

"I'm a fine tracker, too," said Venser. "One of our best. You left that bit out."

Bram uncorked the wine, decided it was what the stew needed after all. He tasted it, found it to his liking. Mostly, he was speaking to the stew, now.

"We're just lost," he muttered. "Both of us. I'm lost for good. I don't know; I thought maybe she could still find herself here."

"I don't know how to help you," said Venser. "You could ride out with us in the spring, if you like."

Bram nursed the stew and said nothing.

"Has Robyn told you where we got Fletch from?" asked Venser.

"Haukmere," said Bram. "All she said."

Venser took a heavy breath. "He was a prisoner of war—one of Jordac's scouts. The storm has broken in the East."

Bram's eyes darted up. That seized his attention.

"Tell me," he said.

"Harrod got him just east of the Danhorn," said Venser. "Before midsummer. The Grand Army was crossing into Surreach when the rebels hit. The Mage himself came, and laid waste to the Third, the Tenth, the Fighting Fifteenth. Lit up the whole Red Heath. They say you could see the smoke as far as Carmac."

"That's ninety miles," breathed Bram. "And the boy?"

"He came from Khihana. I guess Jordac had men in the far South. They brought him up to make bows and arrows for the outlanders. He's well-trained. Harrod's men caught him poisoning the pigeon-cart, so they couldn't warn the rear garrisons."

"He's a long way from home."

"He was on his way to the Fingrun mines when he crossed our path at Haukmere."

"The iron mines? He's a damned child."

"That's what the Censor's clerk said. It wasn't right for a child to suffer a man's punishment. He said nobody would miss one boy out of a thousand prisoners. If we taught him right, kept a tight leash on him, he might one day have a place in the Vigil. And no one would hassle a Havenar for the skin he wears or the tongue he speaks."

Bram nodded. "It's a relief to hear there's still some justice in Haukmere."

"Not much of it," said Venser. "That clerk went to the mines for him, in the end."

"Castor Stannon keeps careful count," said Bram coldly. In the glow of the fire, the boy was marking a stout stave with deep gouges, guiding Aewyn's hands to where most of the wood would fall away and a little bow suited to her frame would emerge.

"He seems well enough," said Venser, watching the concern cross Bram's face.

"No he doesn't," Bram whispered. "Look with your sword eyes. Look how he moves."

Venser squinted, held his breath, moved with him. All he was doing was measuring and notching the wood. But he would not put his back to the door.

"How does he sleep?" asked Bram.

"He wakes in a start, more often than not," said Venser, "now that you mention it."

"Do you put him on watch?"

Venser nodded. "He's got sharp eyes, like Tsúla."

"Don't vary the watch," said Bram. "Same time for him every night. First watch, or last watch, doesn't matter. But put him to sleep and wake him up at the same time every night."

"That'll help?"

"It might." Bram refilled his stew bowl from the wine jug—it was more wine than stew now—as Venser emptied a little purse onto the table with a clatter.

"What's this?" asked Bram.

"Payment for the bow," said Venser, with a jerk of his shaggy head toward the two youngsters.

"Gold," said Bram, holding a tiny coin to the light. "Gull pennies. Where'd she get all this?"

"Darmod Pick," said Venser, waiting for the name to set in. Bram swallowed his wine a little too hard, and the big man laughed.

"That old filcher?" Bram asked. "He coughed this up for her? He's certainly doing well for himself."

Venser nodded. "They're all doing well," he warned. Bram looked at him, then back at the coins, their exquisitely minted surfaces gleaming in the firelight. As of one mind, the two turned their eyes to the boy by the fire, his smile brilliant under Aewyn's barrage of questions.

"Keeps careful count, does he?" said Bram.

"Not a skatt escapes his notice," said Venser. "Nor a bucket or two of Haukmere gold, by my reckoning."

"I'll talk to Robyn in the morning," said Bram, and poured himself another drink.

The next three nights were agonizingly slow for Aewyn. With the return of the Havenari, the cottage had been turned into a sort of barracks. Robyn's men were glad to be back among the women of Widowvale, for a time, but they came and went in a constant procession from the little cottage. Few enough were the moments of peace between their boisterous comings and goings, and fewer still were the moments the girl left them in peace as Fletch set about carving her bow in addition to his usual duties. She was such a constant presence that eventually Robyn handed down her own longbow for Aewyn to try. The pull of Robyn's bow was so hopelessly stiff that she wondered whether Darmod's gift was a terrible mistake, nothing more than an idle ornament of unexpected generosity. But when Fletch (at her daily insistence) set aside the time to finish her bow a day early, it was sized and weighted very differently, and she found it a surprising comfort in her hands.

Over those three days, Corran Oltman came regularly with food for the soldiers, and Arran came down from Grimstead every afternoon with a heavy cask of wine for the Havenari. They were among the last of Grim's own, for the many toasts raised to him had depleted what was left, and the weakness of the season's grapes was a shame that wore heaviest on Arran. He stayed longer than he should have to enjoy Aewyn's company, calling her "sister" and chiding her for her long months of absence. He told her how Karis and the others fared—Rinnie, the youngest, had been learning to read on the knee of his uncle the Reeve—and shared his measure of gossip from the town, as it came to him easily in the company of Grim's wine. He looked more like Grim, except around his lean middle, with each passing day. Corran came and went quickly and silently, sour-faced upon noticing Aewyn's unflagging interest in the young man tillering her bow.

Outside the cottage, preparations for the Harvest Fair hung in the air like ripe apples waiting to drop. Tents were raised and firewood gathered. Old barrels, bottles, and horseshoes were collected for children's games. Alec Mercy brought out his flute and his great bannerhorn, a tremendous fifteen-foot sounding horn of shining bellmetal reinforced with steel. He stood the horn on its stand and hoisted the banner of the Protectorate of Haveïl upon its length, since the town had no proper flag of its own. Its long pennant, a single golden oak leaf on a field of forest green, fluttered in the autumn wind as the townsfolk busied themselves. Alec set up his honey-stand on the edge of the green with the help of Bram, who was given a bottle of Alec's harvest mead for his trouble and had it drunk by nightfall. He seemed sullen and sad, as usual, but worked for Alec with surprising effort and concentration, if not quite finesse.

The preparations for the fair were among the fastest and smoothest in its history, for Poe had come in from the field and was glad to exhaust himself helping any who were brave enough to ask him. He had at last come into his full strength, and he hoisted the massive center cabers of the largest pavilion tents into position as if they were little more than hand tools. Perhaps Aewyn had put him up to it, or perhaps he sensed something of the sacred in their tents and autumn balefire, and felt rather than understood the importance of lending his strength to the celebration. In any case, he came at last among the children and families of Widowvale in the autumn of the Year of Strangers, and was no longer a stranger to them. The women usually raised the tents themselves, as it pleased them to offer the miners a bright spectacle on their return, and when Poe eagerly took on the work of five or six of them, a friendship was cemented that would not be forgotten. None knew, then, that it was to be his first and last festival among them.

It was early on the fourth day of Silmaunt in the Year of Strangers—the year 3413 by Moon-reckoning—that the miners came in from the caves and the camps, weighed down by ore and roughly refined metal, staggering with as much rock in their clothes as on their backs. Unlike the Havenari, whose horns rang in the distant hills as they trumpeted their approach, the miners had no need of horns nor hooves to announce their coming. The thunder of their tools and rock-harvests clattering in wagons, and the roar of their deep voices lifted in song, raised all the clamour they needed:

Ale and cake! Fire on water!
Eat the cake and drink the fire!
Fire for an old man's daughter,
Ale and cake and fire on water,
Water for your heart's desire!

Flesh and fowl! Change of fortune!
Home from hills and home to hold!
Hold each man unto his portion,
Flesh and fowl and change of fortune,
Silver Green has greens on gold!

Lay the boards! Set the table!
Light the fires and burn the bones!
Pass the horn if you are able,
Lay the boards and set the table,
Drain it if you drink alone!

Home and hearth! Hive and honey!
Death to rock and life from soil!
Darkness take the days more sunny;
Home and hearth and hive and honey
Free us from the summer's toil!

There was clamour from the townsfolk, too, as those who had loved ones or relatives (and in many cases, men who were both) among the miners made their way down to the road to see who, indeed, was among the living. The miners who came home to Widowvale were slow and careful in their work: they were free men working for their own purses and not for the hoards of other lords, and they kept each other from the mountain-greed common to many of their profession (which is not so pronounced, in any case, with silver as it is with gold). But rock is sometimes a false friend and a fickle partner, and those who went into the earth, though the miners did not delve deep, did not always return.

The Year of Strangers, as the Chronicles of Widowvale recorded, saw only two losses: Anulf, a quiet man from Adân with few friends, and Owen son of Orin, a small man (like his father) who was nimble in small tunnels and always ready to help a friend. They died together in a collapse some miles south of Minter's Rock, where the soil was soft above them and it might have gone differently for miners with rock in their blood. But Owen was the son of a groom, and disdained his father's humble trade for what could be had mining lead and silver for his own purse. He and his father had had a falling out over it, once. Their feud was settled in death.

Two dead in a year was, for the miners, an average loss; yet their deaths were lamented in the usual fashion and with no less sorrow. Orin the Groom mourned his son the longest, for he had not made amends, and he did not dance or make merry at the festival that year. Owen the Tall, a fellow hiller who had come up from Rahasta three years before, mourned his namesake a long time at the moot-hall. Aside from the tradition of mourning one's namesake, and aside from the older Owen's reputation as a kind and good man in spite of his strife with his father, Owen the Tall was not so particularly tall, and only held the name by way of being taller than Owen Orinsson. In the years to come, to his disappointment, he was known simply as Owen.

But this is not his story, nor the story of any man named Owen.

The Harvest Fair was not the only time the miners returned to Widowvale, but it was the only time of year they all returned on the same day. Some in the distant south and west had been away for months, and some who mined at Minter's Rock for only a few days, but always they were received as if they had come from far off and their journey home was long and arduous. That their work was dangerous, and that Owen and Anulf did not return, added solemnity to the young rituals of the village, and the joy of seeing the others returning to their families (those that had families, at least) seemed all the brighter for that peril. Every man who made it back alive was celebrated, and none with greater joy than Aeric the Miller, who returned to his wife and daughters with heavy bags of silver, and threw them into the grass to greet his lame, scampering dog with both hands.

Having crept away from the village green to take his rest in the woods, Poe caught Aewyn's unmistakable scent, mingled with that of human girls freshly blooded, and followed her up the hill. Hearing low, hushed voices, he crept as quietly as his big frame allowed. When he ran into Aewyn, bounding back down the hill, the two startled each other into a sudden gasp of mingled surprise.

"Poe," she said to him, out of breath.

"I wondered," he said in awkward Tradespeak, which he had been speaking all day, "what place you had got to."

"I went to Maiden's Watch with the girls," she said. "Ali invited me. She said it was time I went."

Poe nodded. "You are a woman now, in my years and even in theirs—though you do not feel like them, somehow. What happens now that you are a woman?"

Aewyn shrugged. "I cannot say," she replied. "All I saw were a lot of naked men and giggling girls."

"It is some kind of ceremony, I think," Poe said. "A very strange one, when the males display their love-parts and the females answer with laughter. Among my kin, that would not be the start of a happy union."

"It did seem strange," Aewyn admitted. "Some didn't laugh. They looked frightened. Ali laughed the hardest, but then, she has five brothers. There was little mystery for her—nor, I suppose, for me."

"Are you to choose a man from among them?" asked Poe. "Is this naked-watching the beginning of a courtship?"

"I don't think so," said Aewyn. "So few of the girls marry the miners, in the end."

"I hope you get a strong one," said Poe. "A man of renown among his kin."

"I don't know what I would do with one," said Aewyn.

"Mate and make children, if you can," said Poe flatly. "I am not convinced you have enough Iun in your blood to breed with them. You look the same, but your smell is…only you. I have no word for it. You are like no man or woman."

"Grim always said that fairies can't have children of their own," said Aewyn, somewhat sadly. "He said that's why they steal children in the night. That's why they stole me from my real parents, he said."

"Your mother, Aelis…" Poe trailed off; the name was too hard for him. "You are the true daughter to your mother."

"I feel it," said Aewyn. "But I don't even know what that means."

They had begun the short walk back to town by now. Poe stopped for a moment, looked off into the heart of the deep wood.

"You should see her again," he said thoughtfully. "If you are a woman of your mother's kin, she can tell you what that means. She can teach you the woman-stories, and show you how it is done."

Aewyn walked on sadly. "She is ever harder to find," she said. "The longer I live in Widowvale, the farther she goes into the woods—away from the village, away from my mind. I fear I have offended her, becoming so civilized. Or perhaps I have just become too ordinary. Long have I lived in the house of Grim—just an ordinary child of an ordinary man."

Poe shook his head. "Grim was an ordinary man, it may be. But by his craft he learned to feed his tribe and make them happy. Rare is the tongue that laughs in Widowvale without his magic upon it. And he had many children, and passed to them his ways. I was not at his side when they planted his body like a seed, far from the sky—but I know none of the Iun, not even Darmod, would have dared call him ordinary."

"Ordinary or not," said Aewyn, "I miss him."

"Then whatever it means to you, that you may become a great legend…in your bones, he has become that already."

They came the long way down the easy slope of the hill in relative silence, before Aewyn stopped on the edge of the green. Poe knew what she was going to say before she said it.

"What does it mean," she asked, "being a karach who is… male?" Her eyes darted with innocent curiosity over his long body.

"Nothing, now," he said, his voice low. "Male, female. Without each other, those words are hollow as two empty pots. What did the females know about teaching me what is male? There are no males left of my kind. And now there are no females, either. So it matters not, man, woman. Only karach."

"That can't be true," offered Aewyn. "Alec Mercy has told me of karach mercenaries in Travalaith, scores of them. Come, we can ask him."

"I would not go into the Iron City for any purpose under sky," said Poe, "not if all my fur were on fire and the Black Wall a great roaring river. There is foul magic there, and even fouler people. If my people are lost there, they are sure to remain lost."

"There is sorrow in you," said Aewyn, her hand reaching high on his shoulder.

"It is not sorrow I have, I think." said Poe. "Only the empty wait for death. My life, like all our lives, is a short time. But when my body is tired and the *mănuk* come to take my spirit away into dreams, then I do not pass into the legend of my children, as your Grim did. On that day, my tribe, too, all our time in the world and the last of our stories, it is only a dream lost without a dreamer."

"That sounds like sorrow to me, my friend," said Aewyn, clutching herself gently and close against the karach's chest.

"Perhaps it is," he said. "I do not know the word so well."

Sorrow was a word nearly unknown that day on the village green of Widowvale. As the gathering swelled, the merchant wagons began to appear, trundling roughly over the grass trail winding up from the Iron Road. They carried all manner of goods from the mundane to the marvelous—huge barrels of salt from the Pale Sea, just in time for pickling and butchering, and bolts of fine-threaded silk from the farms of Selik. Spices they brought from the east and south, strange herbs and flowers in mysterious phials of weird blown glass.

In its first days as little more than a loose trading post of wood huts, the outpost once called Silver had been nigh impossible to find. Even the Havenari admitted it was hard to find still—yet by some miracle of commerce, on the day the miners came in from the camps, their wagons weighed down with lead and their sacks with freshly smelted silver, a string of lost travelers bearing reasonably priced goods from distant lands would somehow stumble upon the hidden vale.

"We are not so hidden as I feared," said Marin the Reeve each year, as sure as the tides.

"Nor so hidden as I would like," said Alec Mercy each year in response.

At this festival in particular, even Karis came down from Grimstead, lured out of the house by her children, and she walked among the townsfolk for the first time in a year. No word was spoken to her of her dead husband, so fragile she seemed, until Bram, having heard at last the news that Grim was gone, wailed in mourning and offered extreme condolences to the widow, which she suffered with dignity and only a few tears of her own.

"You would think him Grim's true wife, the way he carries on," observed Marin over the stem of his pipe.

"It is not the man he mourns," said Alec. "But I've tasted the wines of Grim's final year. I feel like weeping myself."

But Alec did not weep, for Robyn had come at last to the Harvest Fair as she promised, and sprang now across the field as though her soul as well has her body had at last left its plate mail behind it. She wore only her dress of green linen, and her archery brace; when the time came, she would shoot in the dress, then dance in the brace—and outshine the men of the village at both—while the old true-widow Oltman and her sons shook the first rusty songs from pipe, drum, and psaltery with more spirit than skill. Aewyn wove a crown of bright blue knightsage and autumn grass for Ali, and beneath it the girl's golden hair shone with the last radiance of summer, to the admiration of many just coming into manhood. The younger boys and girls had learned that Poe would suffer them to climb him like a grassy brown hillock, and played on his naked back beneath the broad white oak.

"Will you shoot in the tourney this year?" asked Marin. "I'll watch your tent for you myself. Keep Aeric's damnable hound clear of your honeycomb, I will."

"Then I'll compete," said Alec, "and you have my thanks."

"Halgeir had you by only a hair. It could have gone either way."

"But now the Havenari have come home," said Alec. "It won't matter. Robyn can thread a needle at fifty yards, I swear. There's no one who can best her."

Marin shrugged. "She was born in Draden Castle, lad," he said. "She's a blooded Fane. No use competing with that. There's no shame at all in being beat by a woman, but especially not by one of her line."

"Robyn?" he asked, incredulously. Across the field, she caught his stare, smiled, and he smiled back. "Wait… Bram too?"

"Aye," said Marin, "the both of them. Children of Elgar Fane, most likely, going by their age. His children, or young siblings, perhaps. It's anyone's guess what they were to him, now that the Draden Chronicles are all burned. The ink is gone—but the blood remains."

"That would explain why he drinks," said Alec. "It's not funny, I know. But Robyn? A Fane?"

"She doesn't wear the Gold Oak," said Marin. "Nor the gold sheaf of the Dispossessed. I heard some of those who reached the Outlands alive still call themselves Fanesworn. But name me another reason a woman of her age would fight better than any man in this village. The Fanes could afford the best masters, after all. And you know what need of them they had, in the end. We've got a few old Swords and Boards living here, too, remember. Men who were honed for battle, once. But as any smith knows, there's no honing to make up for being tempered by fire."

"I remember," said Alec, and his face darkened. "Even the ghosts in their tombs were masters-at-arms. The Legions had a song about it, do you remember?"

Marin nodded. "A little morality-tale," he said. "A warning to the troops against the worst atrocities of wartime havoc." He cleared his throat, and did his best with the refrain:

> *The wedded rogues who courted doom*
> *Like lustful suitors in the tomb*
> *Found Death a willing maiden;*
> *Two hundred wives in deep despair*
> *Now know the woe of those who dare*
> *Disturb the ghosts of Draden.*

He might have tried the next verse, but his voice flickered and went out like a candle-flame at Alec's scornful gaze.

"I suppose that dirge is no song for a festival," he admitted. "I'm too sober for singing yet, and you, too sober to listen."

"I don't think anyone should sing it," said Alec. "It's a horrid song. But I suppose if it scares some chivalry into the Legions, if it keeps Harrod's undisciplined brutes from reaving and raping, let them sing it. Let the Ghosts of Draden haunt them a while longer."

Marin cocked his head at the tall woman laughing and dancing in the grass. Robyn had taken Aewyn by hands, and spun the girl fiercely through the air. She was a skilled dancer and strong in the arms, and Aewyn was still light and agile. The girl's long hair, now the bright orange of autumn leaves, stood out against Robyn's twirling green dress like a bonfire on wet grass.

"I hope I haven't put *you* off courting the Ghosts of Draden, lad," he said. "Not all of them are really ghosts, you know."

"I know," said Alec. His gaze was serious.

"I shouldn't have told you," said Marin, sour-faced. "I hope it hasn't changed anything."

"It's changed everything," Alec replied. "She can never wear her family name again. I'm going to marry her, Marin, and give her mine."

The Reeve laughed at that, better than he had laughed in a long time, but there was no malice in it. "Marry her? You can certainly try," he said. "But she'll be a hard horse to break."

"Marry her," said Alec. "That's all I said. Never a word about breaking her."

Marin grinned. "Looking to ride her wild, then?"

"Guard your tongue," said Alec, trying but failing to hold a frown. "That's my wife you're talking about." Marin sighed with relief, grateful that the shadow between them had passed. But the haunting melody to

"The Ghosts of Draden" was firmly in his head now, and followed him throughout the day though he tried to forget it. He was careful not to let Robyn or Bram hear him humming the tune.

There was not much time for talking after that. There was business to be done, and games to be seen to; as two of the most important men in town, Marin and Alec had much to do and little of it to do with each other. The butts were readied and the targets painted for the archery tournament, and this year the whole Harvest Fair turned silent so the town could gather and watch.

From the outset, it was sure to be a tight and impressive contest that year; Halgeir the Tall had returned to defend his victory, but Alec Mercy shot like a champion, for he had something to prove and someone to impress. Robyn was the crowd favourite, of course—but the year's prize was a longbow of imported Nalsian yew, the finest Widowvale had ever seen, a carved wonder it had taken Fletch more than two months to make on the trail. It was not really that the bow was of much worth in coin—the finest bow, in those days, was cheaper than the rudest weapon of iron or steel—but a better bow in Haveïl could not be found at any price, not for all the silver at Minter's Rock, nor for all the iron in the Iron City. There were more than a few who reckoned that Darmod Pick would come out of nowhere and sweep the competition. This was not because he was skilled—it was well-known he had a bad eye and couldn't hit the sea from a ship's prow—but it was an accepted fact among the townsfolk that Darmod could do anything at all, and do it just as well as any other man or woman, if only the payment was high enough.

The tournament consisted of twenty or so competitors—all those who passed a series of qualifying shots at distance and speed. Whether by luck or providence or natural talent, or whether because she had been practicing all day with her little bow, Aewyn qualified herself, though she was eliminated quickly as her arms tired and the challenges became more difficult. Halgeir, Robyn, and Alec were (to no one's surprise) among the front runners throughout; Darmod Pick, though he could not on principle fail to try for a prize of such worth, did not qualify at all.

As the rounds wore on and the targets were moved farther down the butts, the fair-to-middling archers fell away, and only one surprising shooter continued to distinguish himself. The second stranger of the year, if Poe was the first, was a withered old merchant of spice and liquor come up from the south. White-maned and attired in forest green, he had come up with the growing caravan of spicers and tinkers, and bought his way into the tournament with liquor and sweet words. Now he stood at Robyn's side and went shot for shot with her. At times the pull of the old man's bow was too much for him, and his arms were shaking with effort by the final rounds, but he hit his mark every time and soon the festival seemed to freeze in its activity so that all of Widowvale might watch.

It was later said, once the day had started to pass into legend, that the stranger split Robyn's final arrow down the middle, or that his last arrow took hers out of the air like a falcon striking a pheasant in flight. Some of the men, threatened by a woman's skill, found comfort in telling the story that her pretty dress betrayed her and bound her broad shoulders, and she fired wide into a tent or a tree. None of those things really happened. The stranger simply placed arrow after arrow through the center of the target, and when the targets were taken away and the Tourney Rings brought, and the arrows trailing coloured silks were dispersed (here Alec's skill finally failed him), the stranger threaded every ring but one in his final round—and Robyn, to the hushed astonishment of the crowd, all but two.

It fell then to Marin to quell the assembly's unrest, for few were happy that a stranger from outside the community had come and taken their prize. All three of the local front-runners were well-loved, and all three were consoled (as was Aewyn, who "did very well" for her first year). But the stranger was so grateful for the town's hospitality, though it was not exactly freely given, that he opened his liquor casks for free to all those assembled. The stuff within was distilled by some secret art, far stronger than Grim's wine, and in very short order the offense was forgotten among gales of laughter and loud contests of boasting.

The stranger sought an audience with the Reeve, then, but was rebuffed. It was time for the fire to be built, and for Alec Mercy to sound his bannerhorn, and send Marin and the children off to the mushroom hunt. Those Havenari who had been eliminated from the tourney (or were uninterested in competing, for they knew better than any the skill of their captain) had gone ahead into the woods to ensure the way was safe, and to scatter a few handfuls of copper skatts for the children among the mushroom patches—fairy gold, it was called. And so the stranger stayed with his wagon and opened small barrels of fruit and nut liquors to any who would hoist a cup as the shadows grew longer and the night began to come down.

Aewyn stayed with Robyn until the sun touched the hills, and together they spoke of technique, of drawing and releasing, of arcing the bow, of reckoning wind and drop, and other things which seemed at first like sorcery to the young girl. But as night fell and the stumbling first notes of an Oltman family jig rose above the crackling of a freshly kindled fire, Robyn's distraction became more apparent.

"You are old enough, I would think," said Robyn at last, "to join us around the fire. There will be songs, at first, though I have no voice for singing them. Or if you feel young enough for it yet, you might catch the mushroom-hunters still. I know you are fast in the woods."

"I know not where I belong," said Aewyn, a small statement that stirred in her the whole weight of a much larger worry. "I know not."

"Nor can I tell you," said Robyn. "You are not like the other girls, Aewyn. Your hair changes even now. You are blooded of the forest court; that much I have seen. I had not thought there were any like you left—but the Havenari have not forgotten their old stories. There is a common path for ordinary women, here, I know—but perhaps it is not for you to follow."

"You do not follow a woman's path," said Aewyn.

Robyn poured herself a wooden cup of the stranger's liquor and passed one to Aewyn. "Every woman follows a woman's path," she said. "Just not the one that is expected of her."

"Do you go to the fire because it is expected of you?" asked Aewyn.

"No," said Robyn wistfully. "Though it is, perhaps, expected of me."

"Is it expected of me?"

"Not unless you choose it," said Robyn. "And if it were expected? That should make no difference."

"If it were expected," said Aewyn, "I imagine I would not go."

Robyn turned her words over in her mind for a long moment. "The will of men is something to be ignored," she said at last. "Not obeyed in fear, but not avoided in spite, either. Do you suppose it's the expectation of the village, that I should wear my clothes if I go down to dance tonight?"

Aewyn laughed. "I suppose it is," she said.

"And do I wear my clothes to please them?"

"I don't imagine you do."

"You know I care not a whit what the men think. So do I doff my clothes to spite them?"

Aewyn shook her head. "I imagine you'd get cold."

"That's it," said Robyn. "Do not wed a man simply because they say that's how it's done. If wise men see a greater destiny for you, do not follow that path because you obey them. But if you are cold, choose a destiny that makes you warm. Even if they call it conventional. A rebel who is not free to conform, if and when she chooses, is a rebel with no freedom at all."

"What if I wished to ride out with the Havenari?" said Aewyn.

"Then you are in luck," said Robyn. "None would call that conventional. When you are older, I will tell you all you need to know of that road, and the history of our little militia."

"How did you become Captain?" asked Aewyn.

Robyn let a smile come to her lips. It was the first time she had ever thought of Toren with a smile.

"I was elected," she said, "but I did not choose the circumstances of my election. I was never meant to hold command."

"And yet you have held it," Aewyn said. "Five years, now, six years this winter, you've held that command."

"Nineteen men I was given command of," said Robyn. "Nineteen. There were twenty of us. Today I command eleven. Twelve, counting myself. We'll be a very unlucky number if I lose one more."

"Is it dangerous work?"

Robyn shook her head. "No. Well, it can be. But none of them have died."

"Where do they go, then?" asked Aewyn.

Robyn sighed and ruffled the girl's autumn hair. "There aren't many men who'll suffer a woman to lead them," said Robyn. "Not in battle. Not doing work like this."

"Eleven's still more than half," Aewyn offered.

"Yes. It's more than half. It would be even more, if I'd been meant for command, properly trained and groomed for it."

"Aren't you? I've heard Alec Mercy say you're the best swordsman—well, woman—in the whole village. And he was a great warrior himself, once."

"I have an excellent teacher for that," said Robyn. "But swinging a sword is not the same thing as leading. I wasn't ready for that. I've done my best, and I've had more help than I deserve from the men who serve under me, but it hasn't been easy, and it's never felt right. If you follow an unconventional path, you'll find the same thing, someday. Unreasonable burdens, unreasonable expectations. And all you can do is take what you're given, and do the best you can with it. The few men who have stayed with me are men who can respect that, whether I'm a good leader or not."

"You are doing the work of twenty Havenari with only twelve," said Aewyn. "In my mind, that means you must be the greatest leader."

"Keep flattering me," said Robyn with a smile, "and keep practicing your archery, and I could be doing it with thirteen, someday."

The fire had risen as they spoke, fed by the villagers, who now rose to dance around its edge. Most of the miners had come out, now, strange tall men whose faces Aewyn did not know, loud hearty men who seemed very different from those who lived in the village year-round. Alec had come, too, and sat with the Oltman family, his patient smile serene in the orange glow of the roaring flames. But his eyes betrayed his destination, and Robyn for all her patience and care with Aewyn could not well hide her own mind on the matter.

"I think I will go in search of Poe," said Aewyn at last. "He has no place of belonging, either. Here by the fire, you might say I don't know if I'm hot or cold."

"If you think that is best," said Robyn. "These things take time. Poe is still at the far end of the green, I think—far from the fire, by the upper tents. Take him a cup of this liquor while you can, if he drinks such things. It's very fine, and there won't be any left when you return."

Beneath the great white oak, Poe was motionless in the lowering sunset. Bits of food—bread crusts, apple cores, bones of pork and mutton—were scattered around him with too much intent to be random; a murder of crows had come down from the forest and were gorging themselves on the leavings of the afternoon's festivities.

"Come," said Poe softly. "Sit. But do not disturb the birds."

Aewyn stepped gingerly around the refuse and handed him her cup to hold while she settled next to him. He tasted it with his tongue, and the face he made was not displeased.

"It is like nothing I have ever tasted," he said. "It smells of all the forest. There is honey and spice, juniper, fruit and flowers. I smell knightsage and lodris—and some secret fire I cannot place."

Aewyn sat with him in silence for long minutes, watched him drink as he tossed the scraps in reach to the crows. After a time she began to do the same, and Poe's words came out suddenly and all at once, guttural in their low reverence.

"We call the birds *mănuk*," he said. "Their droppings are what made the world. All who live on the great flat plains, all who look up and see the stars, know that the learned men of the city lie to you: the world is not really flat, like a map, but round on all sides, like the droppings of sheep. The *mănuk*—it means 'those who carry'—bring messages from the Great Bird, the *Grrăkha*, whose wings are wide and black as the sky. When we die, our body pays the price of passage. The *mănuk* come, and eat their fee from our bodies, and then they peck the soul from our eyes, and bring us home on their wings."

"That is a beautiful story," said Aewyn.

"It is the beginning of a woman-story of the karach," said Poe. "The business of life and death, all talk of coming in and going out, is a female business. I should not tell you such a story. But there are no more women of my kind to make it heard. I thought—no, it is stupid."

"Tell me," she said.

"I have been thinking, this story should be told by a woman," Poe answered at last. "It is every male's place to know these stories, but they are a female's story to tell, not ours. She tells it to the children of her tribe. The sons and daughters know it and live by it, and when the daughters become mothers, they tell it again."

"Are there no stories for fathers?" she asked.

"There are," said Poe. "Different stories. I do not know them. I was too young, yet, to go to the males and learn the man-stories, when…"

Aewyn wrapped an arm around his vast shoulders as far as it would reach.

"When the iron men came."

"I have no tribe," Poe said sharply. "No mother, and no daughter. There are no more mothers to tell the woman-stories, and no more daughters to listen. The stories are mine to hear, not to speak. But now, this year, I see you climb hills to look at naked men, and you tarry at the festival-fires, and you grow tall, and you swell at the breast like a human woman. It is stupid, and vanity—but I thought that if you mate and make children, even children of the *Iun*—I thought one day, once they are growing outside you, you might tell them for me about the *mănuk* and the *Grrăkha*, about snakes and the coming of seasons, about Barrgakh and the eggs, which story I should not tell, but I could one day trust to you. And then when I am called home, the life of all my kind becomes only a dream—but the stories go on, then, with you, and with your children. And they are as stories told from out of a dream. And we are not forgotten."

Aewyn was silent a long time. "I do not know if I will marry," she said. "I do not know if I will have children." The words fell off her tongue unexpectedly, and struck hard.

"You mean to say," said Poe, "that in your bones you already know the opposite." He smelt her tears pooling before she began to sob, raised a brown hand to her face, cradled her wet cheek.

"I do not belong here," she said through a breaking voice. "They call me a foundling, a fairy-child. I cannot bear the touch of wrought metals, and I feel the fairy madness in my bones; even my hair cannot make up its mind. I am a joke made up of fairy curses—nor can I run home to the fairies. I have no right father, and I have less of a mother with each passing year. I go to see her and have no recollection of our visits, if I see her at all. The longer I live here, the thicker the fog grows in the deep wood. I have no home in that world, nor home in this one."

"It is hard to have no tribe," said Poe. "My family, like my stories, live on in my dreams. I am alone in the world, but even I cannot imagine having no family even to dream of."

"I know not who or what I am," she sobbed, "or where I come from, or what will happen to me."

Poe, who had long lain motionless, shifted to drape a heavy arm around her. One of the crows started and took off, beating its wings against the darkened sky.

"So it goes," said Poe, "with all those whose fate is told by stars not yet seen. If I tell you my stories, do you swear to keep them?"

"I am all alone," said Aewyn. "I will never have a tribe to tell them to."

"Then you are my tribe," said Poe. "You are my whole tribe. And I share, from today, all the sacred stories with you, and they pass into dream only when we are both gone together."

"If you speak," said Aewyn, "I will always listen."

Poe nodded. "In the ancient time before before, old Barrgakh was a scavenger," he began.

SIX

THE FIRST EVENING OF THE HARVEST FAIR was an evening of joinings. Under the white oak, Poe spoke, and Aewyn listened, and she learned the unpronounceable names of Poe's father and mother and grandmother; although she could not repeat them, she would have known them to hear them. She learned more of his tribal history than she could ever hope to remember and repeat. She learned too of the Annexation and the Clearances, but not by their political names. She saw them through the eyes of a pup; there were no standards, no house sigils, no petty games of intrigue between the equally awful ruling families of old Travost. There was only fire in the tall grass, showers of arrows, iron-clad men and the howls of the dead and dying. There were other stories, too, some of them solemn, some quite funny, and some she would not find funny until she looked back on them in distant years. But all these stories were sacrosanct to him—to both of them, now—and they shall not be retold here.

At the south end of the green, music played and villagers danced around the fire, and before it was fully dark some men and women took to the fields together, as they had in the old days. Husbands and wives who kept to the worship of the Ten made love in the meadows and hidden among the trees in honour of Kedwyn and Ataur, the Lord of Chaos and Lord of the Forests, as they had perhaps for many years. Ali, daughter of Grim, slipped away from the fire with Ard Oltman and kissed him in the shadows behind the moot-hall; and although they were grateful for the privacy, they deemed themselves sly, and thought their own kisses the only ones traded that night. In spite of his guilt and cares, what Arran finally got up to with Aeric's oldest daughter would have been grounds, in the Iron City, for a lawsuit or a bridegild. What Alec Mercy got up to with Robyn that night none can say, for he was a small man well-trained in the art of stealth; and she, for her part, was wise in the ancient trails of the forest, and when stripped of her armour she moved with an easy grace and gleeful silence.

In the glow of the fire, Karis sat with Orin the groom, mourning her husband and his son, and they shared songs for the dead long after the Oltmans had laid their instruments aside. Those who remained as the flames lowered and the coals glowed orange were only too happy to listen—old maids, some, but a few true widows and widowers, and many who were simply too sad at heart to think on love. In time they were joined by the mothers, those who watched the twin crescent moons make their way in the gathering gloom and wondered after their children.

It was a long time before the children returned to the village, which at first suited their parents best. When the newborn stars had aged some, the children came at last, weary-eyed and dragging sacks of mushrooms and wild forage (and pockets of hidden coins). Most of them wore smiles as bright and curved as the white moon; but four-teen-year-old Gray, who was Grim's middle son, led them home with a set jaw and a look of dread.

Old Orin was the first to reach him, for although he moved slower than the rest, Orin had spent long years listening to the hearts of hors-es, and smelled fear as keenly as any karach.

"You're one Reeve short, lad," he said as the children streamed to their families. Gray cleared his throat and took a breath; when he finally spoke his voice cracked more than usual.

"He sent me to lead them back," he said. "He's still out there. We lost Rinnie."

"Lost him?" Orin looked to the tree line. "Where? How?"

"We don't know. He was with us, and then…gone."

Orin looked to Poe, beneath the white oak, laughing and ducking as the returning children pelted him with mushrooms. "Well, now we know it's not the dog-man," he said. "Go and fetch him for us, lad. Perhaps we can put his nose to use."

As Gray made for the far end of the green, Orin had the pres-ence of mind to tell Karis what had happened, before word reached her from an unkind alarm. Then, he found the Reeve's wife and told her the news, and it was done—the whole town heard it after that, from somebody. There was something like an assembly on the green, and something like a debate—but it was the Reeve who managed such things, and if he was unavailable, it was often Alec Mercy, and if not he, then Robyn, when she was in town. Since none of them had re-turned—many still had not come back to the fire—there was no one to order the concerns of the town. Most were wildly drunk on a liquor whose strength they had underestimated, and worn out from a day of celebration, and the heaviness of an uncanny sleep was upon them. There was no orderly moot, only a chaos of voices, and for a long time nothing was done.

Few of the Havenari were in ready condition, but they volunteered to arm themselves and comb the woods. Hendec, tall and green-eyed, was the soberest of the outriders aside from Fletch, and volunteered to assemble a search party.

"We don't go alone," he ordered, "And we don't separate."

"He's likely just lost somewhere," said some.

"The Reeve would have found him," said others.

"What if Marin's lost as well?" said the Reeve's wife, who put little stock in her husband's sense of direction.

"Lost, or taken," said Hendec, which set the crowd muttering.

"I'll go m'self if I have to," said Karis, brushing off Orin's comforting hand and her own tears. "He's my boy. He's my last."

"Then go with the group," Hendec said, "or not at all. We form a line and we keep it tight. Arm's reach of your neighbour. If we have to make multiple passes, that's fine, but we do not spread out."

The old merchant tugged at his sleeve. "How many have you got?" he asked.

"Maybe a hundred who are fit to walk," said Hendec. "We're lucky the miners are all in town."

"They'll trample any tracks," said the merchant. "A hundred men hard at work, with torches…they'll spoil any scent." He looked to Poe, against whose leg Rinnie's closest brother, Martyn, was crying softly.

Hendec understood, but did not look convinced. "You want to send the karach ahead alone?"

The merchant shrugged. "They're fine trackers."

"Not alone," Hendec muttered, though he had mostly given up. "There are foul things in the wood."

"Not in these woods," the merchant countered. "Not yet." The two shared a curious glare for a moment.

"I'll go with him," Aewyn said, having crept close enough to hear them. The idea was absurd to most, but she had no right parents to refuse her.

"Out of the question," said Hendec. "Robyn would skin me alive if anything happened to you."

"These woods will never harm me," said Aewyn, and she believed it.

"Where *is* Robyn?" someone asked. "Where is the First Spear?"

"Sound the bannerhorn!" said another. "If Alec sounds the horn they'll find their way back! Where is Alec?"

"Send the karach," said the merchant again. "If there are bandits or child-stealers in the wood, sounding the horn will only give them warning." Karis mouthed the word *child-stealers*, but no proper word came out. Poe had heard them by now—or perhaps he had heard everything—and he came before them.

"I am willing to go," said Poe, to Hendec, to the crowd, to no one in particular. "But if the stranger is so eager to see me walk into darkness alone, he should come with me. I do not trust you, stranger. You have no scent, and I trust no one I cannot smell."

"If you can smell the boy," said the merchant, "that will be enough."

"We're going," said Poe, and Hendec nodded reluctantly. They both looked to Aewyn, but knew she would not be separated from the karach.

"We'll follow you," said Hendec. "How much of a head start do you want?"

Poe shrugged. "What is a head start?"

"How long do you want us to wait?"

Poe looked to the searchers assembling. "Ten minutes at least," he said. "I need time, and this old man might be slow on his feet."

"You could leave him behind," said Hendec.

"And walk right into a bandit's trap," said Poe. "He comes with me."

"I'd pity the bandits," Hendec muttered, but said no more about it.

With calm resolve, Poe set off. Aewyn bounded after him, and the old man followed without protest. As Hendec organized the others, and Venser shook off the effects of his drinking to help him corral the miners, the three made their way from the edge of the green past the white oak to the slope Aewyn and Poe had raced down only a few hours before. They climbed first beyond torchlight, and then out of sight of the town as the edge of the escarpment passed away behind them. They stayed close to the mushroom-trails, and Poe made a few small discoveries—patches of mushrooms and hidden coins—but there was not yet any scent to speak of.

Poe was large, very concerned, and determined to move fast. Aewyn was a vivacious fount of energy at all hours of the night, and kept up with him admirably. At first it seemed the merchant lagged behind them, but as the woods grew thicker he moved with a learned grace, slipping nimbly through the forest where Poe was slowed squeezing between trees and Aewyn by undergrowth that came to her slender waist.

"You move well, for someone so old," Poe called after him, when he had fallen far enough behind.

The old man turned away, leaned back toward the town, as if making sure it was not standing right behind him.

"Your sense of smell is terrible for someone so young," he said.

Here in the fragrant woods, the old man had a scent again. It was not instantly familiar, but when he turned back to the pair his features were unmistakable. As he drew back his hood, he unveiled himself and was known to them.

"I know you," said Poe suspiciously.

"Celithrand," Aewyn breathed.

"*Otabia*?" he answered, a question—a greeting.

"I cannot believe I did not know you to look upon you," said Poe. "It is impossible, that I should not know your face or your scent."

"My face I have been careful to keep in shadow," said Celithrand. "Long have I practiced the craft of coming and going in the world without being seen."

"A craft known too well by Grim's children," said Aewyn. "At least, I hope that's what Rinnie plays at."

"Time will tell," replied Celithrand, with a wariness that made Poe's fur stand on end.

"No good can come from this," said the karach. It was a phrase he had learned just this season from Darmod Pick, and it was his first occasion to use it. It would not be the last.

"You have come out of season," Aewyn surmised, thinking back to the foggy memories of her childhood. "That means something more important than a lost child has brought you."

Celithrand frowned and hastened his pace. "More important?" he asked. "A lost child is a very important thing, very important indeed. And may be more important still, depending entirely on why the child is lost, and whether there is still a chance he may be found. Do try to keep up."

"I too am a lost child," Aewyn muttered, but fell into step behind him just the same.

The fog of forgetfulness that wound itself around Aewyn's earliest memories parted somewhat where Celithrand was concerned. He was beloved by the fae, her mother had said; but he was not one of them, and their strangeness did not veil him from Aewyn's memory in the same way. His familiar face was comforting, as Aewyn remembered, but comforting too was Celithrand's regular presence, the natural weight and warmth of him. Where her mother filled her mind only vaguely, like a spirit or a dream, Celithrand had come and gone in the ordinary way, as an old man leaning on a stout cane. He spoke in regular sentences, and wore boots to travel, and he was cold in the winter if he did not find or build shelter. In a sense, Celithrand was her first taste of what it might have been like to know a real person.

The timeworn aeril who led the way into the forest now bore little resemblance to that smiling memory of old. His brow was furrowed with care and concern, but those lines had not all come in the past hour. There were many unanswered questions between them, and answers would have to come. But they could not come now: no matter what outside worlds might have conspired to take Celithrand away from her, or to bring him back, a missing child has a way of commanding the whole world's attention—and of making family out of all those who search together.

There were miles upon miles of wood to cover, but the mushroom-hunt would not have ranged so far. Poe led the way on all fours, ears raised and yellow eyes close to the ground; Celithrand followed with a small torch he had scavenged from wood, bark and sap, and kindled by some hidden art. The trees above them rose tall and black against the sky, like columns of sparkless night against the blanket of stars.

"You say he's Grim's son?" asked Celithrand.

"Rinnie," said Aewyn, before correcting himself. "Marin, really, same as the Reeve. Rinnie's the Reeve's nephew."

"Rinnie!" Celithrand called, his old voice soft and hollow as a reed in the calm air. Aewyn, too, took up the call, and they shouted into the night as Poe padded along in the brush ahead of them.

By scent they found undisturbed brackets of woodchicks and patches of wrinkly chanterelles, some with glistening copper coins strewn among them. These Aewyn collected as eagerly as when she was young. Poe said nothing, but looked often to Celithrand as if expecting direction.

"I can tell you nothing, my friend," he said. "At least, not yet. The men who planted these coins tramped all over these woods. There are a hundred tracks. We depend on you in this darkness."

"Rinnie!" Aewyn called again, and Poe frowned.

"If the Reeve is searching," he said, "strange that he does not also call the name."

"You may be right," said Celithrand. He drew a thin-backed, curved sword that seemed now to have hung on his hip the whole time.

Poe lowered his nose to the ground. "There is scent all over," he said. "Let me find its edge."

"Hurry," said Aewyn. "They won't be long behind us."

There was no sudden moment at which he picked up the boy's trail. There was much walking in circles, ranging ever wider, until the scent of soldiers was weak and only children had picked through the underbrush, scraping themselves on branches, sometimes relieving themselves in the bush. Most did not get far—certainly not out of earshot—but there was no mistaking the one who strayed from the pack, the farther he got from them.

"Here," Poe said. "I have him!"

The name *Rinnie* echoed now through the woods from down the hill. It was clear they had been joined in their search. But the three left those shouts far behind now, moving at speed. None of the Havenari had been this way; there were no trampled circles, no great armoured men stumbling about leaving handfuls of coins for the children. The trail was as clear to Celithrand's eyes as it was to Poe's nose, and they stepped through the virgin undergrowth with haste and purpose.

"Smoke," said Poe, jerking as if unsure whether to halt or break into a run. He paused at once, feeling keenly his lack of a weapon.

"I cannot smell it," said Celithrand. "Can you name the wood?"

Poe shook his head. "I know not the names of all the trees. But I think it has been dried. It is not a wet smoke."

"These mushrooms have been harvested," said Aewyn, fingering a clump of dirt where most of a patch of chanterelles had been dug up. Celithrand knelt, handed her the torch, and sifted the soil with his fingers

"Dry on top," he said. "These were not harvested tonight. Someone else forages in these woods."

Aewyn stood with some concern, looking about her as if frightened. Celithrand brushed off his hands and arose with a smile, sheathing his sword. Poe looked to the two of them, unsure how he should react.

"It is only some forester," he said. "Maybe bandits or deserters, at worst."

"That does not sound comforting," said Poe.

Celithrand clapped a hand on the karach's shoulder as he continued walking. "Let us hope that no greater evil than a few robbers ever comes your way," he said.

"They could kill him," Poe said. "*Iun* hunt their own. They kill children. I have seen it."

"Not when they smell good silver," said Celithrand, "or any good barter, if they be not coin-loving folk. There is not much the *Iun* cannot be compelled to do, if the silver is pure. They can nearly always be bargained with."

"If they have drawn one salt tear from the boy," said Poe, "I swear by tooth and claw they will bargain before *Grrăkha* alone."

The brush was pregnant with a low-lying fog as the three moved towards a little clearing. The sunken hut they found there, to a city-dweller or even most of the townsfolk of Widowvale, would have seemed a rudimentary shelter. Piled with grassy earth and appearing from the south as little more than a bald hillock, it was hardly an impressive structure. But all three of the figures staring out from the trees had lived in the wild for no few winters, and all knew it to be a structure of some permanence, a true house where a single man or a small family might have dwelt for some time.

"That is a timbered mound," Celithrand said to no one in particular; they all knew what it was.

"The smoke is from there," said Poe. "I swear someone abides there. Ready your sword, grandfather."

"*Ibar fulcona luraldeon iara,*" whispered Celithrand, slipping into Viluri as he touched the sword with respect. "This weapon is named. It is not for hacking woodsmen."

"That is not how it seemed to feel," said Poe, "when it jumped into your hand earlier."

"Rinnie!" Aewyn called again, loudly, to the sudden alarm of her companions, destroying any pretense to stealth.

"Hide," said Celithrand, and Poe was quick to agree, seizing Aewyn and pulling her down into the bush.

"Hullo?" called a small voice—Rinnie's voice. The boy's golden head peeped out from the doorway, his timid eyes wide as he searched the tree line. At the sight of him, Poe relaxed his arms, and Aewyn squealed as she ran to him, with Poe fast on her heels and no less overjoyed in his silence. The boy's terror flared as they burst from the trees, and he fell crying into their arms as they comforted him, heedless of the fright they had caused him.

If the little house in the clearing had really been home to bandits or worse, a pair of well-placed arrows from the tree line could have killed them on the spot, so noisy and heedless was their tearful reunion with Grim's last and youngest son. They might have been lain in shallow graves, stripped of their few possessions, and that would have been the end of it. But no such arrows came, and nothing burst from the trees in answer. Perhaps they had been fortunate—or perhaps, for a time at least, this story belonged to them, and it was not about to let go of them lightly.

After some moments, Celithrand emerged from the bush with the guttering torch in his hand. "You should be wary where you drop this," he said, though his smile softened when he saw the weeping child. "Are you hurt?" he asked. Rinnie shook his head.

"I was looking for skatts," he said. "Venser hides them really far away. And I saw smoke, and I followed it, and there was a house in the woods."

"Did you see anyone?" Aewyn asked. Rinnie shook his head, golden curls bobbing.

"No, but I found a treasure," he said, clearly thrilled. "Aewyn, this is for you!" He held up a chubby fist and pressed into Aewyn's palm a tiny pendant of blue glass, glistening on a braided leather necklace.

"It's very pretty," said Aewyn. "But you can't take this. It belongs to someone."

"It's not for me," said Rinnie. "It's for you. Jewelry is for giving to girls, and a soldier can't find any girls out here anyhow. Besides, I want the sword!"

"There's a sword?" she asked him.

"A sword and armour," said Rinnie, his head bobbing. "That's how I know he was a soldier. Maybe from the City."

"Are they in the house?"

Rinnie nodded. "I was playing, but then it got dark. I didn't come out because of the monsters I heard."

"Well, there are no monsters," Aewyn said. "Just my friend Poe here."

Rinnie peered around her at the huge karach, wide-eyed, as Celithrand paced around the clearing cautiously.

"When naughty children go missing and do not tell their parents," said the karach, approximating a smile, "they send me to hunt them down and eat them."

The boy fell to crying again and buried his head against Aewyn's breast. She shot her friend an incredulous glare.

"I do not understand humour," said Poe, wisely putting his teeth away.

"There was a fire," said Celithrand, raising his voice over the child's crying. "It's been out for some time. But someone still lives here, and the Reeve is still missing. Take the boy back to town. I will keep searching."

"What of these weapons?"

"Search the house," Celithrand advised.

"I will take no man's weapon," Poe warned him.

"Take nothing," said the druid, "but see what is to be seen."

The interior of the hut was a single room dug out of the earth, with a crude fire-pit in the middle, furnished with blankets and a single wooden bench. The largest planks framing the roof were branded somehow—Poe could not read—and seemed to have been pried off a wagon and reshaped. There was a bundle of tools made of bone, bronze, and wood, a well-used axe, and an empty chest with real iron hinges. Left carelessly on the dirt floor, as a young boy might leave anything, were a steel broadsword and a cloak-wrapped bundle of plate and chain armour that no doubt added up to a full suit. Poe turned the pieces over in his clawed hands, and a flash of rich blue lining met him from the inside of the cloak. He let go at once, the bundle clattering to the floor, and left the house to find Celithrand had already gone.

"Come," he barked to Aewyn, who had just finished soothing the child. "We must get back."

"What did you see?"

"Death," said Poe, and he seized the child from her, and he was off running.

There was no question of which way he had gone. Where he had eased carefully through the bush, he now trampled, his broad shoulders smashing branches and his clawed feet mashing the fallen leaves.

Where she lost sight of him in the fog, Aewyn could hear the rustle and snap of his graceless travel. She was truly winded, her calves burning, when she reached the lip of the escarpment and half-ran, half-stumbled down its slope to find Poe on the village green, surrounded by Karis, her children, and no small number of the townsfolk, all weeping with joy as they hugged him like a family member—and he, panting hard and shaking with something he could not understand, hugging them back.

It was not Celithrand, in the end, who found the elder Marin. When she had returned from her time in the foggy woods and heard what had happened, Robyn fastened her armour over her muddy dress and organized a proper scouting party out of the five or six Havenari who had sobered enough to move with speed and stealth. She did not search blindly, but searched as she might have searched for a child, with no gift for tracking but her own common sense.

Unlike the child, Marin had had the good sense, in the beginning, to plant a pair of ranger's flags on the edge of the hunt area, indicating his direction of travel. But it was dark, now, and the flags were cut from faded rags and planted low, where the fog had rolled in over them. Robyn combed the whole edge of the field for some time, and found what she was looking for only with great difficulty.

Once the flags were found and a straight line plotted, tracking the Reeve was straightforward. He was a big man and moving fast, having broken into a run not far into the deep woods, and his path was clear where he careened down the edge of a shallow ravine. He was pale as death where they found him on the ravine floor, staring up with glassy eyes, though his barrel chest rose and fell rapidly. At first they did not move him, for fear he had broken something in the fall—but Tsúla let out a blast from his horn straight away to let them know the Reeve had been found. It was answered at once from the town by Alec Mercy's bannerhorn, whose perfect bell-like tone filled the air as clear as day and broke the Reeve, for a moment, from his shock.

"Get me up!" he said, and in his struggles to rise—though he fell again to his knees—they could see nothing so broken that he could not walk.

Two of the Havenari, the largest two, hoisted him to his feet and began the trek home with him. They were joined by Celithrand, who had followed the sound of the horn, and came among them as if he had always been there.

"Marin," he said evenly but firmly. "Can you feel your feet?"

"Get me up," breathed Marin.

"Can you feel your hands?" asked the druid. But the Reeve began to shake, and passed in and out of thought, and could neither hear nor speak.

"What happened to him?" Robyn asked him, but Celithrand waved her away with a hand.

"We take him to town," he said, with such firmness that Robyn took him at his word.

"Move," she said, and they moved.

By the time they had come back to the field, night had completely come down, and the bonfire had cooled to a few small flames over orange coals. The children roasted mushrooms on sticks where there was fire to be had, and Rinnie was among them, looking no worse for his adventure in the stranger's hut. Hendec had stayed with them, sorting safe mushrooms from those that looked suspect to him, and the townsfolk milled about nervously, waiting for their elected master of the town.

Alec met them at the green's edge. "We need a sound house," said

Celithrand.

"Is Marin hurt?" asked Alec. Celithrand pulled back his hood; the fine features of the aerils, and the age of his haggard face, were unmistakable.

"I know you, my lord," breathed Alec. "Take mine. There, across the green, that one."

"Send someone for water," said Celithrand. "Robyn, how well do you know your plants and flowers?"

She looked nearly offended. "Folk who know nothing of plants don't belong out here," she said. "Nor do they last long."

"Good." He handed her a small silver ring. "If one of the merchants has brought up mandrake root from the south, buy it with this. If not, run to the river and find me a flowering nightbell, young as possible. Bring the whole plant."

"Both are poisonous," said Robyn.

"They are," said Celithrand dismissively as he followed the shaking Reeve into Alec's house.

The night was long and dark. Clouds had rolled in to cover the stars, and there were only two furtive crescents to see by as half the town slept and half waited up in silent vigil for their Reeve. Celithrand stayed up long into the night, brewing strange teas and visiting mysterious remedies on the man, who was calmed into half-sleep but moaned and yelled his way through the night on Alec Mercy's table. Alec and Robyn stayed with him; so did old Orin, who had delivered foals and lambs upside-down and backwards, and was the closest thing to a physician Widowvale could offer. Aewyn stayed, too, knowing Celithrand, knowing Robyn, and having lost sight of Poe in the commotion.

"I did not know you at first glance, my lord," said Alec as he returned with the coldest water that could be drawn. "Forgive me."

"I am no one's lord," said Celithrand. "And there are many in Valithar's city who would take issue with your calling me such."

"You were a hero to all of us," said Alec. "Every boy old enough to oil his father's sword knows your stories."

"Even I did not recognize you," said Robyn sheepishly, "though I have seen you many times, in the margins of old books."

"I did," said Aewyn smugly, to a smile from everyone except Orin.

"You'll forgive me, sire," said the old groom, "if I do not take your presence in our woods to be a good omen. You travel unnamed and hooded, peddling spice and liquor, which tells me you do not wish to be seen. And I know well what sickness has befallen this man. My father told me of it, long ago. I know of no way to cure it, but I know what fortunes you have brought here."

"What's wrong with him?" asked Aewyn.

"The men of Travalaith call it Aldwode," said Orin. "Leastwise, they used to. Delirium, if you like. The things this man has seen will unravel his mind. It is kinder to let him die."

"Not so," said Celithrand. "If he lives, he will remember only nightmares. Dreams. Fleeting impressions, the ghost of a memory at worst."

"Then you admit what it was he saw."

"What...did he see?" asked Aewyn.

"A Horror," said Orin. "A nameless creature of Darkness. A beast of the Second Craftsman, who brought Travalaith to ruin. To look upon a Horror, let alone meet it in battle, is to go mad with fear."

"Don't frighten the girl," said Alec dismissively, putting a hand on Aewyn's back.

"I'm as serious as an axe to the face," said Orin. "You tell her, m'lord Celithrand. You fought them. For a thousand years in the Deep North you crossed swords with the Horrors."

"You have read too many storybooks," said Celithrand. "Nothing is exactly what the hero-tales make it out to be."

"I stand by what I said," Orin told Aewyn. "I served my time in the stables of the Grand Army, when I was a lad. I've known old men who saw a real Horror. Not like they were in the Age of Sun, mind you. No dragons left in the world, no sea serpents or titans. But even so, there were plenty of things it's not natural to see. None of those men were ever the same again. They were skittish the rest of their days, like a horse with the panic. Marin's father lost his mind to them, if I remember right. Makes it a special tragedy if he's about to follow his old man out the same way."

Marin groaned in his sleep, tossing fitfully.

"He's not about to leave us," said Celithrand, suddenly impatient. "But there is a way to tell Aewyn what she must know, and this is not it. Nor has the hour come for stories."

"Celithrand," she said, "why…why must I know these things?"

The druid frowned. "You are Chosen. We have spoken many times of such things."

"When *is* the hour for stories?"

"That is a complicated question."

Robyn sighed. "My town is fuller of complicated questions than I would like it," she said, so sharply that even Celithrand paused. Then Marin began to moan and convulse in his sleep, and the lot of them had to sprawl across him until he settled.

"You're hiding something, old one," said Orin.

"These are delicate matters," Celithrand protested. But Orin, who had some of the old man's liquor in him, was far freer with his tongue than usual.

"You're as false as trueblack,"he declared. "We'll see your right colour soon as you hit hot water—and if this is how you travel, I think you're in hot water already."

"Aewyn—" the druid began.

"Aewyn is a child of Widowvale now, outsider," said Orin. "And we don't take well to outsiders who speak crooked."

"We are not working at cross-purposes," Celithrand insisted. "We are allies, all of us. This man's sickness should make us so, even if the circumstance of Aewyn's miraculous birth did not already bind us."

"Orin," Robyn said softly, laying a hand on the old man's shoulder.

"I see no *us*," said Orin. "I see only a small man with a large shadow, blown in from a faraway land and a faraway time, come to us with faraway words. It could be you brought the Aldwode on us yourself. You're running from something, by my bones. And whatever trouble you bring, if you think we'll let this girl, our own girl, be a part of your—" He stopped suddenly, turning about the small house. "Where is she?"

"Gone, it seems," said Alec, who turned just in time to see the heavy door swing shut.

Through the darkest minutes of the night, Aewyn ran, crossing road and fence, passing gossiping wives and concerned friends still waiting for word on the Reeve. She bolted past trade-wagons shut up for the night, and was finally and truly out of breath when she reached her little window in the home of Darmod Pick.

The framed bed he had made up for her had been moved closer to the wall. A hulking shape crouched behind it in the shadows.

"*Otabia?*" she asked.

"It is possible I never eat again," said Poe. "I thought you would never come."

"The Reeve is very sick," she began to say, then thought better of it and settled onto her bed. "I am here," she said, forgetting her own questions in her friend's distress. He seldom came indoors for long, and never to where she slept.

"I do not like these dwellings," said Poe. "But there has been enough ill will in the forest tonight already. I go to the fair at sunrise. I cause no trouble here, you have my word."

"You are no trouble, my friend," said Aewyn. "Even Celithrand brings trouble. I had thought I would be happy to see him. It has been so many years since I was a child."

"What did you talk of?" asked Poe.

"Mostly he did the talking," said Aewyn, "and the others too. I don't know. They were on the verge of fighting about it. Old Orin said there was a monster in the woods, so horrible that if you even look upon it, you fall sick and die, or go mad. They talk of big things—of stories I have heard only distantly. Stories of the sort men come to Widowvale to forget. And already I sense I am at the center of it all."

"No good can come from this," said Poe.

"And you?" she asked. "They called it 'Aldwode,' this fevered madness that took the Reeve. What did you see? What drove you from the cottager's hut in such terror?"

Poe snorted and looked away. "It is stupid," he said. "I fell to panic at the silk lining of an old cloak," he said. "Nothing more than that. You speak of true evils, and the Great Darkness, while I cower behind your bed, affrighted at nothing, like a beaten cat."

"Then you must stay with me the night," said Aewyn, patting the straw mattress, "for you are *my* beaten cat."

"Always in my darkest hour," said Poe, "you find new ways to bring me no relief at all." But he lay down in spite of himself, and slept with his massive head on the edge of her mattress until well into the morning. She awoke in his arms, unsure if the great karach had held her close to protect her from all danger, as a mother might hold her child, or only cradled her for his own comfort as a small child might cradle a doll.

SEVEN

Your welkin is woven of silver-grey silk
And the white moon is fair, fully swollen with milk,
And the red moon is painting with brushes of gold
As she hushes and hushes the babes in the fold.

The summer is come in the cole and the corn,
And the morning sun whispers and waits to be born;
She is hale under hill, where the fae-rivers flow,
Where she hushes and hushes the world in its woe.

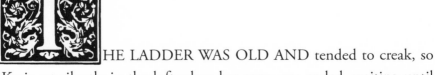

HE LADDER WAS OLD AND tended to creak, so Karis sat silently in the loft when her song was ended, waiting until the air was so thick with sleep that she dared climb down. Rinnie was not even the last of them to fall asleep. For all of her worry he seemed untouched, unconcerned with the day's adventures. And Arran was grown now, and old enough to drink with the men; he had done his duty, and taken his due revelry, and come home late and drunk, and passed into sleep straight away. He seemed to have heard nothing at all of Rinnie's disappearance. It was her second son, Glam, golden-haired like the others but more like her in face than his father, who lay restless long after the song was over, his dark eyes watching her until they, too, were too heavy with sleep to be held open by care. The middlings, Gray and Ali and Martyn, had sworn themselves too old for her songs; but always she sang to Rinnie, and in the months since Grim's death she sang again to them too. Only Glam was well and truly beyond the reach of her rhymes, now. He shared with Arran the hard responsibility seeping into his growing bones, though he was not yet old enough to do a man's work for man's pay.

The winter would be hard, perhaps. It would be hardest for him: he was old enough to know all things, but not to understand as Arran did. The passing of the last generation was always hardest on the secondborn. These things a mother knew.

The soft, unsteady footfalls of an approaching figure echoed on the hill outside as Karis climbed down in practiced silence. By now, she knew the sound of Bram's approach, and could tell him apart from any other visitor at any hour of the night. His steps on the rough stone path leading up to Grimstead were light but uneven, and there was always a lengthy pause at the door before knocking as he collected himself. Having spent her unmarried youth in a Travalaithi alehouse, Karis considered herself a good judge of men, and a better still judge of drunkards. By counting the space between his steps and his knock, as she taught the children to do between lightning and thunder, she could reckon within a half-mug, give or take, how much wine was in him as he gathered his composure.

On this long night of the fair, she heard him stop as she came down, then counted five, then five again. She stilled herself, too, then took a deep breath, and pulled open the door just as Bram raised a fist. He knocked once on the door anyway as its timbers drew back from him. It was not the first time the door seemed to move as he knocked.

"You're come at a very late hour," said Karis.

Bram swallowed and took a breath. "Have you slept, Lady Karis?"

She shook her head and stepped back from the threshold. "Come in if it suits you," she said. "But mind your step, and keep your voice low. The children are fast asleep."

"Don't worry about 'em," said Bram, slumping onto the small bench at their table. "I'm not here to wake 'em."

"I'll keep my own counsel," she warned him, "on when to worry about my children." He raised his eyebrows but said nothing as she rummaged in the small pantry for a mug and an earthenware bottle.

"Will you take a drink?" she asked him, after she had already half-poured it.

"Thank you," he said, "but I've had enough." She tilted the bottle back, caught off-guard for a long moment, then finished the pour and took the mug for herself. By some trick of the pantry, the wine was cold and refreshing after dark, when the sun had gone from the west wall.

"You're out of sorts," she said, fixing him with suspicious eyes. "That unsettles me. What fell wind blew you in tonight, Bram?"

"I know not," he said. "It seemed the place to come." He folded his hands in his lap, at a loss for what to do with them.

"Always has been in times of trouble," she sighed.

"I'm truly sorry," he said. "About Grim."

"You would be," said Karis. The remark seemed not to sting him. They sat in silence a long time.

"He was my friend," said Bram at last. "My only friend."

"He was my only husband," she countered.

"I don't ride with the Havenari anymore," he said. "Even my sister is lost to me. She grieves in her own way, I suppose. A more noble way than mine."

"You've come here to speak nonsense, then" said Karis. "You might do that anywhere."

"You've never liked me," he replied, almost flippantly.

"I don't care for a drunkard around my children," said Karis.

"I don't care to be around children," he shot back. She had a retort for that, too. But she was, as she fancied herself, a good judge of men, and there was some deeper sorrow in him that stopped her. Best customer or no, Grim had been kind to him. She nearly felt his broad gentle hand on her shoulder, and her throat was too tight for words then.

"In the spring thaw, when they rode out," Bram said suddenly, "Grim would come to the house once they had gone, and bring me my wine. We'd open a fat jar together, and talk, every year. He'd tell me about them—the children, I mean. How they've grown. That was enough. Then we'd talk about—other things."

Karis sighed. "I know it," she said. "He had to tell someone, I suppose. Had to let out the things he wouldn't even tell his own wife. Someone he was sure would forget it by morning, maybe."

"Some things you never forget," said Bram, wringing his hands. "They have your hair, you know. Pure gold, like a gull penny, like a pre-Imperial sovereign, before they put the copper in. They'll be golden-haired when they're grown too, like you. Rare beauties, tall and fair. More often, young children go a sandy brown, like Robyn, if they live long enough."

"You've never raised a child," said Karis.

"Nor will I." Karis drained her mug and set it on the table; that seemed a good enough thing to toast.

"Why are you here?" she asked him flatly.

"I just thought," he began, then seemed lost for a moment behind his eyes. "I just thought you might like to know."

"Know what?"

"About Grim," said Bram. "His right name. Where he came from, and why. It's a burden, is all."

"Then it was his burden," said Karis. "I know it, Bram. Some of it, leastwise. And what he kept from me, what he saw unfit to tell his own wife—that's a story he'd never want told again. And it's not for the likes of you to tell."

Bram nodded with respect, then moved to stand. He tested his legs gingerly, but they held him.

"I knew it," said Bram, "and he knew mine."

"Stories," scoffed Karis. "Would you care to know mine? I was a kitchen wench in Travalaith. Parents dead, saddled with a grandfather who fought in the Siege, still lost to the Aldwode fifty years on. Brother gone to seek his fortunes in the mines and send me money for the old man, and I took up as a cook at the Black Bridge Inn, just at the foot of the Stair. Mostly Grand Army soldiers at muster, a few travelers. Grim comes in. He's passing through. Brazen fool comes back in the small hours, wants me to leave with him."

"And you left?" Bram asked.

"What? No, I didn't leave," Karis answered. "Had my grandfather. 'I'll wait,' he said. And three years he was 'passing through' the Iron City, almost to the day. Three years he put away his travels and his future. Then the old man died in the night, and I left with Grim in the morning."

"I never figured you for a scullery maid," said Bram.

"Kitchen maid," she corrected him. "Scullery's for washing up. I could cook, and do it well."

"I don't doubt it," said Bram. "But just the same, if you need any-thing—around the house, I mean—another pair of hands in the coming seasons—"

"I have five boys and a strong girl," she snapped. "Two girls, if Aewyn sees fit to come back to me, now that her indenture's done. We've hands aplenty. We've hands enough. You can take your hands and your Grim-stories and…take them away, I suppose. Take them away."

Bram shuffled to the door, not quite defeated. "You have my sympathies," he said, "and my highest respect. If I had a wife of my own, I'd be glad at the end if she was so content to let my secrets stay in the tomb where they belong."

Karis rose and took her mug to the wash-basin at once, as if to wipe away any trace of the visit. "You'll never have a wife," she scoffed.

Bram nodded silently, weighing something in his mind on the threshold.

"Not again," he said simply, and shut the door. It was the last time they would ever speak.

Dawn, when it came, was hardly noticed. The roosters in a few farmyards crowed up the sun, for they'd had nothing to drink and seemed none the worse for the night of revels. But the sleep of the villagers was long and dreamless, and when they woke under a high sun the events of the previous night seemed as if they had faded into a distant past. Most assumed it had been the grandest festival the town had seen, and prepared to meet the afternoon with groggy optimism, hoping for more of the same.

Word had got round, at least, that Marin had gone missing for a time, and that he had fallen violently ill, but few of the details lingered. He awoke on the long table at Alec Mercy's house in time to empty his stomach onto the floor, and then laid there in a swoon, too weak to walk, though the stranger who cared for him promised he would find his legs again in a day or two. He ordered the stranger away, though, as soon as he had the strength to shake his fist: he swore by all the gods, and by his beard aside, that he would never again take liquor from a stranger, for he recalled a few glasses of the visitor's brew, and a fitful night of unspeakable nightmares had been his reward for it. Orin, who had drunk away the sorrow of his lost son, awoke with no memory of the past day, or of tending the Reeve, though his aid had been invaluable.

To Aewyn and Poe, who had shared only a small cup between them, events were clearer. Aewyn recalled the presence of Celithrand, though little of what he said, and made her intent to seek him out. She roused Poe from a fitful slumber, and gently lifted his great head off of her, and he snorted as he came to.

"Never have I slept in a house on a bed," he said at first—and then, "I have done a terrible thing."

Aewyn sat up and eyed him quizzically. "It's a bed. Just a bed. It's not going to kill you."

"I have told you many woman-stories of my tribe," he said. "Those stories are sacred, not to be told…I have pack-bound you to a tribe that does not exist."

"I don't understand," said Aewyn, but Poe was loath to discuss the secrets of his stories further.

"Neither do I," said Poe. "My head is full of fog. I think some sorcery has been worked on us, and I would have words with the sorcerer."

"We'll find him together," said Aewyn. "There are too many questions without answers."

They rose and made their way to the village green, where the banners and pavilions of the Fair were still assembled, awaiting a second day of less festivity and more commerce. A few grown men and women dozed lazily in the grass. By the spice wagon, Robyn was half-awake, still in her muddy green dress, in quiet conversation with a hooded figure that could only have been Celithrand. He leaned hard on a crooked walking-stick and the bow he had won the previous day was slung over his shoulder. Even its polished nocks shone, carved of something unknown that glistened in the light.

"Good morning," said Aewyn, seeing no need to be uncivil.

"It is good enough," said Celithrand. "Alec and I have been all night with the Reeve. He will survive, and be none the worse for his encounter in a few days."

"Your drink has put a spell on us," Poe accused, never one for small talk.

"Perhaps, of a sort," said Celithrand. "There is nothing unnatural to it."

"There is nothing unnatural to being poisoned, either," answered Poe.

Robyn eyed him warily—but no less warily turned her gaze on the old man. For the moment she said nothing.

"Why did you do this?" asked Aewyn.

Celithrand cleared his throat.

"These are times of great importance," he said, "and of grave danger as well. I travel now under a veil of secrecy. Any memory of me may well put these people in danger."

"If that is so," said Aewyn, "you would not have come, except at great need. And it means you have not come to stay with us."

The old aeril looked away to the sun, well above the horizon now, but not so high that he could not bear to look. Even under a mask of the wrinkles so uncommon to his kind, his cheeks for a moment seemed to shimmer like the skin of a fish.

"No one ever really stays for long," he said. "But you are right. I had not intended to be seen even as much as I have."

"It's good that you were here, I suppose," said Robyn. "The Havenari are trained to resist the Aldwode, not to cure it in others. But if you're a danger to us, my lord, these people have a right to know why—not to be tricked, or drugged, or spellbound, or worse."

"I am a wanted man," said Celithrand. "Marked for death in Travalaith." Aewyn gasped.

"On what grounds?" Robyn asked, eyes narrow with suspicion.

"On charges of treason, I've heard."

"Charges mean nothing without evidence," said Robyn. "Is there any?"

"My answer depends on who's asking," said Celithrand, suddenly wary. "Are you Veritenh's sworn spear still? Do you serve the Vigil? Or are you the law in Haveïl now, answering to the vasil of Haukmere and harrying down every Imperial fugitive who runs afoul of the Kelmors?"

"I'll do both with time to spare," said Robyn, "if they protect the people of the border towns. This one, especially." Celithrand smiled and relaxed his weight onto his walking-stick.

"You've grown into that armour very well indeed," he said. "The petty politics of men have interfered, it seems, with the Godswar. The Mages' Uprising stirs in the East, and now in the South. Jordac grows daily in his power. The Imperator's position weakens, and the mission of his Empire falters. Those who united the Northlands to stand against evil have had a taste of power, now, and are loath to relinquish it. The four of us who founded that Empire—who founded it, I fear, for a purpose lost on the powerful—are surely the greatest threat to its legitimacy. Valithar rules from Cîr-Valithar—but atop the Black Spire he is far from the people and their daily politics. Garim the Mad is lost on the Deep Road, consumed by Horrors or become one himself. Janus Veritenh is dead, and rules only the tomb of his ancestors now: you, my lady, and a few scattered companies like you, are all that is left of his storied Dragons and their Vigil against the Splintered Shadow."

"And then there's you," Robyn said.

"Then there is me," Celithrand conceded. "I am a relic of a dying age. In my time I performed wonders, and men called them magic. Those who sing to their children of the Company of the Owl remember me as a mystic who roams the Outlands in secret. And now a rebellion rises in the Outlands, fuelled by strange magics that frighten the peaceful citizens of the Empire, and the Imperator's servants have no doubt seen their chance to make an end of me."

"They think you're allied with the Mage," breathed Robyn. "Are you?"

"I'm not Jordac's teacher, if that's what you're asking," said Celithrand. "It's a popular rumour, though his lore may already eclipse my own. No, I've nothing to do with the Uprising. But there are enough who'd believe it—and I'm the last rival claimant to the Spire. Eighty-seven years, now, Valithar has reigned as Imperator. He has outlived all opposition. And when I am gone, when his personal scourge has hunted me to the end, his grip on the North will be absolute."

"I thought he was your friend," said Aewyn. "You were Companions of the Owl together. Why would he turn on you?"

"I cannot say for certain," said the old man. "Perhaps he is dead, too, and only his name rules the Empire now. Perhaps cruel advisors have turned his heart. What I do know is this: the Splintered Shadow, the Second Craftsman, is an insidious Enemy. To oppose him by force—to make war against him who created war—it changes you. Though we win what victory we may, some part of it will always serve him, in the end. If ever I had a friend in Travalaith, he is now lost to me. That, sometimes, is the cost of war. We knew it, even then."

"You asked me whom I served," said Robyn. "I will not betray you to the Imperator's Scourge. But we are on Haukmere's doorstep. There's sixty miles of clear trails, at most, from Wescairn to wood's edge. If your presence among us will draw Ashimar's eye, that is something I need to know."

"I hope to be gone by nightfall," said Celithrand. "I had hoped to be gone already."

"Can we be of help to you, my lord? The harvest was rich again. We can give you whatever food and supplies you can carry."

Celithrand sighed and rubbed his face with bony hands. "I would make no such promise," he said, "until you ask if I travel alone." His look to Aewyn was so apologetic, and so sure, that there could be no mistaking his intent.

"You…have come for me," said Aewyn. There was fear in her eyes, but not her voice.

"I had hoped not to," said Celithrand. "But I cannot remain in Imperial lands. I must cross the Miumuranai, and sail to the lands of my ancestors, where even the Imperator's hand cannot reach. And I cannot leave you behind when I do. The days of prophecy are come at last—or will, soon enough. You can remain no longer. You must be made ready."

"It's true, then," said Robyn. "This business about her destiny."

"I'm afraid so," said Celithrand.

Poe snorted. "I don't believe you," he said, so forcefully that the others were lost for words.

"The prophecy—" Celithrand began.

"There is no word in my language for talking about…certain to-morrows," Poe said. "No language trick for talking of days far away as if they had already come. We counted ourselves wise for it. It is the way of the *Iun* to hold false expectations. It is the way of the karach to see what comes, and adapt."

"You have picked a strange friend," said Celithrand, "for one who does not believe in destiny."

"Why?" Poe asked, challenging him. "Why does it matter? The villagers pray to men who walk in the sky. Darmod Pick believes in children's rhymes that make his garden grow and his purse swell at the seams. It makes no difference to me. Why should dess-tiny?" He would have said more, but his ears twitched uncomfortably as the sleepers on the green began to stir.

"We have talked too long, or too loudly," said Celithrand. "We cannot stand here and debate. I must not be seen."

Robyn stood tall and looked westward, toward the river. "We have a house," she said. "You can trust the Havenari...for now."

Celithrand nodded his assent, and Robyn led the way. For Aewyn, who had twice run the whole length of town only days before, the slow walk from the green up to Robyn's long house near Miller's Riffle was interminable. Celithrand moved on bones a thousand years old, with the patience of a man who had weathered every day of them. *The days of prophecy*, he had said—there was always a prophecy of one sort or another, she supposed. But prophecies and legends—and evils especially, save the petty grievances of men like Darmod Pick—had always been the stuff of faraway. Celithrand had raised her from a young age to believe in her own importance, and the legends and stories she had heard from Grim only cemented the notion. It was taken for granted that children of miraculous and mysterious birth—and here she was certainly unique—were always Chosen by the gods for some business greater than themselves. Now that it had come, she waited with some fear to learn what her place would be.

But her long indenture had put the soil of Widowvale under her fingernails. It had soaked her clothes with its spring rains, and burned her fair skin with the same sun that sang up the crops in the fall. Her time in the field had brought her both kinship and purpose—the two things that her years in the forest had denied her. The thought of leaving them now, of never returning to Grimstead, of letting Hettie Oltman's winter rye go unsown, gnawed at her resolve in queer and unexpected ways. She had never worn his promises of a heroic destiny uneasily;

but now they were real, like a debt called to account, and they knotted her stomach and dried her mouth with worry. The affairs of the gods, it seemed, did not suit her any more readily than a marriage to one of Oltman's sons. If her future were of great importance, as he had long said, her simple life was about to change. And if it were somehow more complicated than all that—if there was more to destiny, as Robyn had warned, than merely doing what wise men expected of her—then it would surely become more complex yet.

In the midst of it all was her understanding that Celithrand was not the simple old man of her childhood anymore; she had heard, now, the songs of his deeds, and that renown seemed to make him both more and less than the ordinary man he was before—just as she, too, felt both more and less than her true self under the mantle of his words.

The days of prophecy are come at last. The words haunted her all the way to Miller's Riffle.

Castor Stannon had a taste for art. He much preferred it to war, which largely disgusted him, and for which reason he had begged and beguiled a seat of power as far from the front as possible. Wescairn came by its name fairly; there was nothing at all west of Wescairn unless you ventured into the forest—an errand he took it upon himself to avoid whenever he could. The Kelmors had warlords enough, in draughty keeps and salt-blasted towers all along the Tunderstrand—severe and ugly places for severe and ugly men—and Ashimar was for all his eerie calm the most severe of them all. When the Imperial Scourge had left him, the Censor retreated to his counting-house and poured himself a tall goblet of Rahastan wine. The wine, like the room, was too warm to be comfortable to most men, but Castor Stannon was not like most men. Nor was he much like himself, he thought, as he set his goblet down with trembling hands. It would be a few more hours at least, and maybe a night of fitful sleep, before he had fully regained his customary calm. For now, wearing his calm as a mask would have to do.

Castor much preferred art to war, but here on the frontier, there was less time for one than the other. Only the smiths, whose secrets had come down to them from long generations of master armourers, had time enough for both. The marshy coastal lands of Haukmere were a place devoid of paintings, bereft of sculpture and higher craft, and only the armourers had preserved any semblance of creativity in their art. All four walls of the counting-house, then, were adorned with ferocious masks and war-helms shaped by Haukmere's master armourers. The fearsome visages of wolves, bears, dragons, and three dozen more terrifying beasts stared lifelessly down at him as he sat in uneasy silence. Only the vasils themselves and the legionary generals—ten men under Thurmod, and eighteen under Harrod—were permitted to wear the war helms of Haukmere on active duty. But any man of wealth and taste could possess them, and to his knowledge, Castor held more of them than anyone. Their macabre beauty pleased and thrilled him, and when the outside world or the duties of office troubled him, he would retreat to his chamber and tend to the taxes, while the three dozen great-helms snarled down at him like trophies or severed heads. Sometimes he would turn them over with delicate hands and let the firelight play across their ferocious features, until they so terrified him that he had to look away in spite of himself.

Not one of the masks ever terrified him as much as Ashimar's. The sight of it alone made him feel shaken and small. He loathed these sudden visits, and resented most of all that the war had come to his door. He threw back his goblet. The wine tasted sweet, he reminded himself. It was not sour. It was too expensive not to taste sweet.

The footsteps came just before the door creaked open. They were too light to be Ashimar's. No one else's armour was so well-made, but even so, an armoured and unarmoured man sounded utterly different in these halls. Castor knew well the echoes of his keep, and knew above all the sound of metal.

"Enter," he said. He set his goblet down on the plush chequered counting-table. Sure enough, it was just one of the census-tellers, his arms heavy with stacked boxes of coins.

"Taxes, milord," said the man. "The Protectorate of Haveïl, all accounted for."

"Fine, fine," said Castor. "Lay them here."

The teller lifted three heavy cases up and over the rim of the table. "Aslea here. Widowvale here. Seton here. And there... the outliers."

"Thank you," said Castor. The teller bowed obligingly, patted down the bags, smoothing them, and stood in silence.

"Thank you," Castor tried again. "That will be all."

The man nodded gravely. Castor frowned.

"You are dismissed," he said.

"Begging your pardon, milord—"

"Derec, isn't it?"

"Aye, milord," said Derec.

"Spit it out, man."

Derec's face tightened as he buried his emotion. "He's still here, milord."

"Who?"

Derec cast his eyes up to the fearsome masks. Castor sighed and pushed back his chair. Moving to the side table, peering down the snout of a gilded lion mask, he reached into a cupboard for a second goblet.

"Sit," he told the teller. Derec drew another high-backed chair to the counting-table, bowing his head sheepishly.

"It's just… I'd rather not—"

"Do shut up," Castor urged him, pouring him a half-goblet of wine. "I understand you perfectly."

"I was setting out for the Tunderstrand tonight," said Derec. "His horse shares a stable with mine."

"Eleven wounds, man," sneered Castor. "Leave off and drink that. Learn to say 'yes' to a kindness."

Derec took the cup. "Thank you, milord."

"Slowly, slowly. It's not cheap. Not that pig swill you're used to out here." He rubbed his temples with delicate hands. "These are difficult times, and we all must do our duty. Be thankful for those who get their swords wet for us. It's dirty business, ruling. Men like the Scourge are how men like you and me keep our hands clean."

"Just the same," said Derec, "I'll rest easier when he's back in Travalaith."

Castor nodded and lowered his voice. "I too," he said softly.

They drank together in silence, listening for the sound of hoofbeats as Ashimar's company of bloodguards departed. But no sound came.

"Clear weather tonight," Derec said at last. "I'll make up the time on the road."

"I'm sure you will."

"I'll saddle up quick. I'll be out as soon as that hateful man's headed back from whence he came."

"Whence," Castor mouthed over the rim of his goblet.

"What?"

"Headed back whence he came," said Castor. "Don't say 'from whence.' It's redundant."

"Oh."

When the tension was unbearable, Castor reached across the table and dragged the wide box of Aslea's taxes to his end of the table.

It scraped across the chequered cloth with a pleasing weight. When the thunderous hoofbeats of Ashimar's departing retinue arose at last, Derec drained his goblet with relief.

"Damn," he said. "Tastes better already."

Castor let a thin smile escape the mask of his calm. "Off with you, then."

"You can't hang a man for asking," said Derec, suddenly lighter of cheer. "One more for the road?"

Castor's smile flinched, but did not fade. He looked to the side-table, then to the counting-table.

"If you can promise me I'll be happy with the remittance, I'll grant it."

At that, Derec beamed widely. "It's been a fine year."

"We shall see," said Castor, thumbing the hinge on the counting-case.

"Wait," said Derec. "Leave Fat Aslea for dessert. Start small."

Castor eyed him shrewdly, taking the measure of him, then shrugged and pushed back the first box obligingly. "Show me," he said.

"Widowvale's always smallest," said Derec, laying a lighter box before the Censor with one hand. "More than usual, but still the smallest."

"That is the nature of charity," said Castor as he picked up Derec's goblet. He felt safe, now, turning his back to the door, and did so without a care as he refilled the wine. His hands were steady, now, and did not flinch even when Derec dumped the coins onto his table with a sudden clatter.

"Now that," he began, "is the sound of a bountiful—"

He stopped mid-sentence as he turned around. He handed Derec's goblet back without looking up from the table.

"Wait, how much is here?"

Derec tried to remember. "Just seven or eight sovereigns," he said. "Much of it's in smallcoin."

"Much of it isn't," said Castor. He fingered a handful of little gold coins, stamped all around the edge with shallow ridges so they couldn't be filed down. The Imperator's head adorned one side; on the reverse, an ungainly Haukmere seagull spread its wide wings, backed by the Kelmor crescent moon.

"The Kelmors stamp these in Haukmere proper," he said. "They'd have to ride clean around us to get them. How much of this is gold? Nearly a quarter?"

"One part in five," Derec corrected. "Not quite. Certainly made it nicer to carry."

Castor reached out—not really sorting the coins, just dividing them.

"How many heads in Widowvale?"

"The scroll is sealed, milord."

"It's sealed for me. Open it."

Derec did so and unrolled the census results.

"Sixty-one women—mostly widows, sadly, hence the name—and nine men of working age. Ten men, sorry. There's a retired Havenar in town now. He's exempt, like all Havenari, but he doesn't ride out with them anymore. Paid his head tax, insisted on it."

"And these, what are these?"

"Silver, milord."

"I know what silver looks like, man! They're unstamped."

"Aye. But they check out, milord, at a rider a piece. Weighed them three times myself. They're real. If anything—"

"They've overpaid," Castor agreed. "Not by much. Enough to please me. Ten men?"

"Aye."

"Read me their occupations."

"Aye, milord." Derec spun the rollers in his hand and deftly read down the scroll:

Orin	age unknown, late seventys	animal husbandrye
Darmod	age unknown, fivty-some	sheepherd * farmer
Marin	fourty-eight	forrester * town reeve
Aeric	fourty-five	miller
Owen	thritty-nine	brenner * smith
Jerrold	thritty-seven	mercer
Bram	age unknown, above thritty	invalid
Alec	thritty-one	horse breeder * beekeep
Corran	twenty-one	farmer
Arran	eight-teen	vintner

"Interesting," said Castor. "Tell me about Owen."

"Thirty-nine, born in Carmac, skilled tradesman. Brenner and smith, it says here. They call him Owen the Tall—though he wasn't, particularly. Tall, I mean. Lived on a barren hill south of town."

"Kept a forge and furnace there, did he?"

"Aye."

Castor quietly began sorting the coins back into the box.

"Large as the smelting furnace down below, at Steelgate?" he asked.

"I reckon so."

"How many men did Ashimar leave us to secure the border?"

"A garrison of thirty, milord. More than enough to man the watchtowers and blockade the roads, if his fugitive makes it this far west."

"Unlikely," Castor said. "But we're just as well not to waste them. Call muster in the square; get them ready to ride."

"Something the matter, milord?"

Castor's eyes glinted cold in the firelight as he set the heavy coinboxes aside. "Tack your horse, and mine," he ordered. "I'll explain in the saddle."

EIGHT

OST OF THE HAVENARI, having drunk more than their captain, were only just rising from their bedrolls on the threshed floor as Robyn returned home. A few hastily rushed to cover their nakedness as the visitors arrived. Some had slept in their breeches or even in their long, quilted gambesons, though their leather and mail and been laid aside.

"Good morning, Captain," said Hendec, who was just now waking for the second time.

"It is," she replied. "Hendec, I need you to call muster. Somewhere else."

"You heard her!" he bellowed. Preparations began to hasten.

"I have an ill feeling about last night," said Robyn. "Go lead the men up the escarpment, and sweep the patrol road. I have heard tell of a deserter's shelter, but no deserter to go with it. If you find him, be sure he knows we need not answer to the Grand Army directly. The news he can tell us outweighs the price on his head, if there is one."

"Shall I take them up by the Serpent Trail, then?" Hendec asked.

Robyn waved her hand dismissively. "Gods, no," she said. "It winds on forever. You'd be gone all morning. Just dismount and go up through the broom. You know the way."

As the Havenari made themselves ready, she went to Bram, who was slow to stir. She rested a hand on his shoulder. He was pale and cool to the touch.

"Hard night?" she asked.

"I went…to Grim's house," he groaned. "I drank too much, and tried to unburden myself of secrets."

"So did we all," she said. He began to register that the men were hastily arming around him.

"What's happening?" he asked. His eyes darted to the front door as the Havenari poured out, then to the unattended back door. He shifted slightly under the blanket; Robyn could feel him lift up onto his toes and the fingertips of one trembling hand. His other hand was on the rusted hilt of his sword—he must have slept with it near him—but she brushed the matted hair from his face and hushed him.

"Be calm, dear brother," she said.

"Someone's gone 'round the back," he whispered. His fixed his bleary eyes on the wall, like a cat who hears the scratching of mice in the plaster.

"It's only Poe," Robyn said. "Aewyn and Poe have come to speak with me. But it's a matter of some delicacy. That's why I need the house. Our quiet little farmhouse."

Bram looked around at the walls, the strands of garlic and cured meats hanging from the rafters, smelled the fire in the familiar hearth.

"Everyone's all right," he said.

She stood him up, helped him to his feet, and gently cupped her hands over his.

"Everyone's all right," she agreed. She kissed him on his forehead—she was the taller one, now—and knelt to open his boots that he might step into them.

"I'm sorry," he said. "I was far away."

"It's fine," she said, though she was clearly troubled.

"It's too dark in here," he said. "Altogether too dark."

"There's a lovely sun out this morning," said Robyn, straightening his clothes. "It'll be clear all day. Go out with the others. Get yourself under an open sky and feel the wind on your face. Go bathe at the Riffle; it always does you good."

"If you need—"

"I don't need her," said Robyn. She cupped her hands over his, and took his sword from him, and pitched it lazily into the men's bedrolls. He smiled at her, then, as if he were lifting a heavy weight with the corners of his mouth. Roughly attired, he made his way to the door.

"Give them my best, if you can," he said, and followed the others out—though probably not to muster with them.

"It's clear," she said at last. "Come in."

Poe was the first to enter the house, his long shadow filling the rear doorway just as Bram slipped out the front. Aewyn and Celithrand came together, with the girl helping him over the threshold.

"Our time is short," said Robyn. "Speak plainly and speak truth." Celithrand rubbed at his temples, clearing his throat and his mind.

"What do you know about the Godswar?" he asked suddenly, fixing his gaze on Aewyn. Her eyes went wide with astonishment.

"Very little, in truth," she said. "Just the lessons for children. That Tûr made the world with eleven doors and eleven gods to watch over it. That the Darkness came from beyond, and would have destroyed the whole of Silvalis but for Tamnor, who was wounded eleven times fighting the Darkness, and though he was victorious it seeped into him and corrupted him. I know that the Splintered Shadow is said to live everywhere, and that it calls to him even in his prison Beyond, where Kedwyn has bound him."

"That is more than I knew," said Poe, not without admiration.

"Since that day," said Celithrand, "Tamnor has served as the avatar of that Darkness. Lost to his brethren and his consort, he is the door through which evil comes into Silvalis—the dark Craftsman by whose hand the Splintered Shadow is given shape in a thousand different forms."

"Theologies differ," said Robyn, "on the nature of Tamnor. What happened before the Age of Sun is anyone's guess."

"They differ, certainly," Celithrand conceded. "But since the Age of Sun he has come into the world, now and again, as an agent of its ruin. That ruin has passed into real history. It is no myth what happened a century ago, when Tamnor crossed into Travost and threw down the Towers of the Sun. He loosed a new breed of Horrors across the whole of the northern vasilies. It was a crisis of faith for many that day. It nearly spelled the end of the Tudran faith in these lands."

"That's what happens," said Robyn coldly, "when you pray to all the gods, and none but Tamnor give answer."

"It all seems so long ago," said Aewyn.

"The Age of Sun, aye," said Robyn. "But my grandfather was a boy when Travost fell, and newly a man when Valithar rebuilt it. I never knew him, but he spoke often to my father about the marble towers and the ancient city, like a man long blind remembering his sight."

"The Siege of Shadow and the rout of Tamnor had as well been yesterday," said Celithrand. "Many who endured the Siege thought it was the war to end the Age. In truth, it raged for little more than five years. The Age of the Moons will not let go of us so easily as that. There is another war to come, a war that will outlast the lifetimes of near everyone in this room—but not, Ten willing, the champion who was foretold."

All eyes turned to Aewyn.

"The druids of Nalsin are the last keepers of the *Uliri Imidactuai*—the Mysteries of the Unwatchers—the prophets," said Celithrand. "Long have I studied them, alone and with all the druidlords. For centuries we have puzzled over the champion who would end the Age—the child born of the womb of an êtril, a dyrad of the first forests. The fae as we know them are childless—never dying, never born—and when word came to me that your mother was with child, I knew then that you must be the girl they spoke of."

"The Havenari are no less dedicated to the fight against Tamnor's Horrors," said Robyn. "And yet you have shared no such prophecies with us."

"We did, in the beginning," said Celithrand. "Janus knew the prophecies well. The first Havenari, among other things, supported my search for Aewyn in the early days. Valithar's first Imperial Harper offered a healthy reward for information that led to her."

"Something changed," said Robyn. "I heard none of it. Toren, my predecessor, knew of no such reward—or else things might have gone differently when we found her."

"It would have been before his time," said Celithrand. "We did not know when or where to seek her. But what we found, of course, in the far places of the Empire, was that when we drove Tamnor's Horrors from the city, they went to ground according to their nature. The crudest Horrors, the low creatures that survived the Siege, appear in the form of twisted beasts, misshapen creatures that hunt and kill like wolves or sabercats. But there are other, older spirits. They take different forms and guises—even, in the case of very powerful Horrors, human ones. We realized quickly that if we could find you, our enemy could as well. So we worked in silence, Janus dissolved all central authority, the Havenari became a loose coalition of independent forces, and I searched for you in secret."

Aewyn, suddenly cold, drew her cloak tighter around her.

"You found me easily enough," she said.

Celithrand let out an awkward laugh. "Easily? Centuries I waited, child, and through all the decades of the Reconstruction I hunted you across Tamnor's aftermath. While Valithar was crowned in gold and revered in bronze atop the Shadewall, while he united the vasilies and the old kingdoms to great adulation, I roamed the desolate North, slept in ditches and hollows. I grew old past old on the blasted earth in the hope that you would come. And come you have—in fairer form and better heart than I might have hoped."

"All my life, I have heard these words," said Aewyn. "All my life I have been held to be important—and it has only made me feel small. I am smaller than myself. Always you have told me I had a destiny. But now that we come down to it, it does not *feel* like mine. I am no champion, Celithrand. I am no warrior, and I have no taste for blood. The touch of iron burns my skin. The sight of blood makes me swoon. That's a poor beginning to prophecies about swords and champions."

"I never expected you to be born with sword in hand," said Celithrand. "Well enough for your mother, you were not. There is time, yet, to make you ready. Indeed, your training has already begun."

"A few days with the bow I've given her," Robyn said. "Nothing more. You give me much credit."

"Days with a bow," said Celithrand. "Weeks, on and off, by example, of leadership. Months drawing living things from the earth. Years speaking the language of the *Iun*, learning their ways."

"The village has taught me many things," said Aewyn. "About being a villager."

"I spent long years making things ready," the old druid replied. "I told you in the deep wood, there is not much the *Iun* will not do for silver. By what secret art do you suppose silver was called into those hills—and by whose wagging tongue has word of it spread?"

Robyn looked at him in disbelief and decision. "You cannot mean that the village—we are all here for her sake? By your design?"

"Those who came," said the druid, "came mostly for their own reasons. I do not pretend to know the hearts of men. I only know the land called out for a champion, and the *Uliri* foretold one. And so far, then, was she from the world that needed her, that they had to be brought together. United, like the vasils of the Empire, by a common purpose against a common enemy."

Poe, who had long been motionless, snorted his distaste.

"I refuse to believe," said Robyn, "that destiny alone laid low my family and brought me to this place. Or did your silver buy the scutcheoned thanes of House Fane as well? Our vasil did not fall so that this girl, or any girl, could have a convenient archery teacher. Bram and I—gods, his *wife*, Celithrand—you had nothing to do with it, however much you loved the idea of an Empire. You had no hand in my father's betrayal. That I know. We came here of our own will. Not for Aewyn, whatever love we may bear for her now. Not for any prophecy, either."

"My dead have not died that she might live," Poe agreed. "To suggest it is disrespectful to them. Worse, it is unkind to her."

"All things have unseen ends," said Celithrand, but Poe would have none of it.

"I have heard enough," Poe growled to Aeywn. "You need not pay this prophecy business any heed. Destinies and champions belong in other stories. Not mine, and not yours. We can return to the woods. You can live your life in peace, free of meddling old men. Even a druid has no place in those woods, if we tell your mother what ill-fated designs he has on you." He fixed Celithrand with his yellow eyes and spoke with a measured calm: "We are sorry you have traveled so far.

But she does not like her destiny. She chooses another. You have been my friend for many years, old one. But if she asks it of me, you can expect me to keep her from you."

"I admire your courage, P'ŏh," said Celithrand, pronouncing Poe's true name far back in his long throat with immense effort. "It was always your way to be silent until strong words came. But these things are larger and more long-lived than you or I. You are come now into your full strength, and if you wish to shield her from her fate, you may well succeed for a time. But the flower of your kind blooms only a short while. Aewyn will be timeless, as her mother. In time she will outlive even me. If we prepare her now, perhaps she will even see the end of the Age. But not if she is unready for the inevitable. In two dozen years you will be dead—may the noble crows take your eyes—and the night will come for her all the same. We would do well to make it a little less dark for her in the time that we have."

"If two dozen years, I have," said Poe defiantly, "then two dozen I swear to her. And let the night come when it must. But I suffer no evil in this world, not even a deceiver speaking nonsense in the full bloom of his dotage, to touch her while I yet draw breath." Without standing, exactly, without doing much more than shifting his weight, his bulk seemed to swell in the narrow cottage as the muscles of his shoulders rose and his head lowered.

"Please don't fight," said Aewyn.

"I am not your enemy," said Celithrand, gently but without fear. "And I am sorry to be the messenger. But this peril will come, whether you stand to answer it or no. I would have you both ready to meet it on that day. Or would you claim to protect her, only to let her face the future unready?"

Poe growled wordlessly, but turned the thought over in his mind. His fierce jaws hung open a long time, on the edge of more and harsher words, until he begrudgingly shut them with a snort.

Aewyn felt very small in the silence that followed. "My home is here, in Haveïl," she said. "But if I must come away with you, I will do as you ask."

"Where she goes," Poe warned, "I go."

"I would not dream of separating you," said Celithrand, "and I would not spirit you away in the night from those who helped shape you—not if it can be avoided. I cannot stay the winter, of course—I must stay on the move, and would not draw the eye of Travalaith down on you here. But I will return to you at the first thaw, when you have settled your affairs and said your farewells."

"Where will we go?" asked Aewyn. "I have never even left the woods."

"Westward to the Sea," said Celithrand. "And thence beyond all reach of Travalaith, to Dær Móran, my ancestral homeland. The druidlords will train you in ways of power not seen since the Age of Sun. And it may be that you live out a lifetime, or more, in relative peace before the time comes."

"Will—will I return?" Aewyn asked.

"Certainly," said Celithrand. "But this world may well have moved on before you do."

"I understand," she said.

Poe's nostrils flared. The tears did not stray from Aewyn's eyes, but they were there.

"I thought you wanted to take up the Leaf," said Robyn, frowning. "To ride out with the Havenari, when you were old enough. To be a steward of the wood, and care for the people here as I do."

Aewyn shook her head. "I don't suppose destiny is a thing that cares much what we want."

"Then worms take it," Poe said. "The karach have no destiny. And to my tribe I have bound you with my stories. You have a new destiny, now, if you wish it."

"She has been chosen," said Celithrand. "It will not matter. Destiny has a way of finding us just the same."

"My ancestors did not believe in stories about Chosen Ones," said Poe. "Nor do I. There is no Chosen among my people, and never has been. Only those who *make* choices. And now that we come to it, she wishes no such destiny. She is afraid, old man, do you not smell it?"

"She will be more afraid," said Celithrand, "when the Riddle of Kedwyn is broken."

"I have been lost," said Aewyn, feeling acutely the ache of tears that had not yet fallen. "These long years, I have been lost. And now that I am found, I wish I were lost again. Grim called my destiny a fine tale. He never really believed it. I wish only that he'd been right. But I know…I am meant for something more—no, *other*—than this place. I am sorry to share that curse with those I love."

Celithrand sighed and laid an arm around her. "You have done no wrong," he said. "I too prayed it was not so. The more I came to know you, the more I prayed. But it is as Robyn says—the gods of goodness seldom give answer. At least, no answer we wish to hear."

"I don't even know what to tell the others," said Aewyn. "What will they think when I am gone?"

"I do not mean to steal you away," said Celithrand. "Your destiny has been long years in the making, and there will be time enough for farewells. When I return in the spring, one last time, we will speak of this prophecy, and of many others. In time you will know all that I know. This world is going to ask a great deal of you, and I pledge myself to helping you in any way I can. There is much yet I can tell you."

"But you have said so much already," said Aewyn. "My head is spinning." The old druid rose with a grunt and brushed down his clothes.

"There is more, so much more," he said. "Our years together will not be easy. But they will be my pleasure. I have not stayed the season with you since you were very young."

"If she stays the winter," said Robyn, with some hostility, "I will keep up her lessons in the use of that bow. I made a promise to her, and you ought to let me keep it. If she is a champion of legend, it will not serve her poorly to have some skill at arms."

"As you wish," said Celithrand. "I have not forgotten who founded the Havenari, nor why. Your role in the Siege of Shadow has made you the natural masters-at-arms to begin her training, if you have kept up the old ways."

"I can't blood her against the Aldwode," said Robyn. "Not without the ceremonial blood that I thank the Ten is in short supply. But I can teach her the bow and the spear. There's not much call for the old styles now, dealing with bandits, deserters, settling property disputes, quelling rowdies on the homesteads. But we have not forgotten."

"I should like to train with the Havenari," said Aewyn. "If you had not come, I thought—well, it was my greatest hope to train with them over the winter."

Celithrand waited a long moment before nodding his assent. "As you wish. We have some time, yet. I come to you now out of necessity, for I was evading the Legions in this direction. But I wanted time to tell you everything. Over the next few months, you will—"

The creak of the heavy door interrupted Celithrand's words. Fletch swung it inward and staggered into the room, gasping for breath. The druid hastily threw his hood over his face as the boy stumbled in without a knock.

"Fletch?" Robyn asked, rising to meet the boy. "You were given orders—"

"Pardons—C-Captain," he stammered, small chest heaving. "Hendec—sent me down from the Road. They've picked up some tracks…"

"Follow them, then," Robyn interrupted, a little impatiently. "We're in the midst of something important, here. The others can handle a deserter on their own." The hesitation in Fletch's voice was chilling and immediately out-of-place.

"Not deserter's tracks," he breathed. "A true Horror. What sort, exactly, we cannot tell."

All was silence and stillness. Robyn was the first to move, rising to her feet and belting on her sword. "Show me," she said. As she rushed to the door, the others followed suit.

"I may be of some use," said Celithrand, "though, as we have now said it, the bloom of my strength is much withered."

"I'm coming too," said Aewyn, which of course meant that Poe would not leave her. The druid shot her a stern glare.

"It is too soon," he said. "You are not ready." But she had learned much in her time with Grim's human daughter, and raised her chin haughtily.

"I am the child of your great Prophecy," she said. "If you are so confident in my fate, then I may do whatever I please, and you can rest assured it was all ordained."

"That is not how fate works," said Celithrand, though darker thoughts now held his attention and he had no more breath for talking—not at the pace Robyn and Fletch set ahead of them.

The place was near enough to the lip of the escarpment that readying the horses for the climb would not have brought them any more speed. The five of them climbed straight up and over the steep edge, and pushed back in the same direction they had gone in search of Rinnie and the Reeve. The woods were still and the silence unbroken; there was neither wind nor birdsong in the branches above them. Poe loomed protectively over Aewyn every step of the way: a forest with no birds was a godless place to die.

They stopped, very briefly, at the hermit's hut where Aewyn and Poe had found the child. The karach stopped well back of the hut and Aewyn was compelled to wait with him as Robyn ventured forward with Fletch and Celithrand at her side. The three spent some minutes searching the small one-room hut, and tore at its wattled walls until they were convinced it held no secrets but those Poe had already uncovered. They found, just as Poe had said, the rich accoutrements of an officer in the Grand Army: the deserter's grey tabard and sable cloak were lined with a distinctive and telling shade of blue.

"Cerulean Guard," Robyn breathed as she turned the items over. Outside, Poe's ears twitched uncomfortably as she lifted up the mail-coat; only Aewyn saw him flinch.

"Well-trained," said Celithrand, "and completely loyal. Well-paid, too. A deserter from the Cerulean guard is unheard of—or would have been, twenty years ago. Perhaps times have changed."

"Perhaps," Robyn agreed. "Do you see a mother's drop with his kit? I thought the Ceruleans all wore one."

"Perhaps he wears it around his neck still," said Celithrand. "Or perhaps not. The Cerulean Guard were loyal unto death, once. But those days may be gone."

"Anything of use?" asked Fletch. At the sound of his voice, Robyn picked up the guard's weapon. It was an arming sword, light in hand and well-made. Gauging Fletch's height, she passed it to him.

"We'll induct you properly when time permits," she said, though his eyes were already lost to her as he cracked the sword from its scabbard and gazed with admiration upon the gleaming steel.

With intent to return to the site at leisure, they pressed on and climbed a half-mile or so farther into the hilly woods, meeting up with the patrol road and following it on to where the tracks had been found.

Tsúla and his riding partner Venser were waiting for them on the edge of the narrow trail, flanked by high brambles and blackberry bushes. There was no point in asking them where the trail lay: the verdant wall had come crashing down on both sides of the trail, as if a bull—or several bulls—had come trampling through the foliage. A few slender birch trees surrounding the road had been knocked down at the roots by whatever had come this way. In the cold winters, Aewyn had seen a few felled by the heavy storms, bent and bowed at their height by the gathered ice. But these were healthy trees, or had been, until a few weeks ago, and where they had come down, the grass had died as if the earth had been salted. A whole channel of the forest here, perhaps ten feet wide, had been completely torn apart, and although Aewyn had no doubt she could have made out the tracks of the creature itself, she dared not look any closer.

"A moadon," said Celithrand. "Or something much like them."

"What is that?" asked Aewyn.

"Heavy, stout predators," he said, lowering his voice. "Squarish head, long mandibles. Black or grey, perhaps. Not shaped like any beast of this world. This one's very large, to my relief."

Robyn jabbed with her spear-tip at an overhanging branch that had been knocked loose, gauging the height of the creature. "Not to *my* relief," she said.

"Large means it is old," said Celithrand. "A relic of the Siege of Shadow, likely. Large means it did not come recently from…beyond."

"Do you think this is what frightened the Reeve?" asked Poe.

"I would have been frightened," said Aewyn, which was her way of stating that she already was.

It was not hard to determine the creature's direction of travel. The swath it had trampled through the forest spared none of the low scrub and few of the slender birches. Sparing no caution, Robyn reassembled the entire company before proceeding, following a long path that cut and tacked its way across level ground.

"It walks like a drunkard," Aewyn observed. "Back and forth. Here, there."

"No," said Poe. "It was hunting. This was a chase."

Celithrand eyed the karach with interest. "I think you're right," he said. "How did you know?"

"Look at the trees," said Poe. "Little more than saplings."

"Thirty years old, perhaps," said Celithrand. "There must have been a fire up here. The fireweed is first to come back, then the pine-grass, then blueberries, aspens, willows. These saplings are young birch—thirty years, forty at most. One day all this will be tall spruce trees again."

"But today," said Poe, "It is these thin grey trees, like delicate bones. It crashes through them easily. Look at the destruction. But its smaller prey could not. The man, he has only the strength of a man, so he changes direction here—and here—wherever growth is thick. And the hunter only follows."

"Good," said Celithrand. "You have the makings of a fine tracker."

Poe leaned out at the next change in direction, staring down a tunnel of shrivelled greenery, wide as a trade road, torn through the sunny woods. Wherever the creature's stride met bare earth, the grasses and shrubs had withered in its wake.

"This is not what karach call difficult tracking," he said, and marched on.

The creature's path wound its way across flat earth and slowly uphill onto rocky terrain. Those who had horses dismounted and walked them across the mossy rocks, until the ground was so unforgiving that the trail was all but gone. They had come out at the very east edge of the long escarpment, onto a craggy promontory overlooking the wide woods of eastern Haveïl and the jagged ribbon of the Iron Road. The forest opened up below them on both sides, and distantly they could make out the wood's northeast edge far away, lost in the blue fog of distance where it butted up against the marshlands.

"I have never seen this place," said Robyn. "What a stunning vantage. With a tall enough watchtower here, we could see clear to the ocean."

"The trail ends here," said Poe. "We cannot track it across this lifeless ground."

"There are ways," said Celithrand, moving in methodical steps across the rocks. He stopped at the leading edge of a stony outcropping and peered down into the misty woods below.

"Down there," he said, pointing a bony arm over the edge. The Havenari froze at the word; then, as one, with a grim sense of duty they unshouldered their bows, nocked unsteady arrows, and fanned out along the side of the rock.

Below them, splayed across a lower plateau, was the broken body of a man, his flesh darkened by decay, his mangled limbs hanging at weird angles and the mottled rock browned with the rest of him. Aewyn fell back from the sight with disgust.

"There is our deserter," said Robyn. "Fletch, what can you see with your keen eyes?"

"Less than with my nose," said the boy, leaning over uncomfortably.

"He's right," said Celithrand, deep in thought. "That body should be close to bone by now."

"It is cursed," said Poe. "Stay back."

A few of the bolder Havenari scoffed at that. Venser was already leaning over the cliff's edge, looking for a narrow path, before Celithrand's hand steadied him.

"Even the flies do not approach him," the old druid warned. "Decay is slow because they will not touch him."

"Nor shall we," said Robyn. The men took her comment as an order. Even Venser halted his descent.

"Where did this thing go? It wasn't after prey."

"They may eat the flesh of man," said Celithrand, "but they do not hunt us for hunger."

Aewyn was far back from the edge, now, clutching herself as if suddenly cold. Robyn came and put a hand on her shoulder.

"You ride well," she said softly. "But I'd like Poe to take you back to town now. It is the Havenari's duty, and ours alone, to find and confront this thing. I don't want you to be with us when we do."

Aewyn nodded uneasily, and turned back to the karach, who had himself fallen back from the stench of the body. He needed no convincing to turn back, eager to take her as far away as he could from the body, the soldiers, the duplicitous druid, these unsettling lies about destiny, and anything else he could find an excuse to shield her from.

Back on the cliffside, Venser still leaned out over the body.

"It doesn't look like he was carrying anything," he called up. "He's not out here foraging."

Robyn turned back to him. "What do you think brought him out this far? It's not a short climb, nor an easy one."

Hendec stretched up to his full height and peered over the promontory's edge—not toward the body, but to the far side. He narrowed his green eyes and squinted toward the sun.

"He may have expected pursuit," said Hendec. "You said yourself this was a fine vantage point. Perhaps he came up to watch the Iron Road for signs of unwanted company. You could see a campfire from up here, on a dark enough night."

"Or the smoke of one, in the early morning," said Fletch, joining him. "I can see the traces of a fire even now, by daylight."

Robyn paced back to where the body had gone over the side, looking for signs that the Horror had followed.

"Perhaps," she said over her shoulder. "And a military fire would throw off more smoke than some trader."

"I think that *is* a military fire," said Fletch. "A company our size, at least, or larger."

Robyn turned on her heels. "What? Show me," she said. She left Venser peering down at the body and crossed to the south side of the rock. It was not hard to spot, once she was looking for it. The sun was still to the east, and a narrow plume of hanging smoke was slowly fading against the bright backdrop of the sky and the distant trees.

"That's a huge fire, if it's from the Iron Road," she said.

"I don't think it's blown in that far," said Fletch, squinting. "It looks smaller. I see no split in the trees. Maybe it's come up from near the trade road. Down where it passes the pond."

Robyn stared down at the tree line in disbelief. "What would a Grand Army detachment of that size be doing on the village road? It goes nowhere but to Widowvale."

"Looking for that deserter, maybe," said Venser, who had wandered over. They stared together in silence for a long moment.

"What do you make of it, Tsúla?" Robyn asked when the younger man had come over.

He shielded his eyes against the glare of the sun. "Not much," he said. "I can't make it out without Fletch's eyes," he said. "Is it an old fire? Still burning?"

"I think it's out," said Fletch. "Not long ago."

"Venser?" Tsúla asked. "You rode with the Legions, yes?"

"Don't remind me," said Venser.

"If you were to order forced march by the sun—how long are we after first ride?"

Venser squinted at the horizon, held out a big fist at the length of his arm between the tree line and the sun, counted his knuckles.

"First ride, spurs up, would be about an hour ago, where we stand." he said. "Maybe a quarter hour nearer in the lowland."

"That's a Grand Army detachment," said Tsúla. "No question.

And moving on a tight schedule."

"The Empire is on the brink of civil war in the East," offered Hendec, coming up behind him. "I've heard the Iron City itself is infiltrated by rebels, now. They couldn't spare a whole detachment to mop up just one deserter, not even from the Spire itself."

"Well, they certainly don't need that many men to take the census," said Venser, chuckling.

"They're a week late for that, at least," said Robyn. "The census has already been and gone. We don't even send a runner for the miners until—oh, no ..."

Of all the men assembled, only Fletch saw the shadow cross her face. "What's wrong, Captain?" he asked.

"Mount up," she said. "We have to get back to Widowvale. Now."

Poe and Aewyn had started down the slope on their own, silent in their thoughts, when the sudden commotion of riders mounting horses drew their gaze back up the hill.

"What's going on?" Aewyn called.

Celithrand was suddenly at her side. "It seems the greed of men has caught up with them," he said. "The hills were rich enough for the townsfolk to get by, even with an honest Reeve and honest taxes. I have seen to that. But 'enough' is never enough, it seems."

Although they had led the horses up with due care, the Havenari could ride at speed when they had to, even across difficult ground. They thundered around and past the three figures on foot like a rolling wave and trotted in haste to the tree line whence they had come.

"Let us follow them," said Celithrand, "and see what is to be seen. There is a Horror afoot in the highlands. I would not stay in this countryside a moment longer without an armed escort."

"And they're leaving it to roam free?" asked Aewyn.

"The tracks are weeks old. We can see them only because of the devastation in its wake. But the Havenari will find it again. The young lady seemed to think this a more pressing matter."

"More pressing than a Horror of Tamnor?" Aewyn asked.

"Not all monsters take the form of beasts," he told her. "Come."

"We cannot keep pace with them," warned Poe, but Celithrand was already moving.

"Make haste," he replied. "I know of another way down."

NINE

IT WAS JUST BEFORE NOON that Widowvale began to shake itself out of strange dreams and set itself once again to the serious business of celebration. Before long, the warm smells and boisterous clamour of the Harvest Fair were not so different from the day before. The hum of chattering voices echoed down the valley, and the air was thick with the scent of roasted meat, fresh herbs, and wood smoke.

But there was no music, this day; and by the time the Havenari rode within earshot it was the shouts of the adults, not the children, that echoed loudest on the wind. Robyn's horse nickered at the distant cries, and perhaps at the smell of strange horses, too. They had come down onto the tradeway connecting Widowvale to the Iron Road, the main trunk highway in the northwest; and it was clear now that unfamiliar riders had recently come this way at speed. Fletch rode close to his captain, wishing fervently he were somewhere else, but returning to the village green just the same. Hendec, more than any, understood the gravity of the situation, and had refused to put his spear out of his hands. The rest followed with a deathly calm.

They came into sight of the village green only a moment ahead of Aewyn and Poe, who by Celithrand's woodcraft had descended somehow the steepest parts of the escarpment, and rushed toward the unquiet green. There, amidst the brightly coloured festival tents, the inhabitants of Widowvale had been gathered, and now stood half-awake in confusion. A motley ring of black, brown, and white horses, most of them light coursers, surrounded them, and atop them all sat tall pikemen clad in the blackened mailcoats and purple colours of the Travalaithi Grand Army. Robyn counted more than two dozen of them, all well-equipped and armoured—a sizeable enough force to her twelve men, even without superior arms—and there were a few more horses tied to Alec's honey-tent while their riders went door to door around the green, rousing people from their beds. Orin the groom was just being pushed into place with the others. Karis was stern-faced but stoic in her nightdress, surrounded by weeping children. Darmod Pick looked overtired and positively wroth. Alec affected a front of serenity, but all who knew him could read his concern, as well as a carefully contained fury. Circling the chattering throng with an air of detached calculation was the last of the Strangers for whom that year was named. He was in uniform, but not in armour, and surveyed the crowd from astride the largest horse of them all.

"Now, he looks like a census-teller," said Fletch.

"That's Castor Stannon," Robyn whispered. "He's *the* census-teller. He's the Censor at Wescairn under the ruling vasil of Haukmere… wait, look. Aewyn."

Robyn extended a pointing hand toward the far side of the green.

As the three climbers arrived into the thick of things, it appeared as though the three had been noticed by one of the riders, who walked his horse over more casually than might have been expected.

"Good morning and providence to you," said the rider.

"Good morning?" Aewyn asked, nearly a question. "Is something the matter?"

"You're in no trouble," the soldier said. "Just the same, step into the circle with the rest of the townsfolk, please." They did so with some hesitation, and Celithrand kept himself in Poe's shadow as much as he could.

"Stay in front of me," whispered Celithrand. "Try to look menacing."

"Celithrand," said Aewyn, "what's happening?"

"Hush, child," he said softly. "We're being herded for a head count, nothing more. Stay close to Robyn, when we get to her, and try not to speak. They'll find a few dozen miners who shouldn't be here, fine the town, collect their taxes, and be on their way."

"I have no gift for menace," said Poe, but he dutifully bared his teeth, narrowed his yellow eyes, and straightened his seven-foot frame as much as he could. To his surprise, the display had the intended effect, with some of the soldiers (and the townsfolk) fixing him with unfriendly eyes but giving him as much space as they could. Perhaps it was for the best; Poe was distinctly uncomfortable in the crowd. With all of the miners in town for the festival, there were far more people here than he was accustomed to—and upon realizing just how many miners were in attendance, he understood at last why the Censor had come.

Castor Stannon was of barely average height, but seemed immense on the back of his tall black horse. His hair was black and his beady, darting eyes blazed with the cold blue of the far northern ice. He had a strong jaw but a soft, womanly mouth, and there was something altogether unsettling about his comportment—precise, logical, almost lifeless. Although he was armed for the occasion, the impression he gave off was that of a man of numbers, not of steel. Aewyn watched him through the crowd as Robyn, too, was brought to meet him, with most of her men in tow.

"Welcome," said Castor.

"We don't feel it," snapped Robyn.

"Come now," Castor said with a precise smile. He might as well have not bothered smiling. "It's harvest time. Everyone is welcome in Widowvale in the autumn, isn't that right?" He looked then to one of his mounted men, who nodded approvingly.

"Yes, everyone's very welcome here," he continued. "Miners are welcome. Freemen are welcome. Deserters, why, they're especially welcome. Widows and maidens, just as welcome as the men...though I see we have fewer widows than our records would suggest, after all. Many more wives, though. So many more—and even a karach. Derec, you handled the census this year. How did you miss an entire karach?"

The one called Derec identified himself by shifting uncomfortably in his saddle. Castor ignored him.

"For fifteen years," he shouted, turning back on the gathered crowd, "the town of Widowvale has been recognized by Travalaith, though not always by that name. Silver, you were called once; I can see why. And since that time, Silver has been taxed not by its fortunes, nor by the Imperial land so generously shared with the Protectorate, but by the head. That kindness has been to your advantage." He rode through the muttering throng with measured confidence, pointing to them in turn as if counting.

"But that kindness has been abused," he continued. "There was no plague. The town was never hit by the rot. Your husbands did not die out after all. They grew rich. I'm very happy for you. But they grew rich beyond their due, glutted on the kindness the Empire has shown toward their wives, their children, their poor widowed families. I see now one of two problems before us. Either the head tax has been too low—or else, there are simply too many heads."

At the urging of three soldiers—they took no chances with her, which she took as a compliment—Robyn suffered herself to be led out onto the green with the others. She became at once Castor's new target.

"Surely," he said, "the Havenari would have noticed so many tax fugitives in their regular patrols."

"The mines are far from town, and I know not where," Robyn said, with a straight face that would have made Grim proud. "The miners seldom pay us a visit here in Widowvale."

Castor's blue eyes gleamed cold. "And yet the town is named for their work. And two dozen of them at least were roused, this morning, from the beds of these poor widows."

"Loose morals, nothing more!" someone—perhaps Darmod Pick—shouted defensively from the crowd, bringing a nervous laugh among even the Travalaithi soldiers.

"I don't think so," said the Censor sourly. "But a proper inquiry will out the truth. I would not have come this far out into the thick to level accusations without due procedure." He dismounted from his horse at this, and motioned two men toward the moot-hall.

"Unlock that hall," he said. "And who will speak for the town?"

"I will," said Robyn. Her purposeful step forward was met with a laugh.

"The Havenari are soldiers of the Empire, too," warned Castor. "At least, those Havenari who have not forgotten their place. I will not put Imperial soldiers on both sides of a charge, only to have my verdict thrown out on grounds of travesty. Where is the Reeve?"

"He has fallen ill," said Alec Mercy, who had been led to the green like the others. "He is resting in my house, though I say he will be in no shape to speak for the town today."

Castor rolled his eyes and took no pains to hide it. "Very well," he sighed. "How long must we wait in this insufferable little hamlet for a sick spokesman to recover?"

"What say you, Master? Another day or two?" Alec cast an inquisitive look to Celithrand for an answer, given his role in Marin's care. The druid was closely hooded and averting his gaze, and Alec, a moment too late, wondered why. His gesture of seeking the old man's attention was not lost on the Censor.

"Who is that man?" he asked, icy eyes narrowing. "Bring the old man here."

The rest happened nearly too fast to follow. Celithrand, with surprising agility for his age, made to run for the treeline, but the crowd, suspicious already of the stranger, slowed the stranger's passage enough for the Censor to witness his flight. He was already motioning for the soldiers to pen in the errant old man when Aewyn cried out in shock, completely forgetting herself and any pretense to secrecy:

"*Celithrand!*"

Castor hesitated at the name, but not enough to lose the advantage. "Seize him," he ordered, forcefully but with measured calm. The soldiers, who had anticipated no trouble when they were dispatched to enforce a simple tax dispute, were slow to react. Celithrand threaded through the crowd and was nearly free of them when one of the Imperial soldiers rode him down and caught him by the edge of his cloak. The soldier dismounted without letting go and cuffed the stranger once with a mailed fist—not hard enough to loosen teeth, but hard enough to make the point clear. A second soldier seized his arms, and his flight was ended.

Poe jerked on his feet, and might have gone to Celithrand's aid but the sight of the soldiers brought a choking, long-buried fear back into his gut, and he felt rooted in place. When Aewyn darted for the druid, heedless of her own safety, Poe seized her protectively, as he had seen Grim do at his own trial. She struggled in the grip of his clawed hand, but he lifted her gently until her feet could find no purchase on the ground.

"No one moves," Castor shouted to the throng, more exasperated than angry. "No one leaves." He looked to some of the Havenari, who had drawn steel during the commotion. "Thank you for coming to our aid, my lady, but the Grand Army has things well in hand. I hope your own blades won't be necessary."

"I suppose that's up to you," Robyn replied. They shared a wary glance, like two predators sizing themselves up.

"Put up your swords," Robyn ordered at last. The Havenari, in equal parts relief and resentment, began to sheathe their weapons. As Castor relaxed and turned his attention toward Celithrand, Bram leaned slowly toward his sister.

"Where's my wife?" Bram whispered. She smiled at him, but her face was tight with emotions hard at war with one another.

"Sweet boy," said Robyn softly. "She's still in bed, fast asleep. I don't need her today."

"I've let you down," said Bram. He was shaking. "I should have gone for her. I was here when they came—"

"No, no," she whispered, putting an arm around him. "You couldn't have—you did right."

"I'm here," said Bram. "If you need *me*." His dark eyes stared away into another place, but the trembling in his hands had gone. She held him close, glad for his company, but did not take her eyes from the Censor.

The prisoner was held by no fewer than six men as Castor approached him and pulled back his hood with a gentle, fastidious hand. Despite the mask of wrinkles, the old aeril's face shimmered in the morning light, and there was a starlight in his eyes that was not quite human. Castor rubbed a hand over his smooth chin with concern. No one was more surprised than he to find the old druid there in the flesh.

"Unmistakable," he said. "In the name of the Imperator, Valithar the First and Only, I order you bound and stayed."

"You are making a grave error," Celithrand said softly.

"I have heard those words before," said Castor, "but not as often as you would think. I am a bookkeeper, my lord; I make few errors, and I have only come here to settle old accounts. I did not expect to settle yours. The arrest of a fugitive does not normally fall to me, but to… lesser agents." Here he cast his eyes to a fuming Robyn as the manacles were brought.

"In point of fact," he continued, "in Haveïl, that duty falls most often to the Havenari. Strange, then, that you are here to enjoy the village fair, my lady, yet would not dare to trouble a fugitive from the Empire."

"Who is this man," Robyn asked, "and what has he done?"

Castor cocked his head. "Truly?" he asked.

"Truly," she replied with a shrug of feigned ignorance.

"He is Celithrand, of no other name, druid of Nalsin, Companion of the Owl. He was of old a person of some renown, as I'm sure even you must know. By Imperial edict he is now a traitor to the Empire."

"I have heard no such allegations," she warned.

"I need not repeat them, nor prove them anew," said Castor. "The sentence is already passed. Some months ago, he was found guilty of betraying the sorcerous secrets of the Stormguard to Jordac of Travalaith."

"Never have I heard that name," she lied.

"You will hear it soon enough," Castor warned. "His rebellion in the East is growing. They call it the Mages' Uprising, now—thanks in no small part to this traitor." He gestured to Celithrand, who was being searched and bound at the edge of the green. The assortment of bags, stones, strings, teeth, bits of fur on his person was astounding.

"It is not true," Celithrand called. "But there are worse things to be accused of than treachery against this debased Empire."

"He is condemned by decree of the realm," said Castor, his voice perfectly measured. "His trial is past. The matter is not under dispute."

Robyn scoffed. "Even you don't believe the charge."

"Belief has nothing to do with duty," Castor replied. "Derec, search him to the very bones. Walk with me, Robyn."

He led her away from the others for a moment. The men and women of Widowvale, at first panicked by the spectacle and the intrusion of the soldiers, relaxed into a nervous murmur at the disarming of Celithrand, content for the moment that the eye of justice was off them. It was true, of course, what the Censor had said: the miners were as much a part of the village as anyone, though they lived throughout the year away from their proper homes. Many hoped, and perhaps even believed, that the discovery of such an important fugitive would cause the matter of the head tax to be forgotten. The miners who had wives and children stood close to them, fearful now for the families they had forgone for the sake of prosperity.

When he had gone some distance from the soldiers, Castor affected a sigh. For a moment, a shade of regret seemed to pass over his face.

"You cannot imagine, Captain," he began, "what an uncanny stroke of luck has come to me. I am no Master General. I hold no post in the Cerulean Guard. I am merely the chief clerk in the West from the crumbling, overgrown swamp of Haukmere. I process coin for the lowest and rudest of the old vasilies. The sigil of my office may as well be a reeking bogflower. By chance I am in command, for a span of mere days, of a handful of Imperial soldiers. By chance, I have apprehended the second most wanted man in the Empire nearly by stumbling over him. 'What good fortune,' my wife will say. 'How lucky you are!' And yes, I will be well rewarded for doing my duty to the Empire. But I wish to Tûr I had not found him all the same."

The soldier called Derec approached them with a delicate, gently curved sword in hand. He drew the blade an inch; its steel gleamed with an unmistakable touch of reddish gold.

"He was armed with this alone, milord," said Derec.

Castor eyed the sword with a knowing awe.

"The sentence was passed in his absence some months ago," he said softly and coldly to Robyn. "All that remains is to know beyond doubt that we have the man who was condemned. And that will not be hard to prove, now. Not with this weapon in hand. Half the soldiers here, and anyone who's been to the Spire, would recognize it from the mosaic at Cîr-Valithar." He wandered back toward the prisoner with Derec at his side, leaving Robyn cursing softly.

"It would be a shame," he called back as an afterthought, "to discover Widowvale had been harbouring him."

In his absence, the conversation had grown a little unruly; the crowd was uneasy, and the soldiers had grown uneasy along with it.

"Is the count finished?" he asked.

"And the town otherwise empty," said Derec. "The Reeve is asleep in the beekeeper's house, just as they say."

"Line them up," said Castor. "Count them again, be sure of the score, and then send them back to their homes, or set them free. The taxes can wait until the execution's done. We don't want a mob on our hands."

Celithrand was bound and tied over an empty barrel, with many of the villagers looking on. Aewyn stood near him, having settled down somewhat; Poe was behind her, but not so far behind that he could not grab her again if she attempted something foolish. Castor hoisted the sword and drew the blade. Aewyn gasped but did not move.

"It has a nice heft to it," he said. "The weight of history, perhaps. Tell me, what is its name?"

"Niurwyn," said Celithrand.

"Bird-friend," Castor smiled, brandishing it at arm's length. "A curiously tame name, for a blade of such renown. But that is, indeed, what the songs call it." He sheathed it gently, with care but not with reverence. "And what would you have me do with it?"

Celithrand was careful not to let his gaze stray from his captor's face. "It's mine," he said.

Castor seemed almost bored with this answer. "That's why it is yours to bequeath," he clarified. "Do you think me so corrupt that I would steal a priceless heirloom from your heirs? Your death sentence, as I recall, included no clause of forfeiture. It is your right under law, dead man, to name its inheritor."

"It belongs with the Havenari. They will know what to do with it." He looked then to Bram, who shook his head and glared back with unexplained anger.

"It belongs with my sister," Bram said coldly. "Her alone. I'll sell that for wine if you put it in my hand, first chance I get. I swear it by eleven scars."

"Give it to Robyn, then," said Celithrand. Castor nodded.

"As you will," Castor said. "By naming this sword, Celithrand, and by claiming right of bequest to it, you have also named yourself. I appreciate that you have made my work easy. If you like, I can set the men rummaging through their purses for some old coins, just to be sure. But I have handled a lot of coin for the vasily of Haukmere, and were you not the Rider for whom the little silvers were named? I am certain silver riders issued prior to the Annexation capture your likeness perfectly—though you are taller in person, perhaps, than you were in my purse."

To that Celithrand had no answer. A long silence descended, as Castor considered the logistics of execution, a business which had never before fallen to him.

"Arrange for the execution of the sentence," he said at last to one of the soldiers, who shrugged noncommittally.

"Hanging, sir?" asked the soldier. Aewyn cried out in horror; the muttering of the crowd intensified even as the other soldiers began to push them into rows and columns.

"However it's done," Castor said dismissively. "There's a fine tree at the end of the green. Get on with it."

"You can't!" Aewyn shouted at last; Poe's grip on her shoulder did nothing to silence her mouth. "He's done nothing wrong! He's no sorcerer! He's no criminal!"

Castor Stannon turned to her, then, as if noticing her for the first time. He looked up to the karach, his cold eyes wide and keen. Poe, though he towered over the Censor, took a step back from that stare. Memories of fire and steel, of his mother's fur set ablaze, were quick in his mind then. He clutched Aewyn to his breast, but he was not angry. He was afraid, and although he towered over this soft little man he felt suddenly very small.

Confident in his safety, the Censor approached the girl, slowly and calmly. He moved a step at a time to deny the frightened karach an excuse for action. But he felt the tension just the same as he bent forward slightly, lowering his eyes to the level of hers.

"And what is your name, young lady?"

"Aewyn," she whispered.

"Aewyn," he said, turning the word over in his mouth. "Aewyn. And how do you know this man?" Behind him, Celithrand's face was lined with worry.

"He's my friend," she said, quivering, but sure of herself. Castor's weird unblinking gaze was intense as lightning. It was impossible to tell if her answer pleased or displeased him. He ran a tongue thoughtfully over his soft lips.

"From long ago, you mean," he said at last. "Before he betrayed the Empire."

Aewyn trembled, but did not speak.

"Say it," Castor said. "He was a friend, long ago."

Aewyn nodded. "Long ago," she said. She felt her guts twisting into knots under his gaze. But the Censor stood and turned, suddenly civil.

"Of course," he said. "Long ago, I am sure he was as innocent, as you are even now."

She caught Celithrand's gaze as Castor turned around, and the druid jerked his head up from the barrel so that she could see his mouth.

"Dær Móran," he mouthed to her silently. At his side, Castor turned to a soldier who had returned with some scrounged rope.

"Take those two and send them away from here," he said quietly. "She's overly fond of the traitor, and she's not much older than a child. There's no need to make her watch him dance his last jig."

"And the rest of them?"

Castor looked out on the crowd. Even those who had been turned loose still surrounded the green, peeking around barrels and tents in confusion and alarm.

"Let them see the Imperator's justice done, if it pleases them," he said.

"They're whispering about the Siege of Shadow," the soldier replied. "They say he was a hero once, and a friend of the forest. They say the very trees will not suffer him to be hanged."

"If the wood pardons him, then steel will serve," said Castor at last. He stood aside and allowed the soldier to approach the girl and the karach. He surveyed the prisoner's face, impossibly old and desperate and sad, with an air of detachment. He took count of the Havenari, standing among the soldiers around the green, and wondered if their loyalty would hold, and how his soldiers would fare against them if it came to blows. He was, he knew, a poor judge of such things. After a moment of thought, he summoned both Derec and Robyn to him, both of whom were keenly on edge. He spoke mostly to Robyn, but wanted his words to be heard by his men as well as hers.

"These people are close to panic," he said. "Close to madness. And this man was a hero, once. If the wind changes and they go off all at once, it will be a massacre."

"We are charged to protect these people," Robyn said with measured anger, "not murder them."

"Precisely, Captain. One vengeful folk hero who incites a riot could cause the death of dozens. I will not have that on my head, and neither will you. At the first sign of interference with the execution, any disturbance at all, you will put down the troublemaker without hesitation. I will instruct my men to do the same. I understand that tensions are high. But better to quench one spark before it sets off the barn."

"The Havenari do not take their orders from Haukmere," said Robyn.

"Call it advice, then," said Castor. "And unless your men want to trade your famous spears for shovels, and spend the next two weeks digging graves, I pray you listen to it." Almost as an afterthought, he recalled the heirloom sword still in his hands, and passed it on without ceremony to the woman, who looked down on him in stern but defeated silence.

"This is Niurwyn," he said. "The condemned wanted you to have it. If things go poorly with any of the townsfolk, it will make your job quick and easy."

"Quick, perhaps," said Robyn, storming away without further comment.

"If this town turns on us," advised Derec, "she'll be no help at all."

"If this town turns on us," said Castor, "we put a half-dozen arrows into the old man to ensure the sentence is carried out, and ride for

Wescairn. We came to enforce a head tax, not to put down a rebellion. If the whole town turns traitor, Lord Ashimar will come himself."

"By the Chain," said Derec, shuddering, "I hope it won't come to that."

"So do I," said Castor Stannon, though he didn't sound convinced.

In the shade of a red pavilion tent, surrounded by clay pots of Alec's honey and a few day-old loaves of Alys the Miller's bread, the Havenari tried their best to look as if they were not calling muster. Robyn sat rather than stood in their midst, and in hushed tones she told them of her talk with the Censor. They listened with discipline and deference, but their anger was clear. Fletch kept looking over his shoulder nervously, as if he expected one of the Travalaithi soldiers to ride up behind him at any moment. Robyn knew him well enough to know he was really counting them, marking their positions and the positions of their horses.

"You will not cross swords with the Grand Army," she said firmly, though Fletch did not stop his count. "Your first duty is to the people of Haveïl, and heroism will do them no favours. This affair will be ended soon. Do not mistake me; this is a travesty of Imperial justice. But Castor Stannon is a far sight more reasonable than he lets on, and a damned sight more reasonable than those who will come after him, if this town turns on him."

"Reasonable?" said Hendec, too loudly, and the others hushed him.

"He is a precise man," she said. "There is a certain logic to all that he does. He has already found more trouble than he wished for, and I think if he meets with no more, he will leave us—leave Widowvale—in peace."

"Coin-mongers have no business on that end of a rope," said one of the men. "Though it would not pain me to see him on the noose end."

"No one draws steel," she said, more forcefully this time. "I will not suffer a single man, nor a woman, nor a child from the village to be harmed because one of you impetuous bravos could not keep it in your scabbard. If I see a single hand with a sword in it, I'll pin that hand to your chest with an arrow, and you can wear it there like a medal of shame on your way back to the Capital. Have I made myself clear?"

"Yes, Captain," they replied. It came out as a muffled grumble, and not only because they were keeping their voices low. She caught Venser's uncertain gaze. "Are you with me, Venser?"

"I serve without question," said Venser. "But if you change your mind, Captain, I'll follow you without question as well."

"I do not understand it," she said, "and I do not like it. But we cannot weigh the life of one outsider—and an outsider we are told, at least, is a criminal—against the hundred lives of a village we are charged with protecting."

"From the Empire that would kill them, or worse," said Hendec, still red-faced at the affront.

"Even so," said Robyn. "We swore before the Magistrate of the Outlands, in fairer times, to protect the people of Haveïl from all enemies. I take that to mean from Travalaith herself, if it comes to that."

"If it comes to that," said Hendec, "if you choose to stand against Haukmere, you must know I would stand and fight with you."

"I am her brother," said Bram, "and even I would not. Protection does not always come at the end of a blade."

"Since when have you ever—" Hendec began, though he thought better of it as anger flashed in Robyn's eyes.

"If you wish to join the Uprising," Robyn said to Hendec, her words carefully measured, "we would be sorry to lose you. But Tsúla will count you out, and we'll buy back your kit against the price of your horse—or your sword, if you deem it more necessary than your horse on the way to Selik."

Hendec fumed, but said nothing. Fletch coughed out loud as a Grand Army soldier rode past silently, his horse pacing out the perimeter of the village green.

"I thank you for your words, all the same," she said when the rider had gone. "It seems there is to be an execution. Our lot is not to carry it out, nor to take up arms in defense of the condemned, nor even to bear witness. Our lot begins and ends with keeping the peace, and stopping any villager who is fool enough to give the Imperial Army an excuse. By sword, if necessary."

"Will I be needed for this stupidity?" Bram asked her. Some of the men bristled at his rudeness, but she shook her head with nothing more than sorrow.

"I cannot ask this of you."

"Then I will be at Miller's Riffle with a flask of Alec's mead. Any of you who carry too much anger to be trusted at your post, you are welcome to join me there, and drink until your anger has turned to laughter or sleep."

Tsúla bent his lean body toward the window and peered across the green. "It's not yet midday," he noted.

"I accept just the same," said Hendec. "I object to this whole wretched business. If I am relieved for the day, I want no part of it."

"Let's get going, then," said Bram. "I need to stop by the house on the way."

"You are relieved," said Robyn. "Both of you. Anyone else? Fletch? Venser? Tsúla?"

Tsúla stood and shrugged. "It's nearly time," he said. "They look ready. Unless we all wish to excuse ourselves, we should return." He crossed towards the door, touching Robyn's shoulder as he passed with perhaps collegial affection.

"I predict nothing will come of it," he told her, half-smiling. "There will be some talk. But these are outsiders' problems—the problems of bigger folk, maybe. People come to Widowvale to put those woes behind them. None of them will be foolish enough to risk all that for a stranger they have known less than a day—no matter how good his wine. Except for the fairy-girl, they have no particular attachment to him at all."

Robyn frowned at that. "Where is Aewyn?" she asked.

None of them knew. She had a way of disappearing, after all.

"Get out there," she ordered. "Find her, if you can. And keep them calm. Don't look like you're searching."

The men began to funnel out of the tent. As Bram passed, she took his arm.

"Go back to the house," she whispered. "Get your sword. Keep her with you, and don't stray far from earshot."

Bram turned pale as he listened, but nodded just the same.

"If he turns on the villagers—on the children," she asked, "I'll need her again. I'm so sorry, sweet boy."

Bram's mouth was tight. "Tell me."

"Where will you want them?" she asked.

Bram's eyes were shut hard. The darkness helped him concentrate.

"The moot-hall," he decided at last. "The main door. Send someone ahead to bar the others."

Robyn nodded, and turned to go.

"Robyn?" His voice behind her was so small. She turned back around.

"Hm?"

"Don't let them hurt anyone. It's up to you."

She smiled sadly at him, then set her jaw firmly. "And to you, if I fall."

In a larger city, or even in the Imperial barracks at Wescairn, the arrows loosed at the archery butts would likely have been crowned with target points—narrow, short heads cast from junk alloys with hardly any iron, designed to penetrate targets with as little damage as possible, so they could be used year after year. In Widowvale, much of the target shooting was into nothing more than earthen mounds, draped with flimsy panels of packed straw that would be used as thresh or fodder in the months to come. The time of smiths and fletchers was in high demand, and for these reasons and others, the arrows fired in the annual tournament had hunting heads—the same, in general, that farmers, foresters, and the Havenari themselves used for fowl and large game alike. A full day of shooting might have dulled them, Aewyn knew, but they would fly true and stick where they were put.

"What are you doing with those?" Poe asked her, following her out into the field.

"What I must," she said. "I won't let Celithrand be hanged."

"This is folly," said Poe. "I have seen what the City-men are capable of. If you think you know the *Iun* because you have dwelt a few years in this place of peace, you are sure to die for your mistake."

"If Celithrand is right," she said, "I don't think I will. I have a destiny—and I can't fulfill it without him."

"Destiny," Poe spat. "I know few man-stories of my people—but I do know of Gorrh the Fated, who lived a prophecy of his own. He was destined to bring peace to the warring tribes. Like you, he was told this at a young age. He grew to be a mighty warrior, fearless in battle, for he believed he was protected by the prophecy. Then, like a fool, he sparked the First Great Fire in his tent, and the devastation of the plains in the dry season brought such famine and disease that the tribes could no longer fight the old war. So he brought peace to all his kind, as was foretold, though he burned to death with his cubs." He followed her, insistently, as she crossed to the next archery target. "Destiny we may have. But be not proud of it, for it saves none of us, in the end."

Aewyn tugged hard at an arrow that had buried itself in a stump. It splintered as she pulled it free, and she tossed it away.

"Destiny or no, I am frightened," she said. "But I cannot sit by and let Celithrand die, whatever he has done. You heard them. You know what is about to happen. The Havenari can do nothing; they are Imperial soldiers too, if it comes to that. There is no one to help him but me! I know you fear them, Poe. I know what they did to your family. But Celithrand is my family, and I will not let them do the same to him. I do not ask you to stand with me. But I mean to free him, at any cost. If we can just get him into the woods, he will escape them, I know it! And if it means I must return to my mother afterward, and hide in the deep wood until all who remember my crimes are long dead, I will. If I can do what others cannot, then I must try."

"You make up your bed in a grave!" Poe growled.

She smiled at him, then, and it utterly disarmed his temper. Her sweat was thick with fear—he could smell, he thought, her body readying itself for a fight—but her little square teeth beamed in her tiny, too-human smile, and it softened his resolve more completely than anything he had ever known.

"There is always hope," she said.

Poe snorted in frustration. "Hope there may be." he replied. "But there would be a good deal more of it, if you faced fewer than twenty-five ironmen—or if you had more than nine arrows."

"Then either kill some men," she said, "or help me gather more." In spite of himself, Poe knelt to pry an arrow gently out of the dirt. His ears twitched on his head as he listened to the distant shouts of the soldiers ordering the crowd back from the tree.

"Hurry," he told her. "There is almost no time."

They cleared the targets of arrows in haste—not many people had been out practice-shooting before the soldiers rounded them up—and ransacked two quivers left in a nearby tent. Poe scrounged a few more, following the scent of goose to the fire-pit where some of the Havenari had sat eating and fletching. When he returned, Aewyn was nearly motionless in the field, lost in thought, fastening a tiny blue pendant around her neck.

"Hardly the time to adorn yourself for courtship," he grunted.

"For good luck," she said. "Rinnie gave it to me, from the deserter's house. It didn't feel—right to wear it, somehow, while we might still have found its owner living." She tucked it away under her shirt, cold against her skin, as if to prove that she wore it for herself and not for the approval of another.

"It is no more right to steal from the dead," suggested Poe.

"It was a gift—" she began to protest. She stopped when Poe raised a hand and flattened his ears in warning. He dropped low in the grass and was silent, and finally she heard the footsteps across the field. She followed suit, and lay hidden among the last of the spring wheat until the figures had passed. Looking up, she spied with relief two of the Havenari making their way west, and came up from the earth to meet them.

"Hello," she said, awkwardly clutching her bundle of arrows as she rose. Both men looked at her load with some alarm.

"What you are you doing out here?" asked Bram.

"Gathering arrows," she said. "You?"

Bram's face fell. There was no mistaking what was about to happen.

"We're off to put this wretched day behind us," said Hendec. "We joined the Havenari to protect the Outlands, not to work lethal crowd control for some damned tyrant. Bram and I are more alike than I thought—a coward and a radical. Neither one of us will lift a sword to help Castor Stannon—and call that what you like, but in my mind it makes us the best of the bunch."

"Won't you come with us?" she asked. "We can't just let Celithrand die. We have to do something."

Hendec frowned. "Not so long as I wear the Leaf," he said. "The Havenari do not answer to the Grand Army, and I wouldn't wet my boots to save a drowning Travalaithi, but we're bound by honour not to turn on them. And I care for Robyn's honour a lot more than my own."

"An innocent aeril could die," she said. "Please…"

Both men shook their heads. Hendec was visibly fuming at being forced by oath to pass up the prospect. Bram simply looked sad.

"Come on, Poe," Aewyn spat, without taking her eyes off them. "They won't help us." The girl's look of disdain was so severe that it stopped Bram in his tracks for a moment. He leaned in close and motioned for Hendec to wait. He fought for his words a long time—not like a drunkard trying to find them, but like a man sick at heart with saying them.

"You're both unarmoured," he said. "If the soldiers close, it'll be with the sword, not with maces. They probably come from Wescairn—the master-at-arms there is a man named Gibson. They'll be well-trained, even by Grand Army standards. He's the successor of his school."

"I recognize those words," said Poe, "but they mean nothing to me."

Bram's battered old sword was suddenly resting against Poe's neck—he must have drawn it—and the cold weight of its clean blade was like ice on the back of the karach's broad shoulder. Poe jerked with alarm, but did not retreat.

"Look to my sword," said Bram, "and look at the size of you. See my arm down here. I can't cut you to the heart. You tower over me. You have no collarbone to speak of—karach have not much of one—but your shoulder blades are like temple flagstones. Unless I'm half-swording, and that's another school altogether, my blade's too long for how fast you can come in. I'd hit bone, and couldn't cut through it, not if I were strong as three men. But they will look as if they mean to." Here he dropped his weight and his sword low, as if he had missed his swing wildly.

"They'll swing into this. It's the fool's guard. You'll rush in—"—he dropped his wrist and the point sprang up—"and they come up here, through the false ribs, into the heart from below. They push up from the earth with their legs. Here, at the shoulder, even Venser couldn't cleave you to the heart, not with both hands. But here, if you're coming in with all your weight, a girl Aewyn's size could stick you clean through with just one."

"How do you know this?" Poe asked. Bram sheathed his sword and motioned toward the village.

"Go, if you're going," he said. "But watch for it. They'll get you from below, every time."

"Come on," called Aewyn, already making her way across the field. Poe turned and followed, racing to catch up, his own battle-scent rising. The sounds of swaying grasses and the distant crowd gave way, then, to the sharp knock of wood, followed by an interminable suspended silence. Aewyn took off at a sprint, and Poe kept pace even as his heart plummeted inside him. There was a curse on his tongue, a particularly foul one, but as he lowered himself to all fours and charged like a beast, there was no wind for it.

TEN

DEREC HAD THE HABIT of throwing evens when it came to distasteful jobs. Few things in the world could be relied on, Kellan thought, but Derec throwing evens was just one of those things. He was too lame to throw proper, having taken an arrow through the right shoulder some years back—it was the reason he'd been reassigned from the Grand Army out east to taking the census—and now he waggled his hand over his head like an alms beggar when he tossed lots. But if Kellan had had any faith left in a morally ordered world, it evaporated that morning, when Derec waggled his hand over his head and somehow threw odds.

"My arse," he cursed as Derec laughed.

"Looks like you're the lucky winner, Kellan Fyldron," said Derec.

"Amn't I always," said Kellan.

As far as hangings went, it was an extremely rushed affair. A suitably high piece of furniture to ensure a clean death had to be commandeered, and the rope had to be slung over a bough of the big oak tree, but that was really all it took. On the insistence of some of the soldiers, though, Castor Stannon was forced to establish the prisoner's likeness by sorting through every silver coin in their possession until an old "Celithrand rider" could be found. On the tailside, an armoured knight led a mounted charge against whatever enemies—famine, thirst, the law, the want of a good time—the coin was spent to defeat. On the headside, a stern and sad old druid in a wreath of oak leaves cast his face toward the left edge, as if vigilant against all those enemies he had fought in the name of Travalaith.

There was no mistaking him. This man was a treasure of the Empire, and now a traitor to it. And Kellan Fyldron was about to go down in history as the man who hanged him. It was not an honour he wanted.

"Every druid who wants revenge," he grunted, measuring the rope. "Every white-haired grandmother of the Oldborn who remembers what good he once did. Every uppity little turd who carries steel for the Mage. Every convict slave who could have been free, every man or woman or child whose father or grandfather died of the Aldwode. Every one of them is going to hear my name and come looking for me, all because my big arse is the counterweight on the end of this stupid rope."

"Better yours than mine," said Derec. "And you're twice my size, you lummox. It'll be a cleaner hanging just the same."

"Have you two got it sorted?" Castor Stannon was behind them suddenly, his face unreadable as he strode back to the tree. He had the air of being impatient, and the habit of being thorough. It was an immensely unpleasant combination.

"Aye," said Kellan. "I'm your man."

"Good. If there's to be no further delay, then—"

"There's been too much delay already, sir," Kellan growled. "I say, stick a sword in him and be done with it. Death's a house with a thousand doors. Makes no difference to Dagan how you come in."

"It's not the God of Death I aim to satisfy," Castor countered. "An execution by hanging has a greater air of legitimacy to it than running a man through."

"Aye, sir. It's positively genteel till his bowels let go." With a challenging snort, Kellan hurled the noose over a thick bough and stood holding the slack end, looking incredulous and unimpressed. "We're civilized out here, we are. A passerby might mistake me for a Magistrate."

Castor frowned. "Refresh my memory, soldier. Was I given command of two dozen men?"

"Aye."

"And their tongues also?"

Kellan bowed his head. "Aye, m'lord." He did not wait to hear if there was more, but went to haul up the prisoner. Celithrand was still manacled, and those manacles were bound loosely with rope to a heavy barrel. He did not seem to protest as Kellan pulled a long dagger from under his left arm and cut him free. He had the height and slight shape of an aeril, but even so, he was leaner than Kellan expected. His face was serene but sad.

"It's your time, old man," he said, and Celithrand stood up with some difficulty.

"When one lives long enough," said Celithrand, "one forgets the possibility of death."

"Many things are possible," Kellan said sullenly. "Death is *certain,* if you're patient enough."

Celithrand forced a laugh as the two began walking over. "I could stand to wait a few more years," he said.

"We've found a high-backed chair," said Kellan, matter-of-factly. "The higher you can stand, the better it will go for you. Get up on the arms. I'll try to let you drop some when I kick it out, and I'll hoist you hard. If you're brave enough—some men are—you can jump some. No need to suffer. I'll be as clean as I can."

"I don't suppose I should thank you," said Celithrand sourly.

"No," said Kellan. "I don't suppose you should."

The chair had belonged to Owen, son of Orin; when consulted, the townsfolk decided to give up one dead man's seat to another, and destroy it when the deed was done so no ill luck came back on any man living. It was a tall cedar chair, still sweet-smelling, with high arms. Celithrand placed one foot on it willingly before he froze and had to be forced. He had been alive a long, long time, then—far longer than any ordinary man, even among the Oldborn, and longer too than most of the aerils who had lived in his Age. He was surprised to find that he, like any other, was afraid of what awaited him. He gave thought to how he should have left the world, perhaps long ago, and what uneasy afterlife this end might bring. And perhaps, only for a moment, he thought with some regret of the Imperator, who had once been a friend and comrade to him, a man who would not and should not have sent him to die. Then Kellan's meaty hands were hard on his ankle, twisting it up onto the arm of the chair.

"Come on," said the soldier, not unkindly. "If you've any last words, best get them out of your neck now."

"Take her to the Druids," he called out, loudly, to no one in particular. "To Dær Móran. The prophecy must be fulfilled!" That was all.

When the moment came, Celithrand could not and did not jump. His name and supposed crime were read again, and the sentence was pronounced, and Castor Stannon acknowledged the deed by all his power as some sort of petty official—and then the time for death was at hand, and he was not ready. Kellan, now hooded as an executioner, waited as long as he dared.

"Well?" said Castor Stannon impatiently. Behind the mask, Kellan sighed.

"They never go easy, do they," he said, and kicked out the chair with all his strength.

If Celithrand was accused of teaching sorcery, his reputation was not at all helped by what happened next. Whether by some unseen rot in the great-tree of Widowvale's green, or by some magic he had held in check, the bough of the old oak did not take his weight hard, but bent under the strain like a willow-branch. Celithrand drooped nearly to the ground, the tips of his boots brushing the tall grass, before Kellan cursed and caught him up, hauling him hard against the strain of the bending branch. The old man choked at the rope but his neck did not break; his arms and legs jerked madly as his desperate body tried to dance away from the death that now caressed him, calling him on gently. It would not wait for long.

Kellan spat into the dirt with frustration as he sank his weight and dug into the rope; for all his efforts, this death was going to be a long and hard one. Castor watched intently but impartially, his face a mask that only hinted at a vague displeasure. Derec came over, in the end, to lend his strength to the line as the bough bent a little farther than was right for a limb of such thickness.

The great oak was not far from the tree line that ran the length of the escarpment on the north side of town. Aewyn's plan, initially, had been to come from that direction under deep cover, put an arrow in each of Celithrand's handlers as he was brought to the tree, and hope he had the good sense to make for the woods. She knew him well enough to know that he would be gone within ten paces, and not this Castor nor any of the other dozen new names she had heard and forgotten that day would find him again. She imagined, too, that she could outrun and outmanoeuvre any of the mailed and mounted men once they reached the top of the ridge. But that plan was now lost to her: she arrived around the back of Alec Mercy's house, out of breath and shaking with terror and anger as she caught sight of Celithrand hanging in midair, his manacled hands jerking up and down behind him as his legs kicked tightly together, rocking and spinning him on the end of a fat rope.

Standing more or less out of sight of the soldiers, she hastily nocked an arrow and sighted down the man holding the rope. He was a big, broad man, and a sizable target at this distance, larger than some of the targets she had hit the day before. But she had never taken a human life, nor imagined herself as the sort who would; and now that it came to it, even at twenty times the distance of a sword, she could not will her shaking hands to do the terrible deed. At the end of his rope, Celithrand swung struggling. It felt like it had been long minutes since she heard the drop, but it could not have been. Why couldn't she shoot?

In desperation, paralyzed against the executioner and confronted by her old friend's death throes, she took aim at the rope suspending him in midair. She had heard of such shots attempted, had even seen some trick shooting done in the tournaments. And if she was to be a champion of some kind, now was the moment to put that providence to the test.

"Destiny," she breathed, and loosed an arrow at the rope.

At this distance, in this wind, it wasn't even close. Her first arrow went hopelessly high, whistling through the branches of the oak and vanishing. Her second and third were perhaps two or three hands from the rope, which was swaying gently from Celithrand's weakening struggles. By that time, the sound and path of the arrows had been noted. With a shout of "Archer!" from one of the soldiers, the crowd (for it was a hanging after all) erupted into a thunderous murmur, and the surrounding soldiers kicked their horses toward the prisoner, looking for the source of whatever arrows they had seen. In fright, she threw herself behind the building and bit into her lip in fear, anger, helplessness. Then, with renewed resolve, she emerged from her hiding place again. If she could not touch the rope, she would hit whatever she could.

Kellan let out a sudden grunt. "Ow," he exclaimed, though not loudly.

The pain, at first, had come from nowhere. The sting of an arrow was not completely unfamiliar, but neither was it so commonplace that he knew at once what had happened. He looked down and saw the shaft coming out of his chest; it was clean through his purple tabard, had pushed through his mail-coat, and had buried itself close by the heart in the thick muscle of his chest. Shock, more than the wound, compelled him to release his grip on the rope. He had seen men hit there who died very unkind deaths—some within a few minutes, others hours or days later. But the pain was not unbearable; he tested the muscle and found it ready enough, and praised both his luck and his armour before turning his gaze in the direction of the arrow-shaft. A young girl, fierce-eyed and determined with hair the red of autumn leaves, notched a second arrow. Kellan saw the correction for the first shot, incremental movements as she turned her arrow-point to his companion and raised her aim to his unhelmed head.

"There!" he cried, and pointed towards the girl, who loosed a second shot and disappeared behind cover.

Derec let go the rope as Kellan tackled him from behind, knocking him out of the arrow's path and taking the wind from him as well. Celithrand tumbled weakly to the ground, and Derec waited for the furious orders that were sure to issue from Castor Stannon's mouth. But no order came, save a shriek of pain that barely sounded human. He turned his head in time to watch the Censor go straight down to the earth behind him, with an arrow well and firmly lodged in his eye.

Blood and worse things streamed down his face as his limbs twisted in shock and agony.

"Kill him!" he screamed. "Kill the archer!"

Most of the Imperial soldiers were mounted. Most of the Havenari, for the moment, were not. As the soldiers charged in the direction Kellan indicated, steel flashing into their hands, the Havenari pushed quickly and deliberately in front of the crowds, where mayhem was ready to turn loose.

"Hold the line!" Robyn shouted. "Keep them out of the way!"

But for that one order, the chaos would have been complete. The crowd was screaming and shouting, and many were fleeing from the scene, while the soldiers, now leaderless and under fire, imagined the archer to be somewhere among the villagers who were fleeing. They had gone in the direction of Alec Mercy's house, where Aewyn was pinned. Scattered and disorganized at first, they quickly tightened rank and gained focus as they gauged the distance and pushed their horses to a thundering gallop. They were nearly on top of her hiding-place when the karach hit them.

Most of these men were too young to have fought in the Stonewind Clearances. More than a few had seen full-sized karach before, though Poe could not have known this. Few, though, had ever faced one in combat—and the horses, certainly, had never suffered such ill fortune, nor been trained for it. When he burst from the shadow of Alec Mercy's house at speed, claws and teeth fully bared, the first line of horses reared in terror as the second halted its charge and the third barrelled into the second. Slamming into the underbelly of a rearing horse at speed, ducking the panicked blows of its hooves, Poe pushed his full strength against the overbalanced beast and shoved it backward into the air, toppling it sidelong into the rank behind it in a mass of alarm and kicking legs. The horses panicked—perhaps the sudden smell of a predator did not help matters—and although the riders were seasoned for battle, they were too busy fighting their terrified mounts to give answer with their long pikes. Poe's claws and teeth tore desperately at exposed horseflesh wherever he could find it, for he knew he would not get through the armour of the soldiers (in truth, he was no seasoned fighter and too afraid to contend with them). In a flash the smell and spray of hot horseblood was everywhere, breaking the momentum of the back ranks who were only now catching up with the first. The shriek of the horses was deafening, and suddenly the only smell on the air was the stink of war.

Those at the back had drawn their swords, and echoes of "the karach!" were now in the air. With more strength and panic than technique, Poe seized one of the riders who had fallen stunned from his horse and heaved him bodily, armour and all, into the horse and rider that blocked his most direct path to the old druid, who lay on the ground as if dead. Mounts threw their riders and scattered in his wake, stampeding through the narrow space between the houses. One rider was skilled enough to right himself just long enough to bring his pike to bear, swiping at the karach from behind. Aewyn darted from cover again in time to put an arrow in the soldier's side, but she crossed into the path of the panicked horses and went down with a shriek beneath the onslaught of their hooves.

"Aewyn!" Poe called.

"Go," she pleaded. "Save him!" He could smell the woody scent of her blood—she was hurt—but it was not overpowering, and the riders gathering their wits and rounding on him were sure to be. He held them only a moment, snarling and snapping at the horses, until she had crawled away under Alec's workbench. Now that his blood was up, Poe was more aware than he could have imagined of a battlefield whose descent into chaos was highly selective. Behind him and at his side, a tangle of bloodied horses and men were desperately regrouping to turn back on him and run him down as Aewyn slithered weakly toward safety. Surrounding the clear field before him were terrified townsfolk, held back by the Havenari. The soldiers might have brought him down with arrows, but were hesitating—though he had not the time to determine if it was for fear of the battle, or on orders from their captain. At the edge of the village green, the leader of the city-men was being dragged away from the chaos by a towering brute with an arrow in his chest. Only one man stood directly between him and Celithrand's shuddering body. As the karach lowered into a ferocious charge, Derec met it with steel.

Derec was lame in one shoulder, but he was a seasoned veteran. More than the others, he had seen his share of karach charges. The generation who trained him had seen even more of them during the Clearances. Always the brutes entered the fray in the same manner when unarmed, their dagger teeth bared and leading. Derec drew his sword silently as the karach approached and swung it, too soon, with a ferocious yell.

Poe watched the blade come down and miss him, anticipating his arrival too early and careening uselessly toward the earth. He had the full speed of his charge behind him then, and might have kept on going, burying his claws at full strength; but remembering Bram's words, he broke his charge and turned awkwardly aside as the fallen tip of Derec's sword bounced up and thrust suddenly forward, cleaving into the space where the unarmoured, heedlessly charging karach should have been. It was this strike, the committed killing blow, from which Derec's recovery was slow. By the time he had stopped the forward thrust of the sword, the massive karach was inside his guard. What happened then was a grisly end fifteen years in the making, as Poe's terror turned to desperate fury and the purple-cloaked warrior, like enough to the one who had burned his family, seemed suddenly as soft and wet as so much mutton in his jaws.

"Kill it!" came Castor Stannon's wail across the green, and indeed the men who were rallying were ready to try. But having reached the object of his explosive charge, and not being naturally inclined to the carnage he had just wrought, Poe had no interest in standing his ground to test whether Bram's advice would serve him just as reliably twenty times in a row. With as much gentleness as he could muster while his nerves buzzed and his breath came with ragged fear, Poe hoisted the old druid into his arms and made for the treeline. A desperately hurled dagger or two nearly cut short his flight—one of them, twirling end over end, caught him hard in the side of the neck with its pommel, a half-turn away from ending his story. But there was no catching him after that: the light coursers of the Travalaithi Grand Army were swift as the wind, when they chose to be, but with the stink of an ancestral predator all about them, and drenched as they were in the blood of other horses, they were not inclined to give pursuit. Trained though they were for battle, the horses fought their rising panic and their own riders in equal measure, and those few horsemen who spurred their steeds on could not immediately coax them to a full gallop. Some of the men poured into the trees; some dismounted there in the hopes they would find the karach hiding in the undergrowth. Most, after the display on the village green, simply hoped they would bravely seek him without a shred of success.

It was those men, in the end, who were the most satisfied. Poe knew the terrain, and knew whither he was headed; and even on level ground, he could run faster in fear than they could in confusion. When the soldiers returned to the village, many people had fled to hide in their homes, and the Havenari remained with the rest of the murmuring crowd. They, too, were out of sorts, but the Havenari conducted themselves with discipline. Not one of them had struck a blow or loosed an arrow in the chaos. Robyn had dismounted her horse and was sitting, exhausted by the ordeal, in the honey-tent with the beekeeper. One of the Travalaithi soldiers dismounted and approached her.

"Anyone hurt? Any one of you, I mean."

"Nothing serious."

"The beast got one of ours."

"I'm sorry," said Robyn.

"It took the prisoner. Can you ride?"

"We can ride," said Robyn, "and we know the woods."

"Good," said the soldier, extending a hand. "Then you can lead us."

Robyn paused for a moment, thinking. "I'll leave half my men with you," she said at last. "Let the rest of us go on ahead. We'll move faster without you. I've seen karach run." The soldier nodded and she motioned for the Havenari to go collect their own horses.

"Mother of Sorcery," the soldier sighed. "It came out of nowhere. Our commander's fallen, I think—poor little coin-tender. If he lives long enough, he'll have a grim story to tell Lord Ashimar."

Robyn shivered at the name. "He'll send someone, no doubt. A larger force."

"Or come himself."

"I'm sure that won't be necessary."

"Haukmere takes the forest lands very seriously," said the soldier. "You are not alone out here. The Grand Army has not withdrawn its support just because there's fighting elsewhere."

Robyn smiled politely. "I don't think I can tell you what that means to me."

The soldier immediately dispatched three of his comrades to the west, east, and north. Riding all-out to the Aslea in the north and the nearest military posts on the Iron Road, they carried the news that Celithrand had escaped from Widowvale, and that all the roads and ports should be shut from Haveïl to the sea. Bram and Hendec were making their way back now, having come running at the sound of battle, and

Fletch brought them up to their captain as the force regrouped. Neither looked particularly surprised to hear what had happened.

"What of the girl?" asked Bram.

"There was no girl," Robyn insisted, with a sideways glance that shut him up. "It was a karach, plain as day. The one who lives somewhere near town, and sometimes preys on our flocks. He killed one of the Army. Tore him clean apart. And he put an arrow in the Censor's eye."

"A fine little bow he must have had," said Fletch, earning a glare from his captain.

"We're going after them," she said. "Him and the prisoner, I mean. I'm leaving now to try and catch them before they've gone far. Bram, I want you with the Grand Army, soon as they've seen to their horses and their wounded. Gather the fastest riders for me, and lead the others up the Serpent Trail, quick as you can, and meet us by Maiden's Watch."

"Quick as I can up the Serpent Trail," Bram said, momentarily confused; then he nodded with a brother's wisdom. "I understand you completely, Captain. Tell me when your men are ready, sir, and we'll join the pursuit."

Aside from Derec, whose untouched face in death bore a shock the others found deeply unsettling, it was the horses more than the riders who had come off the worst. One soldier had broken a leg where his horse fell on him after they were thrown back, and one had taken an arrow an inch deep into his hip; but some of the horses were mortally wounded, and Orin was sent for, in the hopes that his old hands could see them out of this world as gently as he brought foals in. One was so far gone that he had to lay two gentle fingers against its open eye to be sure it was still in need of his knife. Most of the people had begun to scatter by the time he opened its veins; like so many folk, they were awed well enough by the action and spectacle of the battle, but had no stomach to witness its aftermath. Those who lingered behind heard

Orin weeping as he methodically ended the life of this crying stallion and two others—not only because it so grieved him, but because he had seen the karach at gentle play with the town's children, and wondered sorely that a creature of such good heart could be led to wreak such hurt.

The village was calm for only a few minutes as it reeled from the disturbance (it was only a matter of time, some said, until the karach went berserk). It was not yet midday when the bustle began again as wounded soldiers and the surviving horses were moved under guard to Robyn and Bram's house; Castor Stannon, not yet dead, was among them, though he was so delirious from pain that even his own men had ceased paying any heed to his mad orders. Orin looked up as the Censor was carried past by his protector, a stony-faced brute without the slightest regard for the arrow in his chest. For a moment, perhaps, he thought of opening the Censor's neck, too, ending the same suffering to which he had condemned these horses—and probably condemned Poe, too. But Orin had seen too much death already, and had no taste for more of it. And so he carried out his duty, weeping softly and sick with grief, as the soldiers who could ride assembled their hunting-spears and prepared to go after the karach and his fellow escapee.

The autumn breeze was cold on Orin's naked back. Unlike the Reeve, and Grim before him, who had got fat with age, Orin had run to lean, and the wind blew through him now more easily than in his youth. But he had few clothes—and one shirt only worthy of a festival. He refused to claim it from the grass, shivering though he was, until water was brought up to clean the blood from his hands and arms. In the time it took to send a boy for it, Robyn was off up the hill with half the Havenari, fanning out in pairs as they made their way into the trees.

By the time the boy had returned with a splashing bucket, the soldiers who could fight had set off with the other half, taking the winding trail to the northeast with more haste than speed. They were ready for a fight this time, though, and the loss of their coin-counting superior had put a true military man back in charge of the force. Their steel weapons and mail-coats, worth perhaps more than the entire yield of Silver that year, shone in the sunlight as they spurred their horses to a frightful gallop—a speed, old Orin knew, they could barely keep up until they had run out of sight of the foolishly awed townsfolk. While the armed men departed, racing away toward the thrill of the hunt, the rush of the battle, and the glory of the Imperator's justice, Orin emptied the bucket of brown water over the bloody soil, scattering the flies that had landed, and set himself to finding out who, among the villagers, would help him clean and haul away the filth that such glorious warriors always seemed to leave behind them.

Ard Oltman was younger than his brother Corran, and not so bright, but he was a big-framed boy and a hard worker. He came with a shovel when the time was right, and a strong back to work it.

"We'll not bury the horses, boy," said Orin. "Not today. More than likely, we can use the hide and the bones. Maybe even the meat, if all things here have gone to ruin."

"What about him?" Ard said, pointing to Derec's corpse. A small-cloth had been draped over his face, but nothing large enough to cover the whole body had been spared.

"I'd forgotten him," said Orin. "He deserves a decent burial. The soil will serve better for it here than at Haukmere." His eyes narrowed as looked up into the trees, as if squinting at something just beyond his sight.

"Take some help with you," he said. "South of the road where the miners are buried. Ready the grave, but don't put him in until his fellows have returned to bid him farewell. Just keep digging. We're going to want a larger grave opened up, too. Large enough for five or six men, at least."

Ard followed his elder's gaze up into the tree line. "The karach is not small," said Ard thoughtfully. "But a hole the size of five or six men, if you ask me, is more than you'll need for him." Orin looked from the trees to the seven grunting miners nearby who, on his suggestion, were working their hardest to haul the first of the horse carcasses away from the green.

"Maybe," said Orin as he watched the work being done. "But for five or six men it'd be just the right size. And if they do corner him, that's what we'll need."

There was no time to stop, no time to inspect his burden or even reckon whether the old one would live—whether he was already dead. The tree had brought him down gently, and he had not dangled there long, though it seemed longer in the rush and strife of the moment. But Celithrand was old beyond reckoning to a karach; he had seen fifty generations or more of their kind, and there was no telling how fragile an aeril became in such extreme age. Did his meat dry out, or his bones turn to dust? Few aerils still remained in the world, and their reputation as an immortal and magical people led to their frequent confusion with the fair folk of Aewyn's supposed parentage—they, too, lived apart from ordinary men and women and had little to do with them. But unlike the fey spirits of the wood, Celithrand's kind were only immortal by the short reckoning of the karach, and Poe wondered whether in their final days even the aerils grew weak of limb and frail of body.

The wind had picked up along the ridge, and Poe ran with it at his back. He ran towards Maiden's Watch, and cut right and upwards before the cliff edge. There was a horse trail some distance up, and if he could cross it before the riders reached it, he might stand a chance.

But he could not hope to outrun them—at least, not over this short distance—and the old druid was a fragile burden. He carried him as gently as he could, but the gentleness cost him speed. His great heart seemed to roar in his chest, bidding him run all-out or else stand and fight; but he had no weapon to fight with, nor the heart to use one. The warm taste of raw human flesh was in his mouth, and it did not displease his tongue. After more than a year among the villagers, hearing their stories and playing with their young, he was not sure how he felt about that.

He turned back only once, breathing hard, before he slipped into the trees. Something nagged at him even as he fled, and when he turned into the wind it came back to him again: the smell of Aewyn's blood. Maybe the smell of bone. He thought of the horse trail for a moment, watched his window slipping away as he stood on the high hillside— then, with resignation that it might be the end of him, laid Celithrand gently down and went back for the girl.

She had made it no further than the edge of the tall grass, and was there crawling on her belly with a leg splayed strangely behind her. His whole life, he had seen her bounding effortlessly through the wood; now, watching her inching forward on her belly like a wounded animal made him powerfully sick. Her breeches were soaked with blood, she was barely moving, and Poe could not imagine how she had crawled away from the chaos of his desperate fight without being seen or followed.

"I'm here," he whispered as he reached her shivering form. "I'm here. Come."

He went to move her and her ear-splitting scream as he lifted her was enough to flatten his ears and make him cringe.

"I'm sorry," he breathed. "I'm sorry. I'm sorry." The whole span of her, head to foot, was so much less than the span of his arms that he hoisted her like a babe in his left arm and cradled her mangled leg in his right. With enormous, bloody, clawed hands, he lifted and carried her as gently as the children carried handfuls of eggs in the harvest races. He could feel the unnatural give in the leg. It had broken clean through.

"Celithrand," she murmured as he carried her. "Celithrand…"

"You saved him; he's alive," Poe whispered, and hoped that it was so. "Now we escape together, we run far away from this place. Whatever destiny you want, it is yours. I have denied you for the last time."

She tried to give answer, but the agony as he moved her was too much. She had not the heart to tell him how badly she had been trampled. She had seen a horse with a broken leg once, in the village, and she knew what soon became of it.

When they came again to the top of the escarpment, Celithrand was wheezing weakly. His breath was shallow but sure, and he had begun to stir, pulling at the ropes that still bound them. Aewyn gave another cry of pain as Poe shifted her to one arm to cut him free.

"We make for the deep wood," Poe said.

"Stop," Aewyn urged. "Please, stop."

"I am so sorry," said Poe. "The hurt is nearly over."

"No," she gasped. "Don't cross…they're coming…"

"We must make the trail," said Poe. "We're nearly there."

He carried her and led Celithrand through the trees into the thick of the wood. Ahead of them, the blast of Tsúla's horn shook needles from the trees. Poe froze in his tracks.

"Impossible," he said.

"I told you," Aewyn answered. "The Havenari…" Gently, with silence rather than speed, Poe began to step sideways into the deeper growth, shielding his burden from brambles with the breadth of his back.

"I had not thought they would be the ones to hunt us," he whispered. "The ironmen I could evade in these woods. But the Havenari—

they are cunning trackers, swift riders, and they know the land. I cannot escape them. You must not be seen with me when I make my last stand."

"No," Aewyn answered. "This is my doing. I loosed...the first arrow."

"You loosed—what?" Celithrand managed to ask. His voice was a hoarse rasp.

"I had not stopped to think you would—everything has gone so wrong," said Aewyn.

"I have seen the ironmen kill," said Poe. "You cannot fight them. There is no chance. I tried to tell you."

"And yet here you stand," she shot back at him. "Fighting the ironmen."

"I could not let you die," said Poe. He was weeping, too; she had never known if he could. She raised a frail hand to his long cheek.

"Poe," she whispered, but could say no more. He laid her down gently and turned toward the trail.

"Have you got your breath, grandfather?" Poe asked. "Can you take her, or hide her?"

Recovering his senses, Celithrand only now saw the pain that she was in. He touched her leg lightly and she wailed.

"How—"

"The horses," she answered him. "I just...they came so fast."

Fumbling with her clothes, he saw the bruises first, great purpled patches already rising where she had been lucky. But her leg was broken, and a sharp horseshoe had taken some of the meat of her leg besides. He wasted no time in removing his cloak.

"Have you a knife?" he asked.

"If I did," said Poe, "I would have need of it." But Aewyn pawed desperately at a pocket, and there Celithrand found the little obsidian knife he had brought her many years before.

Celithrand sucked in his breath as he cut away the breeches on her wounded side. "That's bad." He laid a hand across her forehead. "Very bad."

"Is it the end of her?" asked Poe. "Tell me true. Those who are coming for her, if they mean her ill, are dead if they cross me. But they too are my tribe now. I do not want to hurt them if I am defending only—only her last breath…"

"You should not have moved her," said Celithrand. "The sharp bone could have bled her dry. I'll need to splint this."

"She was moving on her own," said Poe. "The damned girl does not know when to—"

"Here!" rang a familiar voice. It was Fletch's. He sounded near enough, suddenly, to be hit with a thrown stick. Poe dropped to his belly in the undergrowth. He could smell the horses now, and the riders, too.

"How many?" whispered Celithrand. Poe held up two clawed fingers and readied himself. Aewyn's silence was punctuated by steady groans of pain and shallow breaths. To Poe's ears, she may as well have been singing, so loud it seemed.

"Good eyes, lad," called another voice—Robyn's. "Can you see which way they're going?"

The boy came into view, his own bow in hand, an arrow loosely nocked but not yet drawn. Poe readied himself to come from the bushes, but hesitated as the boy turned his back.

"They haven't crossed the trail," said Fletch, dropping his voice. "They're close."

"So small," he whispered. "Barely a man." Aewyn had known the karach long enough to read the conflict, the disgust, the sorrow in his body. She reached up weakly, held him by the chest, shook her head.

"Poe, be at peace," said Robyn's voice, so distantly and so softly that only he heard it. She rode in a few more paces, toward the flattened turf where their flight had ended.

"Be at peace," she said again. "I come as a friend."

He narrowed his eyes with doubt, hesitating. Her horse nickered, picking up the scent of blood.

"Hush," she said to it, brushing its neck with her gauntleted hand. "Easy, Acorn. Easy." She scanned the trees, looking for signs of movement. "Poe? I am here to help you. There is not much time. Does the old man still live?"

"We're here," Aewyn groaned suddenly, though it pained her to speak up. Poe looked back at her, nearly snarled, but the trust in her eyes drained the anger out of him.

"Here, then," he grumbled.

Perhaps twenty paces away, Robyn turned her horse and came forward, swinging her leg over it as it stopped short. Fletch looked up and saw them, too.

"How is he?" Robyn asked.

"He lives," said Poe, still wary. "But Aewyn is in a bad way." Robyn looked, and recoiled when she saw the wound and the blood from her shredded breeches.

"Fools," Celithrand said again. "Should have left me."

"Gods," Robyn muttered. "What happened to her? Can you do anything with that?"

Celithrand shook his head. "Not much without my bag," he said. "It's clean enough. I can try to set the bone. But the wound will turn without—"

In answer, Robyn tugged the old man's satchel from her horse's saddlebags and threw it at his feet.

"Make this right," she said. "Work your magic. Make her whole."

The old druid looked up with surprise. "How did you find—"

"You must have escaped with it," said Robyn. "And with a couple of waterskins, too, damn you." These she set down beside Celithrand, who was already mashing dried leaves into some kind of paste.

Between Poe's strength, Celithrand's healing craft, and the medicines of the old wood, they managed to reset the leg well and construct a crude splint for it. With the last of Celithrand's strange liquor they washed and bound the wound as Aewyn whimpered in agony. Fletch watched the ordeal in great worry with a hand at his mouth, lost without direction. Robyn, for all she could assist, was helpful enough; but time was passing, and she knew they had precious little of it. Celithrand whispered things in the language of the old wood as he worked, and his bony hands were passing wondrous in their skill. But Fletch paced before him so nervously that Robyn had to send him away.

"What shall I do?" he asked.

"Plant an arrow and watch for them," said Robyn. "Up on the trail." She threw him one of the waterskins. Fletch ran back up to the trail, searching for a depression in the packed earth that was sheltered from the wind. When he found one to his liking, he took careful aim and sank an arrow into the earth, and gently poured the water out around the shaft until enough of a murky puddle had been made to reflect the upright shaft in the noonday sun. And there he lowered himself carefully to the earth upwind of it, and watched on his belly, and waited in silence.

"Don't use much of the water," Robyn called after him. "They'll need that to run."

"We can't run," said Celithrand. "Not with her in this state."

"You have not much choice," said Robyn. "They've sent their fastest riders to warn the post-wardens. The Grand Army will tighten around these woods like a fist. You have to get away, and quickly."

"If they reach the sea before us," said Celithrand, "the way will be closed."

"You must have a hidden road," Robyn prompted.

"I can go over the cliffs," Celithrand said with a shrug. "But Aewyn? Like this? She would never survive the climb."

"You cannot leave her!" barked Poe. "For what she has done to save you, she is as good as dead!"

Celithrand turned even more pale. "What has she done?"

"I fought," Aewyn breathed, half-conscious. "I fought."

Poe tapped the side of his head. "She put an arrow straight into the eye of their chieftain," he said. "He still lives—or did, when I left town. But I think he has seen his last sunrise."

Celithrand shut his eyes; whether it was from pain or sorrow was hard to tell. Aewyn's own tears were loosed by the news, and streamed down her cheeks though she was too weak to weep loudly.

"She loosed that arrow to save your life," said Poe. "You cannot let her face certain death while you make your escape!"

"They're not looking for Aewyn," said Robyn, to the surprise of everyone. "I don't think a one of them saw her."

"Not even when they rode her down?" asked Celithrand.

Poe hung his head. "It did not happen that way. In that moment, all their attention was on me."

Robyn touched the Karach's shoulder. Only now did she realize he was trembling.

"Oh yes," she admitted. "They definitely want you dead. They will kill Poe if they find him."

Poe looked her in the eye. "And the Havenari?"

Robyn's mouth drew tight. "We will kill you if we find you," she said. "We must not find you."

A single realization cut the gathering storm of Poe's worry like a bolt of lightning.

"She cannot run," he said. "And I cannot stay."

"You're dead, if you do," said Robyn. "And if they find you with her—the least they'll do is kill you in front of her." She looked back down the hill with firm concern. "I think they've had enough of hangings, too."

"But her destiny—" Poe sighed. "The prophecy, and such."

"I thought you didn't believe in prophecies," said Celithrand, recovering a little of his strength.

Poe snorted. "I don't. But she was beginning to choose it. I wanted—as she wanted."

"I want—to—" Aewyn started, but did not finish. Celithrand tied off bandage and splint alike, and wrapped her in a blanket with bloody hands.

"I've done my part," he said. "Change this bandage in three days—and every day, after that. It will heal clean with time. But time and rest is the heart of it."

Robyn jerked her head to the west. "You know what lies ahead of you. Are you well enough to make the climb, old man?"

"I scaled those cliffs a dozen times in my youth," said Celithrand. "If anything, a thousand years of erosion will have made the rock face more gentle."

Aewyn gathered her strength and pulled him close. "A thousand years of erosion," she breathed, "has been no more of a friend to you." Celithrand laughed sharply, and Poe too, though it turned to a weighty silence in his chest as soon as he understood.

"I have sworn to protect her," he said.

"And that is why you cannot be found with her," said Celithrand. The slump in Poe's frame as the heart went out of him was felt by all.

"I'm so sorry," said Aewyn. "I meant to do good. To do what is right. I've ruined my destiny, haven't I?"

Celithrand dared not answer her directly. "This is not what I foresaw," he said. "I am an old fool. I did not expect things to go this way."

"I cannot leave her," said Poe. "But I cannot stay. But I cannot leave her."

Celithrand tried to rise, but his full weight was still too much. "I cannot take her to Dær Móran," he said. "My errand has failed. I have failed. They will all be coming for me, now. The soldiers. Ashimar. Even the village will not be safe for her."

"Then let her ride out with the Havenari, as she once wished," said Robyn. "We'll take her far from here. We can ride through the winter, at need. Keep her on the move, as soon as she is healed enough to sit a horse. You need to take Poe and go, before your window of escape is shut forever."

"Go?" asked Aewyn, tears still welling. "Where will you go?" Even in her sorrow and agony, she saw the steely conviction in Robyn's eyes. The First Spear had hidden away all trace of warmth, now; she had seen hard times before, and now that they were come again, she would not dance or laugh or wear her dress again until they were past.

"To Nalsin," said Celithrand. "To Dær Móran, and the halls of my ancestors, for a time. To the isle of the druids, whither I would have taken you, whither the grasp of Travalaith does not reach."

With a momentary thought, Robyn unbelted the sword at her waist. "This belongs to you," she said.

"Niurwyn," said Celithrand, and took it. "You have my thanks."

Poe, still in denial, let his great head sway from side to side in disgust.

"My place is here with Aewyn," said Poe. "She is my tribe." He hesitated, snorted, muttered softly. "My whole tribe. All my people. She is all that stands between my people and dreamless oblivion."

"Captain!" called Fletch from the road. The reflection of his arrow was twitching, almost imperceptibly, in the surface of the puddle, as the shaft stirred tiny ripples in the water.

"Gods," Robyn sighed, rolling her eyes. "We have no time at all. Can you make it, old man? If you take this one with you, can you beat Castor's rider to the docks at Lockmouth?"

"If we go now," Celithrand conceded. "If I abandon her, and go home to the druidlords empty-handed, with no child of prophecy and little hope for the Godswar. If I am prepared to fail in my errand, we can make it. But I fear it will not save her. There will be questions when you take her back in this condition. Questions for which there are no easy answers. Questions that Ashimar may take great delight in asking."

Poe took a ragged breath and waited until both of them were silent.

"*I* did this," he said.

"What?" Robyn asked. Poe gestured with his snout toward Aewyn's splinted leg, and the open wound that stained Celithrand's makeshift poultice a ruddy brown.

"I have done it before," said Poe. "I have broken the laws of men when it suited me, and then fled like a coward when my reckoning came. It is a credible story." He brushed an enormous hand gently over a stray forelock of her autumn hair.

"Tell them it was me," he said. "She came after me, tried to stop me, tried to talk sense. So I did this to her. They cannot possibly question her story then."

"Poe, no…" Aewyn grasped at his fur.

"They adore her, Poe," Robyn warned. "The whole village has come to love her. If I tell them you did this to her, they will not forgive it. Not ever."

"Captain!" called Fletch. "They're coming!"

Robyn cursed under her breath. "You cannot come back after this. They will hunt you. *We* will hunt you. If we find you…"

"Take her," Poe urged, holding out one of her spindly arms as if offering. "You must keep her safe for me." But as he reclaimed his clawed hand, there was a smaller white hand in his that would not let go.

"I don't want to leave you," Aewyn said, clutching suddenly at his chest.

In spite of her fragility, he wrapped her in his muscled arms and surrounded her with his bulk. "You can never leave me," he said. "Never."

"Captain!" Fletch urged, as loudly as he dared. Celithrand made to stand, and seemed much improved on his feet with the passage of time.

"You will see him again," said the druid. "I swear it."

"Go," said Robyn. "Go now. I will not let you down."

She would not have been strong enough to take Aewyn from the karach if he had not let go. But his massive hands, far down at the ends of his arms, seemed to release her of their own will. He watched, as if he were already far away, as she passed from him and into Robyn's embrace. Distantly, in moments when the breeze was still, they could now hear the hoofbeats of men coming at speed.

Celithrand had shouldered his pack, hoisting himself with the aid of a curved stick he had found in the brush. He was unsteady, but the fire of determination was in him, and for just a moment, he cast as noble a shadow as he must have long ago.

"Come," he said. "All is not lost until they see us together. Come with me."

Poe turned his feet, but he remained fixed on the girl as Robyn pulled her away. With three clawed fingers he tapped at his breastbone.

"My stories are your stories," he said.

She repeated the gesture. "*Ossili ei, ossili lai.*"

She could not watch him go for all the tears in her eyes. Robyn held her tightly, but the woman's breastplate was cold and hard, and the touch of the steel was painful on Aewyn's cheek.

"No," was all Robyn said, and that only once. When next Aewyn raised her head, the druid and the karach had gone, though in what direction even she could not tell. The thunder of hooves was audible now, and Fletch began working his arrow free of the soil.

"I'm sorry, I'm sorry," Aewyn wept, clutching at Robyn's breastplate like a child. "I'm so sorry. I've ruined everything." Her leg burned and left her dizzy, but Celithrand's woodcraft has done its work.

"I wish I could have done as you did," said Robyn. "Gods and fishes, how I wish it." Her own eyes were not so dry as she called her horse, but her jaw was set firm by the time Bram rode up the long trail at the head of the search party.

"Captain," he nodded to his sister. "We came as quickly as we could. No sign of the prisoner or his rescuer." He looked back at the uneasy soldiers, all of whom had been run to fatigue on the twisting road, but were ready for a serious fight. "Or perhaps his accomplice," he added. "Whatever the less kind word for a 'rescuer' might be."

"I found a trail," said Robyn, "and traced it here. He laid the old man down here—and then, nothing. Druid's magic, I'll wager. There'd be no less trace of them if they turned into starlings and flew away."

"Is that Aewyn? Mother of Sorcery, what happened to her?"

Robyn met his eyes. "She tried to stop him. The karach did this to her. Tore into her leg and got away."

"Did he," Bram said. He didn't believe it for a moment, but she knew he could be trusted to repeat it.

"The leg is broken. I've set it as best I can. She can't ride. I'll need Fletch to help me cut a litter to get her back to town."

Bram, looking to the men with him, who were still gnashing and eager to put their swords to the beast who brought down Derec. One or two looked with pity on the wounded girl and vowed to kill him slowly for it.

"I'll take them all the way up the ridge," said Bram. "We can't be sure they got past us until we've waited them out." With a nod from his sister, Bram spurred his horse onward and led the men up past Maiden's Watch, through the wide grove where Grim had first met the karach some years before, and upward until the trees crowded together so tall and thick that they had to dismount and lead the horses by hand.

Bram's patrol was the first and largest, but by no means the only one led up into the deep wood during the last two days of the Harvest Fair. The soldiers were tireless, ranging ever wider, and the Havenari rode with them and on their behalf, scouring the forest for the fugitive, the karach, or any other menace, as was their duty. For all that Aewyn wanted to ride out with them, she was for some weeks a prisoner of the bed they made up for her. One by one, from furious Darmod to suspicious Venser, the townsfolk would come to wish her good health, and to promise her that the monster who savaged her had finally gone too far. At night, when it grew too dark to search, she would simply lie before the open door of the little cottage, comforted by the hearth-fire on one side and the cold night air on the other. For hours upon end, lost in a haze of pain, she would watch the trees, hoping to catch momentary sight of Poe, or Celithrand, or at least some sign of their passing.

There were some in the village who did not really expect them to have gone far. Heartbroken by Poe's betrayal of Aewyn, the townsfolk would send a search party out night after night with torches and long spears; and more than once, she thought she caught a glimpse of Poe's eyes burning bright green in the glow of their torchlight—but always, then, she would wake on her bedroll under the dusty rafters and know that even that glimpse of him, even the smallest flash of his sad eyes, was now no more than a dream.

The first thing to come back to him was hunger, a hunger so powerful that the faint smell of fresh-baked bread on the wind was more insistent than the pain. But the pain came right behind it, and it kicked the breath from him before he could even open his eyes. The whole side of his head burned like fire and he was suddenly dizzy. He tried to turn onto his side and retch, but could not move his head for the agony. His stomach heaved as he lay flat on his back, but there was nothing left in it to drown him with.

"Well tan my doubting arse," said a deep voice. "I thought you were a dead man, Stannon."

Castor Stannon heaved again, gasping for breath, clutching at nothing in the air as he drew his first deep breath in days. His whole face burned too fiercely to concentrate on the rest of his body in any real detail—but aside from an ache in his back and a burning in the pit of his stomach, nothing below the neck seemed too worse for wear.

"Where am I?" he asked, his voice hoarse from disuse. "What's happened?"

"It's the twenty-fifth day of Laeamaunt," said the other. "You're in a little pisspot of a border town. Widowvale, sir. And you and I are the two luckiest men in it."

"My head hurts," said Castor. "I can't get up."

"Don't try," said the voice. "I'll come to you." A long, dark shadow loomed over him, and coarse hands lifted a wet fragrant cloth from his face with surprising gentleness. He opened his eyes—one of them, anyway—to look on a towering, broad-shouldered man in black, balding hair cropped short, smiling down at him the way a wolf smiles at a lame sheep.

"Don't strain yourself," said the big man. "I've saved your life, and that's worth something. If you take sick and die before I get you back to Wescairn, I've done spit-and-fiddle, and that's worth nothing."

Castor took a deep breath, smoother this time, and collected himself quickly. "Kellan, wasn't it?"

"Yeh," said Kellan, nodding. "Still is. You've got a good memory. Smart man."

"What happened to me?"

"You took an arrow to the eye. I dug it out."

In the gleam of his good eye, Castor's impassive countenance was a broken mask belying his terror. "The arrow?" he asked. "Or the eye?"

"Yes," said Kellan, turning away. He placed a heavy book back on a shelf—Castor found the gesture odd, for some reason, fixated on it. Whose house were they in? Who would have an old book? Why would an unlettered soldier have taken it down? His mind leapt to any thought at all to evade the grim truth of his maiming.

"You saved my life," he said, more a question than a statement.

"Whole town figured you for dead," said Kellan. "I got you inside. Dug out what I could. Cleaned out your eye-hole—whatever you call an eye-hole, I don't know. I'm no physician, and no great healer like the cellwives you'd find in the Capital. But I know enough to burn a bad wound with a hot iron before you bleed to death. Men lose an arm or a leg in the field, it can save their life. I imagine an eye's not much different. They've got an old man who cares for the horses. He's helped keep you alive, too, though I don't think it pleases him."

"This can't be," said Castor.

"I felt the same way," said Kellan. "Thought we were done, both of us. An ambush like that, caught completely unprepared. You straight in the eye, me close by the heart. Like I say, we're lucky men. Fearful ugly, the both of us. But I got used to being ugly years ago, and so will a pretty man like you, in time."

Castor tested an arm to wave feebly at his bandaged face. "You call this lucky?"

Kellan undid the lace at the neck of his black tunic in response. There, partially obscured by the thick black hair of his chest, a small brown scab had formed over a nasty wound to his chest muscle.

"This could have gone one inch deeper," he said. "One damn inch. Ended my tale right there. You, my friend, didn't have another half an inch to spare. But by the grace of whatever god you take serious, some backwater village yantan with a weak arm weights his bows here for gamebirds, not for war. Another five pounds on that string would've done us both. D'you know there's some bone back in there?" He gestured at Castor's eye. "I didn't know that. Thought it was just a big hole till I saw yours. Learn something every day."

Castor frowned. "Must you keep talking?" he asked.

"You rest up, then," said Kellan, seemingly unoffended. "I'll be here, by the fireplace. If you want for anything to get healthy, just call out." Castor shut his eye and felt the big man's shadow begin to drift away from him.

"Bread," he said at last, though he hadn't even meant to say it. "Bread. And some weak wine."

Kellan smiled. "You're a harder man than I gave you credit for," he said. "Won't underestimate you again."

The days ahead (there were already three behind, Castor learned) were patchy and surreal. Kellan hardly left his side, except to bring him food and water, and never left him alone with the townspeople. One of the villagers, a smaller man named Alec, came and went with hot poultices that smelled of honey and forest herbs. The pain never really went away, but in time he began to adjust to the sight of one eye, though the dead socket burned like a pitch fire anytime he moved his good eye inside his head. He found his balance greatly disturbed, and could not walk but a few steps, and those with a cane. But as the days passed and more of the townsfolk marvelled at his survival, Castor Stannon began to understand just how close to death he had come.

The soldiers he had been assigned were furiously combing the forest for the karach, but found no trace of him. The Havenari, concerned with the people, lent no men to the search, but set about raising defenses in case the karach returned for more blood. The taxation matter had been all but forgotten; tracking down the traitor and Derec's killer was now the highest priority, though perhaps (Castor hated to admit it) the hunt was a personal one. All of the men, men who had mocked his command under their breath all the way from Wescairn, were astonished to see him alive. More than one of them had seen men take an arrow to the eye, and all agreed it was not the sort of thing most men could survive. The Censor had some degree of respect after that, even from the seasoned warriors—but from no man more than Kellan, who seemed convinced that all men were marked for death, and seemed genuinely pleased to watch him cheat it.

"Tell me about your family," said Kellan one night, quite unexpectedly, as they were sitting up in Robyn's house. Castor had, by then, regained his usual calm, though perhaps the loss had not yet fully sunk in.

"You're asking because you presume a Censor to be an important person," said Castor.

"Absolutely." Kellan saw no need to hide it. "I don't want any reward from you, don't you worry. But you're no doubt a rare prize to House Kelmor. You've held your post a long time, and you're made of better stuff than ever I reckoned."

"And you mean to collect for saving me," Castor said. "And what do you suppose I'm worth? A good pension, paid out in gold sovereigns? Some pretty, fat-boned Kelmor cousin arranged for your wedding-bed?"

"Women I've no use for," said Kellan. "If it's got to be something, I suppose it's men for me. But even they can't be trusted, and Kelmor men least of all. I've no desire to share a bed with Ashimar's kin. I'll take your gold in a pinch, but even gold invites trouble. I'd sooner see it in silver, or wax iron, or weedmead if it please you."

"I'm a censor," said Castor. "Nothing more. My life's not worth a pension to them."

"Then you're undervalued," said Kellan. "You're made of solid stuff, little man. Don't forget, the Imperial Harper himself was born a censor's son. If some fat Kelmor treasurer won't unlock the family coffers, maybe Ashimar will, ere this is over. Your life is worth that much, I swear, if it's worth a shaved farthing."

"Ashimar is not the giving sort," said Castor coldly. "Nor has he any claim to Haukmere. He gave that seat up forever when he became the Imperator's personal scourge. You're stuck dealing with Lady Esha and Arin Kelmor, I'm afraid; and those two are tight-fisted. Believe me, for I've kept their accounts."

"We'll see," said Kellan. "They may change their mind when they hear the tale of how I fought off a mighty karach to save your hide."

"Suppose I tell them how it really happened," Castor suggested.

Kellan shrugged. "Yeh, you might at that. I suppose I'll have to share my reward with you to keep you quiet. You back up my story just once, my Lord Censor, and I'll be able to afford to bribe you to back it up forever."

Castor tried to shake his head, but thought better of it. "No," he said. "You mistake me for a different sort of man—aside from which, I don't trust you. For a man greedy enough to cheat the Kelmors out of a reward, you are too ready to give up your claim to half of it."

Kellan seemed to consider the remark a long time. He returned to Alec's shelf (for it was his house where he lay), selected another book, sat down again before answering.

"I like money well enough," the big man admitted. "But I'd sooner have half the money, and half the enemies, than an abundance of both. Taking on enemies for coin is a popular business these days, but it's how too many people end up dead."

"I have a wife," said Castor. "Corinne. I'll tell her you saved my life. We're not close, but she might cook you a pheasant for it. Not much else."

"I'm frightfully fond of pheasant," said Kellan.

After some days, the last of the year's strangers came to Silver. Two riders from the Kelmors' seat of power in Haukmere, light scouts, had come in search of the soldiers who were due back from Wescairn some time ago, and became lost themselves in the woods where the trail had somehow grown over. The Havenari picked up their trail and brought them to town, where they marvelled at the disarray of the scattered soldiers, who seemed as much defeated by the forest itself as by the karach who was surely beyond their reach by now. They asked Kellan for his version of events—as the constant companion of the censor, they seemed to mistake him for the highest ranking soldier, and he told them the whole story as the village had come to accept it. While he distinctly remembered his fleeting glimpse of the young red-haired girl who had shot him, he made no mention of her, for reasons he could not quite understand.

When Castor was well enough to sit up and write with a pen, he first sentenced the karach to die more officially, then passed his summary judgment on the matter of taxation, hobbling carefully to the moot-hall to deliver it to Marin himself.

Although the penalty was not as severe as many feared, it was a final affront to the carefree spirit of the last festival days of Silver's year. For the Year of Strangers, numbered 3413 in the Age of the Moon, taxes were ferociously high: the miners, all able-bodied men, swelled the head count of the town considerably. Despite all their time in the mines and camps to the south, the miners were treated as residents; this seemed fair enough, as they were the unsung source of the town's prosperity. For concealing their relationship to the miners, and presenting themselves as a town composed largely of widows, spinsters, and old men, the township itself was fined two dozen pounds of silver, and ten times that weight in lead.

Marin arranged to see the amount paid over the course of several years, contingent on a survivable yield after taxes, and a writ of censorial order to this effect was negotiated before the people, signed and sealed by Reeve and Censor alike. After the mad events of the weeks prior—a traitor at large, a public hanging, a desperate attack and the furious hunt that followed—the quiet formal drudgery of these civil negotiations seemed to reassure the skittish townsfolk, who were utterly divided on the matter of Poe, that things were returning to normal. After commandeering a small wagon for the soldier with the broken leg and those whose horses had been killed, most of the Imperial soldiers set out to return home the day after the contract was signed and sealed. Three men, Kellan among them, remained behind with Castor until he was well enough to travel, and they observed with wonder that a few days returned to the world of figures, contracts, tax edicts, and Imperial law seemed to do more for him than all the kindness and shared meals of the townsfolk put together.

"When you're ready to travel," said Kellan, "it's best I take you home to your keep and your coins. They're what's healed you this past weeks, more than anything I've done."

Walking restlessly from one end of Alec's house to the other, Castor tested his stride without the cane. His legs were strong enough; from the beginning, they were never really hurt. Only his balance was off, but it was rapidly returning.

"I shall be ready in another day or two at most," he said. "But all you want, I think, is your reward."

Kellan shrugged. "I just don't like to be stationed in a place I don't belong. If that karach is out there, his fear won't last forever. If he's there at all, he'll start hitting back at the patrols. We'll be throwing good men after bad before the end of it."

"I never expected to hear sound command strategy from a footman," said Castor.

"Been a footman a long time," said Kellan. "Learned that lesson firsthand from the Ghosts of Draden."

"You fought with the Old Wolves? I didn't think any of their lot survived."

"I was eighteen," said Kellan. "They needed men, and they paid, and they were a road away from a home I didn't much care for. The fighting in Selik was fine. But turning on our own nobles, the havoc we made in Creslyn Wood and the folk we killed—that wasn't fine. We were never meant to be there. Stick your neck out long enough, and Dagan always notices. Necks are sacred to the God of Death, so they say."

"You don't believe in the gods," said Castor. Neither did he, particularly.

"I believe Harrod's Wolves should've left Draden Castle well enough alone once all the men were dead and the castle burned," Kellan said. "I believe, gods or no, the old catacombs were no place for dumb shites looking to make an example or a romantic evening out of the survivors. The house was gone. The point was made. Every one of those men could have done their job, taken their coin, and gone home to Travalaith, as I did. Only they didn't. They let their loins, or their swords, or their wolf brains get the better of them, and the ghosts got them, and now they're all ghosts themselves."

"I don't think you believe in ghosts either," said Castor.

"What I believe," said Kellan, "is that men are fools, especially smart men, and it more often than not gets them killed. Whatever happened down there, it's because men who had no business there didn't know enough to leave things well enough alone. I mean not to make that same mistake. Soon as you can ride straight, I'm done with this town, and I'm not coming back."

"Send for the horsewife," said Castor. "See if that old man thinks

I'm ready to have done with these bandages."

"As you will, sir," said Kellan with a nod of thanks.

When the bandages finally came away, Jerrold the Mercer sewed an elegant eyepatch to cover the wound, adorning a cupped patch of black leather with a button made from a small silver coin where the iris would have been. Even Kellan praised it as a dramatic improvement—though he was quick to add that covering any part of Castor's face, maimed or otherwise, could only be a change for the better. It was not until some days later, after he had grown well enough to make the journey home, that Castor observed the coin to be a pre-Annexation silver rider, sewn with the horse on the inside and Celithrand's oak-wreathed profile, stern and sad, looking toward Castor's good eye with wisdom and regret. He laughed at it coldly when he saw it, so hard that his wife rushed upstairs from the street to see what had happened.

"I think I'll keep it," he said. "Some things a man cannot afford to forget."

ELEVEN

ITH THE DEATH OF DEREC, the loss of the horses, the wounding of Aewyn, and the escape of a traitor to the Imperator, Poe was swiftly marked for death as well, and there was little the Havenari could do about it, except to enforce the Censor's decree as lazily as possible. The outcry when Aewyn came home on a dragged litter was worse than it was over the hanging, and there was no shortage of homes who offered to care for her while the Havenari went to work finding the fugitives. She stayed next to Robyn and Bram's house, at the home of Aeric and Alys and their daughters, and for weeks she wasted in bed but was always kind to those who visited. As the days wore on and the manhunt proved fruitless, she was touched and horrified to hear that Darmod Pick had ridden to Wescairn himself, and put a private bounty of three gold sovereigns on the karach's head for what he had done. It was a princely sum for a shepherd, and fronting it in gold, he said, would bring the sort of mercenaries and bounty hunters that could see it done.

With mock concern for the town's well-being, Robyn stationed nearly all of the men in Widowvale for the whole time of Castor's recovery. At her direction, they raised muddy ramparts and a low, hasty palisade of sharpened stakes, in case the karach returned to menace the village. None of the Havenari dared to admit what they all knew—that the defenses would prove just as useful against the Grand Army troops, if it came to that.

She listened with some amusement to the reports as Castor's soldiers tramped endlessly through the bush, looking for some sign of Celithrand and Poe. They came across the deserter's hut, and ordered his remaining belongings returned to Travalaith, but what few tracks that they found seemed to lead nowhere: she was sure they had picked up their own trail more than once. Her men were swamped entirely with the raising of the town's defenses, and there were none to spare to lend the soldiers aid. Of all the men, Fletch alone she dispatched, to ride west through the forest at all speed and notify distant fellows among the Havenari of the goings-on at Widowvale. It was only with this mission that Aewyn realized there were other bands of the Havenari throughout the wood, and perhaps even beyond. To her they had seemed like little more than a town militia; now that her friends were marked for death, their invisible numbers and reach seemed truly terrifying. But Robyn assured her that Fletch's report was kind to them, demanding that the other cells of the Havenari take up the pursuit with minimal, even cursory effort. Aewyn wondered how the other bands would respond to the demands of a woman—whether her rank would be enough to satisfy them. She wondered, then, whether she too might someday make something of herself with them, and hoped

Robyn would tell her more about the organization in time.

Fletch was a small, slim boy and a fast rider, but the other camps were many leagues distant, and it was several days before he returned. Castor Stannon was already taking short, stumbling walks around Alec's house in the cool of the evening when Fletch came up the village road, drenched in sweat and looking as if the horse had dragged him the last mile. The horse, too, was slick with sweat that foamed at the saddle, and it snorted unevenly as he pulled it short. Robyn, shaving down stakes for the palisade with some of the others, set down her tools and motioned to the others.

"Tsúla, fetch some water," she said. "Venser, go find Orin and bring him."

Fletch's legs barely held him as he dismounted. "Came as fast as I could," he said.

Robyn took the reins from him, looking the horse over. "I see that," she said. "This is no way to treat a horse."

"There's news from the Surreach," he said. "Conscriptions…of the Havenari. Many of the old bands are gone, joined up with the Grand Army to fight in the East. Not by their choice."

Robyn sighed. "Did you find any of the rest?"

Fletch nodded. "At Cloverheart, on the edge of Orrath. They weren't wearing the Leaf, but I know my own kind when I see them."

She ruffled his raven hair affectionately; even his head felt loose on his skinny neck. "Good man," she said. "We'd best get you watered, too. That's a savage ride."

Orin was brought, and took no joy from the state of Fletch's horse. He set the men about washing her, then scraping her dry, then washing her again, and so stern was his glare that they dared not question him. Robyn and Fletch, both eager to escape the blame of that gaze, retreated to her house to speak.

"Start from the beginning," Robyn said at last, once a mug of weak ale was in his hands.

"There are no recent signs of our quarry on the forest roads," he said. "I do not fear for the fugitive, or the karach. If they can get across the Iron Road, the lands south of it are unpatrolled."

"You're very sure of that," said Robyn. "Surely you didn't comb the whole forest."

"I didn't have to," said Fletch. "I rode to Cloverheart, found the Havenari there. A large band, at least. Forty men, or fifty. They've forsaken the Leaf. They call themselves the Knights of Tûr, and claim to be mercenaries. But I know what they really are."

"They're evading conscription," Robyn said. "Clever."

"They're sworn to no vasily, either," said Fletch. "It's why they've settled near Cloverheart. As far as the soldiers from Haukmere know, they hail from Orrath. As far as the Legions stationed in Orrath know, they're woodsmen from Haveïl. Their First Spear says it preserves their independence."

"And who holds First Spear?"

"They call him Elwin, Lady. A big man, Oldborn, I think. Elwin Êtriel."

"Êtriel," Robyn said, turning the name over on her tongue. "Êtriel…fairy-maiden. that's a man's name?"

"Do you know him?" asked Fletch. She shook her head, but poured herself a mug of ale as well.

"He wasn't in command when I swore my oath."

"Well, he's in command now. He's united all the Havenari who weren't conscripted. All except us, that is. Says there's greater fights on the horizon than the massacre at the Danhorn."

"In the East?"

"Aye, Lady. The Battle of the Danhorn was the start of a major offensive. Jordac's raised an army of sorts. They slipped away into the lowlands when the fighting was done, and the Legions lost them under cover of night. It's why they're conscripting the Havenari, if you get me. They need men who know the Outlands, men who can track—and fight monsters, if it comes to that. Captain Elwin says it's all petty politics."

"Not to the thousands who died," said Robyn. "But this changes things. Any sign of Hendec?"

"They haven't seen him," said Fletch. "Likely he made his way east. Whether he makes for the Capital or turns south toward Carmac and on to the Uprising, I've no guess."

"I have my guesses," said Robyn, "but I'd like to know for sure. He was a good man."

Fletch nodded as if confused, as if his innocence and wisdom were fighting within him. He let out a troubled sigh.

"Then he is a good man still," said Fletch, "and I wish him well."

In the yard behind the small house, in the stillness of their uneasy silence, both heard the rhythmic slap of Aewyn's arrows striking a soft target. In spite of Celithrand's miraculous hands and a few weeks of bed rest, her leg was still too weak to put her to use raising the ramparts, but she could hobble about with a small cane, and had returned to her archery as best she could to curb the boredom. Robyn had no intention of putting her to work in full view of the soldiers: it was a stroke of some fortune that no one had identified her or connected her to the attack, and Robyn was content to keep her sheltered for now—though she knew she could not protect the girl forever.

Fletch followed his commander's eyes to the shuttered window. "Is she coming with us?" he asked.

"It seems best for everyone," said Robyn. "Celithrand spoke of a prophecy. He said it was her destiny to go south with him, to go become some kind of Chosen One and prepare herself for the coming Godswar, and such. That road is lost to her, now—if indeed it was ever really hers."

"You don't believe him?"

"He was just a man, in the end," said Robyn. "A very wise man, and powerful, perhaps, in ways he did not show. But all men see what they wish to see."

"In Khihana," said Fletch, "we have a proverb."

> *Malba mald'un, malba t'anhad'un,*
> *Tsat'eba hālzita ekt'elun.*

"What does it mean?" asked Robyn.

"It means something like, 'love your lover, and love your friend, but only trust the stars in the end.' It means to say, the truth is always written in the stars. But it is only men, after all, who read them. And the stars are never wrong—but men are wrong about the stars all the time."

Robyn nodded thoughtfully. "I do not think he meant her harm. He wanted, for all of us, what he thought was best. Perhaps he wanted it so badly he was willing to dance on a rope for it. But now that it comes to it, I am happy that fate has brought her to us instead."

"If you can convince her to choose us, you mean."

Robyn smiled. "Now you're learning," she said. "I'll have to be on my guard."

The regular sound of Aewyn's arrows stopped as she slowly limped up to retrieve her shafts. Robyn moved toward the door.

"Don't tell her she has a place with us," said Fletch hastily. "Tell her instead that we have a place for her, if she wants it."

Robyn nodded. "I had always hoped, ever since she taught us to wattle our storm shelters, that she might one day join us. We have much to teach her, but she is wise in the ways of the deep wood already. And if the conscription of the Havenari reaches this far from the Capital, that's where we're going, to keep clear of them. We'll have more need of her than ever, now."

Fletch beamed at that. "You mean not to fight with the Army."

"The Havenari were raised to keep the Vigil. We were not bred for civil war."

"Then should we not go south to join the Knights of Tûr?"

"Our home is here in Haveïl," said Robyn. "Though you seem awfully taken with the south company."

"Elwin is an inspiring man," said Fletch. "I think he will do great things for the Havenari, whether they hold to their old name or not."

"Time will tell," said Robyn, though her mind was already elsewhere.

The target Aewyn had brought in from the butts was a disc of coiled straw, unpainted and heavily worn. For four days, now, Aewyn had been shooting to exhaustion against the side of the little house; the ground was littered with broken shafts where she had missed the target altogether near the end of the day, loosing wild shots with her spindly arms shaking. She shot until her muscles and shoulders ached from the strain. It was a nice break from the monotony of her recovery for something else to hurt, for a change.

It was yet early in the day, and there was a stillness to her that Robyn found comforting as she made her way down the little field. The girl had stepped back almost into the river today, and while it was no great distance by Robyn's standards, her arrows were hitting their mark.

"Relax your hold on it," Robyn offered as she approached. "No need to grip it as tightly as it seems to have gripped you."

Aewyn nocked and loosed another arrow. Her form was good, especially shooting on a bad leg, but she clutched the bow hard and her jaw was set tight.

Robyn turned back to the target. "You're a natural talent," she said. "Better than I was, at your age."

"Not good enough," said Aewyn, as she nocked another.

Robyn put a hand over the girl's clenched fist, pushed the bow down until Aewyn had no choice but to meet her gaze.

"I can't tell you that you did the right thing," said Robyn. "Nor can I tell you that you did the wrong one. All I can say is that it wasn't time, perhaps, for you to hold a grown man's bow. And not only because you're small."

"I see the Censor," said Aewyn. "Wandering about the town. I see what I did to him. I'm walking again. I'll get better. He won't ever get better, will he?"

"But he won't get any worse, either, now that he's on the mend," said Robyn. "Even a forty-pound bow would have killed him dead, with an aim that sharp. You did what I couldn't, Aewyn. Gods know I wanted to. But I couldn't, for reasons you'll understand when you're older. The way I see it, you saved a man's life without taking one in its place, and that is always worth something. There are many other ways it could have gone. Most of them are far worse than what came to pass."

"But if I'd only hit the rope—" the girl began.

"Come inside with me," said Robyn.

"I'm practicing."

"First rule," said the older woman. "Never shoot angry."

Fletch was already hard asleep in Robyn's bed by the time they came in, nearly as exhausted as the horse he had ridden into town. The air inside was hotter and drier than usual; a roaring fire burned in the pit, and the crucks and timbers above it were dressed with river-fish and Darmod Pick's salted mutton. To Aewyn, the house smelled like the changing of the seasons, and it was no longer altogether pleasant to her. The longer she dwelt in Widowvale, the more she could feel the slow march of time—not around in circles, as time passed in the deep wood, but onward in a straight line to an unknown destination. She sat close to the fire, savouring its dry heat as the older woman thought of where to begin.

"When I was a little girl," Robyn said at last, "from the time I could crawl till my fifteenth summer, I had the best library of any little girl in the whole of Creslyn Wood. I grew up with the old legends. I passed my days surrounded by storybooks, among the heroes of the Age of Sun. At eight or nine summers old, I was reading the lays of Ithuriel the Fair and her many suitors. I never cared for the princess or her trappings, though. From the first, I admired the minstrel Llor, who was cunning and brave, and shot golden arrows from the strings of his magical harp. The Lay of Ygilemë and the Bandits, which Bram can still recite—at least, he could last year—was where I first saw it written that a man could shoot out a hangman's rope at a hundred yards."

Aewyn nodded sagely. "How is it done?" she asked. Her earnestness brought a smile to Robyn's face, but the older woman shook her head.

"Gods and fishes, how I tried to do it," she said. "Years, I tried. They cut me my first bow at nine. I remember my father would have no peace from me until they did. I tried to do everything you hear of in the old legends. And in all my days as an archer, from that day to this, I have never seen it done—least of all in the heat of battle. And that, after a fashion, is where you were."

"Celithrand said I'm destined to be a mighty champion of the people," she said. "I thought my time might have come early."

Robyn sighed. "He has believed in you a long time," she said. "He almost died for that belief. But—how do I say this—he has believed it so long, now, that in his mind it can only be very real."

"It must be real!" said Aewyn. "Celithrand is a great and wise man.

All of the aerils are, and he most of all."

"Wisdom, I've found, comes as often from simple folk as from great folk," said Robyn. "More often, maybe."

"Poe doesn't believe in prophecies either," said Aewyn.

Robyn hesitated. "Prophecies," she said at last, "have a habit of coming true in ways even the prophets don't expect. That doesn't mean they're untrue. But neither are they the sagas of the future, telling us word for word who is bound for what destination, or meant for what end, as if it's already come to pass."

"Celithrand seemed so certain."

Robyn lifted another log onto the fire. "Are you?"

"I was," she said. "That all ended when I...when I hurt the poor censor."

"There is a man in the South," said Robyn. "Fletch said the Havenari have a new First Spear there. They call him Êtriel."

"Fairy-born," said Aewyn. "Daughter of a fairy-maiden. That's a man's name?"

"Yes."

"Do you think he's born of a dryad, like me? Are there more like me?"

Robyn smiled. "There is no one like you, Aewyn. As to his parentage, I cannot say. I know only the news Fletch brought back. He's rallying the Havenari. Some have been called to the Grand Army, but he seems to be keeping them to their purpose."

"To fight the old monsters?" asked Aewyn.

"Yes. Until what happened at the Fair, I thought it was a ceremonial duty. Someday I'll tell you the history of the Havenari—the history of that duty. All I can tell you today is that we've fallen far from it. We're a town militia, Aewyn. We hunt poachers, keep a sort of tribal justice in the Outlands, those parts that'll have us. We haven't trained hard to fight the Horrors since the days of the Siege. Until this new man, a veteran with the cognomen of a fairy-child."

"You think he's Celithrand's true champion," said Aewyn.

"Perhaps," said Robyn. "Perhaps not. I think he's now the second person I know of who could be—and I don't know that many people. I think if you wanted him to be, wanted it with all your heart, you could twist the words of the prophecy until he seemed to be exactly what they meant. But if there's a second possible reading, there could be a third. If a third, why not a fourth? Countless others, maybe. Perhaps he's a hero destined for legend—or just a fool destined to die for defying an order of Travalaithi conscription. Maybe he'll get all the Havenari south of the Iron Road killed for deserting the call of the Grand Army."

"You think he will?"

"Time will tell. But it's possible. That's why I'm in no great rush to join him. His actions could be the saving grace of this world, if you believe in prophecies. Or they could be absolute folly that destroys our whole order. More likely, like most people, he's something in between the extremes. But committing to absolute folly is a rare thing in wise men. It's something they most often do when they believe too hard in destiny."

"I'd like to meet him," said Aewyn. "I'd like to see if he's truly my own kind."

"Fletch describes him as Oldborn, aeril-blooded from the days they lived among us...closer to Celithrand than what you are. Our roads will cross with his, in time. But I'm in no hurry. I mean to go north."

"North?"

"The Êtriel is right about one thing. We've fallen from our purpose. If that beast we encountered is a true Horror of Tamnor, we have to find it, and do what we can to keep it away from the villages. I'd like...we'd like you to come with us. Soon as you can walk and ride without pain."

Aewyn looked confused. "Of course," she said. "But I thought you didn't want me on the trail with you. Just before the soldiers came... you sent me back to the village."

"The village isn't safe for you now," said Robyn. "Not with Stannon's men about. There's a queerness about you that's hard to miss. Sooner or later, one of them's bound to take notice of you, and he'll start asking the wrong questions. It seems prudent to take you away with me, as long as you know you're not protected from on high. Destiny means almost nothing in the world, Aewyn. We'll all end up somewhere different than we are now, no matter what you call it."

"I have felt different for so long," said Aewyn. "I thought I was... special."

Robyn smiled. "There are no prophecies about me," she said. "Am I not special?"

"Of course you're—"

"I'm practically a princess, you know. The young lads at Draden Castle, in my day, thought I was dainty as shit." She spat into the fire for emphasis. "At least, I'm as close to a princess as anyone has been, ever since the Baron-Kings replaced the true royal line in Travost. Whether that makes me special—"

Aewyn smiled. "You *are* special. That's not what I meant."

"You are a marvellous girl," said Robyn, "with a destiny and a purpose. And that purpose need not be foretold, and it need not be understood, nor play out in the way you expect. Carry your little prophecy, recite it every night if you like, but this one thing I will tell you: do not live your life according to the will of men who call themselves great. Remember what Poe told us at the house. There are no Chosen Ones, Aewyn...only the ones who choose."

"Then I am certain of only one thing," said the girl. "I choose to come with you... if you'll have me on this ride."

"Of course we'll have you," said Robyn. "So you should get some rest. We ride as soon as your leg will suffer it."

"I...don't have a horse," Aewyn said.

"Neither does Fletch," said Robyn. "His is done with the road for now. Maybe for a long time. But we'll put you and Fletch on Hendec's horse, and leave while the soldiers are deep in their cups."

"Is Hendec not coming?"

Robyn frowned. "We had words," she said at last. "The Havenari are not free enough of Imperial influence for his tastes. He's gone east to fight in the wars of men. He, too, has chosen his own destiny."

With some excitement, Aewyn waited some days in absolute impatience. She set about stretching and strengthening her leg as it healed, and gathered what few possessions she could. She wondered whether it was too late, now, to fetch the rest of them from Grimstead—if, indeed, she had need of them. She thought of her carved bird-whistles, nestled along the top edge of the children's loft, and wondered what use they would be against the horror that awaited them.

When next she came to Robyn's door, her leg was ready enough, though her eyes betrayed that the rest of her was not.

"If there's no room," she said, "if there aren't enough horses...I'd be content to wait until you ride out in the spring."

"You're wise to be afraid," said Robyn. "All the more reason I want you on this ride. If it's a Horror of Tamnor we face, we'll need every lucky charm we can get."

Aewyn stepped gently through her bow and began to unstring it for travel, as she had been taught. In the distance, over the crackling of the fire, she could hear the approach of the other men, who had passed the evening in the company of townsfolk they saw too seldom, and might not see again until the next ride was over. When she had done away with the cane, they knew their time was short.

"I thought you didn't believe in such things," she said. "Lucky charms and prophecies."

"I believe the people who are too sure of anything in this world are most likely to be wrong about it," said Robyn. "That includes myself, most of all."

On the morning after Fletch's return, Marin woke early and made love to his wife, who was not half so shrewish and humourless in the quiet of their home as she liked to affect in public. When their passions had turned to sweet words, she counselled him on the matter of the manhunt for Poe, for he had a great facility with people and a bold presence in the hall, but she was wiser than he and of sounder judgment, in the end. He could do little to change the mind of the Grand Army, but the Havenari were another matter and might, with his guidance, be persuaded to lay the matter to rest. He had not forgotten that the karach had found his beloved nephew and namesake in the woods before something more terrible did. For that reason alone, he resolved to put an end to the matter, or at least to alter the severity of its terms as best he could.

Dressing hastily, Marin came down from his house atop Grefstead. He crossed the barren fields of its sister estate, Grimstead, whose grapes had long been taken in by Karis and the older children (and eaten off the vines, perhaps, by the younger ones). He came westward with the rising sun at his back, past the village green and the great-tree, already called Traitor's Oak, past Alec Mercy's house in the shadow of the escarpment, past most of the miners' houses, past Darmod Pick's pasture and down the hill to Miller's Riffle, where he expected to find the hearth burning and the smell of breakfast from Robyn and Bram's cottage, filled to the brim with soldiers still at rest.

The house was dark and empty of life. The scent of bread from

Alys the Millwife's immense stone oven wafted down on a cold wind, but from the low cottage downriver there came no sound.

The golden light of dawn cast hard shadows against the fence and the bushes; Marin did not see the lean, stooped figure seated against the fencepost until he had nearly passed the gate.

"You're hours late," said Darmod Pick, rising. "They've gone in the night."

Marin nodded, looking up at the cottage with narrowed eyes. "Didn't expect to find you here," he said.

"I had some business with the fairy girl," said Darmod. "Knew she might be riding out with them this year. Fool knows, she's been talking about it every autumn since I can remember."

"She's been with us a long time," said Marin. "Do you think she'll be back?"

Darmod shrugged. "She still loves the monster that hurt her," he said. "More than I've ever seen a child love a pet. A good deal more than most wives love their men, for that matter."

"I've come to lift the hunt on Poe, if I can," said Marin.

Darmod scoffed. "After what he's done?"

Marin nodded, his mouth tight. "I don't think that was the whole of it," he said. "He could have left her crippled with that wound. You think he would have?"

"If she'd got in his way," Darmod offered.

"There's not enough of her to get in his way," said Marin. "He could have batted her aside like she was nothing. What I figure is, she was the little archer who put that arrow in Stannon's eye. Somehow the tale of the karach has grown in the telling."

Blindsided by what he knew at first listen to be the truth, Darmod let out a laugh. "I don't suppose Grim wrestled him into submission and carried him back to town, either."

"We've all got our stories," said Marin. "Anywise, I'm here to make peace with Poe, at least among the Havenari. Is Bram somewhere about? He can get word to the others, if they're already gone."

Darmod laughed. "Listen to this one: Bram rode out *with* them."

"Impossible."

"I swear it," said Darmod. "Back in his uniform, mailed and mounted. Stone sober again, too. At last, a sign that things are setting themselves right around here."

"I don't think it's a good sign," said Marin. "The list of things that would pour Gilbram Fane into his armour again is very, very short. And none of them are good."

Darmod's grey eyebrows darted up. "Gilbram Fane? The Ratcatcher of Draden? Thought he died when their own thanes betrayed them."

"Does that surprise you?"

Darmod whistled low. "Smarter men would've killed him first. Well, we've all come out here to have done with our old lives, haven't we? I never thought the Iron City would have so much reach, out here in the thick. But now we wait and see just how much the Imperator cares about Master Stannon's eye. Might be those ghosts have an admirable way of not staying dead."

Marin turned back toward Darmod's house, and the shepherd followed. "What do you think the Imperator will do?" he asked the shepherd.

"I think the Imperator, or whoever else, would find it easier to replace Castor Stannon than to bring that karach to justice," said Darmod. "You tried that once yourself, didn't you? We got nothing but trouble for it."

"Trouble? Your holdings and purse are twice what they were before you bought his labour."

"I bought the girl," said Darmod, "and it was that bony little thing who came every day to the yoke. The season of the plough belonged to her. Not to the savage who killed my sheep and fled the punishment.

I don't forget, and don't you forget it, either. Any boon I've had out of this mess, I owe to her." He paused for a moment, as if kind words were the sort of neglected heirlooms he had to dust and oil before putting back into service.

"I owe her a great deal more than I've let on," he finally added, turning his eyes away. "I'd meant to give her Shimble."

"The yearling filly from Alec Mercy? It's too soon for her to take a rider."

"Too soon for a grown man in armour, certainly," said Darmod. "But maybe just about ready for a girl her size."

"Orin would have a fit if you saddled a filly that young."

"No matter. She took Hendec's horse, in the end."

"Hendec's horse?" Marin furrowed his brow. "Did Hendec stay behind?"

"He went East," said Darmod. "Left days ago, I think, to join the Mage. Left his horse, sold back his kit, kept his sword and his bow. Went south to seek passage east on the Iron Road."

Marin was caught off-guard by that. "He said nothing of it to me."

"I haven't heard much of his reasons," said Darmod. "Only know what I saw. Was that old sack of bones really the man they call Ce-lithrand?"

"He looked enough the part," said Marin. "And I've never seen the like of that weapon he carried. Niurwyn, they called it. Bird-friend."

Darmod laughed. "Gods, that's a grisly name," he remarked.

"I thought it rather tame, myself."

"You've never spent a day on a battlefield, then," said Darmod. "I've no doubt that sword fed a hundred flocks in his lifetime. Ce-lithrand was a hero of the Siege of Shadow, mind you. He was a hero of a lot of things. He meant something to the people, once. As much as the Imperator ever did. He might have had the Spire himself, if he'd seen fit to push for it."

"That much I knew."

"And hanging him in a field, like a common horse thief…it didn't sit well, even with me, and the fire of youth is ground right out of me. I reckon it was a turning point for a firebrand like Hendec. He's wanted to turn on Travalaith for some time, I'm sure of it."

"Whatever his reasons," said Marin, "he's a good man, and I'm sorry to see him go."

Darmod looked back toward the escarpment, toward the deep woods, as if expecting to hear the sound of horses. The trees glistened cold in the light; the morning was turning bright without getting any warmer, and Aewyn was nowhere to be seen.

"It's a good season to be sorry for things," he said.

If Marin had come a week sooner, he would have heard the falling-out between Hendec and Robyn, which was civil but uncompromising. He would have seen the big man storming off southward down the village road and the resigned understanding of his companions. As it was, he was only a few hours too late to catch the twelve horses, with Aewyn and Fletch taking Hendec's place, as they mounted the steep slope of the escarpment and forged their way nimbly into the woods. With the town settling down and the anger fading among the Censor's troops, it was time the Havenari were away again. But even Marin did not know what terrible errand had occasioned such an early departure—nor, after his own ordeal in the woods, did they think it wise to tell him.

They climbed with stern purpose up the Serpent Trail, patrolling the whole edge of the escarpment on their way back to the body of the deserter. At midday they came onto the promontory and stopped for water. This time, Robyn suffered Venser's curiosity and allowed him to make the climb down to the body. A few minutes of prodding it unceremoniously with a stick—even he would not touch it directly—suggested that the deserter's limbs had been mangled not from the fall, but in direct confrontation with the monster.

"Aldwode or no, he was a fighter," said Robyn.

"As you'd expect from a Cerulean," said Bram.

They found the deserter's dagger nearby, badly rusted, worn dull from too much use as a utility knife. It showed no sign of having struck true before it was lost to him. With some difficulty, Fletch spotted the signs, down below, of the creature's passing, and tried to establish a fresh trail. It was slow going, though; it had been weeks, now, since the original trail, and they quickly learned that the obvious carnage of its passing in the highlands had been characteristic of a charge at speed.

"It stampedes there, and slithers here," said Tsúla, and that was the truth of it. In stealth, it could move through very small places indeed, and Robyn wondered with some concern whether their long spears would be much use where the trees were thickest.

Aewyn rode capably but in troubled silence. Her heart was miles away from the chase in that moment, though how many miles she could not tell. As he had in the summers of her youth, Celithrand had slipped back into myth, only this time he had not gone alone. There was a natural hunter in Poe's blood, and he could be stealthy when he wished, but there was a completeness to his disappearance this time that was hard to forget.

For much of the afternoon—for the whole climb down into the northern valley and the heart of the old wood—she dwelt on the earliest days of her youth, recalling Poe's days as a cub smaller than she was, and the startling speed with which he surpassed her, of the endless long nights they spent in burrowed shelters and at play in the high grasses. She thought of his gentleness, first with her, and then with Grim: the vintner never learned, not really, just how delicately Poe had handled him, like a guilty child with a glass toy that was not his own. In her hand was the little black knife the druid had brought her so long ago, the one she knew Grim had secretly coveted and perhaps even stolen, sometimes, for the vines and trellises along Grimstead's southern slopes.

Grim was gone, now. Poe was gone. Celithrand, too, had vanished under circumstances that made it unclear when, or even if, he might return. The little knife felt ugly in her hand, like a prize of pity. She nearly dropped it, once. One day, if she lived as long as everyone had said she might, she knew she would lose it, too. You could lose anything, if you lived long enough; it was just as her mother had said it would be. *The outside world is a world of loss. Silvalis gives you more than you could ever imagine—and then takes back from you still more than that.*

It was strange that here, in the ranks of the Havenari, the memory of those words should come back to her. Her memories of her mother were faint at best, having faded long ago. She recalled the heart of her mother's woodland as if out of a dream. Whether the mists she recalled were real, or whether they were the only way she could fathom the timeless spell on that place, was beyond her best efforts to determine.

But in that hour she saw her mother's face, and heard her mother's voice. The name Aelissraia, like wind in the trees, quickened on her lips and flew away from her mouth, and she started at the sound.

Fletch leaned back in the saddle suddenly. "Did you say something, Aewyn?"

The hush of the forest was broken. Somewhere above them the mournful chittering of a kingfisher suddenly ceased.

"We should not be here," she said, though at first she did not know why.

"What?" said one of the men.

"This place is sacred," she added hastily, and knew in that moment that it was true. She was again in her mother's land. All things here were suddenly familiar. She could remember faces, conversations, whole years at play. She was no longer cold in the chill of the wood.

She was home.

"We follow our quarry," said Venser, who had never seen a Horror before and—it was now clear—was unadvisably keen to look upon one.

"If it has come here, to this sacred place," said Robyn, with a little more sensitivity, "it is all the more reason why we *must* be here."

An unexplainable fear gripped Aewyn's insides at that thought. Her legs, already weak, turned to jelly beneath her; she might have fallen, had she not been firmly in the saddle. Her stomach, though full since breakfast, felt hollow and sick. She could feel her mother's presence here, somewhere—beyond the lake whose shores she could only now remember. The kingfishers told her just how near to that water she had drawn.

But hers was not the only presence. Something else, something darker, called to her blood.

Aewyn's veins flooded with some hot urgency. It seemed to come down from her head, fill her lungs and her chest, spread like fire to her limbs. The forest seemed to reel around her. Her mouth was dry, and her hands on the reins were soaking wet.

"Sister," said Bram, somewhere up ahead. He called Robyn that in town, but never on the trail.

"I feel it," she answered. "Close ranks and string up."

The Havenari brought their horses together, flank to flank, two and three abreast. Two by two, they dismounted to string their bows and hang arrows at the ready. Swords were drawn, too—the woods here were too thick, now, to be sure they'd get off a volley of arrows if they were taken by surprise. Their spears—more bladed, slashing polearms, really—were too long to use effectively in the thick. And no one wanted a bow in hand when the thing was fast upon them. Celithrand had called it a *moadon*—none but he had seen one, or even rightly knew what it was. This time, every sword-point swayed with uncertainty; only Bram, who hesitated and did not draw, had steady hands. When bows were made ready, they rode on.

In the back ranks, propelled by something not quite understood—filial concern, a sense of jealous reverence, some ancient and silent call to her blood—Aewyn inched back from Fletch, shifting nervously in the saddle until he was used to the feel of it. Then, with a still and silent grace, she swung her weak leg quietly over the saddle and slipped off the mount onto the strong one, walking beside the horse with easy steps until it had grown accustomed to walking with its herd. The horse raised its ears with curiosity and Fletch, ever in tune with it, leaned forward and scanned the tree line. They rode in restless silence only a short distance before Tsúla called a halt to the procession.

"Tsúla," said Robyn, waiting with some displeasure.

He leaned toward Fletch's horse. "Pardons, Captain. But young Fletch appears to have lost some cargo." Robyn's look of confusion lingered only a moment before she recovered her wits—but not her temper.

"Mother of Sorcery!" she shouted. "Where is she? Did you see her?"

"No."

"Did you?"

"No, Captain."

She wheeled her horse suddenly, startling some of the others. "Are we not on the most dangerous hunt of the last five years? Are you not looking out?!"

"I was looking out," Fletch offered. "Not in." He rubbed the back of his neck like a guilty child. Robyn, riding over, might have cuffed him with her gauntlet if he'd been even slightly bigger.

"Well, look out now, boy," she ordered. "Bram, with me on point. Fletch, take the rear with the Two Blind Hawks here."

"She might have got ahead of us," Venser offered.

"Why would she leave us?" said Bram. "It makes no sense, none that I can see."

Fletch held up a hand for silence, and the whole company complied at once. He silently slipped down from his horse, his eyes darting almost hungrily through the shadows, eager to make up for their lapse. The breeze had altogether calmed.

"Fletch?" Robyn whispered. She was high in the saddle, muscles hard and tensed, until she saw him visibly relax. The trees closed tight against the road here, and he had to get right into the nettles to retrieve a glinting, fist-sized piece of metal. He held it up for the others: it was a dented stirrup, blackened by long exposure to the elements, and something else.

"Is it stamped?" Robyn asked. Fletch turned it over.

"Yes, but something's eaten it away. I can't make out the maker, but it's the same, exactly, as yours."

Robyn held out a hand. "Bring it here," she said.

"Hang on," said Fletch. A tall thicket just within the trees was rustling in the still air, and he inched closer, raised an arm toward it.

"Aewyn?"

A soft squeaking sound, like the coo of a baby, came back in response.

Fletch reached out his hand. "I think I've found her over here," he began to say.

The lake, of course, was precisely where it should have been. Aewyn's feet knew every step of the way, even through the mist, even weighed down by coarse-soled riding boots and a troubled heart. Through layers of green that multiplied as the lake-water grew invisibly nearer, Aewyn climbed with the ease of a fast-returning familiarity, even when the land dropped off suddenly and began its descent into the thicker fog below.

With practiced ease Aewyn shed her boots and the heaviest of her clothing on the stony white shore. It was faster by far to swim across to the narrow peninsula than to make the trek around, and she was not so distracted by the numinous beauty of the hollow that she dawdled in her errand.

The motionless afternoon air was cool, and the water here had a biting chill--but as she approached the heart of the forest, the cold seemed lost on her, as it had been in her youth. The lake itself was blanketed with a thick fog that smelled faintly of juniper, cedar, lodris in bloom. Her hair was damp and glistening when she reached the grassy peninsula, though she had not ducked her head under the water. The autumn, perhaps, was dying before its time this year.

Aewyn heard before she saw that she was not alone. Her mother's voice, when she heard it, was unmistakable, though the song was new and mournful:

> *Iarthundon fei iarasu*
> *Ionai cruthandairova*
> *Hani emai hallom*
> *foriammaillas*
>
> *Ap şiil sae vectelim*
> *odondi lentumvei*
> *f'lurithal eştona*
> *Ionlurind graivect.*

The words Aewyn could make out were certainly Viluri—an old form of it, certainly, but undeniably familiar. Beneath the melody, there seemed no other song; but Aewyn felt more than heard a far older language beneath the words, a language of young rivers and patient stones. Where it came from and what it meant she could not know.

Her mother sang without ornament, but with a starkness and clarity tinged with sorrow. She might have gone on all day, all year, if Aewyn had not interrupted.

"Mother," she said. The voice stopped abruptly, but the song of the forest continued; it echoed through the fog like something out of a dream.

"Homeward you come," said her mother, "at a very late hour."

She stepped from the fog, then, resplendent in a cloak of autumn. Where Aewyn's hair had gone the ruddy orange of a pumpkin, her mother's untamed curls were shot through with bursts of fiery red, harvest gold, the blazing yellow blondes of rapeseed and mustard. Her skin had the creamy softness and precise colour of a peeled birch tree; she was naked, as far as nakedness went, but there was something otherworldly about her that seemed to defy the very notion.

"There's a Horror loose in the wood," said Aewyn.

"There are more than one," replied her mother coldly. Aewyn shuddered at the words.

"We've been tracking one," she said. "It killed a deserter from the city."

"Yes," said the dryad.

"It was coming this way."

"Yes."

"I thought you were in danger."

"And so you came."

Aewyn nodded. "Of course I came."

The dryad turned away. "To do what?"

Aewyn shook her head for want of a reply. "You're impossible," she said at length, mostly to herself.

"And I grow more impossible every day," said her mother. "That will be my end, Aewyn. Not these monsters. You would do better to protect the Iun you have left alone in the deep wood."

"The Havenari can take care of themselves," said Aewyn.

"And I cannot?" A cold breeze picked up, thinning the fog. The tremendous branches swayed curiously overhead as the first few drops of an autumn rain began to dapple the stones at their feet. Aewyn shivered in the wind and felt, more than ever, like a visitor in this place.

"There's more," Aewyn said, though she had not known it until this moment.

"I thought so," said her mother. "Have you eaten?" The sweet scent of fruit and honeysuckle was carried on that fog too, wafting down from the slopes that surrounded the lake.

"I have been speaking with Celithrand," she said, ignoring the question. "He came home to take me away—my destiny, he said, is at hand. He spoke of the *Uliri Imidactuai* the Mysteries of the Blind Watchers, and read the old verse to me. He called me a champion of mankind, a great warrior...or something."

"Your destiny belongs to you alone," her mother said. "What path you walk, what company you keep, even the very world you live in. All these things belong to you, now."

"But the prophecy—"

The dryad silenced her with a raised hand. Her countenance was washed in a gentle sorrow.

"Celithrand has long been kind to you, Aewyn," she said. "Old and wise he must seem to you. But he, like all his prophets before him, are children born under the Moons—young in this world. He did not rise from the sea, nor was he born into the old magic. That Age has been gone a long time, Aewyn. And men who are not born into magic will take it for themselves, or make their own, wherever they can find it."

"You do not believe him?"

"Long have I tended my wood," she said. "Long have I smelt the air and listened to the crashing of the distant waves. Before the *Uliri Imidactuai*, or any *Uliri*, before Luna herself cried down the aerils, my feet danced ripples in the edge of still and dreamless oceans, and I sang upon a green heath under untroubled skies. What the wise foretell may come to pass, as it has since the beginning. But that truth does not equal destiny. It does not weave a spell of their words. And the worded folk of the world would do well to remember that."

The dryad reached out—Aewyn had not realized she was close enough—and touched the girl's cheek gently. Her voice softened. "Celithrand has believed your whole life that there was something special in you," she said. "In that, child, we are in agreement. But there is vanity in prophecy—his, and yours. He has sacrificed much for you, and more than a little of it, I think, needlessly. He has moved the earth for you in ways you do not yet understand. It is by the strength of his belief that all these deeds have come to pass. So I dare not deign to say that prophecy is without power. Through him, prophecy has brought you such things as I could never give you. It has brought you a home, first and foremost, among those who are most like you."

Aewyn flinched at the words. "You considered me a child of the forest, once. Your own child."

"You will always be my child," said the dryad. "And those of my kind do not *have* children. That you were born to me, in the fashion of a daughter to a woman, is a miracle unto itself, prophecy or no. You are my miracle, Aewyn—my own reminder of the lasting grace of a love that the First Children should not feel."

A cool breeze stirred the waters of the lake, and a passing cloud, for only a moment, spun a fleeting shadow over Aelissraia's sad face.

"You are loved," said the dryad. "I have made you, and birthed you, and I see myself in your eyes with pride. But what do I know of a woman's affection? The newest mother or the smallest babe among the Iun knows more of a mother's love than I."

"I don't understand," said Aewyn. "Your words are riddles to me." There were tears in her eyes, but true to her words, she could not fully comprehend why.

"That is inevitable," sighed her mother. "You will understand less and less as this world takes you from me. My words were simple to you, once. I wonder what you will make of them when you are gone, if you remember them at all."

Aewyn was silent a long time, nodding solemnly as the rain picked up. There *had* been something else, after all, though she had not at first known it.

"I've come to say goodbye," she said, discovering the thought only as it left her mouth.

"Yes," said her mother. An unquiet rolling thunder boomed distantly in the sky.

"Poe is gone. Celithrand is gone. And you tell me you, too, are fading."

"I wish I had something to give you, child," said the dryad. "I will leave you nothing, when you go to them—only a memory, and the fading ghost of memory at that. It is a meagre dowry for one so loved."

"Mother," said Aewyn, and it was all she could say. She gripped her mother in her arms and pinned her tightly to her breast. The dryad flinched, then relaxed. This was what men and women of the village often did to each other when parting for a long time.

"Hush, child," said the dryad. "We have time, now, to talk as we once did, though I fear you will not remember it. Let me hold you and sing to you, and quell the shadow within you while I can. Let me make you whole again, as once the old magic could have, before it was taken from the world." She touched Aewyn's leg—her hand was full of icy, chilling water—and as the numbing chill of it passed over her thigh, deadening the pain, she washed away the grisly scarring from the horse's hoof as washing away a stubborn stain. A scar in the shape of a thin red crescent, where the raw iron of the horseshoe had struck deep, was the only scar that remained.

"The others are in danger," she said sleepily.

"Hush," said her mother. "Even now, death is already come and gone with its prey. There will be no more of it if you tarry. Not even if you linger till the whole wood is gilded with dusk."

TWELVE

ENEATH TWO FULL MOONS, eight long years past, with the guarded pity of a stern and half-loveless father, Toren had mixed the last drops of an inky, fetid ichor with the heartblood of a living stag and a sacramental wine from the vineyards of Veritenh. The stink of a few drops of that rancid fluid had turned Robyn's stomach; she was a lean-faced and bony girl of twenty-one, and she had retched twice before forcing a few drops of the hideous concoction down. Bram, who by then would drink anything with wine in it, heaved once and was done with it, though it disagreed with him for days after. There was none left for the Blooding of Tsúla, when he came, nor for Fletch, when they conscripted him at Haukmere and saved him from the mines. Robyn might not have thought of it, for she had buried the memory deep and had no desire to recall it. But the overpowering stench that came from the shadows as the trees parted brought it all back to her; and when she swooned and fell senseless to her knees, the foul taste rose again in her mouth and pulled her from the edge of a nightmarish vertigo that shook her to the bone.

Fletch, who stood closest and had never been Blooded, let out a sound like a lost sheep as the darkness closed around him. The whole forest wall disappeared in an instant behind a great mass of shadow and sinew as it came, and so light was its step that not a tree branch or the snap of a twig betrayed its coming. Only the crackling of leaves as they withered and died gave warning of its desperate lunge, and in the moment it came, Fletch fell to the Aldwode and was already lost beyond reckoning when its jaws swung open like the doors of death themselves.

There was no hope. There was no time for words, for a last stand, for the kind of deed that would be sung about. The Havenari would remember for years after with solemn pride that he died with his hand on his sword, as if the Travalaithi deserter's weapon had been eager to avenge its master. But the immense presence of the shadow-wreathed moadon was too much, and his sword-hand went slack, in the end. Those who stood like statues in thrall to its unholy bearing, who could not reach for their own weapons in the long seconds to follow, would remember that too.

It rolled through the bush, through the sapling trees, through the boy, like a wave of locusts howling through tall grass. The force of its impact might have killed Fletch on the spot, so furious was its charge, but he went up in its mandibles and was so rent from himself that none could say whether his end was here nor there. They stood nearly to a man transfixed—even Venser, who was a seasoned and Blooded veteran, and boastful beyond belief when his blood was up. As tatters and drops of the boy's body spattered his hollow, gaping face, something old and strong woke in him, and he was the first to give answer.

The slashing head of his long spear was the weapon of choice for it, but so tight were the trees and so fast and slick its slithering movement that he could not find its flesh in the roiling shadow. The blade bounced awkwardly where it struck, swinging into its leathery hide so hard that the impact numbed both his hands. A long, rusted crack split the head of Venser's spear and he fell back, roaring in pain and alarm.

"To arms!" he called, though his deep voice quivered.

"To arms!" someone answered, though no one came.

The others stood shaking a moment longer. Robyn drew her sword almost absently but her jaw was fixed; she could mouth no order, and none of the Havenari seemed ready to comply.

Venser's courage held long enough to swing a second time, then a third, with his ruined pole; but its attention turned to him, and it fixed him with its many bottomless eyes, and when it jerked its head toward him he was nearly motionless with awe. Its whole head tore sideways, showering him with the blood and bone of its first prey as its jaws struck his arms hard, bouncing the weapon from his grasp and nearly taking him from his feet. It was only when he tried to lunge for the weapon that he realized his arm was mangled beyond use, shattered into a sack of bones. He reached for the sword at his belt with his good arm, but the thing swung back around, knocking him to the ground and blasting the sense from him, though the razor edge of its jaws did not land square enough to tear through his mail.

Too frightened to close with it, the Havenari fell back and nocked arrows with mixed results; most of the arrows skipped off its hide as if fired against a castle wall. Robyn caught it straight in the eye, so true was her aim, but its head was such a mass of eyes that it seemed hardly the worse for it. It turned its terrible gaze on her as she shot again, into another eye, and lunged on at her, impossibly fast, as she tried to nock a third with shaking hands.

"I need her!" she cried, a moment before its gnashing jaws blasted the air from her chest and sprawled her onto her back. She tried to rise, tried to take in enough air to cry out again, but the plate was caved in flat against her ribs and she could draw no breath.

Steel rang out as its chittering jaws plunged downward. The point of a sword—Bram's sword—plunged hard into the thick centre joint of her breastplate and fixed itself firmly in the polished steel as the creature struck. An inch above or below the brace point, the tip of the blade might have pierced her to the breast; but lodged in the strongest square inch of her armour, the blade caught the full brunt of the Horror's lunge on its gleaming edge and spread the force of the blow across the whole breastplate, sparing it from crushing her any further. Bram jerked upwards as the gnashing teeth came in and cut deep into the flesh of the monster's gums.

Muscle against muscle, Bram could not hold its weight off of her, but he turned his sword hard, wedging it against its anchor point, and wrested the monster's head aside with a desperate yell. It wheeled on him in time to taste the sword's edge twice more as Bram crossed the centre line of his sister's body and sliced with quick, even strokes where the meat of its face was softest.

"Back!" he urged. "Get back! It's too big! We can't hold it!" He snapped the tip of his sword out again and it came back bloody.

The string of the cuts and the sound of his voice seemed to drive some new fury into the Horror, and it advanced again with the deadly caution of one predator against another. Bram backpedalled steadily, turning it from Robyn's body as its mandibles and then its skittering forelimbs thrashed, thrust, cut at him, jamming the blade against its rapid strikes. The jaws struck his sword so hard that they shook apart the rusty cross-guard, which began to crumble away in flakes as it spun and danced in his hand. But the blade beneath did not bend; it began, at last, to remember.

"Spears and swords!" Robyn commanded at last, almost uselessly.

Those who could draw their weapons knew already it was time to do so. Those who were stunned in the creature's wake could not be helped. The moadon reared, and the shadows around it seemed to deepen as it lashed out with a chittering tangle of forelegs; Bram caught them against the edge of his blade, though the force of them sent him down and drove him to a knee.

"Over me!" Bram called out. Rising to his feet, sucking in a great gasp of foul air, Venser struggled to free his sword with his good arm. He jerked it from its scabbard and let it fall into his hand as Bram's sword licked a twitching claw away from one of the forelegs.

"Well, I'll be damned," said Venser, as he staggered to his own weapon.

Tsúla, who had never been Blooded, was on his back screaming blindly, though he had not been struck; Roald, one of the old veterans, had taken up his spear and thrust hard against its chitinous side. Where the spear could not penetrate, still it could hold the creature straight on in the direction it was facing, lest it twist round unexpectedly and take them by surprise. It jerked sideways as Roald struck it, sensing the fight had been joined. In that moment, the bony plates of its neck opened and Bram's sword lunged home. Blood or something like it spilled out, black and steaming. As it turned back to him, Bram snapped off the crumbling edge of his rusted crossguard with a hard pull and wedged it hard into the wound. It nearly took his hand off for the effort, but as it snapped its head around to Roald, then back to Venser, the gap in its neck plates did not fully close. It must have felt the cold winter air against the open wound, and known its weakness, for it turned from Venser and threw its whole weight forward against Bram again, who dove backwards as it barrelled in and came up just outside its jaws.

"South!" cried Robyn.

Bram ducked his head, threw himself back down, as an arrow whistled just over his head and into the thing's vulnerable face. He recovered his stance too late to catch a jab that sliced open his cheek—but in time, barely, to keep it from taking the rest of his jaw with it.

"West!" Robyn cried, and he ducked left.

There was some unseelie cunning to the creature—it seemed to wear its wicked intelligence like a long shadow—but in the frenzy of battle it could focus on nothing but killing. Bram held its attention and its jaws, and flicked his sword-point into soft flesh when he could.

One by one, the Havenari found their wits and brandished whatever weapons they had to hand: it was determination, more than skill, that wore it down, and as the Havenari began to remember their training they fell into tight formation, walling it in with their spears and holding it at bay as well as they could. One or two of the men carried maces as well as swords, and tried them where the hide was thickest, or took swings at its clawed and scrabbling feet.

Tsúla could move no closer to it under his own power, but he had taken up another spear and could thrust it, at least, into the predictable path of the beast as Bram lured it forward again and again onto his spear-point. At first the wounds served only to make it more furious, and Bram was hard pressed to do more than preserve his own skin. But as the wounds multiplied, the thing began to slow, and Bram began to retaliate—first with desperate, harmless flicks of the sword-edge, then with hasty jabs, then with swings of steadily diminishing finesse and more raw power as the creature began to slow and the meat of its face slowly fell away in pieces.

When enough of it had been done, and Robyn had exhausted her quiver, she moved in to stand shoulder to shoulder with her brother, and her sword's fresh edge cut smoothly and deeply where Bram's had hacked away the armour of its leering insectoid face.

It could not even be said when the Horror passed over from living to dead. So unbroken was its intent, so pure its purpose, that it fought on well past the certainty of its own death, well past the endurance of some of the men. Venser, wielding his heavy sword in his weak hand alone, struck at its flank again and again until pain and exhaustion caught up with him and he slumped against its writhing side, nearly falling beneath its trampling feet. The others renewed their assault when he fell: none really knew whether it had struck him again, whether it had killed him, whether it would kill them all, whether dying at the hands of a Horror of Tamnor was somehow a viler end than dying from a fall or an illness or a knife in the back.

"Regroup," Robyn called, hoarsely, when her sword-arm seemed ready to give out and the creature lay still. Its shadow had gone out; it lay out grey and leathery in the afternoon sun and in spite of its twitching mandibles was probably dead long before the rain of blows abated. Until the most panicked of the men could be calmed, blade after blade and spear after spear found their place in its flesh. It was impossible to tell then whether the sickening dread in the air was some power of the creature, or the logical reaction to such an attack. It was impossible, too, to tell when they ceased to battle a living foe and passed on to hacking at its corpse.

Bram's hands were steady as stone, but his fingers were bruised nearly blue when Robyn closed her own around them. She looked down at him to find the tears running down his face as he stood motionless before the monstrous husk of the moadon.

"We killed it," she said, though he did not respond.

She could hardly brush the tears from his face with a gauntleted hand, but she peeled away the last traces of the flaking, rusted iron cross-guard from his sword. Beneath the rust, the unmarred stamp of House Fane—a four-rooted oak, ringed with a narrow annulet—was capped by a simple maker's mark.

"Good steel," said Bram. "Though I've ruined her edges both."

Robyn brushed her thumb over the maker's mark as she embraced her brother.

"Tysen would be proud," she said.

Bram studied the blade ruefully for a moment.

"And Gilbert... Elana... Silandra?" he asked. She wrapped her shaking arms around him.

"Especially her," Robyn sighed. "Her most of all."

The metal shone brightly—as brightly as when he had last oiled it and put it away—but both edges were pitted and gouged where the monster's keen jaws had hit it. He tested its balance in his hand, found it true.

"That, at least," he said, "was the workthe she was meant to do."

Robyn smiled wistfully, and might have said something else, if Tsúla hadn't interrupted.

"Captain," he said with a heavy face. "Fletch is gone. And you'd better come have a look at Venser."

There are dreams that come and go in the night as silently as if they had never been. So, too, come dreams that end only with the waking of the dreamer, strange windows into inner worlds that force their way into memories, some as close as a monster's breath, some as distant and sad as the buried dead's last memory of starlight. And then, in extraordinary times, come those that linger on long after sleep—dreams that rise and walk with the dreamer into the misty world of early waking.

So it was with Aewyn, who found herself wandering in thought, not far from a trail, within range of voices raised in argument. She had talked with her mother for moments, or for months; she could not now tell which. The kiss of a dryad—for she had certainly had one—had shrouded her memories in fog. There was a perfect and drowsy peace in that moment, but also an intangible sadness. It was like rising from a familiar bed for the last time.

A pungent reek in the autumn air brought her back to her senses abruptly. It smelt of blood and scat and fouler things, and it hung in the breeze like a billowing shroud. The trees here, she saw, had already begun to wither. She knew, somehow, they would not last the winter.

Robyn was the first one she saw, kneeling in the lee of what seemed like a massive grey boulder. She was bent low over a heap of kindling, trying to strike a fire with trembling hands. Her dull armour was un-buckled and smashed in at the breast; it gleamed under striped ribbons of red and black—and her face, caked with blood and dirt, fared no better.

"Robyn!" she called. The older woman looked up but hardly ac-knowledged her. Her hazel eyes were ringed with red and wide with mad terror. She looked up only long enough to see that Aewyn was no threat—perhaps not even long enough to recognize her—before she returned to her work.

"Damn it," she spat. "Bram, help me."

As Aewyn came closer, she could see Bram crouched over Venser, who lay splayed on the ground, clutching at his shoulder with grim resignation. The arm below that shoulder was ragged and torn, impos-sibly twisted like the branch of an old dwarf beech.

"Venser?" he asked.

"Go on, help her," the big man grunted. "It won't get any more broken now."

Bram turned himself about with some difficulty and staggered to his sister. If he was not the first to spot Aewyn, he was the first to pay her any heed.

"Come here, you," he said.

"What happened here?" she asked. "Are you all right?" Bram shared a glance with his sister that, even to Aewyn, seemed somehow

wordy. The older woman rose. The stench in the clearing was everywhere, but much of it was on her.

"Come," she said.

Aewyn walked with her around the great grey mass while Bram
struck the fire. On its far side she could make out the head—a many-
horned, many-eyed thing. It had the face, if it could be called that,
of a wolf spider, dominated by four bulbous, lidless black eyes, beneath which a row of smaller eyes glistened like plums in the mocking
shape of a grin. Some had been pierced by arrows buried almost to
their fletchings, and sent up an awful stench where they had leaked
their black innards. Below them were two opposed sets of mandibles,
crushing jaws as long and thick as her thighs, coated in blood and still
twitching. It had not been dead long, if it was indeed dead. It was not
long departed from life, if indeed it had even been alive.

"Do you remember your parting with Celithrand?" Robyn asked
her.

"Yes," she said.

"Do you remember taking up the Leaf?"

Aewyn nodded. "I was accepted."

"You swore yourself to us."

"Yes," she said eagerly.

Robyn's eyes pooled with sadness for only a moment. Then she
backhanded the smaller girl, hard, across the face. A plated gauntlet
made the blow no less ferocious, and Aewyn fell almost to her back,
reeling in pain and confusion.

"Never desert the company again," said Robyn, in a tone Aewyn
would not soon forget. Blood streamed at the corner of her mouth as
she rose, fell dizzily back to earth, and climbed back to her feet with
the aid of a nearby trunk. Her limbs shook like the legs of a newborn
fawn: it was no gentle city knighthood, this.

"The men are gathering dry wood," said Robyn. "Take what they bring you and arrange two biers, one large and one small. Opposite sides of the road."

"Biers…" Aewyn breathed, which earned her a stinging glare. "Yes, Captain," she finished hastily.

Tsúla was first back to the road, his arms loaded with fat branches and his saddlebags slung over his own shoulders, likewise burdened. She thought at first that he was bent low by their weight, but his ashen face was downturned even after he had dumped them out.

"Tsúla?" she asked. He shook his head, hollow-eyed and broken, and went back for more wood.

A pair of the others, men Aewyn had seen casually but who were less known to her, followed suit. They all came through the thicket in their time—all save one. Then Tsúla came anew. She struck out an arm; she would not let him depart again with downcast eyes.

"Where's Fletch?" she asked.

He shut his dark eyes tight and sighed. "Underneath," he said. It was all he could manage.

She was not prepared for what awaited her.

It was hardly the first corpse Aewyn had seen in her short life. There had been the deserter from Travalaith—only a few days before, it seemed. The year before that, she had been with Grim when he died. But where Grim's corpse had been something like an old, abandoned house, vacated quietly in the night, the house of Fletch's spirit was made a ruin. A hideous gnashing of jaws had driven him from it and laid waste to it entirely; his keen dark eyes were gone, lost somewhere in the mass of him. Aewyn could not bear to look on him long enough to learn what other parts of him were left, or where they had come to their final rest. She bit her fist in grief and backed away and looked on him no more.

"Firewood," said Robyn coldly. "Stack it." She drew her sword and approached the creature.

Aewyn felt the weight of a man's hand, then, before he spoke, though he had approached in silence. These were strange times indeed, that a bloody hand on her shoulder should bring her comfort.

"There are none, dear girl, who can bear to see him," said Bram. "Not you, nor me."

Aewyn's tears were her only reply. They streaked hot down her cheek, and stung in her right eye, which had begun to swell up.

"You could not have saved him," he whispered. "None of us could, though we tried. Gods, how we tried." The quiet was split by a leathery crack as Robyn swung Fletch's sword struck the creature's neck and clove down a few inches. With a coarse grunt and a foot laid aside of its head, she pulled the blade free to swing again. It was no work for her own sword, and would ruin the blade before it clove through. But the weapon was of young Travalaithi steel, poor in its make, and the boy would have no more need of it.

"I have never seen such a thing," said Aewyn.

"It is a moadon," said Bram. "We think. It is a lesser Horror, in any case, a spawn of Tamnor, or of his lieutenants. A terrible living relic of a dark time. Its blood is poison. Its very being is poison. I would tell you not to touch it, if you did not already feel sick at the thought."

"It came out of nowhere," called Venser from the ground. "Hit us fast. All that training, all they give us…no damn good."

"Is it dead?" Aewyn asked. She sat down on a stump beside the wounded man, and looked out to Robyn, who continued to cleave into it in anguished fury.

"It ought to be," said Bram. "Safe practice is to take the head off, though, it seems to me. Then burn head and body together, if they'll burn. That's good enough for most things. But these are no ordinary beasts. It is nothing like a bear, or wolf, or sabercat."

"We're not even rightly certain it is a moadon," said Venser. "None of us have ever seen one. No Horrors of this size have been seen since the Siege of Shadow. The fool I was, wanting to see one for myself."

Tsúla threw another pile of firewood onto the ground, then returned vacantly to the woods.

"What's he at?"

"Aldwode," said Venser. "We've all been Blooded, save you and him. He fought well, considering. But there's one remedy for it, and it takes time to prepare. Repetitive tasks keep him from going too far mad."

"Celithrand knew of another," said Aewyn.

Venser winced as he adjusted his mangled arm. "Gods willing, he's a hundred miles from here by now. We get by on what we've got."

Staring into nothing, her eyes directed earthwards, Aewyn could not help but note the little river of red blood—Fletch's blood—spilling into the creature's darker stuff.

"Did he fight well?" she asked. Bram unstoppered his flask—not his waterskin—and took a long draw of it before answering.

"He would have," Bram said.

"Never saw it coming," added Venser. "He had no chance."

For the first time, Bram's eyes softened. "Venser, there—he took it head-on. Even Blooded men can lose themselves at the sight of these unsouled monsters. Sloppy technique, of course—" here he kicked the dust affectionately at the wounded man—"but he fought with such valour, at least, as would be worthy of song."

Venser tilted his head disapprovingly, though he dared not shrug his shoulders.

"I tried to save him," he said simply. "They write no songs for them that *try.*"

Robyn had, by now, made it most of the way through the thick leathery neck of the creature. The stench was overpowering, in any case, and she had to stop. She let go of Fletch's smoking sword, which clattered to the stained earth, and walked back to the others. Some of the men had begun building the biers. She motioned for her brother's flask and he reluctantly surrendered it for a moment.

"I gave her a job, Bram."

Bram patted her on the back and nodded to the firewood. "Best get to it," he said. "Live in the work, if you can. Nowhere else."

Aewyn nodded, and joined the others while Robyn took her place on the stump.

"How are you?" asked Bram.

"I think I'm going to throw up," said Robyn. "Venser, how's your arm?"

"No polite word for it," he said. "Let's call it 'broken,' at least. That's the only term fit for a lady's ears."

"This deep in the old woods, I might find you some lodris," said Robyn. "Help you sleep. It could soften your memory of the fight, too. Maybe strip it from you completely, if I can prepare it right. I saw Celithrand do it once. Might mix some of it for Tsúla to keep him calm until his Blooding."

"I'll have no sleep here," said Venser. "Let me ride, Captain. If I can't ride, by Tûr and the Ten, just let me walk. I can't make it far, but I'll have no part of this evil place. If I have a mile in me, if I have a hundred feet, give me that."

"We'll talk once the boy's at rest."

Venser frowned. "He deserves a decent burial. A memory stone, maybe, to tell of his deeds. Not to be tossed on the fire like a damned roast."

"His ways are not our ways," said Bram. "In Khihana, cremation would have been a royal death. Only the very wealthy could burn this much wood. Fletch will go out like a king of his people."

"He should not have gone at all," said Venser. "I failed him."

Bram laid a hand on his good shoulder, searched his wits for consoling words, and found none.

"We have all failed him," Robyn said, her breaking voice raised, seeking a trace of the presence it usually commanded. "Too long we have been a ceremonial guard. Too long we have kept the peace against stock-thieves and outlaws. Ninety years, now, the teachings of the Dragons of Veritenh have come down to us. How low our swords are fallen! What a rude town watch have we become! We bleed our towns-folk for coin as if we were scutcheoned vasils, and the worst we've been ready to fight for it are wolves and poachers. The people of Widowvale, and of Aslea, and of many other towns besides, have hard bought our bluster and pageantry. And now one of our own, a child at war unready for horror, has bought them most dearly of all." She sighed and threw down her dented breastplate, for want of something else to throw down.

"I wish Toren were here," she said. "Gods, though I hated him. I wish he were here now."

The Havenari had gathered about her by now, but none dared venture a response. Aewyn fell to her knees in a scatter of firewood, clutching the earth in her grief. Robyn said no more, but completed the biers alone. If she for a moment stopped moving her jaw, or her hands, she feared she might be of little more use herself.

The pyres were lit in silence. Bram's little source-fire was smoking and guttering under some foul concoction of the monster's ichor, but the flame served well enough to kindle the others. In a few minutes' time, the boy called Fletch with the unpronounceable Southern name was laid to rest by fire. The Horror had to be burned where it was, for the combined efforts of the men could not move it. Aewyn watched it burn with ferocious curiosity, mostly because she could not bear to look on the pyre behind her. In her hands she clutched her little bow of elm—the weapon she had used against a man only a few days before. She felt as if Fletch were there somehow, in the wood; but his presence did little to comfort her. She knew, then, how close she had come to ending a life, and in the moment of Fletch's burning she did not suppose she would ever have the stomach for it, now, under any conditions. The last images of her future as Celithrand's champion, thundering across the battlefield on a stallion like the heroes of the Hanes, were forever replaced her mind by the gleaming smile of a dark-skinned boy taken out of the world too soon.

The stench of the moadon as it surrendered its skin and fat to the flames was like nothing else of this world. Venser, too weak to move himself away from the smoke, emptied his stomach at the smell and was hoisted onto his side to keep him from choking. Some of the Havenari said prayers to Tûr or the Ten, or to their own personal gods, while Aewyn simply gazed at the pyre with weary resolve, watching the eerie flesh rise and fall as its natural spirits left it. Roald returned from the woods with Robyn's bow and a young doe, whose blood they saved before preparing to roast their supper.

As the flames tore on through the hide, the undulations grew more pronounced, until the distended belly was so disturbed by the flames that Aewyn saw fit to point it out.

"Someone give me a sword," said Robyn, rising.

The monster's hide was as tough in death as in life, and it was no easy work slitting it open. Fletch's dull sword was unwieldy, and refused at times to bite; but by sheer determination Robyn slit the underbelly to let the gases out.

What emerged froze her in her tracks. It—they—were unspeakable copies of the original, three of them, rendered in perfect miniature, slime-covered and keening with the unmistakable, unearthly noise of their mother. If they were unready to be born, they were no less ready to die.

"To arms," she breathed, more terrified than bold. "Men, to my side!"

Aewyn recoiled at the sight when the first of them spilled out. It seemed to fix her with those unsettling rows of insect eyes; but these were different and altogether more terrible than the lifeless eyes of the corpse. They had in them a blackness like the blackness beyond the stars, some unspeakable cunning and malevolence belied by their monstrous forms. The first came free of the flesh as the other two emerged, staggering slightly, but undeniably proceeding toward her.

Bram's battered sword flashed in his hand, ringing out as it hit home, but failed to penetrate the creature's hide. As the recoil shook him, he clutched the weapon by its chipped edge and threw all his weight down on it, guiding the tip of the sword through skin and bone and whatever else might have been inside its target.

The others were barely a step behind him, some falling on the impaled creature with whatever weapons they had close to hand, others turning to the remaining spawn. Tsúla was first to reach them, but in the gaze of those terrible eyes a shadow seemed to fall upon him and he shrank back in despair as his allies streamed around him. In a few moments it was over: stirred to life by the urgency of death and of fire, the little spawn sustained themselves on rage alone, being unready for survival outside the womb. But the sudden shock of this secondary assault was enough to unsettle every one of them—and in the long, uneasy peace that followed, their fears only grew stronger.

"Unless that was some insidious design of the beast," said Bram, "I believe those were babies."

"Gods and worms," Robyn breathed. "It's not possible."

From the ground, Venser let out a resigned sigh. "Nothing about them is possible. Would that Celithrand were with us now—if that's really who he was."

"If they bear young in the manner of ordinary beasts," said Bram, "there must be another one out there. There can be no mother without a father."

Robyn's reply was sharper than it might have been. "Yes, we've all figured that out, now; thank you, Bram," she snapped.

"There's been no word of it in Widowvale," he said, ignoring her tone.

"It may be the outlying villages have heard or seen more," Venser offered. "If not Widowvale, maybe Aslea. Maybe Seton, up the way, was in its path."

"That's the direction we've been travelling," said Aewyn. The sound of her own voice surprised her, as if it were coming from somewhere far away.

"My wife's in Seton," said one of the men whose name Aewyn had not yet heard. She watched the colour drain from his face. "Or she was."

Robyn stared long and thoughtfully at the twitching spawn before kicking them back into the fire consuming their mother. "Our duty is first to the towns," she said at last. "Roald, see about cutting a splint for Venser's arm. We'll search for tracks till that's done. If we find only the one set, we ride for Seton, wet-kneed and through the night, if we can. Venser, can you ride?"

"Aye," he said. "Get me up in the saddle, and I can stay in it." Bram slipped past Aewyn and into the brush. Her eyes turned to the smaller of the pyres on the far side of the road. The licking flames had risen to claim the body, which already seemed smaller than she expected. Stripped of his armour, which was too valuable to leave with him, Fletch was smaller than even Aewyn remembered.

"We should bury him," she said. "Fletch's bones, I mean."

"His people burned their dead on a pyre," said Robyn.

"But the men of Widowvale bury their children," replied Aewyn. "Was he not one of ours, too? Did he not make Haveïl his home?"

Robyn frowned and looked down at the smaller girl. One of Aewyn's eyes was wide in innocent earnest, and the other was starting to swell and darken from the gauntleted backhand. Without ceremony she jerked her head toward Tsúla's horse, which was heavily loaded with gear on account of his small size.

"Take the shovel," she said at last. "We'll bury him if you can dig deep enough by the time we're ready for the Blooding."

The labour of digging earth was no new chore to Aewyn. The round-bladed shovel was smaller than most farm tools, sized for packing on the horse; but Aewyn was accustomed to the little tools she had used with Grim, and the repetitive labour of digging came rapidly back to her. She was small and her arms were spindly, but some of the men marvelled just the same at how easily she set spade to earth. Her technique and familiarity with farm work made her appear far stronger than she was; and those men who favoured burial as their end looked upon her with newfound admiration.

By some art unknown to Aewyn, and with some guidance from Venser, Robyn prepared a foul concoction over the fire and distilled it to a single clay vial. Pouring a few drops of it into Tsúla's waterskin, he took a long draught of it, and would have thrown the waterskin away if Robyn had not brought it over.

"Drink," she said, and Aewyn's mouth burned a little—but not overmuch—with the acrid taste of something vile and altogether unnatural.

"Am I one of you, now?" she asked.

"Drinking a potion doesn't change who you are," said Robyn. "To be a Havenar is to live by your word, and by your deed. Those alone."

The mood of the Havenari was strange and divided. Those who had known Fletch the closest, who considered themselves his fast companions, were in some ways the slowest to grief. Tears came easily to the men who had looked on him as a boy: one or two had young sons of their own in the forest towns, and saw the boys' faces in him. Those who saw a comrade in arms were stern and sullen, and wore their grief within—Robyn with more anger than most. Some men wore their tears upon their faces, as rain collects on hard clay. Bram was impassive and unflinching in his tending of the fire and his collection of the boy's blackened bones, a task he performed, like Aewyn's digging, with the ease that comes from practice. As rain falls on softer soil, the tears did not linger on his face, but wound their way deep into him where none could see.

A real rain, too gentle to be cleansing, broke overhead as the fires died down. Aewyn's arms and back burned with the effort, but still she sank the shovel-blade into the earth, hollowing out the ground with a steady rhythm as if to the beat of some inner drum. Grim had often sung as he worked, in a low half-spoken voice that came between grunts of exertion, a means of keeping time. They were work-songs, most of them, ill-rhymed and repetitive. But one of them, a harvest-song, came to mind as Aewyn carved out the hole to plant Fletch's bones, like a winter wheat, out of season with all the rest of the world.

> *The girls have all gathered for harvest.*
> *The boys call the beasts to the stone.*
> *The red moon is redder than heartblood;*
> *The white moon is whiter than bone.*
>
> *The seasons of harvest are sudden;*
> *The winters are all ever-long,*
> *But precious and few are my verses,*
> *For my days are as short as my song.*
>
> *My vines are a garland of garnets;*
> *I've gilded the furrows with gold;*
> *The river shines brighter than silver;*
> *Stars glimmer with riches untold.*

My boat is but laden with memories,
My barrow is narrow and small,
But bury me under the moonlight,
And I'll be the richest of all.

Aewyn's tears, it seemed, had come only in the form of sweat. She was drenched and muddy by the time Bram laid the boy's remains in the little hole she had made.

"Grace find you, lad," he said simply— then, to Aewyn, "let me cover him." He took the shovel and hastened to fill in the little grave; the loose soil, damp from the gathering rain, was heavy but yielding. They were none of them master healers, but with a degree of effort Venser's arm was roughly set and splinted, as Aewyn had seen Celithrand do with her leg, and he was hoisted into his saddle. The horses, hastily watered as Bram filled in the grave, were unsettled by the stink of burned flesh, and by the Horror that had come among them, and were champing and snorting nervously, eager to be on their way.

"To Seton," called one of the men, vexed to see if those in the village were living or dead. The men organized rapidly. Aewyn stood over the grave, seeking words of farewell that did not come. The rain had drenched her autumn-red hair and soaked it almost to the deep brown of late summer. In her hands was the little bow of elm he had made for her, its arms splayed wide as the wet string began to slacken. In time, Robyn was at her side; with eyes half-closed, Aewyn felt the woman's broad-shouldered figure block the rising wind before she felt the hand on her cheek. The single knuckle of Robyn's gauntlet brushed gently where it had struck, not with threat but with something like tenderness. The wrought metal stung her sharply, though, where it touched, and she flinched out of her reverie.

"Mount up, soldier," said Robyn. She gave Hendec's old mare a swat in Aewyn's direction, and it loped over obligingly as she headed for her own saddle. Even the horse seemed to understand that Robyn was in no mood for hesitation.

The rain picked up suddenly as the Havenari walked their horses back into patrol formation. At the head of the line, beside his sister, Bram hoisted his wineskin nearly to his lips before distastefully casting it, half-full, down into the dirt.

"Gods, I hate the rain," he said.

With a sharp cry, Robyn kicked her horse into a long-strided trot, and the others followed suit. Standing forward in the stirrups, Aewyn thought back to her time in the woods with her mother and wondered if it was well spent. Her mother's words already seemed to fade into mist, and their time seemed longer ago and farther away now than her parting words with Poe, her time at the Harvest Fair, the seasons at the plough that were now behind her. Her time in Widowvale was so vivid, such a part of her, that she began to understand the changes her mother had told her of.

The business of prophecy seemed far away, too: the rain and the trail, now, were all she knew. Robyn, posting high in the saddle as she led the Havenari down the hill and away, seemed a long way herself from the carefree woman in the green dress, and Bram farther still from the drunkard still mocked by the men of Widowvale. Her mind over the next few miles turned to Darmod's fields, and the far meadows of his sheep, to carrot seeds shaped like tiny mace-heads, to the widow Karis and her children, in whose vine-wreathed fields she had spent the last years of her childhood—and finally, to the trail, and the forested hills below, and the villages that lay beyond. She felt with uneasy certainty the weight of Fletch's little bow upon her narrow back, and knew then that the time for farming was past.

In the jagged foothills beneath a high cliff, on the steep edge of a long gorge many miles to the west, Poe sniffed at the air and shivered, though not from the cold.

"That smell is no smell of this world," he said. "There is smoke and ash, and some…thing, a dead thing, too terrible to name."

Below him, Celithrand crept up from the stream, his back bent like a willow-branch under the weight of full waterskins and a tremendous dirty bag of roots and saplings.

"There, perhaps, burns the last of the Horrors of the Siege," said Celithrand. "I cannot smell it, myself, but I know too well the scent you speak of. Were I close enough to make it out, though, I should much prefer the scent of one dead to one living."

"I am sure to be happier," said Poe, "when it is burnt and the land reclaimed it as though it had never been."

"That will never be," said Celithrand. "The land will heal in time. But always will it tell the story of its wounds to those who know how to read the scars. Do you see water that feeds this land?"

"I see a stream from the high hills," said Poe. "It must feed the river that runs by the town."

"Today," Celithrand nodded, "it runs into the river that turns the wheel that grinds the wheat for Widowvale's bread. Şarcruthamar, my folk called the stream, at its distant source. Long ago, in days of great storms under wilder moons, this was a mightier river by far. All this valley is a deep scar of that time, riven in the rock by old waters. It has no name, that I know of, in younger tongues. It is only a stream, now. But its banks tell an ancient story."

The old man, leaning heavily on the cane he had cut for himself not long ago, picked his way up the hill with storied sure-footedness. Once or twice he stumbled, and Poe thought he might fall, but they had made the treacherous descent down the rocky cliff to the northeast, and came out soon from the shady trees onto a trail that, after some days in the deep wood, seemed as wide and finished a way as the Iron Road itself.

"I know this place," said Poe. "How is it that we have come so far south?"

"The deep wood has many paths," said Celithrand, "though men do not see them. In time, I hope, the path to Widowvale will grow over like these ancient ways—impassable to all who would come, but free to those that leave."

"That is a good wish," said Poe.

"It will be best for the town, now," said Celithrand, "if it has no more to do with Travalaith, or its soldiers, or its jockeying vasils. A season or two of fruitless searching, if it comes to that, will take the wind out of Haukmere's forge."

Poe snorted. "What is in Haukmere?" he asked.

"The worst you can imagine from the ironmen," said Celithrand. That was good enough for the karach, who hurried his pace on the old roads until it was all that the old druid could manage to keep up.

"These evil men accuse you of treason," Poe said as he pushed through the underbrush. "This means betrayal."

"Yes," said Celithrand.

"All my life," said Poe, "I have never known you to have dealings with the ironmen. Betrayal, as I understand it, is a crime against family or friend. A traitor breaks faith with someone who trusts you. How can you betray a stranger?"

"Treason to the realm is something like opposition to those who control the realm," said Celithrand.

"So you are a rebel. A member of this Uprising."

"No," said Celithrand. "Well, yes and no. But I am now a fugitive, I suppose. I am a bit baffled by the Mages' Uprising, myself. It has sprung up in a generation. It has little enough to do with the war we fought against the dark powers. I concern myself with the wickedness of the gods, until the day that the wickedness of men has grown to eclipse it. The specifics of the accusation—that it was I who taught Jordac in the ways of magic—those are certainly false. I have heard many stories of that man, but have never met him."

"Then why accuse you?"

Celithrand began walking, then, along the edge of the road but within reach of the trees. He was not accustomed to sitting still as he spoke.

"The politics of the Iun are of little concern to me," he began, "and the nature of my crime is political. When the Siege of Shadow was lifted, I stood beside Valithar, who was my brother in arms, and who became Imperator in the years between. I had equal claim to the viceregency of old Travost, if we had pursued it. I suppose in the eyes of some, that makes me a claimant to the Empire itself."

"You could have come to us," said Poe. "Lived all your days in Widowvale, free from their grasp."

"I came there only once, and was captured immediately," Celithrand pointed out. "And my life is in no one place, not while my strength endures. Do not be fooled by the strife of men, my friend. There are yet terrible evils in this world. The petty evils of small folk are of no concern while such things last."

Poe shrugged. "I know nothing of dark gods," said Poe. "The karach have stories of cowards and tricksters, light-stealers and—pardon me—traitors. But in our stories there are no gods of darkness. Wickedness is the work of men, and of caitiff karach with no honour, not the work of gods. The Iun who say that great power brings evil, I think, are mistaken in their understanding of what power really is. The power that brings evil is not true power—it is merely vanity clad in might."

"So you have become a philosopher," said Celithrand, not unkindly.

"Philosophers can read," said Poe.

"I will teach you to read," said Celithrand, "and many other things besides. I will teach you all you need know of Tamnor, who is the source of wickedness both great and petty. And perhaps of reading, too; there is some disagreement on the matter."

"Tamnor sounds to me like an excuse," said Poe. "A story made up by wicked men too cowardly to own their own evil deeds."

"When you confront true evil," warned Celithrand, "you will see how it eclipses the petty feuding of ordinary folk."

Poe spent a few moments in silence before he spoke, turning the words over in his mouth. "Those who think themselves above the petty feuding of ordinary folk can still be hanged for it," he said at last. "And those who are hanged by ordinary folk may not live to confront true evil. Your life's story, old man, was very nearly finished that day."

Celithrand rubbed the back of his neck. "I have not forgotten," he said.

"It was no lord of darkness who took my tribe from me," said Poe. "It was no monster of legend that ran my mother through and burned her. It was no dragon that burned the village of my father. It was men, Celithrand. Small, vile men in black mail-coats, with weapons as ugly and coarse-edged as if they had been hammered by children."

"You still have a tribe," Celithrand reminded him. "She knows your stories, your mother's stories, all too well."

Poe snorted. "Now she too is lost to me. Again over treason. Again over politics."

"You will see her again," said Celithrand. "I swear it. And when you do, you will have learned much about the nature of evil, and of virtue with it. You will see the forest of Nalsin, so unlike this one, and the wide sea, and you will dine in the halls of my ancestors. When the time comes to return, I will not keep you from her. And until that day, I will teach you all that I know of this world."

"You have lived two dozen of my lifetimes," said Poe. "The karach have many blessings, but long life is not one of them. If you would teach me all that you know, old master, I hope it pleases you, lecturing to the empty wind when I am gone."

"I will teach you the language of birds," said Celithrand. "If the *Grrăkha* wills it, they will carry my lectures home to you a hundred years after your spirit is sick of them."

They traveled in silence for a time, burdened by thoughts they were both unready to share. Neither one was a stranger to the woods, and in time they moved with such an easy grace that songbirds who had ceased their singing as the pair passed now grew bold enough to serenade them. When Poe spoke at last, and shocked them into silence, it was as if the whole mood of the forest had changed.

"Tell me again of the prophecy," he said. "The one for which you nearly gave your life. The one I can now safely say has failed to become truth."

Celithrand might have bristled at the comment; but under the weight of profound exhaustion, he let the remark go. "The *Imidactui*," he said, "sometimes called the Unwatchers, or the Blind Watchers, were the last seers of the Age of the Sun. They foresaw the rising of this Age, the Age of the Moons, which will come to an end when the Chain of Night is broken and Tamnor returns to the world. They tell of a champion born of a fairy-maiden—a chosen warrior raised in the wood—which for centuries seemed to make no sense. Creatures like Aewyn's mother do not have children. All the stories in the Hanes about fairy kidnappings, changelings and the like, they come because the êtrili have no natural born children of their own. So none have understood what these words might mean, until now. Until Aewyn."

"And you believe her the dryad's natural child."

"Yes," said Celithrand.

"How is this possible?"

The druid frowned. "I don't know," he said. "But the *Imidactui* are never wrong."

Poe rested his tongue for a moment, deep in thought. At last, he ventured a reply.

"Are you?" he asked.

"Am I what?" asked Celithrand.

"Ever wrong," said Poe.

Celithrand felt at the marks on his neck and considered the question.

"Sometimes," he muttered.

"And if you are wrong about Aewyn? What then?"

To this Celithrand had no reply.

"Since the great fires of my youth," said Poe, "I have watched over her. Probably by your doing, old trickster, but so it is. I brought her food in the woods, and gave her warmth in the winters, and taught her what woodcraft is common to the bone-walkers of my tribe. I did this because she became my family. I know that you made this so. You brought me to her, when I should have died, and made it so that we became tribe. I think that you are wise in the ways of metals, too. I think you found the riches of the town, if you did not call them up from the rock by magic, so that the strongest city-men would come, and she would learn the way of the warrior you think she is. I have never said it, for you saved me when I had nothing. But everything she is, I think, you have bent toward your vision of these ancient words."

"I have done all I can to help her," said Celithrand.

"Why?" asked Poe. "Why help a child of prophecy? If she has a true destiny, what does she need from you?"

"The prophecies speak of a champion, and a great war," said Celithrand. "They are silent, alas, on the matter of who will emerge the victor."

"And now that you are wrong about her," Poe pressed again. "Now that she is not your champion. What then?"

Celithrand stopped walking, then, for the first time in what seemed like hours. Poe caught the scent of the ancient's tears even before he turned round.

"Dire times lie ahead," said the druid. "That much is certain. If she is truly chosen, she has no need of me. If she is not—if I am wrong—if I have been wrong in all of this—then she may have no destiny at all. There will be war, and that war will reave the world. The champion will see it through to its end. But if she is just an ordinary girl—"

He sat down suddenly, wearing his years on his care-worn face.

"I could smell your doubt," said Poe. "You have carried it a long time."

The druid ran a hand through his white hair and sighed. "I was certain, for a time. I put her on this path. And then—she became my child, P'ŏh. *My* daughter. As much as she was ever Grim's, or Aelis-sraia's, or her true father's child. If she is not chosen by Fate—then neither is she protected by it. And this war that comes may take her away from me."

"Now you know the doubts," said Poe, "that plague ordinary men and families in an age of heroes."

"I have been a hero in a hero's age," said Celithrand. "It is different, perhaps, but it is no life of glory. I have been the one for whom great lays are sung and statues raised, over whose shoulders men and women drape the heavy mantle of their hope. And I have seen so many laid low by fortune, so many who gave their all to the War of Shadow, and whether by destiny or cruel fortune it was I, not they, who found fame as a hero of renown. They were laid into pits in the end, their bodies too numerous to count, and no songs were sung of them, and they passed from this world into a dreamless sleep, as if all that they were had never been."

Poe laid an enormous hand on him. "You speak of the greatest sorrow of the karach," said Poe, "if sorrow is what I think. A sleep without dreams—no dreams of your own, no dreams of your tribe to carry you on—that, to karach, is the most wretched sorrow of all."

Celithrand met the karach's gaze with a look of profound woe.

"Those who fell to the Horrors—not even the worms would eat their eyes," he said.

Poe lowered his head well below his shoulders. "Crows take your eyes," he whispered.

"Crows take yours," said Celithrand. "And Aewyn's, most of all."

"Yes," said Poe. "Most of all hers."

They sat in silence a long time. The sun crossed overhead, gliding through a clear sky, as the two dwelt in heavy thought.

"I have decided to help you," said Poe, at last. "Speak, and I listen. These things you foresee, she may be none of them. But she is all of them to me. She is my hero, and my champion, though all the rest of the world forget her."

"She will thrive with the Havenari," said Celithrand. "Robyn will be good to her. They all will, in time. They will give her more, in the end, than the men of the Iron City ever give to their women. And when trouble comes—the trouble of gods or men, as you choose—you will be glad for all she has become."

"I am glad of all she is today," said Poe. "For that there is no need to wait. It is I who am not enough. It is I who fail her, again and again with her people. I know not what lessons you teach, but I cannot go on without wisdom. And since the wisdom of my people is lost to me, now—your wisdom, I think, might suffice."

Celithrand smiled for the first time in a long while. "You, too, have a great destiny, my friend," he said. Poe raised his ears at the thought.

"No more prophecies," he said; but then, after a pause, "what is my destiny, then?"

Celithrand chuckled as he stood to his feet uneasily. "I have no idea," he said. "Let's go in search of it together."

All that day and into the next, they ranged across the face of Haveïl, over high desolate heaths and thickly wooded hollows, resting in forest lawns and hustling through the untended chases of self-proclaimed lords and over barren meadows freshly cut for the encroaching winter. With walking-songs and stories of old they passed the long hours in the highlands, chasing the dried and forlorn paths of ancient waters to shield themselves from the high winds. They dined as they pleased on hare, quail, pheasant, and for Celithrand, the berries and fruits of a dozen strange trees.

For all their ease, they were not unsought. Patrols came went, even on the old roads, and the whole host of the Grand Army that patrolled the coast had been called inland to hunt them down. But Poe's senses were uncommonly keen, and Celithrand whispered strange sounds to the forest birds as they walked, and they seemed to answer him in kind. Only once, in a narrow ravine winding that penned in all travelers, did they come so close to a patrol that Poe could see them from the tree-line. These were not Havenari, but fully armoured troops of the Grand Army, though they moved with an ease and familiarity on the trail that unsettled the ancient druid.

"They dress like City-men," said Poe when he was sure they had passed. "But this is their home soil. I feel it."

"We are a long way from Travalaith, now," said Celithrand. "Perhaps there is a new outpost in these hills. There wasn't, last year."

"The wilderness is too crowded, now, for my taste," said Poe as they took the hard climb up the side of the ravine and left the well-travelled trail far below them.

On the late afternoon of the third day, with the pale ghost of the white moon overhead, the sound of rushing water and the cries of many birds came to Poe's ears, and he stopped short.

"I have never heard a river rage so fiercely," he said. "We had best build a raft or cut some floats to ford it." But Celithrand said nothing, only doubled his climbing speed with a sudden exuberance, and with a bony hand on Poe's broad neck hoisted him to the top of the ridge.

"Look," he said. "Look."

A thin curtain of flowering broom was all that lay between them and the sea. On the far side of the swaying highland reeds, under an overcast sky of hazy light, lay the shimmering silver mirror of the Miu-muranai, the Sea of Joining Skies, so wide and bright and serene beneath the canopy of the world that an endless ribbon of grey mist, glowing faintly on the distant horizon, barely seemed to divide the waters from the heavens. The rush and hiss of the waves came only from the rocks below, where white-winged gannets and gulls played at fish above the churning shallows. As Poe rose to his full height, towering over the golden broom in stunned silence, all he could see in the whole world seemed made of silver light.

"Never in my days," he said, "have I imagined such wonder. It is a water without beginning or end."

"It is," said Celithrand, with no small measure of his own joy. "And yet you will cross it with me. Come down with me to the sea, P'ŏh. We will find a fisherman to take us south, along the coast. There are sailing ships aplenty in Lockmouth, if we can reach it before night-fall."

"I wish to go down with you," breathed Poe, his whispered voice low and reverent. "But I seem to have lost my feet, and all my breath with them."

Celithrand reached up, touched the karach's trembling shoulder, guided him forward onto the gentlest slope of the high hill.

"Come along," he said.

HERE ENDS THE FIRST BOOK
OF THE *TRAVALAITH SAGA*.

AFTERWORD

Aewyn and the Havenari will soon return in

The Season of the Cerulyn
being the second book of the *Travalaith Saga*.

New reaches of the Travalaithi Empire and the sprawling darkness of the Iron City itself will be revealed as the Empire plunges deeper into civil war. The Havenari find themselves wrapped up in a web of seduction, espionage, and brutal violence as the Mages' Uprising lives up to its name.

If you enjoyed this book, **please leave a brief review** on Amazon, Goodreads, or the social media platform of your choice. Independent authors & small presses simply do not have the same marketing support as the major publishing houses. Your support is more precious than gold, and I try to read it all: it not only enables me to keep writing new books, but gives me the valuable feedback I need to help make each new book better than the last.

You can find me on the Web at **Lukemaynard.com**, where you can follow my writing and music, and sign up to be notified whenever I have a new release.

Thank you for taking a chance on *The Season of the Plough*. I look forward to our next meeting.

—*Luke R. J. Maynard*

ACKNOWLEDGMENTS

Don't be fooled: the term "indie publishing" is a misnomer. Producing an indie work requires support, counsel, and a few swift kicks from a whole village of people. Without them, this book would not exist, or would have been much inferior.

Eldest thanks are due to Jessie and Brett, who gave me characters worth telling stories about, and to Emily, who gave me an extraordinary skald in whose difficult, ornate, rich voice they simply had to be told. (Her story, and how she came to tell it, is yet to come).

The youngest of my thanks go to my beta readers and editorial team, and chiefly to Riley Kirkwin, who was First Spear among them—nor has any spear ever boasted an edge keener than her eye for detail.

I'd like to acknowledge Herb Hunter, Marilyn Scott, Inge Evans, and Larry Garber for teaching me to be a good-ish writer (that is, to be a master thief). Thanks to Neil Brooks and my twenty-three other literature teachers, for showing this master thief where all the treasures of the ages lay waiting to be plundered.

Thanks to Jamie Ibson, who has endured my worldbuilding habits for more than 25 years. Thanks to Scott R. Jones at Martian Migraine Press, who taught me by example how an exceptional Canadian micropress should be run: with absolute integrity, professionalism, and kingly patience, no matter how many trolls & goblins are at play within your sub-subgenre of choice. Thanks to Kathryn Sandford, who knows no fear, for showing me that I didn't need anyone's permission to chase my own stars by my own rules.

I'd like to thank my mother, who has supported me as a writer from my first alphabet blocks to this; and the family and friends who were instrumental in keeping me going all the days in between. Natalie & Ashley, Matt & Megan, Jen, Amy, Karen, David, Judy, Shannon & Megan, Justins I & II, Daniel, Madison, Erica, Aladdin,

Sol, and Yukimi: the world is full of half-written stories left behind by earnest writers who simply give up on them. Thanks to your kindness and support, this story is not one of them.

Finally, a heartfelt thanks to the readers who took a chance on this largely unknown book by a largely unsung author. If there are more to come, it's because you supported new writing from an unknown indie publisher. Don't stop reading.

About the Author

Luke R. J. Maynard is a writer, poet, scholar, lapsed medievalist, musician, and wearer of sundry other hats in the arts & letters. Born in London, Ontario, Canada, he received his PhD in English Literature from the University of Victoria in 2013, and his *Juris Doctor* at the Unive sity of Toronto's Faculty of Law in 2019.

Luke's first CD, *Desolation Sound*, was released in June of 2018. *The Season of the Plough* is his first novel. Luke currently lives in Toronto.

Made in the USA
Monee, IL
13 May 2021